PRAISE FOR
L.A. W...

"Truly GRIPPING." Malorie Blackman

"THRILLING and ROMANTIC."
Ruth Warburton

"Will have you THRILLED, SCARED and
HEARTBROKEN." Teri Terry

"HEART-STOPPING." Mizz

"WONDERFUL, ORIGINAL." The Sun

"Packed with SUSPENSE
and DRAMA." The Daily Mail

ABOUT THE AUTHOR

L. A. WEATHERLY was born in Little Rock, Arkansas, USA. She now lives with her husband and their cat, Bernard, in a draughty Victorian house in the Scottish Borders, where she spends her days – and nights! – writing.

L. A. Weatherly is the author of over fifty books, including the bestselling *Angel* trilogy. Her work has been published in over ten different languages.

Catch up with L. A. Weatherly on facebook

@LA_Weatherly

laweatherly.tumblr.com

BLACK MOON

L.A. WEATHERLY

USBORNE

HOPE IS REBELLION

There is no past that we can bring back by longing for it.

– Johann Wolfgang von Goethe

PROLOGUE

FEBRUARY, 1942

COLLIS AWOKE FROM THE FAMILIAR NIGHTMARE with a start. His arm throbbed; the pain was red-black. He lay in a double bed. His chest was bare and his right bicep had been bandaged.

At the memory of shooting himself, the dream-images of Harmony Three faded.

Collis propped himself up on one elbow, wincing. He stared around him. He'd never seen this lavish bedroom before.

More memories returned: the wound had bled badly, soaking rapidly through his handkerchief. He'd pretended to pass out in a field near where Amity had assassinated

Gunnison, and then really must have. All he recalled afterwards were urgent voices and mumbling to someone that Amity had shot him – that she'd gotten away.

Had she gotten away? Or been captured?

Mac and Sephy had been arrested, he remembered then. The pain of this was even greater than his wound.

Collis sat up all the way, gritting his teeth and pushing himself on his good arm. Breathing hard, sweating slightly, he spotted a small bottle and a glass of water on the bedside table. He picked up the bottle and studied it. Painkillers. Glancing at the water, he longed for one or, even better, a few. He shoved the bottle roughly back into place.

The door opened, and Kay Pierce peered in. She entered, closing it behind her. "Collis! You're up."

He tensed and tried not to show it. "Hi, Miss Pierce. I mean…Madame President."

"Oh, call me Kay."

She came over – small and slim, with a pointed face and blue eyes. Her upswept light brown hair was in stylish curls that didn't really suit her. She wore a tailored skirt and a jacket with broad shoulder pads.

"How are you?" She sounded genuinely concerned – yet Collis knew from Mac that President John Gunnison's former Chief Astrologer had apparently had it in for him.

His temples pounded. *In no mood for this shit, that's how I am.* But his instincts were still there and he gave a weary, rueful smile. "Been better."

"I bet. Here." She leaned over and rearranged his

pillows so that they'd prop him up. She was so close he could smell her perfume and wariness prickled through him.

He sank back against the pillows. "Thanks."

Kay sat on the side of his bed. She nodded at the painkillers. "It's been a few hours. You can have one."

Collis had no idea if she was lying. But thinking of Mac and Sephy again – shot, if lucky, or else already on their way to a correction camp – he didn't need more urging.

He shook out a small pink pill and took it. There were lots. Too tempting. He'd flush them down the toilet later, or he'd be popping one whenever he wanted some welcome oblivion.

He longed to give the painkiller time to work its numbing magic, but knew what he had to say next. "What's been going on?" he asked, putting the water down. "Has Vancour been caught?"

Kay grimaced. "No."

He hid his rush of relief. "*Damn* it," he muttered.

In every lie, a truth. It was how you made people believe you. Collis thought of Mac as he said it and knew bitterly that he'd gotten the helpless anger just right.

Kay tapped her red-painted nails on the covers. "What exactly happened?"

What had happened was that when he'd seen Amity shoot Gunnison – had realized in a panic her fate if captured – he'd lunged forward and grabbed her. He'd hustled her out of the stadium amid the chaos, shouting that he had her. There'd been no thought to the plan.

He said, "We struggled. She got the pistol and shot me. Then she grabbed the keys to the Shadowcar and took off."

Kay's sigh sounded peevish. "We figured as much when you were found. Were you trying to cut across the fields behind the stadium?"

"Must have been. It's kind of a blur."

"I can imagine." Her gaze lingered on his bare chest. A wry smile touched her lips. "What's it like getting shot?"

The question took Collis by surprise, and he snorted. "It hurts," he said. "A lot." Then he recalled Sandford Cain, Gunnison's right-hand man, collapsing onstage too. "Is Mr Cain okay?"

"The doctor says he will be. The bullet lodged between his ribs. He needed surgery." After a pause, Kay added, "Mac Jones and Sephy Geroux got away."

His pulse leaped. He gave a disbelieving laugh and massaged his forehead, playing for time. "Yeah…I heard their names called. Resistance, right?"

Kay's eyebrows shot up. "How did you know?"

"Started to suspect Mac recently. I went to Johnny with it. I thought that's why they were being taken in."

"No, I had my own suspicions. Mac wasn't as smart as he thought. But now they're still out there, somewhere." Kay gave a small, unhappy laugh. "Guess the Resistance will be after *me* next."

"Don't worry, we'll weed the scum out." Collis's heart was singing. Mac and Sephy, free. *Oh, Mac, you wonderful, clever bastard,* he thought fervently.

Kay traced her nail on the bedcover. "I shot Cain, you know."

His thoughts stuttered. "I…you what?"

She looked up levelly. "I'm the one who shot Sandford Cain. Not Vancour. Me."

The stadium's stage had been crowded with officials for the Harmony Treaty that would forcibly annex Appalachia to the re-formed Can-Amer. Collis hadn't had a clear view. He'd assumed that Amity had shot Cain as well as Gunnison.

He studied Kay, apprehension cold in him. Her freckled features were expectant. "Why are you telling me this?" he said slowly.

Kay rose and crossed to the window. They were still in Washington, he realized: he could see the ancient ruins of white, staid buildings beyond.

"Because I think I can trust you," she said, gazing out. "I admire you, Collis. You're very good with people. Johnny always spoke highly of you."

Johnny probably had; he'd seen Collis as a kind of good-luck charm. Collis had taken advantage of it at every opportunity.

"What about Cain?" he asked finally. His arm still throbbed as his mind spun. What perception of him did Kay have? What exactly should he be playing along with?

She shrugged as she looked over the city. "I saw my chance and took it. Wish my aim had been better, that's all. We'll see if we can work with him or not."

We?

Kay turned. "I'm thinking of relocating the capital to New Manhattan," she said brightly. "Biggest city in the country. It deserves to be the capital, don't you think?"

"Sure," he said. "Good idea."

"Plus it has wonderful shopping," she added with an impish smile. "I've cast your chart, by the way."

He swallowed. "Oh?"

"Mmm," she said, nodding. "You have a bright future. Jupiter in Gemini, trine with Venus. A new age of communications."

If she actually believed in astrology, he'd eat his socks. "Well...I guess a new age is fitting," Collis ventured. "Given the circumstances."

Kay came back and sat on the bed again. To his surprise, she took his hand. She turned it over and traced the Leo tattoo on his palm. He flinched, reflexively closing his fingers.

Kay looked up. The emotion in her blue eyes seemed genuine.

"No, don't be ashamed of it." She smoothed his hand open. Her fingers were warm. "It's a badge of honour. You've been to one of those places and survived. That means something. And you'll keep surviving."

It was the memory of Amity's touch he'd winced at.

She'd often traced the tattoo, not realizing it marked him as a former correction-camp prisoner. She sure as hell knew it now.

"I guess you're right," he muttered.

To his relief, Kay released him. "I'll let you get some rest. But there's a role for you in my regime, Collis. We're the most powerful country in the world – I need a right-hand man I can trust."

I could finally have enough money, he thought. Enough to not be a garbage Reed any more. Enough to be worthy of winning a Vancour.

The knee-jerk thoughts brought a familiar self-disgust. At least his actions were what counted – thankfully no one knew the crap that went on in his head. The main thing was that with a role like that, he could aid the Resistance more than ever.

Collis let a disbelieving grin spread across his face. "I'm left-handed," he said. "Can I still be a right-hand man?"

Kay smiled too. "I know you let Amity Vancour go."

In the sudden silence, she studied him, rubbing a finger over her lips.

"So what can we do about that?" she said.

Under Kay Pierce's rule, we're bombarded daily with propaganda seeking to rewrite history. Don't be deceived. The facts are these:

In March 1941, former Peacefighter pilot Amity Vancour – "Wildcat" – was made the scapegoat of the World for Peace scandal that rocked the world. The charges against her were lies. She'd found evidence that dictator John Gunnison was illegally manipulating the old and noble practice of Peacefighting – two fighter pilots pitted against each other to resolve conflicts between nations – to further his own ends.

"Wildcat" sought to expose the corruption. She was arrested, framed for murder and sent to a correction camp.

She escaped. In February, she shot Gunnison as he overtook the entire continent via his infamous "Harmony Treaty". Kay Pierce, formerly Gunnison's Chief Charlatan (aka his Chief Astrologer), seized power.

"Wildcat" escaped once more. She remains at large, working with others in the Resistance to bring down Pierce.

Gunnison was a madman. Kay Pierce is every bit as dangerous: a scheming liar who uses astrology to control and terrorize. We must fight her regime, or die.

When the time comes, be ready. Fight with us.

– *Somewhere in*
New Manhattan

PART ONE

MAY 1942 – SEPTEMBER 1942

CHAPTER ONE

MAY, 1942

THE CLOCK'S TICKING HAD NEVER seemed so loud.

Distractedly, I scanned my cards. Heat blanketed the shabby apartment, barely stirred by the small electric fan. Taped-up newspaper covered the edges of the closed window blinds.

I put down the three of spades. Mac, sitting across from me with his shirtsleeves rolled up, raised an eyebrow.

"And here I thought you were hoarding threes."

"Think again, pal." I managed not to flick another glance at the clock and took a five. I did need threes, as it happened, but couldn't concentrate.

Mac was leaning back, brown hair rumpled, one foot propped on his battered chair.

"Interesting," he drawled. He stretched forward to snag my three.

His guise of normality made it easier to act the same. My brother Hal and Sephy, Mac's girlfriend, were working on astrological charts at the other end of the table…and Hal didn't know. He had no idea that tonight was make or break for the Resistance.

Mac discarded a four. I swiped it up. The cards felt sticky. Ever since we'd entered New Manhattan, the heat had been oppressive, as if the weather was on Kay Pierce's side and knew what we were up to.

From the Harlemtown streets below, a Shadowcar's siren wailed. It chilled the back of my neck. Across the city at the other safe house, Ingo was waiting too, if all was well.

I gave in and looked. Five to nine. Five more minutes and we'd know.

When I threw down another card, Mac took it. "Gin." He showed his hand.

I groaned, glad of the distraction. "Really?"

He tossed the cards down and stretched, deceptively relaxed. "Shouldn't have taken your eye off those threes, kiddo."

Hal glanced up but didn't comment. In a different lifetime, he'd have asked what had happened – maybe joked that he guessed I wasn't such a card shark after all.

Now wasn't the time to try again to put things right with him, even if I knew how. Yet as our eyes met, I hesitated.

"Want to play?" I asked. "Vancour versus Vancour?"

My brother's face was a male mirror of my own: olive skin, light brown eyes, sleek dark hair. He gave a small grimace and returned to his chart.

"Need to finish this," he muttered.

I didn't really blame him. It still hurt.

Sephy gave me a quick sympathetic look. She and Mac were the ones who'd been there for Hal during those long, grey weeks after I'd shot Gunnison. It was a lot more than I'd managed.

Restless, I went to the tiny kitchen. I wasn't hungry, but opened the icebox and took out some cold cuts from the deli downstairs. The owner, Jakov, gave us free lodging and helped out with food when he could.

"Anyone want some?" I said.

"Sounds good." Mac gathered up the cards. "Grab the telio, will you, pal?" he added to Hal. "Might as well catch the further burblings of our glorious leader."

Hal gave a sour grin. "If we have to."

"Well, it sure is *my* favourite time of day," said Sephy. Her wavy black hair was caught up in a green scarf, her neck long and elegant.

"Yours too?" I concentrated on the cold cuts I was putting on the table, distrusting my ability to look casual. This was it. Any minute now, we'd know.

Hal snapped on the second-hand telio set. It whined into life. From the twin curlicue speakers, soft music bounced through the room: the famous crooner Van Wheeler.

"*Oh, life's so okay…we all say…with Kay! Kay! Kay!*"

They'd started showing film clips as music played. On the small, round screen, Kay Pierce was getting into a gleaming auto, blowing kisses in grainy black-and-white.

As he sat back down, Hal glanced in frustration at the chart he'd been working on. "Do you think we'll be able to actually get *rid* of her soon, instead of just…?"

The charts he helped Sephy doctor had already saved several people who'd have been found Discordant otherwise. Sephy had been one of Pierce's astrologers. She knew how Pierce's mind worked – what astrological dictates she might think up next. We'd started a newspaper too, using an ancient printing press hidden deep in the tunnels below the city.

None of it felt like enough.

I shrugged, afraid Hal would hear the truth if I spoke.

"Hope so, buddy," Mac said easily, reaching for a slice of ham.

"There's Collis," Sephy said, straightening.

I stiffened. My ex was now Pierce's speech-writer and "special advisor". We watched as he stood beside her on the screen, the pair of them waving from the balcony of her Centre Park palace. Collie was kind of saluting the air, one hand on Pierce's back. His shapely mouth was twisted in that smile of his.

Hal shook his head. "Man, he's a good actor."

"He has to be," said Mac quietly.

With an effort, I bit back a response. I was the only one

present with call to be bitter about Collie's acting ability.

Reaching for a piece of cheese I didn't want, I thought of our potential meeting tonight with the deposed President Weir. My guts tightened. We needed it so badly…but if it went ahead, Collie would be there too.

He and I had grown up together – been best friends. When he'd turned up on the Western Seaboard Peacefighting base after four years of silence, we'd fallen in love. I'd have laughed in the face of anyone who told me he was a spy for Johnny Gun and a crooked Peacefighter.

I'd believed in him almost right up until the moment he'd turned me in.

That was over a year ago. I'd ended up in Harmony Five. Yet when he'd rescued me after I shot Gunnison, he'd kissed me.

A man can change, he'd said.

I'd been in such shock that I hadn't protested the kiss – or even known if I wanted to. After waking up from the greyness, I did know: if I'd been myself I'd have stopped him, and if Collis Reed had any sense he should have realized that. He couldn't actually think I'd take him *back*, could he?

The thought filled me with angry amazement – and sadness. How had I gotten it all so wrong?

At nine o'clock exactly, the Harmony symbol's grey and black swirls appeared – a distortion of the old yin-yang, blood and black in real life. A trio of female singers warbled, "*And now it's time…for all of us…to end the day with KAY!*"

"Good evening," said Pierce in her thin, stilted voice. "I often ask myself, what does Harmony want from me? As you know, I think there's a purpose to all things. Astrology simply helps us discern it…"

Unlike the earlier images, this was live. Kay Pierce was sitting at a microphone right now, probably in a room cooled by fans blowing over ice blocks, reading the notes Collie had prepared for her.

Hal carefully drew a symbol on his chart. "Her burblings are as enlightening as usual," he said.

"…and so, as I often stress when I meet with my advisors, clarity can be achieved by…"

Clarity, following the mention of a meeting.

Collie had just given us the all-clear.

Mac's gaze met mine. Electricity sparked briefly in his brown eyes. Across the table, Sephy's shoulders relaxed a fraction.

I cleared my throat. "No surprises there then," I said in response to Hal.

After Pierce finished, dance music came on, slow and sweet. Sephy casually resumed work on her chart. My pulse hammered, out of time with the music. It was really happening.

I dealt a hand of solitaire, trying to concentrate only on the gentle slap of cards. Forget Collie. The Resistance *had* to get ex-President Weir on board if we hoped to succeed. Nothing else mattered tonight.

Mac finished his sandwich. "Hey, Amity, you want to

have a look at that spot in the tunnels you told me about? The one we could use as a cache?" Our script had begun.

"Kind of late," I said, forcing myself to sound casual.

"Ah, it's too hot to sleep anyway. And we might not get a chance tomorrow."

"All right – shouldn't take long."

For a change, I was glad of the distance between me and Hal – otherwise he'd likely have wanted to come. As Mac and I stood up, he started putting his things away.

"Think I'll take a shower before bed and cool off," he said to Sephy. "Night," he added to me, a touch too late.

"Night," I echoed.

When he'd vanished into the bathroom, Mac's and my movements turned hurried. We grabbed up our jackets – it was cold in those ancient tunnels that spiderwebbed under the city.

At the door, Sephy and Mac quickly embraced. "*Be careful*," she said.

Mac linked his pale fingers with her dark ones. "We'll be fine. I promise," he said softly. He jostled her hand. "Hey, you could always agree to marry me, if you're really worried."

"Get back safely and I'll consider it."

"You're a witness," Mac said to me.

"I am," I agreed, trying to smile.

Sephy squeezed my arm, and I knew she'd guessed that I wasn't looking forward to this.

"Hurry back, both of you," she said.

A route led into the tunnels from the deli's cellar, but we didn't take it – we were due in less than an hour; not enough time to travel solely underground. We hurried around the corner, where there was a drugstore with a payphone.

Mac ducked inside. I kept to the shadows, praying a Gun wouldn't pass. I gripped my arms and gazed at the shabby brownstones, and a tattered poster for an act at the Eros Theatre: *Harmony Hugh and His Hepcats.*

Ingo should have left the other safe house by now. *Stay safe,* I thought fiercely to him. *Please.*

Mac was back in less than a minute. "Dwight's on his way."

We waited at the rear of an unlit parking lot. Mac's fedora sliced a curved shadow over his face as he leaned against the brick wall, hands in his trouser pockets, watching the street. Headlights from autos with gleaming front grilles passed occasionally.

I knew him well enough now to guess what he was thinking. I nudged him. "Go on. I won't tell Sephy."

He gave a quick, rueful smile. "That obvious?"

"Maybe not to a blind person."

"Ah, what the hell. Thanks, pal." He reached into his jacket's inner pocket and drew out a pack of cigarettes. Cupping a hand around his mouth, he lit one with a quick scratch of flame from his lighter.

"Listen," he said, putting the lighter away, "if this goes as we hope, I don't want Hal involved. I don't even want him to know about it until he has to."

I let out a slow breath. It wasn't really a surprise – Mac had been reluctant to let Hal even come into New Manhattan with us. But I knew how desperately my brother wanted to help defeat Pierce. Like me, he needed to feel he was doing something to obliterate our father's legacy.

"I agree," I said quietly.

Mac blew out a puff of smoke and glanced at me. "You sure? I know things have been kind of tough between you two. Keeping a secret this big from the kid won't help."

My lips quirked humourlessly. I gazed at a bus's high, curved shape as it passed, an advertisement for Capricorn Cigarettes on its side.

"I'm sure," I said in a low voice. "He's only fifteen, Mac. I don't want him involved in a murder plot any more than you do."

CHAPTER TWO

FIVE WEEKS EARLIER, I'D SAT beside Ingo on a sofa in a safe house in Bayon, New Jersey, staring at a man I'd seen only once before. Around thirty, with thinning brown hair: Grady, the best of the Resistance, according to Mac.

It felt as if he'd just punched me in the stomach.

As Grady's words hung in the air, Ingo breathed something in Germanic and closed his eyes. Hal sat at the dining table, stricken. Across the room, Mac had sunk onto the arm of an easy chair.

Sephy remained on her feet. "Can you repeat that, Grady?" she said faintly.

Grady stood in the middle of the living room, slapping

his fedora against his hand. His voice was thick with reluctance.

"I showed the photos of the nuclear weapons to the right people in the European Alliance," he said. "President Brochu telegraphed other world leaders: Russo-China, Africa, everyone. No one's going to act. They prefer to try to negotiate with Pierce – stay on her good side."

Pictures that Ingo and I had found while on the run came in a vivid mental flash: a mushroom cloud against a grey sky; two fat, bloated bombs; smiling scientists.

"But...they *have* to help!" I burst out, gripping my cane. "Don't they understand what's at stake? What exactly did you tell them?"

"That the fate of the world depends on them taking action," said Grady heavily. "I'm afraid they're more concerned with the fates of their own countries."

"They won't even send covert aid?" asked Ingo.

"Money, supplies?" added Mac, voice rising. "*People?*"

"No," said Grady. "Nothing that might endanger their relationship with Pierce."

I started to speak again and couldn't. We'd known there might not be much in the way of armed forces – the world had been demilitarized for a century, wholly unprepared for Gunnison's illegal army over a year ago. But not even *aid*?

We were about to enter New Manhattan. Kay Pierce's bastion was a closed city now. Mac hardly had any contacts left.

Grady slowly sat too, still slapping his hat against his palm. It was the only sound.

"I'm sorry," he said. "I gave it everything I had."

"Yeah, I know you did, buddy," Mac murmured. He slumped back against the armchair, gripping his head as he stared at the ceiling. Looking ashen, Sephy touched his shoulder.

"We still have to fight her," blurted Hal, his hands balled into fists. "We *will*, won't we?" He looked around the room. His eyes didn't meet mine, and a pang went through me.

"Yeah, we'll still fight," Mac said quietly. "We've just got to figure out how."

He leaned forward and cracked his knuckles, his jaw hard. "All right, we've got some decisions to make. Looks like we're on our own."

An hour after Grady left, I'd perched on the picnic table atop the flat, airy roof, gazing across the river. Kay Pierce's new capital city stretched out in a glittering mass in the sunset. I rubbed my arms, chilled despite the warm evening.

When would all of this end?

The door opened and Ingo came out. "Thought I'd find you here."

The roof had become a favourite spot for us both, this week we'd spent waiting for Grady. We'd played chess up here a lot, or Ingo would strum his guitar.

He sat beside me, propping his forearms on his long thighs. He wore the same tan trousers and white shirt he'd been given when we were in hiding. My faded dress was second-hand too. Neither of us had much.

I shook my head, still staring at the skyline. "How can they do it?"

Ingo knew I meant the world's inaction. He gave a wry snort. "Never underestimate the human capacity to stick your head in the sand, I guess."

His face's left side was unmarred. The right was a crinkled mask. The burn scar puckered tightly from forehead to chin, making his eye droop, pulling at his mouth. Earlier, I'd been reminded how most people first reacted to Ingo – Grady, who'd already met him, had greeted him without the startled flinch I'd seen from others this past week.

I knew how much Ingo must hate it. He never mentioned it, never showed it.

Traffic rumbled below. The air hinted of the ocean up here – fresh and clean. Yet in a last shard of sunset, I spotted a giant Harmony flag flying over New Manhattan. I felt brittle as I watched it.

"Are you okay with what we decided?" I asked Ingo.

"Yes, oddly enough."

I glanced at him. "Oddly enough?"

He lifted a shoulder. "Sanctity of life, and all that." It had been part of our daily Peacefighting oath, back when we were opponents and the world was sane. We'd vowed to honour the sanctity of life. To fight fairly and well.

What a crock.

Ingo's almost-black gaze was level. "What about you?" He knew, maybe more than anyone, how shooting Gunnison had affected me.

I sighed, twisting my cane between my hands. "It's even worse this time. Premeditated."

"It is."

"But, yes, I'm okay with it too. We don't have much choice now, do we?"

"Well, we could always choose to say to hell with it and forget the whole thing. But given how stupid we both are about these situations, naturally we're going for the 'noble path' instead." He gave the words ironic quotes.

"It hardly feels noble."

"Hardest path, then."

"We both *are* pretty stupid, aren't we?" I said, and Ingo gave a one-sided grin at that, the scarred half of his face barely moving.

"Ah, what the hell," he muttered, gazing at the city. It was darker now – twilight – and the skyline looked spiky, ominous. He ducked his head close to mine. "Quick, what does it remind you of?"

I didn't hesitate. "The woods around Harmony Five."

"Yes, me too. Do you have a terrible feeling of déjà vu?"

I had to smile despite my apprehension. I'd been thinking of our escape from Harmony Five too, of course.

One of Mac's contacts was going to smuggle us into the city the next day in his van…with luck.

"Sneaking in this time, not sneaking out," I said.

"True. I think maybe we're doing it wrong."

I hesitated, studying him. His dark hair was just getting long enough to curl again. "Are you really having second thoughts? Mac could probably get you to Nova Scotia – you could—"

His mouth twisted. "Stop," he said quietly. "I'm kidding. You know that."

I could still hardly believe Ingo was here. He was supposed to have taken a ship home to the EA two months ago. I'd learned only the week before that he'd stayed to help the Resistance.

Ingo had been a Peacefighter for the European Alliance. I'd fought for the Western Seaboard. In Harmony Five, we'd joined forces to escape; on the run together, we'd become friends.

Since shooting Gunnison, I'd been locked in gloom, unable to find my way out. Seeing Ingo again had unlocked something. I'd cried in his arms on this very roof – he'd held me close without saying a word. Even after my tears had dried, I'd stayed pressed against him, feeling his heartbeat against my cheek…and had known it would have made a difference, those dark weeks, if I'd realized I'd soon be seeing him again.

The knowledge was a little unsettling. I looked down, fiddling with my cane.

"I wish *Hal* would go to Nova Scotia," I said finally. The small island was still a free country. Our mother was there.

Ingo's gaze was on me. After a beat, he glanced away and nodded. "He's young. I'd be worried too. But I guess you can't tell a boy who was in hiding in a closet for nine months that he's not allowed to fight the regime that put him there."

"That's exactly what I'd like to tell him."

Ingo smiled slightly. "You're his big sister. Worrying about him is your job."

Worrying was an understatement. Remembering severed heads on a chain-link fence, I glanced down at the Aries tattoo on my palm and clenched my hand shut.

"You know, I'm not sure why I'm even doing this, except…" I trailed off.

"I know," Ingo said softly.

A harsh laugh escaped me. "I want to be over it, Ingo. I don't want to *care* any more about Dad's thrown Peacefight. All I want is to move on. To…be happy, if that's possible."

Ingo looped an arm around his knee, studying me intently. "Does it feel possible?"

"Maybe," I whispered, staring at the Harmony flag's dark, shifting shape. "But not until everything he put into place is gone."

Ingo touched my arm, his fingers warm against my skin. "Amity. Your father didn't put all of this into place."

"He was the catalyst."

"A catalyst isn't the same as a cause." He gave me a gentle nudge and let his hand fall. "Come on, you remember enough high-school chemistry for that."

"I do?" I glanced at him with faint amusement. "I never took it. I went to Peacefighting training school at sixteen."

"Ah, well, that explains it. If you'd taken chemistry, you'd know these things."

"I thought poetry was the answer," I said, deadpan. Ingo had introduced me to poetry when we were in hiding. Before, my literary taste had run mostly to adventure stories and books about flying

"A poem about chemistry," he said. "One must exist. 'Hail to Thee, Fair Periodic Table', or something. I'll find it for you and then it'll all make sense."

"Somehow I doubt it. But thank you. What about you – does happiness feel possible?" Then it hit me; I leaned quickly towards him. "Your family. Did Grady bring word?"

He shook his head. "Nothing."

I'm sure they're all right. I didn't say it. We didn't do platitudes, Ingo and I.

"I'm sorry," I said, touching his shoulder. "I hope you hear something soon." For all Ingo knew, they still thought him dead.

He grimaced and scraped his hands through his hair. "Last I heard, a late frost had killed off half the vineyard...

Erich was taking extra jobs to stay in law school; Lena was going home on weekends to help out... That was over a year ago."

"Sure you don't regret staying?" My heart tightened as I said it. I wanted so badly for him to be happy.

He glanced at me; a wry smile touched his long, angular face. "When do I ever not say what I mean?"

I smiled too. "True."

"No. I don't regret it," he said quietly. "I just wish I could be two people at once, that's all. Neat trick, if I could do it."

I nodded, understanding. I'd heard nothing from Ma either, though I didn't expect to until we got a network set up.

A network: that was what we'd talked about for most of the last hour. Mac had explained that his dozen or so New Manhattan contacts would be limited in what they could do. At least there were two safe houses. One, an apartment above a Harlemtown deli, would be our main base.

We'd discussed doctoring Discordant birth charts, spreading the truth about Pierce's regime, rallying people to action. Ingo, who'd gone to boarding school in New Manhattan, knew some of its ancient, forbidden tunnel network. We could use it to covertly travel the city, maybe even to help people escape. Grady had agreed to set up a "railroad" network to the north, to help people reach Nova Scotia if we managed it.

And after Mac had asked Hal to go to the drugstore for more ice, we'd agreed our main objective...

Getting rid of Pierce for good, with the help of Collis Reed.

The van's hidden compartment was close and shadowy, lit only by a small ventilation grille. As the engine vibrated around us the next morning, I was hyper-aware of Hal sitting on the other side of Mac – of wanting to hide my fear from him.

At the checkpoint, no one moved. Dwight, the driver, had managed to get permission to leave the city for his uncle's business. It was unusual for a hardware store; I was terrified he'd be challenged.

The low murmur of Guns came from outside. One slapped the van as if bored, and we all flinched. In a rush, I saw again the heads on Harmony Five's fence – weather-beaten, glittering with frost. I screwed my eyes shut, trying not to shake.

On my other side, fingers linked through mine. My gaze flew to Ingo's. Despite his own fear, he gave a small smile. I exhaled and held tightly to his warm grip. It helped as no one else's could have – like me, Ingo knew first-hand what could happen to us.

When we started moving again, Ingo and I still held hands. We didn't let go until the van finally stopped and we knew we were safe.

That turned out to be relative.

Dwight was eighteen but younger-looking. Mac had

known his parents back in what used to be the Central States. When he opened up the van's hidden compartment, he was pale.

"You, um…probably didn't hear what the Guns were saying," he said.

I'd just gotten out after Ingo; our gazes met in alarm.

Mac's expression sharpened. "What's going on, buddy?"

We were in a dimly-lit garage. Dwight glanced at its closed door. "A Gun was killed earlier today," he said in an undertone. "Knocked down in traffic. It sounds like it was an accident, but…Pierce has retaliated."

"Retaliated how?" said Hal faintly. Sephy squeezed his shoulder, her narrow, high-cheekboned face apprehensive.

Dwight was breathing hard. He let out something almost like a laugh, shoving a hand through his pale hair and looking again at the door. "She's…she's decreed that…"

I didn't want to know…but when Mac headed towards a dusty window beside the garage door, I followed.

The others came too. Peering out beside Mac, nausea lurched; I gasped and pressed a fist to my mouth. No one spoke. I glimpsed Hal's expression and wished wildly that he wasn't seeing this.

Bodies, hanging from lamp posts. One after the other, stretching away down the street. The traffic passing underneath seemed muted – cowed. The nearest body was an old woman in a flowery dress. Another was a dark-haired boy no older than Hal. From their bloody torsos, they'd all been shot first, then strung up.

They dangled motionless, without even a breeze stirring them.

"Fifty people," whispered Dwight. "She's decreed that from now on, if a Gun is killed, fifty people will be shot."

CHAPTER THREE

NOW, FIVE WEEKS LATER, MAC and I were about to climb into Dwight's van again, but this time its false back was gone – Dwight had removed it so his aunt and uncle wouldn't suspect.

He arrived promptly, picking us up in the dark parking lot. Mac and I sat in the rear as he drove us through the Harlemtown streets. "Holy moley, I can hardly *believe* it." Dwight glanced at us in the mirror, his hair looking almost white in the passing street lights. "The meeting's really going ahead?"

"Looks that way," I said, tension making me curt. Neither Mac nor I mentioned Collie. Only a few of us knew he was our contact.

"Nothing's agreed yet, don't forget," Mac told Dwight. "But, yeah, fingers crossed."

Former Appalachian President Arthur Weir had been under house arrest here in his native New Manhattan since Kay Pierce seized power. Dwight gave a low whistle, running his hands up and down the steering wheel.

"He'd be good," he said. "Well. *Anyone* else would be good. So long as we get rid of her, I don't care if we put a duck in charge." His eyes flicked to mine again in the mirror. "Hey, Amity, what did one Resistance worker say to the other?"

I smiled slightly. "I don't know, Dwight." It was a common refrain.

"'Know a duck we can put in charge?'"

"Don't joke, it may come to that," said Mac.

New Manhattan had twelve sectors now. When we reached Arnhem Street, we were on the far edge of Gemini, skirting Cancer.

The sectors had primarily been set up to establish checkpoints, but in a spirit of fear, people had embraced them. Through the van's side window I glimpsed a restaurant: Gemini's Delight, with an emblem of golden twins. Beside it was a hairdresser's: Twins' Tresses.

I gazed at the signs in apprehension. A week after our arrival, a man had resisted arrest and a second Gun was killed. Fifty more random people had been shot, their bodies strung up along Concord Avenue.

Even if President Weir agreed to help tonight...when

the time came, would the city stand behind us?

Dwight pulled up in the shadows behind Blake's Bar and Grill. He killed the engine and hopped out. As Mac and I emerged, an alley cat hissed and scrambled away.

Dwight darted a look at Blake's, rubbing the silver ring he always wore. "Will you be okay? Want me to wait for you?"

Mac clapped Dwight's shoulder. "Better not take the risk. Just get on home, buddy. Keep on their good side."

Dwight nodded tensely and glanced at me. "Good luck, doll-face." As always, he said it faux-gangster tough.

"Later, gator," I replied with a faint lifting of my lips.

After Dwight drove off, Mac and I went to the double basement doors that lay against the ground. I acted as lookout as Mac took the key from under its loose brick. The owner was another of our handful of sympathizers.

We crept down the stairs. The basement enveloped us: cool, dark, smelling of hops. A pile of dusty tables and chairs sat stacked against one wall. We edged behind them to an old door tucked away in the corner.

Mac creaked it open. Another dark stairway with earthen sides. We peered down, listening. Guns occasionally patrolled the upper tunnels.

There was no sound. Mac groped for the hidden gasoline lantern and offered a small grin. "Ready to go meet a president?"

I irritably pushed away my reluctance. "Ready."

Half an hour later, we were deep underground in a

section of the old sewers, a cavernous space that Ingo and I had found weeks ago: two storeys high, criss-crossed with ancient pipes. Its ceiling vanished into shadow in our lantern-light.

These abandoned subway tunnels and sewers were once the veins of old New York. Nearly two thousand years ago, the ancients had destroyed themselves in what we called the Cataclysm. Centuries later, New Manhattan rose atop New York's ruins. It had disused tunnels of its own.

The entire forbidden network spanned hundreds of miles and once linked several islands. The blast and time had altered the coast. Now, New Manhattan Island, nineteen miles long, was alone.

When Ingo went to boarding school here, a small band of his friends had explored its tunnels every weekend, sometimes throwing parties deep underground.

Back then it had just been a lark...until Kay Pierce took power. Closing her new capital city had trapped it in a nightmare. People were executed these days for even mentioning the tunnels, so full of covert possibilities.

By now, Ingo and I had mapped much of its main system. But the one thing we needed desperately – a route out, to help people escape – had so far eluded us.

I shoved my hands in my jacket pockets as Mac and I waited, my fingers tight. Mac started to say something – then four resounding clangs came from the pipes further up the tunnels. They echoed in the high, gloomy space.

Neither of us moved. I licked my lips and checked my watch. Exactly twenty seconds later, there were two more clangs.

Mac picked up a piece of lead and rapped out three quick beats of our own.

I stared at the main tunnel. *All that matters is what this means for the Resistance,* I reminded myself sharply. *You'd have had to see him again at some point anyway.*

Footsteps approached. Three men appeared in the shadows. One was average height with prematurely greying hair. One was tall and thin, with a half-scarred face framed by unruly black curls.

The third was Collie.

As arranged, Collie had covertly smuggled President Weir from the midtown brownstone where he was being held. Ingo had met them both and brought them down here. Mac glanced at me as we headed towards them but didn't speak.

We met the small group halfway across the dripping chamber. Mac offered his hand to President Weir. "Pleasure to meet you, sir."

Weir shook with Mac. "Likewise, Mr Jones. Thank you for arranging this."

"Shall I keep watch?" said Ingo.

Mac nodded. "Thanks, pal."

Ingo's eyes caught mine as he headed back into the tunnel. His small smile was troubled, sympathetic. It helped to know he understood how I felt.

Mac introduced me to President Weir. I kept my gaze from Collie as I shook his hand.

"It's very good to meet you, sir." Nerves stilted my voice.

Weir was young for a president, in his forties. His eyes were hazel and sombre, but he smiled dryly: the last time he'd seen me, I'd been on a stage shooting Gunnison.

"It would be difficult to forget you, Miss Vancour," he said. "Thanks for meeting me."

"The pleasure's mine," I said. As Mac said something else to President Weir, I knew I couldn't put it off any longer. I turned to Collie.

His hair was longer than when I'd last seen him in person, combed back from his strong-featured face. His blue-green shirt matched his eyes. He fiddled with his cuffs.

"Amity," he greeted me softly.

My spirits sank. From his expression, I hadn't been wrong – he *did* have hope. Surely he knew it was impossible? Yet as I stared at him, to my surprise my anger, my unease, faded.

What was left?

His throat moved. He stood motionless under my scrutiny. Belatedly, I put my hand out.

"Collie," I said, and we shook.

There weren't any chairs. The four of us sat on discarded pieces of pipe, our shadows long in the lantern-light. Mac outlined the plan: the Resistance would spend several months gaining support in New Manhattan before making a strike against Kay Pierce, Sandford Cain and their council. We'd then reinstate Weir as president over Can-Amer.

"You mean you're planning an assassination attempt," said President Weir.

"Yes," Mac responded simply, unflinching. "Not just an *attempt*, with luck."

Collie winced slightly at this. I had a sudden hollow memory of aiming at Gunnison; pulling the trigger. As I'd said to Ingo, it was worse this time – premeditated. Yet I longed to get it over with.

Mac explained further: the moment Pierce, Cain and the council were disposed of, various Resistance members would take over key points of the city – a telio station, the airport, the capitol building. Mac and others would then parade Weir through the streets, shouting that Pierce's reign was over and Weir was back in charge.

He finished, "When we get you to the capitol, we'll have a crowd of thousands with us. We'll put you back in power."

His level tone made the plan sound foolproof. All of us knew that if the city wouldn't stand behind us, it was anything but. The silence of the tunnels pressed down.

Weir's mouth was grave. "The European Alliance definitely won't help us depose her?"

"No one will," said Mac. "The world's left us on our own. It's this or nothing."

"If I consider this, I have to know that my family will be safe," Weir said finally. His wife and two daughters were under house arrest with him.

Mac glanced at me. We'd known he'd say this.

I leaned forward. "With luck, we can get them out of the city through the tunnels if need be."

Weir shot me a keen look. "You have a route out of the city?"

"Not yet," I admitted, cursing the fact. "But Ingo – the man who brought you down here – and I have just spent weeks mapping the tunnel system. We're close to finding a way out, I know it."

Half-bluster, half-hope. Mac was worried, I knew, but gave no sign.

"The second we have one, we can hook up with helpers to the north," he said. "They've agreed to form a sort of 'railroad' to get people in danger to Nova Scotia. It'll all help to boost morale, so that when the time comes, we can put you back in power without a hitch."

"Raising support is where you come in too, I suppose," said President Weir to me.

I nodded, disliking it but willing to do it. I'd do anything to get rid of Pierce.

"Everyone already knows who I am," I said. "So I guess we have to use that."

"Wildcat," said Mac with a small smile. It was the name the press had denounced me under, but we'd decided to use it – turn it around.

Mac counted off on his fingertips. "One, an underground newspaper – we've already started that. Two, Amity will begin giving wireless broadcasts, as soon as we source safe locations for them. Three, helping people found Discordant by doctoring their birth charts, or smuggling them out of the city. Word will spread: Wildcat's on the loose, and Pierce's days are numbered. People will stand behind us when we need them to."

He reached into his jacket and pulled out a copy of *Victory*, our newspaper. He handed it to President Weir. "We distribute those all over the city. They go on park benches, in library books…people are reading the truth."

President Weir scanned the single folded page. "Pretty risky for all of you, making it so obvious that you're here."

I shoved away the image of hanging bodies and shrugged brusquely. "There's no help for it, if we want to raise support."

"But ultimately, success will depend on the assassination plan itself." President Weir glanced at Collie. "How do you propose to do it?"

Collie shifted. "Well…not me specifically. But—"

"With his help," finished Mac. "Don't worry, any plan we put in place will be rock solid. But probably the less you know about that part, the better."

President Weir fell silent, clearly deep in thought. Mac waited patiently, though I saw a flicker of tension in his eyes. It matched my own. Without Weir's familiar presence at the helm, we'd face a probable military coup once Pierce and Cain were gone. Pierce had the army on her side.

Yet part of me was still conscious of Collie – the way he was sitting with his arms propped on his knees – and of my mysterious easing of mood where he was concerned. Why was that?

Then it hit me. I'd dreaded stirring up old feelings tonight – hadn't wanted to relive the pain. But at some point, without my even realizing it, the pain Collis Reed once caused me had faded.

The relief came from how little I actually felt on seeing him again.

My attention snapped back to President Weir. "I'll only agree to be involved if you can find an escape route through the tunnels," he said. "My family *must* be kept safe if things go wrong."

"We'll find one," said Mac firmly, rising and offering his hand to President Weir again. "Then we'll get word to you. With luck, we can attack by the end of the summer."

He sounded completely confident. My guts clenched at how much he was depending on Ingo and me. But at least we'd cleared this much of the hurdle. I let out a breath and stood up too.

As Mac and President Weir said a few last words to each other, Collie turned to me, jiggling his hands in his jacket pockets. "Amity…I wonder if maybe we could talk in private for just a few…"

He faltered at my expression. From somewhere, water dripped with a faint echo. Once I'd dreamed of hurting

Collie as badly as he'd hurt me. Now I just felt tired and detached – maybe even a little sorry for him.

Mostly, I wanted to leave.

"I don't think so, Collie," I said softly.

His small smile was bitter. "Yeah…forget it."

Just like the safe house in Bayon, you could go up on the roof of Jakov's, though there wasn't much of a view – just a sea of dingy brownstones and the lights of an occasional elevated train flashing past.

When Mac and I returned later that night, we went up. Mac smoked another cigarette while we waited for Ingo. He sat sideways on one of the two battered deckchairs, not saying much, his brow furrowed.

"Want to spill it?" I said finally.

He blew out a puff of smoke. "Let's wait for Manfred."

I nodded. Hugging my good leg, I looked up at the washed-out stars. Jakov kept pigeons; they rustled in their coop.

When Mac and I had come in, I'd been surprised to find Hal still up, working on an astrology chart. "Find the cache okay?" he said. He'd directed the question at Mac, though his eyes had flicked belatedly to me too.

"Yeah, I think it'll work really well," I'd said, my voice falsely cheerful.

Part of me had wanted him to ask questions about the mythical cache, even though I'd have had to lie further.

He'd just nodded stiffly and turned back to his chart. Mac had pretended not to notice, which made it worse.

And I'd known it was my own fault.

After I'd shot Gunnison in February, I'd made my way to the safe house where Hal was. Mac and Sephy had followed. I barely knew Mac then; all I knew was that he was a leader in the Resistance and had been a double agent under Gunnison.

Sephy had turned out to be no-nonsense and kind. When I could think of it, I'd been glad, because my brother had needed someone like that. A few days before I'd shot Gunnison, he'd learned that our father had thrown the civil war Peacefight. Then, though he'd only just found out I was still alive, I'd left him again without even a goodbye.

It was me Hal had needed those two months after Gunnison's death. Yet I hadn't been able to find my way out of myself to reach him. I spent entire days curled on an upstairs window seat, my thoughts as grey as the sky.

A memory came.

"Amity?"

Hal's voice. Outside, the oak trees shifted in the breeze, their branches bare. I stirred myself to lift my forehead off the window and look at him.

"Yes?"

He stood in the bedroom doorway, fists tight. "I just… thought you might want something."

I shook my head. "No. But thank you."

Later Sephy came to the door. "He's hurting too, you know."

"I know," I said, staring out at the trees.

But I hadn't moved.

I sighed, gazing at the pigeons' dark, feathered shapes. Since coming out of the greyness, I'd apologized to Hal; tried talking to him. He'd accepted the apology but a distance remained, like a pane of glass separating us.

It seemed the crucial moment had already passed, and now I wasn't sure how to get him back.

With relief, I pushed it all away as the roof door opened and Ingo appeared. He came over and sat beside me. "You're looking grim as hell, Mac – what's up?"

Mac stubbed out his cigarette. He studied us levelly, his features clear in the city's ambient glow. "Okay, you two, give it to me straight. We need that escape route. Can you do it?"

"With luck," I said.

"'With luck' doesn't fill me with joy, kiddo. You've had almost a month down there already."

"There are over three hundred miles of tunnels, you know," Ingo pointed out dryly.

"Exactly. Listen, if it's not possible, tell me now, and we'll figure something else out – though who knows what."

Ingo and I looked at each other. "From studying old maps, we think it's possible," I said slowly. "The northernmost tunnels are full of cave-ins – but we've gotten close a few times, Mac, we're sure of it."

"If there even *is* a way out," said Mac.

Ingo's dark eyes were still on mine. He glanced back at Mac. "I think there is. When I went to school here, a friend of mine said he'd found a route that went all the way under the river to the north. He wasn't the type to make up stories to impress us."

"Wish you could get hold of the guy and ask for directions."

"Yes, that would be more convenient than scrabbling our way through cave-ins, I agree."

Mac sat playing with his lighter, scraping the flame into life and then snapping it closed again.

"I don't have anyone spare to help you," he said finally.

The other dozen or so core Resistance members were New Manhattan residents, like Dwight. They had jobs, lives; they needed to avoid suspicion. The tunnels we had to reach to explore further were already over a day away.

"I won't even have *you* to spare in a few weeks, kiddo," Mac said to me. "As soon as we're ready with those wireless broadcasts, we need to get going on them, pronto."

"We'll find a route out," I said. "We *will*, Mac. We'll leave tomorrow morning. All right?" I added to Ingo, and he nodded.

"We're both good at maps," he said to Mac. "We'll figure this out if it kills us."

"Soon," said Mac. "I'd say 'no pressure', but I'd be lying through my teeth."

"We understand, don't worry," I said softly.

Mac nodded and stood up. He clapped Ingo on the shoulder and briefly squeezed my arm. "See you both tomorrow, before you go."

A pigeon trilled as he passed. The roof door closed behind him.

I exhaled and looked at Ingo. I tried to smile. "You shouldn't joke about figuring it out if it kills us, with all those cave-ins."

"Who the hell said I was joking?" Ingo swung himself wearily around so that he was lying lengthways on the deck chair, his long legs beside me. I knew he had an extra reason for wanting a route out of the city – he couldn't get word from his family without one.

I stayed where I was, thinking, tapping the chair's worn wood.

"The old Lexington Avenue line," I said. "The part of it we found that branches off – remember?"

"Yes, I was thinking the same." Ingo scraped a hand over his eyes. "The northernmost route – we can try the sewers around there too. It's a place to start, anyway."

"Agreed." The journey would take several days at least and I sighed, thinking of Hal. Being away again wouldn't help matters between us.

"Was it all right, seeing Collis?" asked Ingo suddenly.

I looked at him in surprise. He lay with one arm under his head, studying the stars. As I watched, he turned his face towards me.

"Fine," I said after a pause.

I nudged him. Ingo shifted and I stretched out beside him. I gazed up at the pale moon, taking in its faint craters. "I was dreading it, a little," I admitted. "But there's just… nothing left. I don't even hate him any more."

"Well, I suppose that kind of thing does kill a relationship," said Ingo wryly. He knew about my arrest fourteen months ago, when Collie had turned me in.

"I just wondered," he added. He cleared his throat. "I'm glad it was all right for you. I was imagining how I'd feel if it was me, seeing Miriam again."

"How would you?" I turned my head towards him. The ruined side of his face was close to me, its puckered folds shadowy.

Ingo lay still. His arm under his head moved as he shrugged.

"Reluctant. Unhappy. But ultimately relieved, I think, to realize she didn't have any effect on me any more." His ex had betrayed him, too, only days before my own arrest.

It was late; the elevated train had stopped running half an hour ago. I nodded, feeling the long warmth of Ingo beside me and listening to the silence of this city that was never totally silent – the faint drone of traffic, an ambulance siren off in the distance.

"Yes," I said, and smiled at the stars. "That's exactly it."

CHAPTER FOUR

MAY, 1942

KAY PIERCE LAY PROPPED ON one elbow, gazing down at Collis.

He was asleep on his stomach, one arm looped around the satin-cased pillow, his ribs moving faintly with each steady breath. His sandy hair – so immaculate during the day – was rumpled, full of dark gold shadows in the glow from her bedside lamp.

Kay resisted the urge to stroke the silky-looking strands. She jostled his bare shoulder.

"Hey," she said.

"Hmm?"

"*Hey*," she repeated, shaking him.

Collis gazed up blearily.

"You have to get out," she said.

He peered at the gold clock on her bedside table. Almost four a.m. He yawned and drew her close. "No, not yet," he murmured. He kissed her hair.

Kay pressed briefly against his firm torso, savouring the feel of him. Then she pulled away. A glass of water sat beside her lamp. She dipped her fingers in it and flicked them at his face.

"Out," she said.

Collis's eyes flew open and he sat up, swiping at his damp cheeks. He gave a rueful grin. "All right, all right," he said. "Madame President."

He kissed her bare shoulder and got out of bed. Kay stayed where she was, taking in his lean athleticism as he dressed. The dimpled wound on his right bicep was his only blemish.

Collis didn't bother with his undershirt; his own room was just down the corridor. Trousers on, shirt hanging open, he bent over her, his lips briefly demanding on hers.

"Sure I can't stay?"

"Very."

Collis eased her back onto the sheets and held himself poised over her. "Really sure?" he whispered against her mouth. His warm lips slid down to her neck. "You can feel what you're doing to me, can't you?"

She could, and was half-amused, half-irritated to realize that she wanted him again too.

"*Out*, Collis," she said, pushing at him. He kissed her once more, gently, and then got up.

"Are you ever going to let me stay an entire night?" he asked. His eyes were pure green tonight. Sometimes they looked blue, sometimes a mix of the two. Kay shrugged and pulled her knees to her chest.

The fact that she wanted him to stay meant that she'd throw him out every night without fail.

Collis gave a half-smile, as if reading her mind. He picked up the glass of water and took a sip. "You should try that water-flicking trick against Cain," he said, toasting her with the glass. "It might startle the bastard enough to solve all our problems."

Then her speech-writer and special advisor was gone, slipping out the door and easing it shut behind him.

Kay smiled slightly. The deal she'd offered Collis when he'd first awakened from his gunshot wound over three months ago had been accepted, as she'd guessed it would be – and was working out even better than she'd hoped. They were two of a kind. She'd known it for a long time.

Her smile faded at the thought of Sandford Cain. "Problem", indeed.

The pale-eyed Cain had been Gunnison's right-hand man, renowned for his brutality. Kay had a sudden flash of his clubbing Mrs Lloyd, her former neighbour in Topeka. His bland expression had barely changed – only from the twitch of his mouth had Kay realized how much he'd enjoyed striking the woman unconscious.

Kay started to bite a fingernail, then caught herself. She might have enjoyed it too, come to that – she'd loathed Mrs Lloyd – but having Cain still alive, working under her, when he possibly knew too much about his own bullet wound…that was worrying.

Very.

Kay's palace had once been the finest hotel in New Manhattan. Six hours later, she and Collis stood on its west balcony, smiling and waving to a cheering crowd. It was late May and glorious. People stood pressed together, filling the expanse of Centre Park – a mass of fedora hats and bright summer dresses, with Harmony flags flying above them.

"You look gorgeous," Collis murmured to her. The sun hit his hair, turning it flaxen.

"Not so bad yourself," she said, a broad smile plastered on her face.

"Got a good night's sleep," he said.

The throbbing cheers washed over Kay, lifting her spirits. They were for *her*, a sign of all she'd accomplished. The scene echoed the many Harmony Rallies that she'd attended under Gunnison, down to the dozens of grey-clad Guns in attendance, boots gleaming as they surveyed the crowd.

Back then, she'd had no idea that she'd one day become John Gunnison's Chief Astrologer – and much more. She'd just been a frightened citizen like all the rest, cheering loudly so that no one would suspect her.

At the thought of Gunnison, something hardened within Kay. She arched her eyebrows at Collis, who handed her a sheet of typewritten paper. She lifted her chin and stepped close to the microphone. It was large and rectangular, with a Harmony symbol at its base. Her diamond scorpion brooch glinted.

"Thank you," she said, and heard her voice bounce back with a faint whine. She read the speech Collis had prepared, speaking of the need to remain vigilant about the Discordant menace – to keep a close eye on others and report anything suspicious.

"We have come far, but we have not yet won," she informed the hushed crowd. "With your help, we will." She raised her voice and punched the air. "Harmony for ever!"

The flags waved in the breeze. On cue, the crowd cheered again, a roar of sound that buoyed her.

So far it was no more than what Johnny had done, maybe. But it would be. Kay thought of her secret plans and smiled.

Johnny was dead. She was not.

Later, she strode down a cool marble corridor, her heels tapping out a quick beat. Collis walked beside her, tall and solid. She handed him the speech without breaking stride and he put it in his briefcase.

They turned a corner and Cain appeared.

His reflection wavered in the marble as he headed towards them with several cronies in tow – none as bland-faced as he, but all with smiling faces, shielded eyes. Kay stopped.

Cain nodded as he drew near and halted. "Madame President." His tone indicated nothing but respect.

"Sandford, good morning," said Kay briskly. She'd never been able to bring herself to use Johnny's nickname for him, "Ford". She wished she could; it might lessen her fear. *Why* hadn't her aim been better that day?

She indicated Cain's briefcase. "Did you receive my memo?"

"Yes, I did." Cain passed his case to an underling, who drew out the pieces of paper. Collis – immaculate in a double-breasted suit despite the day's warmth – leaned against the wall, watching.

"*Noted Discordants*," read Cain. His pale gaze met hers. "Very interesting. I'll check them out when I have time, of course. But I see nothing to worry about."

Kay stiffened. Some of the names were random, to keep people on their toes. Others were potential dangers to her regime, gleaned from various sources.

Cain knew this.

"They've already been checked out," she said sharply. "All that needs doing are the arrests."

Cain gave a small smile. "With respect, Madame President, you've put me in charge of Special Investigations.

I'd be failing in my duty if I didn't investigate. But thank you, sincerely, for the information."

His bowed head stopped just short of irony. He and his group continued down the corridor.

Their footsteps faded. It felt as if the walls had grown eyes. Kay motioned quickly to Collis. They went into an adjacent room and she closed the door and pressed her fingers against her pounding temples.

"Do we have a copy of the list?" she asked.

"Of course," said Collis quietly.

The room lay in shadow, its heavy curtains partly drawn. Kay leaned against a table. "I'll have to bypass him and go to the Head Gun," she murmured. A blatant move – a direct confrontation to Cain's judgement. Her stomach chilled. She glanced at Collis.

"Are we any closer?" she asked.

He knew what she meant. He propped himself beside her and nodded. "I'm trying. We can't move too fast without raising suspicion."

"I *will* get rid of him," she said.

Collis's gaze was steady. His hand closed around hers. "*We* will."

Kay exhaled. Maybe Collis's trustworthiness only extended as far as their deal…but she knew Collis down to his core and that didn't worry her. Meanwhile, his fingers were warm – firm.

His grip tightened. "I've been thinking that a new meeting room might help," he said in an undertone.

She frowned and looked up at him. "How?"

"We need one that's more secure. Down in the basement, maybe. Someplace where we're certain no one's watching or listening."

Kay considered it. "Yes, maybe."

The thought of the basement reminded her of something and she crossed to the window. It looked out to Can-Amer Avenue.

She propped her hands on the sill, gazing down at the streaming traffic. A line of tall grey Shadowcars slid past. Pedestrians bustled across when the light changed, some of the men carrying their suit jackets over their arms in the heat.

Beneath it all lay the tunnels. Kay imagined them: cool, vast, endless.

"You said that the Resistance uses that ancient tunnel network," she said without turning around.

Collis's reflection appeared beside hers as he joined her. "Yeah, that's what Mac told me."

"Let's get more Guns down there. Experts."

His eyebrows drew together as he glanced at her. "We can't clamp down *too* hard. The Resistance can't know that I—"

"They won't. We'll do it gradually. But I want all the main sections mapped." She couldn't dispose of Cain – yet – but *here* she could flex her muscles.

Collis nodded, playing with one of his cufflinks. Another new pair, Kay noticed, amused. Armanti and Manti, even, with the trademark *AM*. Collis Reed cut an impressive figure these days.

Money and power. Just like she'd known.

Kay turned and perched on the broad window sill. Standing in a bar of sunlight, Collis looked every inch the ex-Peacefighter hero. It amused her further: if the world only knew. She trailed a slow finger down his chest – circled his belt buckle.

"Will you see to it?" she said sweetly.

Collis's smile was knowing. He caught her hand and kissed it.

"What else is a right-hand man for?" he said.

CHAPTER FIVE

MAY, 1942

THE CAVE IN MIGHT HAVE BEEN THERE for almost two thousand years. It felt as if Ingo and I had too, endlessly shifting these ancient shards of concrete, while darkness pressed against our lantern's glow.

We were *so close*.

Ingo pulled another rock free and chucked it back into the abandoned subway tunnel. A clattering echo.

"Keep playing – this is driving me insane," he said.

"Whose turn is it?" I said, distracted.

"I don't remember. Yours."

I tugged at a stubborn piece of rubble and blew out a breath. How far had we gotten? Five feet? Six? I resisted the urge to take out our map and check – I'd done that over and over, until Ingo had threatened to take it away altogether.

"I'm waiting," he said.

"Bossy."

"Pot, kettle."

I smiled slightly and thought before settling on a "First or Favourite" we hadn't already done. "All right – favourite class at school."

Ingo paused mid-motion and looked at me.

"It's a perfectly valid question," I said.

"Which we must have already done a dozen times."

I wrestled with the rubble, jerking it back and forth. "I don't think so," I got out. "I always thought…it was too obvious…so I never asked."

Ingo tugged another rock loose. "Fine, I believe you," he grunted. "History."

No, we hadn't asked it yet, because that surprised me. I wiped sweat from my cheeks and looked at him. "Really? I thought you'd say literature."

He shook his head and lobbed the rock behind us. "Reading always felt private to me. History though… I liked learning what had happened in all those places in the atlas."

I finally wrenched the stone free and paused, eyeing the rockfall. It stayed stable.

"I didn't like history," I admitted.

Ingo's good eyebrow shot up as he glanced at me. "You? I'm surprised."

"I'm surprised *you* liked it. All that memorizing of dates."

Ingo helped me heft a large shard aside. "Ah, so you never had a good teacher then…I didn't like it either, until I got Frau Berger. What was yours?"

"Math." I reached for another dusty rock. "I loved how logical it was, like working out puzzles. I'd do all the problems really fast and then draw airplanes."

Ingo gave a tired grin and swiped his wrist over his grimy forehead. "All right, *that* doesn't surprise me. Okay, first time you got drunk."

I was struggling a shard free. It came loose with a scrape and the pile of ancient debris shifted abruptly, lurching us sideways. I held back a yelp and Ingo grabbed my arm, holding me in place. We stayed motionless for several beats, staring at the ceiling.

Finally he let go of me. We exchanged a look…but neither of us suggested stopping.

My heart still pounding, I twisted to heft the rock down the tunnel.

"It was when I was fifteen," I said, as if nothing had happened.

"With Rob the bad-boy boyfriend?"

"Yes, exactly." I glanced at him; my tension faded a little as I smiled. "If you already knew, why did you ask?"

Ingo craned for another stone. "Details, my friend. You know the rules."

"All right, it was at a party. Ma said I couldn't go and so I snuck out through my window and climbed down the fire escape. Rob had stolen some cherry brandy from his parents' liquor cabinet and we drank it on the way there."

Ingo gave an amused wince. "The whole bottle?"

"It wasn't full. But we each had a few swigs, and I thought it was *delicious*. Like drinking cherry lollipops."

"Ugh."

"I know. And then we got to the party and there was beer, and someone had brought the dregs from one of their parents' cocktail parties that they'd collected in a milk bottle—"

"You can stop now. I'm feeling sick."

I wrestled another shard free. "Nope, you get to hear the whole sad story. I had three beers and a few gulps from the dregs bottle *and* some wine that someone had brought, and I danced for hours even though I'd never danced before, and then I threw up on the way home and Rob couldn't get me back up the fire escape. And so he had to ring our doorbell and when Ma answered I threw up *again* on the doorstep, and she was *livid* – not that I remember much about that part since I'd pretty much passed out by then. I didn't drink again for almost two years."

Ingo had started laughing halfway through this. "I don't believe it. That's even worse than the first time *I* got drunk."

"At home?"

"No. Of course not."

"Why do you look so surprised? You grew up on a vineyard."

"Exactly. Dad started us off with a splash of wine mixed with water at dinner, then a quarter glass, then half, and so on. I could drink responsibly by the time I was twelve. No, it was when I was in boarding school—"

We both froze at a creaking moan.

Our gazes clashed. We scrambled to our feet, staring at the dark ceiling.

I licked my lips. "Maybe we only…" I started, and then the groan came again. A crack shivered open above the cave-in. Pebbles pattered against the rubble. Behind us, a few larger stones fell, landing with quiet thuds.

"Get out!" cried Ingo. He snatched the lantern; I was already lunging to grab our backpack.

The darkness swung crazily in the lantern light as we raced down the tunnel. Pieces of falling masonry came steadily now, pelting at our feet. I cried out as my weak leg tried to buckle, and Ingo put his arm around me, hurrying me on.

The world erupted. Noise roared through me – shuddered up through my shoes. Panting, I risked a glance back and saw the bend we'd just come around disappear under a black, shifting curtain.

Finally it ended.

We jogged to an unsteady stop and stood clutching our knees, trying to catch our breath in the dust-choked air. The bullet wound in my thigh throbbed – dazedly, I wished that I still carried my cane.

"We'd…we'd better go and see," I said in a faint voice.

Ingo scraped his hands over his face. "Yes," he said at last. "Let's find out just how depressed we should be."

We held our arms over our mouths and headed back, coughing, until we reached a new, solid barrier of debris.

Neither of us spoke. Ingo held up the lantern as I took out our hand-drawn map and spread it against the wall. I touched our location. Ingo put his own finger where we'd just been digging.

We gazed at the distance between the two.

"I wish to hell that I didn't know the scale on this thing," Ingo muttered. We were standing close, arms touching.

Fifty feet. I choked out a laugh. "So…I guess the answer to how depressed we should be is 'very'."

"Unless it's 'extremely'."

Wearily, I put the map away. "No, let's go with 'very'. Save 'extremely' for the time we *don't* run fast enough."

We looked at each other. And although nothing was funny…after a beat, Ingo's mouth twitched. An answering snicker escaped me – after the hours of hyped-up hope, it was that or cry.

Once we'd started, we couldn't stop. We slid down the wall to the ground, shaking with helpless laughter.

"You realize…you realize that we've probably both gone insane," got out Ingo.

"I can't think of anyone better to go insane with," I gasped.

"I'm not sure that's a compliment."

"Statement of fact, pal. Statement of fact."

When our laughter finally faded, there was only darkness, and the weight of two cities above: one ruined, one modern. I stared at the cave-in, taking in its jagged shadows.

We'd been so close.

Finally Ingo sighed and got up. He reached a hand out to help me, his fingers firm against mine. He let go the moment I was standing.

"You know," he said, "I'm not sure pilots should spend so much time underground."

The days passed in a blur of tunnels—digging out cave-ins, exploring even deeper in the abandoned labyrinth. The tunnels were treacherous but had a weird beauty: the way our lantern-light stroked across the ancient bricks, or revealed arch after arch heading off into the blackness.

You could tell from odd artefacts that after the Cataclysm people had lived down here, maybe for centuries. We found dusty makeshift shelters, weird murals, signs for "roadways".

Once we rounded a corner, and I gasped. Bones. Thousands lay stacked in a curved alcove across from an old subway control room. We'd found several "graveyard" chambers piled high with skeletons; some centuries-ago person had made this one into artwork. The scrolled ends of femurs made geometric patterns. A line of ribcages had skulls inside.

I shone our light over the structure in wonder. "Was the artist insane, do you think? Or just bored?"

"Or both," Ingo said. "One doesn't preclude the other."

"Personal experience?"

"Ho, ho."

The thought of a bored maniac was amusing, in a grisly way, and I smiled. "It needs a name."

Ingo straightened from where he'd been examining its base. "Yes, you're right." He came over and took the water canteen from me; he took a swig and absently handed it back, studying the bones intently.

"'Maniac's Delight'," he said.

I wrinkled my nose. "Really?"

"All right, *you* think of something."

"You're the creative one."

He gave an amused snort as we started walking again, our footsteps echoing. "I am? Since when?"

"Well, you're the one who reads poetry, anyway."

"Oddly enough, there are very few poems about a shitload of bones stacked in an abandoned tunnel."

"'Ode to Bones'," I said, and he barked out a laugh.

"Now *that* is even worse than mine," he told me.

Just as we'd already done for weeks, Ingo and I spent almost every moment together. Sometimes frustrated, sometimes hopeful – but always talking. We often lay awake in our bedrolls, sleep impossible when there was so much to say to each other.

Though it was cold down here, we kept our bedrolls

separate. On the run together six months ago, we'd slept pressed together for warmth every night and thought nothing of it. Now this was something to be avoided, as definitely as if we'd discussed it. I wasn't sure why. It just seemed like a bad idea.

But night after night, I listened to Ingo's steady breathing a few feet away, and was glad he was there.

Whenever our supplies ran low, we had to return to Jakov's, or to caches stocked by the others. In the upper tunnels, especially under the West Side, we had to choose our routes carefully to avoid the Guns we occasionally saw.

Each time we returned, it was harder to tell Mac that we hadn't found the route out yet.

Two days into our latest journey, we were both edgy. We'd spent over three weeks now discounting various routes in the deepest, most ancient tunnels under the island's northern tip. If a route out existed, we had to be getting close.

When a new passage branched off from the one we were exploring, Ingo paused and took out the map. "This section's worse than a rabbit warren," he muttered, glancing at his compass. "I think the ancients were just building tunnels for the hell of it."

I checked the twine we used to measure distance. "Or to torment us. Fifty-two feet."

"Thanks. And, yes, that too. They thought, 'How can we

make life as difficult as possible for a pair of pilots-turned-cartographers a few thousand years from now…'"

He crouched and spread the map on his leg. His hand, as dirty as mine, made careful marks. As he worked, my gaze lingered absently on the line of his thigh – the way his dark hair curled so crisply against his neck.

The need to record everything slowed us down, but was vital. And despite our urgency, it was satisfying to see the map grow, bit by bit, a perfect representation of the tunnels.

I liked it that Ingo understood this – that he felt the same.

When we finally put our gear down tiredly hours later, we were in an abandoned subway station, its tiles still eerily fresh-looking. We compared our hand-drawn map against the ancient chart on the wall and it ignited us again.

"There, you see?" said Ingo, pointing at the Broadway Line. "All the way under the river. That *must* be the route Will found." He rapped the wall. "If we could just get around these damn cave-ins."

Will had been his boarding school friend. From Ingo's tense frown, I guessed he was thinking not only of the Resistance, but of hearing from his family. It seemed to be weighing on him – he'd been uncharacteristically quiet for hours.

"Look…maybe here." I traced the newly-drawn branch on our map. "It might run adjacent to the cave-ins…what if there's a service tunnel that cuts across and connects?"

Ingo grimaced, rubbing the stubble that grew only on

his left jaw. Most of the service tunnels we'd found ran parallel to their main routes.

Finally he glanced at my thigh. "Could you manage it, even if we found one?"

He was right; my wound was aching. "I'm fine." The possibility, however slim, made me too edgy to sleep. "You're not tired, are you? Want to go check it out?"

Ingo studied the map again. "All right. Might as well." He quickly packed up our bedrolls and shot me a grin. "Who knows, maybe we'll get lucky for a change."

We didn't.

We spent hours exploring the ancient sewer. No service routes. No way to cut across. By the time we finally made camp in a niche in the sewer's curved wall, it was after three in the morning. We were both quiet with discouragement, too exhausted to be hungry.

We put the lantern on low. The shadows drew closer. The ancient concrete was cold, even through my bedroll, and I hugged myself. Ingo lay gazing at the arched ceiling, the unmarred side of his face grim.

Distantly, a slight rustling came – a rat, maybe. I stiffened. For a change, Ingo didn't tease me about it.

Silence.

"I asked Mac to get in touch with Collie," I said out of nowhere.

Ingo's head turned. He looked at me in surprise and I sighed, remembering a conversation I'd had with Mac the last time we'd returned to Jakov's.

"For Hal." I rolled towards Ingo, propping myself on one elbow. "He doesn't know yet that we've been in contact with Collie. They've always been like brothers. I think he needs to see him, if Mac can manage it. Especially now, when…"

I trailed off with a weary shrug. Ingo knew about the current distance between Hal and me.

He was silent for a moment. "Good," he said. "I hope 'Collie' can work his magic."

"There's no magic," I said, nettled. Ingo never called Collie by his nickname – he'd given it an ironic twist. "They've just always been close."

"My mistake."

"What's with you?"

"Nothing. I'm delighted for them."

"Fuck off, Ingo," I said, and he stared at me – then got it. It was what he'd once told me his sister Lena said, to let him know he was out of line.

"Fine, I'm sorry," he said. "Forgive me if hearing about Collis Reed isn't what I feel like doing just now."

"What *do* you feel like doing?"

"Not talking at all, if that's the best conversation you can manage."

He didn't often get in this mood. It annoyed me when he did. I didn't bother answering. I lay studying the ancient stonework, irritably counting its patterns – wishing I was tired enough for sleep.

At last Ingo sighed and rubbed his temples. "I apologize,"

he said in a low voice. "I know how worried about Hal you've been – I'm glad he'll get to see Collis. I mean it."

I looked over at him in the dim light. "Accepted," I said finally.

"Today's Erich's birthday," he said.

"Oh," I said softly, suddenly understanding. Erich was his brother. They were as close as Collie and Hal.

Ingo lay gazing up at the stonework. His tone was too level. "He always goes home for it. Everyone will be there. If they still think I'm dead, it'll be…"

"Don't think about it." I stretched to touch his arm. "Tell me about another birthday instead."

His good eyebrow arched. "Whose?"

"Anyone's. One of your favourites to remember."

After a pause he shifted onto his side, facing me. "All right. It was Dad's seventieth two years ago. My family always makes a big deal of birthdays – everyone comes, all our cousins, neighbours, everyone. There's a special meal, outside if it's warm enough. You can see the vineyards… smell the olive trees…the kids run around, playing…"

Wistfulness touched me at the look on his face. It reminded me of how I'd felt about the farm I grew up on. The rambling old house with its surrounding woods and fields had once been my whole world.

"So we threw a surprise party for Dad," Ingo went on. "We had it the day before his birthday, so he wouldn't guess. Lena and I had letters going back and forth for months, planning it."

"Erich?" I said.

"He helped get everything ready. Quite a covert operation, apparently. And he picked me up in Pisa when my ship got in. I'd saved up all my Peacefighting leave so I could be there."

"Were you seeing Miriam then?"

"No, thank fuck."

I laughed. "Why 'thank fuck'?"

"Because I might have been demented enough to take her home with me, and it would've been a disaster." Ingo gave me a dry look. "Are you determined to talk about our exes tonight?"

"No. Go on."

Ingo smiled slightly, his eyes remembering. "At the party, Dad pretended to be annoyed – he kept demanding to know why we were all making such a fuss. 'I'm seventy, not dead!' But when he first realized what we'd done – when he saw the decorations, and that I was home – he had tears in his eyes. Later, he took me into his study…" Ingo stopped.

"What?" I said.

He hesitated, his expression battling sadness. "He told me he was proud of me," he said. "When I became a Peacefighter he didn't try to stop me, but it wasn't what he wanted – I knew that. It wasn't even really what *I* wanted; I just got swept up in it. But he told me that he'd always seen himself in me…and that when I finished my term and turned twenty-one, we'd have a serious talk."

Ingo was twenty-one now – he'd had a birthday in Harmony Five.

"About the vineyard?" I guessed.

Ingo nodded slowly. "Erich's never been interested. And Lena wants it as a place to come home to, but not to run it. Dad knows how much I love it. All of it – every vine, every stone of the house. It's been in our family for over a hundred years."

I swallowed, thinking, *He could be there now, if he hadn't chosen to help fight.*

As if hearing my thought, Ingo's mouth quirked wryly. "Maybe that's partly why I had to stay," he said. "Because I care so much about my home. And if Pierce isn't stopped..." He gave a bitter laugh and shoved his hand through his dark curls, gazing at the ceiling. "Ah, hell, that sounds so...stupidly noble, saying it out loud, and I'm not. But it's true, I guess."

"I understand," I said quietly.

Ingo turned and looked at me, his mouth still wry but his eyes warm. "Tell me about one of yours."

"Homes?"

"Birthdays, you noodle."

I snickered. "Noodle?"

"Go on."

I thought for a minute. "When I was seven," I said finally. "Dad took me up in his Firedove. I think it might have been the first time he let me take the controls. It was..." I shook my head, not having words – remembering aiming the Firedove at a cloud and then lifting it higher – the feeling of soaring, the smell of machine oil, the Dove so responsive at my fingertips.

"I can imagine," said Ingo, his tone soft.

Recalling Dad's hand occasionally guiding mine as I steered, sadness touched me. Would I ever have a memory of him again that didn't bring back what he'd done?

"Don't, Amity," murmured Ingo.

Glancing at him, my muscles eased. We exchanged a small smile.

"The birthday," he said. "Don't leave me in suspense."

I let out a breath. "And that night, Ma had baked a chocolate cake."

"Your favourite?"

"Isn't it everyone's?"

"No. Mine is tiramisu."

"Sorry, but that's just wrong. And I got a pile of adventure stories, and probably lots of toys and board games, and they let me stay up until midnight."

Ingo propped his head on his hand. "You didn't have any friends over?"

"I wasn't really close to the girls in my class," I admitted. "All I cared about were airplanes and climbing trees. Besides, we lived a few miles outside of town. Collie was there," I added. "Sorry. Not to bring exes into it again."

Ingo shrugged. "He was part of your life. If you have good memories of him, I'm glad."

"You must have some of Miriam."

"Oh, ye gods, you *are* determined to talk about our exes tonight."

"Don't you?"

He looked tiredly amused. "My good memories of her take place almost exclusively in bed, if you want the truth. And even then she'd usually pick a fight just afterwards, which tended to take the shine off it." He grimaced. "Maybe back then I found it exciting. Who knows?"

"I can't picture you putting up with that," I confessed. The Ingo I'd known so well for the past seven months would have little time for game-playing.

"No, me neither," he said. "Not after almost a year in Harmony Five."

I'd become very conscious of the long lines of his form — the nearness of him. I went silent, playing with a loose thread on my bedroll. "I was in love with Collie, but... I had no idea who he actually was," I said finally. "So I wasn't in love with him after all. He was just...a fantasy."

"I suppose I've never..." Ingo hesitated, looking as if he were searching for words.

"What?" I whispered.

"Friendship has always been more important to me. So I suppose I've never mixed the two. I've never been with someone who I really like...who I also love."

We gazed at each other. The stillness of the tunnels beyond the small glow of our lantern felt absolute.

As the silence grew heavy, I could sense Ingo about to speak. A feeling oddly like fear came.

I straightened. "All right, first or favourite," I said. "First time you were ever grounded."

When I woke up, I was in Ingo's arms.

I lay motionless, gazing at his ruined face. We'd talked for a long time the night before, playing the game and sharing stories about our pasts, and must have fallen asleep without turning off the lantern. I had a vague memory of half-rousing, freezing cold, and dragging my bedroll next to Ingo's, pressing against him the way we'd done so many times in the past. He'd put his arms around me without waking up.

He was still asleep. I studied his eyelashes – pitch black, surprisingly long against his pale skin. Even at rest, his arms had a wiry strength.

Something seemed poised within me. I frowned and shook it away. *No. Ingo's my friend.*

I edged from his embrace. He murmured something and rolled over.

When I checked my watch, I saw that it was time for us to get up anyway. I dragged my bedroll a few feet away again and then gently shook his shoulder.

"Hey," I said. "Rise and shine, lazybones."

Over the next twenty-four hours, we mapped a rough, zigzagging route along the partially-collapsed Broadway

Line. In places we had to squirm through narrow passages, praying there wouldn't be another cave-in.

At last, after dropping down from an old sewer, we suddenly found ourselves facing an underground river coursing past.

On the other side, we could see light.

We stared at it, hardly daring to hope. "Feel like a swim?" said Ingo.

"I've never felt more like one," I said fervently.

The water was waist-high and smelled bad. We made it across, battling the current. The opening was an old grille set in the ceiling; through it hung long strands of moss. Blue sky showed through the slime. No sound of traffic.

Ingo, almost a head taller than me, wrestled the grate off. When we climbed cautiously out through the square hole, neither of us knew what we'd see – we could be emerging into a city park for all we knew.

Instead we found ourselves in a quiet patch of woods, with New Manhattan in the distance. We gave a jubilant whoop and spontaneously hugged, Ingo lifting me off the ground.

"We did it!" he cried. "*We did it!*"

We were both filthy, wet with mud. I laughed, exultant, holding onto him. We could set up the "railroad" – Ingo might soon have word from his family – President Weir would commit to our plan.

The thoughts tumbled past. Ingo put me down almost immediately, both of us still grinning...and I suddenly realized what else this meant.

It was almost June. I'd begin doing the wireless broadcasts now, and Ingo would start getting people out of the city – it had been decided for weeks that that would be his role. Through Sephy's astrology work, there were already many desperate to escape.

From now on, until – if – Pierce was defeated, I'd see Ingo only when he returned to Jakov's to stock up before taking another group out. I'd never know whether my friend was safe until he got back.

The thought left me hollow.

"I'll miss you," I said without thinking.

Ingo was studying the New Manhattan skyline, the scarred half of his face to me. At first he didn't move. Then he glanced at me, his dark gaze slightly unsure – questioning. For a moment I felt unaccountably awkward.

After a beat, Ingo gave a rueful smile.

"I'll miss you too," he said.

CHAPTER SIX

JUNE — JULY, 1942

I RUBBED MY PALMS ON my thigh. "I don't know what to say," I muttered to Mac. I'd prepared notes, but looking over them, they seemed trite and stilted.

Mac and Dwight had readied numerous locations for our secret broadcasts. The boarded-up shoe factory still smelled faintly of leather. I sat at a long, dusty table. In front of me, the wireless set's switches and dials reminded me a little of a Firedove.

Mac leaned against the table. His voice was low, as passionate as I'd ever heard it.

"Tell them not to lose hope," he said. "Tell them you're Wildcat, that you're here, that they've got to find ways to fight that won't get them killed but that will keep the spirit of victory alive. Wake them up, Amity."

"You'd be better at this than me," I said softly, shaken by his intensity.

"Nah. They don't want to listen to some bozo they've barely heard of, who used to work with Sandford goddamn Cain. They want you, kiddo." He touched my shoulder. "You can do it. Be our voice."

I turned on the wireless set. Its dials glowed yellow as it hummed into life. I glanced down at my notes, frowning, thinking. Slowly, I slid them aside.

Mac checked his watch. At seven o'clock exactly, he murmured, "Go."

Trying to ignore my thumping heart, I leaned towards the mic.

"This is Amity Vancour, the voice of the Resistance," I said. "The press call me 'Wildcat'. I'm here to tell you that you're not alone."

My voice sounded squeaky. Angry with myself – *come on, Amity, you can do this* – I kept talking, pushing myself.

Somehow words came, though I stumbled several times. I urged people not to give up hope – to keep victory in their hearts.

We only dared broadcast for five minutes at a time; we knew the Guns were sure to start seeking us using wireless waves of their own. That first night, the five minutes felt like five hours.

When I finished, I slumped back in my seat. I had little

recollection of what I'd actually said; for those minutes my whole world had been the microphone.

Mac squeezed my hand and smiled.

"Good job, Wildcat," he murmured.

I got used to broadcasting more quickly than I would have expected. It helped that my only visible audience was Mac. He was always there, willing me on with his eyes.

He reminded me of Russ, my old team leader. He made me want to be better than I was. Having spent so much time in the tunnels, I'd missed a lot of what was happening in the city. In the glimpses of its streets that I saw now, while being covertly driven somewhere to broadcast, there were Guns everywhere.

Spotting them never got easier. It always brought back Harmony Five.

Kay Pierce relished showing people what would happen if they put a toe out of line. The street lamp on the corner of Central and 42nd was a favourite of hers. We avoided passing it whenever possible, but sometimes had no choice. Once, Dwight was driving us and I knew from his sudden silence and the whiteness of his knuckles what was coming up.

Mac, in the back of the van with me, didn't tell me not to look. He wouldn't; he faced things head-on. From his expression, he was thinking, *This is what we're fighting.*

The bloodied body of an old man dangled limply

from the street lamp. A sign reading *Dissenter* hung around his neck. I felt empty. I stared at his features, obscured by a dark, moving mass of flies in the heat…and thought numbly that Harmony Five had been better that way, with its frost instead.

The fear was constant. I hoped Ingo would be safer in the tunnels, but the Guns' presence down there had increased. They seemed to be mapping it themselves. We could barely use the routes under the West Side now. We tried to keep the shadowy passageways that led to the deepest routes, heading out of the city, hidden.

But we were doing it – helping people to escape. "When I take a group out, I get to know them a little," Ingo told me on one of his fleeting return visits. "You can't help it. And I also know what would happen to every one of them if we hadn't found that route."

From the expression in his eyes, we were both seeing a barbed-wire fence…Guns in greatcoats.

I cleared my throat. "We should find your friend Will and thank him."

Ingo smiled. "Screw that," he said softly. "Thank *you*. I'd have gone crazy searching down there alone."

Whenever he left for another journey, I knew almost a week would pass before I saw him again. As the summer burned on, I listened tensely to Pierce's nightly telio speeches, dreading to hear that he'd been caught.

Worry for my friend became a way of life. Missing him became a way of life.

Meanwhile, word spread about our illegal broadcasts. We'd mentioned them in *Victory* and people were listening, tuning in secretly on ham wireless sets – telling others, gathering in small groups to hear.

Soon Pierce was proclaiming on the telio, "'V for victory' is a sham! Drawing the Resistance's symbol just proves you're a traitor like Vancour – don't believe her lies! For a Harmonic society, we must all…"

Mac grinned when he heard this. "Thanks, buddy," he said to the invisible Collie behind the scenes. It made me smile grimly too – Collie had managed to promote our new symbol even while Pierce was denouncing it.

The idea about drawing a V for victory had come from Hal, the second week I was broadcasting.

When he'd asked Mac if he could come along to a broadcast, I'd hoped it was a good sign. Even with me around more now, things hadn't improved much between us. That sense of a pane of glass separating me from my brother was still there.

This time we were broadcasting from the top floor of an abandoned house in Hell's Kitchen, with Dwight standing guard below. Through the window, a red sunset bled across the sky. The buildings of New Manhattan rose against it.

The tallest, the Majestic Building, had a giant Harmony flag flying from its iconic spike. The same flag I'd seen from across the river before we'd entered the city. Of all Kay Pierce's actions, flying her symbol from the beloved Majestic was one of the most hated.

As we set things up, Hal looked out the window, studying the flag's red-and-black swirls. From the line of his jaw, I wondered if he was thinking about Dad too – if he wanted to move on as much as I did.

I hesitated, and then went and stood beside him. He was tall for fifteen. Though I was five foot eight, he had a good two inches on me.

"Terrible view, isn't it?" I said.

"Yeah, it is," he said after a pause, jamming his hands in his back pockets. He glanced at me with a small, rueful smile.

A few minutes later, it was time. At seven o'clock, on Mac's signal, I leaned close to the mic. Hal was sitting on the battered table. I felt very aware of his scrutiny.

"This is Amity Vancour, the voice of the Resistance," I said. "The press call me 'Wildcat'. I know you see terrible things every day here in New Manhattan – I see them too. You're afraid that you or someone you love might be next."

Despite myself, I glanced at my Aries tattoo and clenched my hand shut. "I understand your fear," I said roughly. "But there are still things you can do to make a difference. If you see a copy of *Victory*, read it, pass it on…"

I noticed Hal out of the corner of my eye then, idly sketching a V in the table's dust. The next words flowed, as if I'd planned them:

"…and draw a V for victory wherever it's safe! With a pencil on a park bench, maybe, or in chalk on a building. *V for Victory!* Draw it, spread the word!"

When the broadcast ended, we began packing up hastily. Mac's grin lit his face. "Kiddo, that was inspired! A rallying sign is exactly what we've needed."

I felt jubilant. "It was because of Hal." I pointed to the scrawled V on the table. "*Thank you,*" I said fervently to him. "I wouldn't have thought of it otherwise."

He'd been wrapping up the antenna's cable. Startled, he looked at the V and then at me.

Slowly, he smiled – a real smile, for a change. "Any time, Sis," he said.

Then he hesitated, playing with the cable. "You said we're going to fight." He looked at Mac, his expression taut, hopeful. "Are we? Is there a plan yet?"

Mac shook his head. "Not yet, buddy. But I hope we're getting there."

I had to look away as I put the wireless set in its pouch. Mac was lying. There *was* a fledgling plan in place. It focused on a new secure meeting room that Kay Pierce was building deep in her palace basement. One of the abandoned tunnels led to a chamber directly below it.

"Explosives," Mac had said tersely to Sephy and me just the other night. We'd been up after Hal had gone to bed, talking in undertones. Chilled, I'd gone motionless, imagining it.

"Can we get them?" Sephy sounded as if she were steeling herself.

Mac had nodded. "Jimmy," he said. One of his contacts; an ex-thief who worked in construction now.

Murder. Premeditated. I thought of my Peacefighting vow to honour the sanctity of life and didn't know what to feel. As I slowly ran my hand over my mouth, all I could see were hanging bodies…heads on a fence.

I let my hand fall. "All right," I murmured, almost to myself. Then I glanced at Mac. "When?"

"We don't know yet," he said. "Collis is keeping me informed. We all just have to keep doing what we're doing for now."

With Hal's help, Sephy was doctoring charts night and day. "We wouldn't do anything else, babe," she said. Her green scarf looked emerald against her black hair; her brown eyes soft and level.

For a moment it was like I wasn't there. Mac's expression was conflicted as he put his arm around her, drawing her close. She pressed against him.

I could see in his eyes that he'd give anything if she was someplace safe, far away from here.

"Hey, Amity, why did the Resistance worker cross the road?"

I sighed. "I don't know, Dwight."

"To fight the other side."

I half-groaned, half-snorted.

The abandoned subway platform that hid our printing press was shadowy, lit by a single lantern. *City Hall,* read its faded tiles. Dwight, taking a day off from his uncle's hardware store, was helping me lay out page one of *Victory*, laboriously creating each word letter by letter with small wooden blocks. Across the room, Anton and Susannah worked on page two.

We all tensed as murmurs came from the tunnel – someone talking to our guards. Then Mac appeared, hefting himself nimbly onto the platform.

He came over. "How's it going?"

"Fine, if I don't end up strangling Dwight," I said, and Dwight grinned at me.

"You wouldn't do that," he said. "You like me too much."

"I do?"

Mac was checking the layout. "Good stuff." He clapped Dwight on the shoulder. "Nah, don't strangle him, kiddo," he said to me. "We'd have to find someone else to cart the wireless equipment around."

"That would be a pain, it's true." I glanced at him. "Any news?"

He shook his head. "Saw two victory Vs on my way here. Better than none."

"There was one on my street yesterday," Dwight offered. "The Guns were bitching about it."

"We'll get there," muttered Mac. He met my gaze and gave a small smile. Troubled, I returned it, hoping he was right. New Manhattan was still scared – how could it not be?

I was too. No amount of anger at myself helped the fact.

Yet according to the rumours stirring in the city, twenty-year-old "Wildcat" had strode up to John Gunnison like a warrior and shot him in cold blood. She led the Resistance single-handedly. She probably laughed whenever she saw a Gun.

They'd gotten my age right, at least.

Mac went over to speak with Anton and Susannah. Dwight and I worked in silence for a while, the only sound the faint *click* of letters.

Finally he cleared his throat. "Hey, doll-face…can I ask you something?"

I glanced at him in surprise. He sounded serious for a change. "Okay."

He hesitated. "I know, um…that you probably don't like to talk about it. But…" His gaze flicked to the tattoo on my palm. "What – what are those places like?"

I stared at him. He flushed and played with his silver ring. "This, um… This was my mother's," he said. "I'm originally from what used to be the Central States – she was taken when I was twelve. So I just…wondered."

I licked my lips. I hadn't realized this was why he lived with his aunt and uncle. "They're not good places, Dwight."

"I know. Will you tell me anyway?"

So I did.

As we kept working, I told him about solitary, where I'd been beaten and had no sanitation, no food. About seeing bodies carried out. The executions; the hunger; the cold. The severed heads that still haunted my nightmares.

When I'd finished we'd completed the front page, yet neither of us had reached for the ink. Dwight leaned against the table, pale.

Why were words so inadequate?

"Maybe she didn't suffer much," I said softly.

Dwight swallowed. "That's what my...well...what someone I dated last year said once. He said that if I don't know, why assume the worst?"

From his expression, the memory of the guy he'd dated wasn't helping either. He gazed down at his ring.

"When Mom gave me this, the Guns were at the door," he said at last. "She just said, 'Hold this for me, okay?'" He grimaced. "I've wanted to ask you for a while now. Stupid."

I was so awful at this kind of thing. "Listen...maybe it's better to know," I said roughly.

Dwight gave me a quick glance. I'd never noticed how blue his eyes were before.

"Do you believe that?" he said.

"I'm not sure," I admitted. "But I would have had to find out too."

He nodded slowly. Then he sighed and straightened. "Anyway. What the hell. This paper isn't going to ink itself."

"I can tell you're trying to think of a terrible pun," I said after a pause, and he grinned gratefully at me.

"Ain't no such thing," he said.

* * *

Though things didn't go back to normal between Hal and me, they at least eased – on the surface anyway. We were able to receive letters sometimes now too, passed along to us from person to person via the outside network. Ma's last letter had reached me in June.

She'd asked me to keep Hal safe – a thought that haunted me.

Ingo had finally received word from his family too. His relief had been palpable when he'd shown me the letter during one of his brief stays at the safe house, translating as he read. They were all fine, his mother wrote, and overjoyed that he was alive.

His sister Lena had enclosed a separate note that made him laugh: *It's just like you to decide to stay when I miss you so much. Be careful, you big idiot, or I'll have to come over there myself.*

Hal's frustration at not doing more hadn't escaped Mac's notice. Though Mac still didn't want my fifteen-year-old brother involved in a murder plot, he started giving Hal other jobs whenever Sephy could spare him – letting him help print new editions of *Victory*, delivering messages via the tunnels. He drove with Dwight sometimes, too, to learn the Resistance's routes and safe houses.

Ma's plea goaded my conscience, but we were all in the same danger. "He's the steadiest kid I ever met," Mac told me once. "I wish to hell that times were different for him."

During those long, hot months I was aware that the Resistance was growing behind the scenes, becoming dozens-strong. And occasionally members were captured. Pierce always crowed about it during her wireless broadcasts; they were shot and strung up for all to see. So far there was no one I'd known, or who'd had vital information. Neither fact was a comfort. It felt as if a noose were slowly cinching around us.

I met other key members that summer: Roddy, Anton, Ernest, Mabel, Jimmy, Susannah. All different ages and races, linked by their determination to bring down Pierce – their willingness to risk their lives. Ernest and Mabel ran the other main safe house; *Victory* was written there.

Anton was around Ingo's age and, like him, Germanic – he'd come from a village not far from Ingo's, though his family had moved to New Manhattan when he was fourteen. In snatched moments from Ingo's escape work, they talked sometimes in their native Germanic, playing chess occasionally.

I liked listening to the guttural-sounding language – liked hearing Ingo's voice saying such unfamiliar words. Other times, Ingo would play his guitar, or the two of us would just sit and talk.

Whenever he was back, it felt as if I could breathe again.

CHAPTER SEVEN

JUNE – JULY, 1942

COLLIS GLANCED UP AND DOWN the gold-edged palace corridor. Deserted. He eased open a wood-panelled door and slipped inside a small meeting room. He locked the door behind him.

He left the lights off, the thick curtains drawn. In the gloom, a mural showed Kay with a scorpion perched on one hand and the scales of justice dangling from the other. She was Scorpio, with Libra rising. "It means I'm ruthless but like nice things," she'd smirked once.

Neither of them believed in astrology, yet that was a pretty damn accurate description.

The thick rug muffled his footsteps as he went to the mural. He snagged a glass from a nearby table and pressed it against the wall. One of the scorpion's black eyes was covered by an almost-invisible panel. He stroked it open and peered through into the next room.

Sandford Cain's private office. Cain sat in one of two plush armchairs, speaking in an undertone to another man opposite him. His associate's suit was as expensive as Collis's own – *Giordanni,* thought Collis automatically – and one dark eyebrow had a scar through it. He murmured something back.

With practised ease, Collis alternately put his ear to the glass cupped against the wall and watched through the peephole.

"Who the hell is he?" the stranger was saying.

"Nobody. Johnny's old good-luck charm."

"Right. Well, he's someone *now,* my friend. If she goes, will he try anything?"

"Not if he knows what's good for him. I tell you, he's negligible."

"He's another wrinkle. I don't like wrinkles."

"Let me worry about that."

They were talking about him. Despite himself, Collis felt anger at Cain and grim pride at the stranger's summation: *he's someone now.*

Actions were what counted, he reminded himself sharply. Not his stupid, automatic thoughts.

Cain rose. He glanced towards Collis and Collis froze. But Cain was only crossing to a sideboard. Collis hardly breathed as Cain stood scant feet away and poured a pair of drinks. The clink of crystal came clearly. Collis could see a small, pale mole beside Cain's nose that he'd never noticed before.

Cain turned; he went back to the table and handed the man a drink. Whiskey. Collis stifled his immediate urge to have one himself. "The question is, how?" Cain said, swirling the amber liquid.

"How suspicious do you want it to look?"

"I don't really care. The bitch shot me."

"She's got a lot of support though. Keaton."

General Keaton was the head of the military, and Cain's friend was right. As Collis had found out soon after waking up that first day, Kay had wasted no time in getting Keaton on her side – increasing his salary, letting him know that the military would be supported throughout her regime. Keaton didn't like Cain, who'd spoken out against him in the past.

"I'll take the chance." Cain took a swig of his drink. "I'm not carrying on as lackey to a twenty-year-old girl."

"Hey, she ain't doing so bad," smirked the other man. "Gunnison would be proud of his little mistress, rest his nutty soul."

"Yeah, she slept her way to the top – but she won't stay there."

"You pissed because she's sleeping with Mr Negligible instead of you?"

Collis tensed. To his relief, Cain said, "We don't know that."

A chuckle. "The guy's twenty-one, in her office all day, and easy on the eye. Hell, *I'd* do him."

As the conversation continued, the two men ruled out shooting Kay from the park as she stood on her balcony – too uncertain, given the distance and the number of Guns she always had patrolling. Similarly, Kay had taken a leaf from Johnny's book and had everyone who came into contact with her searched, so attacking her elsewhere was tricky too.

"Good old-fashioned poison, I'm telling you," said the other man in an undertone. He drained his drink. "Easy to smuggle in and untraceable if you do it right. You could even be the one to find the body and try to revive her. Boohoo, too late, how sad."

"Good," said Cain. "I can't risk an all-out coup at this point. When?"

"Give me a few days. I'll arrange it."

"You'll be well rewarded."

"Oh, I know that, buddy."

The meeting ended soon after, with Cain showing the man to the door. Collis heard the sound of their murmurs from out in the corridor. Then Cain re-entered the room. He ran a hand through his hair and smiled – one of the first times Collis had ever seen him do so. It sent a shiver down Collis's spine.

Cain sat at his desk and started to write something.

Collis drew away from the wall and eased the peephole shut. Without a sound, he put the glass down. He went over to a table near the curtained window and hefted himself softly onto it.

Faintly, the sound of traffic drifted up from the streets below. There was a hanging point nearby: the street lamp at Can-Amer and 60th. Until two days ago, a body had hung there – a woman executed for aiding Discordants.

Collis sat in the gloom for some time, thinking.

The broad space of the underground rendezvous point felt clammy. "So you tipped her off?" said Mac, his features half-shadowed in the lantern-light.

They were sitting on a length of abandoned pipe – the same place Collis had sat when they'd met down here before, with Amity and Weir. Collis tried not to think about the look of finality on Amity's face when he'd asked if they could talk.

"No choice," he said, tapping a fist against his opposite hand. "If Pierce is taken out with Cain still there…"

"Yeah, I get you. That was always the problem with getting rid of Gunnison, too." Mac sighed and pushed the brim of his fedora up. "Must have helped on the trust front though," he added with a rueful smile. "Not a lady alive who doesn't like being warned about a nice poison-plot."

"Sure, it helped." Collis glanced down at his gold cufflinks – the finest he'd ever owned. The weeping walls depressed him. They reminded him too much of the coal mine at Harmony Three, where he'd been incarcerated for almost a year when he was seventeen.

Not that he'd worked in the mine long. He'd made himself too useful to the Guns for that, hadn't he?

He straightened. "She's put extra security in place," he said shortly. "She hasn't let on to Cain that she knows, but he's obviously guessed. He's eased off for now – he doesn't know who the mole was."

"She's not getting rid of him?"

Collis shook his head, recalling Kay's fear and anger. "She's looking for a way. He's got too many supporters in the palace to do it easily."

Mac snorted. "Knew it was on the agenda. She's not a lady who likes sharing power, is she?"

Thinking of the many conversations that he and Kay had had on the subject of doing away with Cain, guilt touched Collis. *Just tell Mac about your deal,* he thought. His friend, a seasoned double agent, must suspect anyway… yet somehow Collis couldn't admit the extent to which he'd become entangled with Kay Pierce. His own motives felt murky to him.

Actions, not thoughts, he reminded himself grimly. He was here now; that was all that mattered. But the idea of losing Mac's good opinion paralysed him.

"I brought the map," Collis said after a pause. He reached in his pocket and handed it over.

Mac studied the hand-drawn map of the palace intently.

He rubbed his jaw. "So the secure meeting room is in the works?"

Collis pointed to a chamber. "Right over that section of the tunnels you told me about."

"Yeah, good…it'll take a few more months for us to be ready, though. We've got to have the city on our side." Mac handed the map back. "Got it. Thanks." Mac never forgot anything – never took notes.

"Got a light?" asked Collis.

Mac passed his silver lighter over and Collis set fire to the map. Watching it burn, he said, "It'll take time from my end too. Getting the two of them and all their cronies in one room won't be easy."

Mac smiled. "You'll manage it, pal. You've got the golden touch."

Memories of that very morning came to him – Kay had said something similar. He grimaced. "Yeah, Mr Glib… that's me."

"You okay, buddy?"

Collis let the paper burn almost to his fingers before he dropped it and ground the charred remains out with his heel. "It just…gets me down, you know?" he said at last. "Being in there on my own."

"Tell me about it," said Mac mildly. "I've been there. Hard to hang onto your soul."

This was so similar to what Collis had been thinking that he couldn't go anywhere near it. He gave a casual shrug.

"Yeah, I'll be all right. What the hell, it's only a soul."
He handed the lighter back. He hated asking but couldn't
help himself. "How's Amity?"

Mac's eyes were sympathetic. He smiled. "Fine. Doesn't
like broadcasting, but has lots of opinions on it anyway."

Collis felt his own lips tug upwards. "That sounds
familiar."

Mac scratched the back of his neck. "I like her a lot," he
said finally. "And I like you too. So that makes it kind of
tough."

Collis tried to sound flippant and failed. "What – that
she hates my guts?"

"You'd have to ask her that. But listen, pal, you want my
advice? I'd try moving on."

Collis wondered if Mac suspected that, technically,
he'd been moving on with a vengeance.

"Thanks for the advice," he said.

"Not sore, are you?"

Collis looked down, lightly tapping his fingers together.
"Not at you. Guy named Collis Reed I wouldn't mind
taking a pop at, though."

Mac smiled slightly. "Nah, go easy on him. I hear he's
not so bad."

Collis wanted to argue but didn't. As idly as he could,
he brought the conversation back around to the Resistance,
and tried to find some small thing he could use that would
keep Kay happy.

* * *

Four months ago, after Kay had told him that she knew he'd let Amity go, silence had pressed down in the bedroom.

Collis's wound had been throbbing as badly as his head. His initial response – to feign offended anger – had died as he saw his Gun uniform lying on a chair.

The breast pocket was open.

He'd had a notepad in there; he had a sudden vivid memory of scrawling down the address of Sephy's friends for Amity. Alarm pulsed. How deeply had his pencil scratched the paper? Was the top page indented with the address?

He couldn't see the notepad's outline in his pocket. Kay would have had no reason to take a blank one.

Oh, holy hell. *She knew where Amity was.*

Only seconds had passed. Kay's expression was level, waiting for him to speak.

"Yeah, you're right," he said. "I let her go."

Kay raised an eyebrow. Collis went on instinct. For whatever reason, he'd sensed that she genuinely wanted him to work with her. And as he'd learned over and over – Amity flashed painfully into his mind again – someone who wanted to be convinced was easy game.

"I gave her some money and an address to go to," he said. "She took them, all right – then shot me for landing her in Harmony Five. I was an idiot."

"What address?" said Kay.

"Oak View, Morrison Road, Huntersville." He prayed

that Kay didn't know Hal was there too – and probably Mac and Sephy by now.

From the slight flicker in her gaze, he'd been right; she'd known the address already. "You weren't going to tell me?"

"No. You'd have had me shot."

She smiled at this. "Honesty. Good. I learned the value of that from Johnny, you know. I tried to deceive him too, when we first started." She tapped her teeth with a fingernail.

"Oak View, Morrison Road, Huntersville," she mused, drawing out the words. "Shall I send Guns there now?"

"Go ahead. I'm finished with the bitch." Collis managed to sound bored. For Amity and the others to have a chance, he knew he had to play this perfectly. He'd only had one painkiller and longed for another.

Kay looked dryly amused. "So how much of your liaison with her was for show?"

As far as Collis was aware, Mac was the only one who knew he'd been in love with Amity since he was fourteen. "All of it, to start with," he said. "But…I guess I came to care for her. Enough to not want her to die, anyhow."

Kay wrinkled her nose. "I wouldn't have thought she was your type."

Collis tried to hide how startled he was that Kay had formed an opinion on this. "Oh yeah?"

"I was at her trial," said Kay. "She's awfully…intense, isn't she? Doesn't exactly seem a laugh a minute."

Collis squelched a memory: Amity wearing only his shirt, laughing as he threw them both onto her bed back on the Western Seaboard base. Her face had been open, alive, her eyes sparkling.

"She's not so bad, for a Discordant," he said.

"Don't bother pretending to believe in 'Discordant'. We both know there's nothing to it."

He swallowed. "All right."

Kay gazed out the window. "But, yes, these things can get tricky. Johnny and I…" She made a face and broke off, her face fleetingly angry, vulnerable.

"Emotion gets in the way," she said finally. She paced a little, gripping her elbows tightly. "You know what the only useful emotion is? Fear. It keeps you on your toes. Ambition's pretty helpful too."

In a flash, Harmony Three came back to him. The water barrel had frozen once, and no one had bothered to get them anything else to drink. Collis thought of the man he'd betrayed to get out – and, despite his nightmares, as usual could feel only a weary thankfulness that he'd managed it.

"Holy hell, you've got that right," he murmured, gazing at the ceiling, and knew he didn't have to worry about sounding sincere. Something in him was broken – gone – he'd realized it years ago.

"You might as well know it all," he said after a pause, because he knew she'd have guessed. "I was with the Resistance too. Well, supposedly."

Kay turned and looked at him, the ancient Washington ruins framed in the window behind her. She waited.

"I was compiling info for Johnny," he said, since Johnny was lying in a morgue and couldn't deny it. "But as long as I'm being honest, I'll tell you that I liked Mac. Kind of hard not to."

Kay sat on the side of the bed – poised, studying him intently. His palms felt clammy. Why hadn't the painkiller kicked in yet?

Then, remembering what had happened on almost his last day in Can-Amer, Collis suddenly knew what Kay was waiting for.

"Oh, and I got Vancour's brother out," he added, his voice casual. "Mac saw his name in one of your files and was worried that the kid was in danger. I was trying to keep his trust."

Kay smirked slightly and studied her nails. "Yes, I had spies in the Western Seaboard Records Office," she said. "I knew Halcyon's paperwork was stolen – then a boy fitting his description turned up in Topeka. What was he doing there?"

Collis shook his head. "Mac got him out of the WS. Maybe he thought Vancour's brother could be a rallying point for people – I dunno. He didn't tell me everything."

Kay looked privately pleased with herself. "I planted the name that Mac saw," she said. "And he fell for it. That's how I knew for sure about him and Sephy."

Collis shrugged, thinking, *Shit, shit.* "Yeah, thought it might have been a plant."

"Where's Halcyon now?"

He struggled to keep his icy muscles relaxed. "Same address."

Collis had been the one to rescue Amity's brother and mother from the Western Seaboard. They were like family to him – a hell of a lot closer than his own had ever been. He *had* to get to that address in time to warn Amity and Hal.

"Amity Vancour doesn't seem to trust you very much any more," said Kay after a pause. "Given that she shot you."

"No. I guess not."

"What about Mac?"

"Sure, Mac still trusts me." Collis hid the faint tendril of hope that had just broken through. He managed a wry smile. "I was a good Resistance worker, you know. And I told Mac everything. He thought I was on the up and up."

"If the Resistance continues –" Kay mused – "and we both know that it will, in some way, shape or form…"

Collis yearned to supply the rest of the thought. He somehow kept silent. Kay studied him.

"If I leave Vancour alone, the Resistance will think they can trust you," she said finally. "She'll team up with Mac, most likely – all of them together in a nice, convenient little group. The question is…would she work with *you*, as an inside person? Or would she refuse to go anywhere near you?"

The hope felt desperate, hard to contain. "I think she might work with me, if Mac put in a word," he said, recalling the expression on Amity's face as he'd pulled the trigger on himself. He cleared his throat. "When she shot me…it was out of character. She was still overwrought from killing Johnny."

It struck him that neither he nor Kay had bothered to pretend any distress over Johnny's death. This small detail alone seemed to show how deep he was already in.

Kay nodded slowly. Her mouth twisted. "Another question, of course, is whether I trust *you.*"

"Do you?"

"Should I?"

"No," he said, and she smiled.

"Honesty again. Good. Well, I might be persuaded to trust you, Collis Reed, because I understand what makes you tick. I've been keeping an eye on you, you know. We're very much alike."

It was true and he knew it. Self-disgust mocked him. If he hadn't been so guilt-ridden over Amity ending up in Harmony Five, would he have ever joined the Resistance? No – he'd have kept working for Johnny and tried to get as much out of it as he could.

That was then, he thought. *This is now.*

Sunlight glinted on Kay's light-brown hair, bringing out faint reddish tints. Her voice turned businesslike. "So here's the deal: I'm going to need someone who can infiltrate the Resistance and keep me updated on what they're doing. And I think if I give you what you want, you'll do it."

The painkiller was finally working. His emotions felt distant enough to control.

"What do I want?" Collis said.

"Power. Money. Prestige. And maybe…a warm body once in a while, no strings attached." Kay smiled and studied his chest again. She didn't touch him but it felt as if she had. "Neither of us like strings, do we?"

His bullet wound still throbbed, but distantly. He forced himself to take Kay's hand. He could think through the implications of the deal later; all that mattered now was surviving and keeping Amity and the others safe.

"You've got me pegged pretty well." Collis stroked his thumb across her palm.

Her blue eyes glinted. "Then we have a deal?"

"I'm your man," he said.

In the four months since, Collis had embraced his role. *Sometimes you've got to play a long game,* Mac had told him once. Collis did this now with a vengeance.

He was all Kay's.

He gave her no reason to suspect him. He advised her matter-of-factly on things he found stomach-turning but to his disgust he had a talent for – how to control the populace, for instance. In doing so, he could never fail to recall Harmony Three…or suppress a faint feeling of *better them than me.*

"What about kids?" he'd said back in June.

He and Kay had been in her office. She'd propped her chin on her hands with a smirk. "Why, Collis, are you suggesting we have them?"

He'd managed a natural-sounding laugh. "No, the kids in Can-Amer. Young teenagers. We could use them more, couldn't we? Call them Harmony Helpers or something. Let them have rallies, meetings – talk about how great Kay Pierce is – keep an eye out for Discordants." They both still used the word to mean "divisive elements", even if neither believed people to be Discordant by their stars.

A slow smile had spread across Kay's face. She'd come and sat on his lap, twining her arms around his neck. "Have I told you lately you're a genius?"

"No. Overdue," he'd said, stroking her spine.

And even though he'd *hated* the idea of "Harmony Helpers", fucking *hated* it, some inane part of him had been pleased that he was playing his role so well…maybe even pleased at the praise from Kay.

Kay had implemented the idea immediately. The Helpers were thugs who spied on family and neighbours. *Well done, Collis,* he told himself whenever he saw their red-and-black uniforms.

Yeah. Well done.

Mac trusts me. Collis kept repeating this to himself. It was his touchstone. Mac Jones, the best judge of character he'd ever met, had listened to almost everything Collis had done and decided that something in him was okay after all.

Collis would never understand it, but would be grateful to Mac for ever.

He didn't tell Kay about his meetings with Mac though knew she was aware – that his very freedom to slip away from the palace meant he was probably being followed. Smuggling President Weir out of house arrest had taken weeks of secret preparation, and was one of the few times he was confident he hadn't been tailed.

As the Resistance's activities became more overt – the newspaper, V for Victory, Amity's broadcasts – Kay grew restless. "Maybe we should just get rid of them after all," she muttered, listening with tight anger to Amity's voice on the wireless.

Collis had shaken his head, pretending casualness. "Another Resistance would just form eventually. One that I wouldn't have any connection to."

"*And?* At least it wouldn't have Amity Vancour in it! If we string up Wildcat, people will think twice."

His guts lurched. "Listen – trust me," he said. He stroked her upper arms. "Something's in the works with the Resistance. You and I are going to use it to get what we need."

Kay went very still. "Getting rid of Cain," she breathed. He nodded.

"I want details."

"I can't give them to you. You have to be able to act naturally when the time comes."

She frowned, studying him. He met her gaze steadily.

Finally Kay looked down at his cufflinks – his newest pair; the gold ones that each had a small diamond at one corner. She touched one and gave a tiny, private smile.

She slipped her arms around his neck. "All right," she said. "But it better not take long."

The ruse made keeping Kay's trust even more vital. Collis was still feeding her information about the Resistance, though it sickened him to do it: the identity of minor players, the odd hint about their less important plans. He always protected the core group. And, of course, Kay knew that to keep Mac's trust, Collis gave information in return, though not the scale of it.

Collis longed to tell Mac about the deal. But it would be selfish; his own craven need for absolution. Mac was better off not knowing – not having to sacrifice his own people.

In the past, Mac had been in Collis's position. Once, back on the Western Seaboard base, he'd sentenced three dozen of Collis's former Peacefighting teammates to correction camps.

Collis had been there, thinking of Harmony Three and trying not to throw up. Mac had also saved over seventy of them, risking his life to do it. Logically, Collis knew his situation was similar.

But his recurring nightmare came all too often – he'd wake up sweating, hoping he hadn't shouted out. He couldn't shake the fear that the dream symbolized who he truly was. Maybe the only reason he wasn't telling Mac about the deal was that he doubted his own motives for working with Kay.

Because if he was honest, he liked the money. He liked the power. He liked it that nobody, ever, thought of him as a garbage Reed any more. Standing on the palace balcony waving with Kay, one hand on her back as thousands cheered, gave him a rush. He couldn't deny it.

Everyone in Can-Amer might hate him, but they sure as hell respected him now.

CHAPTER EIGHT

JULY, 1942

THOUGH THE DOOR LEADING TO the deli's shop section was closed, the only light I dared in the kitchen was a candle. Its flame gleamed against the countertops.

It was nearly midnight, but I hadn't been able to sleep – I couldn't stop seeing a scene from hours earlier. I studied the meats in the icebox that Jakov had set aside for tomorrow and took them out. I loaded the ham in the slicer and started turning the handle.

Doing the next day's prep work for Jakov usually soothed me. Tonight the magic didn't come. I sliced all the ham and the turkey, and then, still restless, looked for something else to do.

Mayonnaise, I realized with relief. Jakov made his fresh,

and he was almost out. Though in my old life I'd never cooked at all, I'd started studying cookbooks sometimes, late at night here. Something about the neat lists of ingredients and instructions felt calming.

Just now I needed that badly.

I'd been at Ernest and Mabel's in the Leo sector that afternoon, working on the paper. They were a retired couple who used to live in Paris. Mabel had been a dancer back at the turn of the century and wore outrageous flowing scarves; Ernest was scholarly, with a kind laugh. A framed print of the ruins of Sacré Cœur hung on their wall. They drank espresso from small, dainty cups.

When we'd heard the shouts and sirens, for a heart-stopping moment I thought we'd been discovered. Then it became clear that whatever it was, was happening further down the street.

The three of us had glanced fearfully at each other. I slowly put down my pencil.

"Come on," said Ernest finally.

Pressing close together at the small window, we'd opened the blinds a razor-width more and peeped out. We'd seen it all: the woman dragged stumbling from a house down the street by Guns while a crowd shouted at her. Her head had been shaved. The Guns tied a rope to a street lamp. The woman was forced to stand on top of a Shadowcar. They put a noose around her neck.

I felt dizzy – realized that Mabel and I were gripping hands tightly.

The Gun had proclaimed through a megaphone, "For collaborating with and abetting Discordants, and therefore showing herself to be one of them, this woman is sentenced to death."

They hadn't given her any last words. She'd said some anyway.

I repressed the memory with an effort – I couldn't bear it. With the candle's flame flickering gently, I got out the eggs and the vinegar from the icebox. I broke the eggs into a large bowl and attacked them with a hand-beater. I liked the mechanical way it whirred, and how the yolks swirled away into the thickness of the whites.

Watching the eggs churn, I tried to forget what had happened before the Shadowcar the woman had been standing on had driven off at speed.

Don't think about it. Don't think about it.

"It must be like having pixies in your kitchen," observed a voice.

I started and turned. The door leading down to the cellars had opened without my hearing it. A tall man with dark, curly hair came in. He shrugged out of a small backpack and rested a lantern on the worktop.

The breath sagged out of me. I leaned against the counter, the beater forgotten in my hand.

"You're back," I murmured. Unaccountably, tears sprang to my eyes.

Ingo came over and touched my arm. "Amity?"

He looked weary, his clothes and skin grimy. In the

candlelight, the burned half of his face appeared melted, tugging his eye downwards more cruelly than usual. The unmarred side was frowning with concern.

"I…" I swallowed hard and wiped my eyes. "I'm fine," I said roughly. Then I realized I was still holding the beater, dripping mayo onto the floor. I swore and put it back in the bowl.

"You're back earlier than I thought," I said, struggling for composure.

Ingo let his hand fall from my arm, though he still stood close. "Yes. What's wrong?"

"I'll tell you later," I said finally. "Just…something that happened earlier. I'm fine, I promise." I wiped my hands on a dishcloth, taking him in. The relief was like diving into a cool lake.

"Seriously, how did you get back so early?" I asked softly. "I wasn't expecting you until tomorrow."

Ingo regarded me for a moment. Then he went and washed his hands and opened the icebox door. "I had a bit of luck." He swiped a tired hand across his jaw. "Is any of this for us?"

"The pasta," I said, and he took out a bowl covered with tinfoil. I handed him a fork and he ate standing up – quick, hurried gulps that I recognized from my own eating, as if someone might take it away any second. Harmony Five did that to you.

"There'd been a cave-in," Ingo went on. "It must have happened last week sometime. I had to try a new tunnel coming back – the one near the Chambers Street sewer, remember?"

I started beating the mayo again. "I thought that one was caved in too."

"No, we were wrong, but you have to crawl for a while. It opens out and connects with the main Midtown line."

"A shortcut?"

Ingo nodded, still eating. "A good one. It cuts at least half a day off the route, though some of the groups won't be able to make it through that tight passage."

Any shortcut was good – the round-trip journey would still take him nearly a week. "So you got everyone out all right?" I asked.

"Yes, I hope so. Three of them – parents and their little boy. He was only four. We saw a group of Guns on the way down to the oldest section," he added.

I stopped mid-motion, my gaze flying to his. "They didn't see you?"

"No, though we had to hide for a few hours and try to keep the boy from crying."

My chest tightened. I slowly put the finished mayo away in the icebox, imagining it. After that afternoon – what had happened to the woman – I could see it all too vividly. If Ingo was ever caught…

I let out a shaky breath and leaned against the counter, rubbing my forehead. Ingo hesitated, then put the bowl aside and came and propped himself beside me.

His voice was quiet. "Are you going to tell me what happened today?"

I was very aware of his closeness. My neck felt damp in the warm kitchen, my hair too heavy. It would be even worse upstairs, with its stifling rooms and the thick air of July weighing everything down.

I glanced at Ingo and tried to smile. "Do you...want to go up on the roof for a while?"

He looked down at me, his dark gaze level. An odd lightness stirred in me as we studied each other.

"Yes, I'd like that," he said gruffly. "I'll take a shower first and be up."

CHAPTER NINE

SEPTEMBER, 1942

MAC AND I NEARED A BEND in the abandoned sewer and hooded our lanterns. We peered around the corner.

Guns, clear in their own lantern-light, had just emerged from a tunnel a few hundred feet away. We jerked back. *No – not when we're so close to it finally happening,* I thought wildly.

"Lead the way," Mac murmured.

I was already scanning my mental map. "Come on," I whispered. We hurried back the way we'd come and quickly climbed up a service ladder.

Twenty minutes later, we were in another tunnel, narrower. We half-jogged through the silent gloom until we came to an opening in the wall. I hefted myself into it;

Mac followed. We paused, listening.

Nothing.

We exhaled and glanced at each other.

"You and Manfred are two of a kind when it comes to this place, aren't you, kiddo?" said Mac with a rueful grin. We started down the passage.

The thought of Ingo brought a dull ache and emotions I didn't want to examine. In a rush, that night on the roof almost two months ago came back. I pushed away what had happened and cleared my throat.

"Yeah, I suppose," I said.

Finally we reached a ladder ten feet below street level. We climbed upwards, Mac ahead of me. He paused at the top and murmured the code word. I heard a faint reply.

"It's okay," he said over his shoulder, and I relaxed a little.

We emerged in the basement of the abandoned building in Hell's Kitchen. Dwight sat waiting, his arms wrapped anxiously around his knees. "Coast is clear," he said, scrambling to his feet. "I've got all the equipment."

"Good work, pal – thanks," Mac said, stripping off his jacket.

I quickly did the same. It was September, still hot as summer. Up on the third floor, it would be stifling. Underneath I wore a light sleeveless dress.

Dwight stuck his hands in his denims pockets, arms stiff. "Hey, Amity, hear the one about the Resistance worker who spent all her time in the tunnels?"

I glanced warily at him. "No, what?"

"Her friends thought she might be a mole."

I made a face, then snorted despite myself. "That's terrible, even for you."

"Yeah. Sorry."

Mac was busy checking the equipment. He slung the pouch over his shoulder. "All right, come on."

The three of us went up to the ground floor. The building was gloomy in the twilight. Graffiti covered its inside walls – including a large, scrawled "V" that had appeared a few weeks ago. As always, my gaze snagged hopefully on it.

"Keep watch, okay, buddy?" said Mac to Dwight, who nodded and posted himself near the dilapidated front door. From a bar across the road, faint neon light blinked on and off against his tense, young-looking face.

One more week, I told myself. If we were lucky, that was all any of us had to stay safe for now.

Ten minutes later Mac and I were on the top floor. I rubbed my hands on my skirt and glanced at my watch. At exactly seven o'clock, I leaned forward.

"This is Amity Vancour, the voice of the Resistance," I said into the microphone. "The press calls me Wildcat."

As always, I told people to hope – to know that we were here – to have faith that fear of Pierce hadn't killed everything good. Mac stood propped against the wall, smoking a cigarette, listening intently.

My eyes met his as I said, "Remember, we'll take real

action at some point. When we do, fight with us."

They were no longer empty words. With Collie's help, we had a plan in place now, centring around the new meeting room in the palace basement. On September 17th there'd be a status meeting. Kay Pierce and her advisors would be in there with Sandford Cain.

I knew Mac would have preferred to wait. The "V" on the wall downstairs still didn't have enough company; the number of them we saw didn't make us totally confident. But Collie said this meeting was the only one he could arrange.

Now or never.

Mac glanced at his watch and held up two fingers. I spoke more quickly: "Meanwhile, if you feel able, attempt small acts of sabotage. *Don't* hurt the Guns – you know how harshly Pierce retaliates for that. But maybe there are phone cords that can be cut, or auto tyres that can be—"

I broke off as a rhythmic shouting came from outside. Mac hastily stubbed out his cigarette and went to the window. I licked suddenly-cold lips and went on, glancing back at him:

"…auto tyres that can be deflated. Anything you can do to make the Guns' lives uncomfortable is useful – make them realize that we're awake, not cowed; that we're ready to fight."

Mac came over and scrawled a note: *Something happening next street over. Keep going. I'll check with Dwight.*

I nodded, but before Mac could move, footsteps came banging up the stairs. Dwight appeared, breathing hard.

"The Guns figured out which area we're broadcasting from!" he gasped. "They've got a huge group of Harmony Helpers – hundreds of them, searching houses all up and down the street at once!"

Mac swore. "The cubbyhole under the stairs," he told Dwight. "Go, *go*!"

Dwight pounded down the staircase. Three floors below, I heard faint thunder: a troop of Helpers rushing in.

My pulse beat through my brain. My gaze flew to Mac's.

Muffled shouts: "Find the Discordant scum! Find the Vancour bitch!"

In a daze I turned back to the mic. Somehow my voice stayed steady as I murmured, "The Guns have found us. We may be about to be captured. If we are, keep fighting. V for Victory."

The second I finished, Mac jerked the cord from the back of the wireless set. He fed it quickly out onto the darkness of the fire escape and then closed the window.

My lungs felt too tight to breathe. I rose slowly, gripping the table as images of Harmony Five assaulted me. The clamour from below grew louder. They'd reached the first floor now.

A trio of cabinets were set into one wall. Mac flung open the bottom one and slid out a shelf.

"Inside," he whispered. "There's a hiding place."

"It's no use, Mac."

"Get in!" He grabbed up the wireless set, shoved it at me with the mic.

I swallowed hard, clutching them. "What…what about you?"

He motioned up at the smallest of the cabinets. "I'll take that one. *Hurry*, kiddo!" He pushed me towards the opening.

Shaking, I crawled inside. Mac Jones didn't use any location unless he'd first made it as safe as he could. He'd hacked a hiding space at the back of the cabinet months ago.

I crouched in it, deep in the musty, cobwebbed space between the wall joists, hugging the still-warm wireless set. The square of light showing the empty room split in two as Mac slid the shelf back in place, then vanished as he closed the cabinet door.

Darkness. I heard Mac heft himself up into the smallest cabinet. All at once the shouts were very close, coming from the next room.

"Anything?"

"Not yet."

"Keep looking! Find the bitch!"

I pressed against the joist, sickly conscious that there was only a thin layer of wood and plaster between us. The door to our own room banged open.

"Hey! Smell that?"

"Cigarette smoke! Shit, someone's been *in* here!"

"Get the window!"

The antenna. I bit my lip to hold back a whimper. The sliding rush of the window, the clanging of feet on metal.

The vision came vividly: a grimy cabin in the Yukon where Ingo and I had crouched, trembling, holding weapons to each other's throats as Guns battered at the door.

Ingo. Pain winced through me. Please, no, I couldn't die without seeing him again – things had been so strange between us—

My cupboard door swung open. I was shuddering so hard I was sure they'd hear. I squeezed my eyes shut, cringing my head away. When the door banged closed again, I knew it was a trick and didn't move.

"Just shelves. What about that one?"

A muffled yell came from outside the room – was repeated up the stairs.

"The tunnels!"

"There's an entrance to the tunnels in the basement!"

"Quick, before they get away!"

Shouts, thumps. Clanging footsteps scrambled back up the fire escape. Someone banged against the table and swore. From through the wall I heard people racing from the other room too, so that I was caught between the tumult.

The noise faded away down the staircase. Slowly, silence descended.

I didn't trust it. As my heart hammered in the darkness I counted the seconds: three minutes, five, nine. I stayed huddled against the joist, not daring to stir.

When a rustle finally came from above, I gasped. I'd almost forgotten about Mac.

I heard him drop to the floor. As he opened the cupboard door I went limp. It must be safe now – Mac's judgement was infallible.

The rumour that I was the one in charge of the Resistance was laughable.

"You all right?" Mac asked softly.

He half-crawled into the cupboard to help me out. My muscles were stiff. As I emerged into the shadowy room I staggered.

"Fine," I got out. I rested the wireless set on the table.

Mac touched my arm and started to say something. We both tensed at the sound of a hesitant tread. As Mac lunged for the door, Dwight appeared, hugging himself.

Mac let out a breath and gripped his shoulder. "Glad you're okay, buddy."

Dwight looked close to throwing up. "Yeah, but, Mac…they're down in the tunnels. That was our only entrance in this sector."

The tunnels. My chest clenched as it hit me – Ingo was still somewhere in the upper levels. He'd left with his last group just this evening.

Mac shoved a hand through his unruly brown hair. "All right, we'll have to risk the checkpoint," he said finally.

"Meanwhile, let's hope they don't explore too deeply over by the Park Line, or we're screwed."

The old Park Line went under Kay Pierce's palace. It was where everything would be happening next week.

I turned abruptly away and slid the wireless set into its pouch, which had rested unnoticed in a shadowy corner. Dwight watched the stairs as Mac went and snagged the antenna off its hidden ledge.

Our attack had to be successful. It *had* to be. I buckled the pouch with short, angry motions and cleared my throat.

"A point for future reference," I said to Mac.

He glanced up. "What's that?"

"You might want to stop smoking, pal."

He gave a humourless laugh. "Oh, man, you ain't just whistlin' Dixie. Come on, let's get the hell out of here."

CHAPTER TEN

MAC AND I SAT SQUASHED together behind some boxes in Dwight's van. As we slowed for the Gemini checkpoint, Dwight muttered back to us, "Okay, I know these guys. Fingers crossed."

"If you're caught, we hijacked you," said Mac shortly.

I almost felt too drained to be frightened. I heard Dwight roll down the window. Voices.

"Evening, Dwight. ID, please…thanks. What are you carrying back there?"

"Some goods for my uncle's shop."

I licked my lips. Dwight wasn't a natural actor like Mac and Collie. He sounded strained – falsely casual.

"What kind of goods?" From the Gun's tone, I could

practically see him craning to peer in the back. I sat motionless, glad of Mac's solid warmth beside me.

"Just…canned goods from Taurus sector, mostly. Listen, um…I need to report something," Dwight said. "Can I give it to you, sir?"

Interest flared through the Gun's voice. "Sure, what is it?"

Dwight went into a long story about Wildcat's broadcast and how he'd heard a wireless set back on Bronson Street illegally tuning into it. "I'm not sure which house, sir. But I definitely heard it."

"All right, thanks. We'll check into it." A snort. "I wish you were telling us you'd seen Wildcat herself."

Dwight gave a strangled cough. "Yes, I – that would be – holy moley, sir, I'd come straight to you."

Mac tensed as apprehension spiked through me. But the Gun didn't seem to notice anything amiss. "Fine. Get on home, now."

The van started moving. I slumped against a box as the neon lights of the city began flashing past again.

Mac exhaled. "And so we live to fight another day," he murmured. "We won't need too many more, with luck. Thanks, buddy," he said, raising his voice to Dwight. "You did fine."

A few minutes later we pulled up to the back of the deli. Dwight swung open the van's rear doors. As Mac and I climbed out he caught my eye and managed a queasy grin.

"Hey, Amity…what did one Resistance worker say to the other?"

I shook my head.

"'Ever think of getting into a safer line of business?'"

I smiled faintly. "Not much of a punchline."

"Not much of a business. Ba-dum-tish." He hunched a shoulder. "Night, doll-face. See you tomorrow."

Sephy and Hal had heard my hastily-ended broadcast, punctuated by the dim shouts of Guns. Back in the shabby apartment, Sephy flung herself into Mac's arms with a cry.

"I thought that was it, damn you," she choked out.

Mac stroked her back. "We're fine," he murmured against her neck. "We're fine."

I sank onto the sofa, massaging my aching thigh. Hal glanced at me, his face tight.

"So what happened?" he asked.

I sighed, wishing I could shield him. But we had enough secrets from my little brother already.

"They almost got us," I said.

Mac looked resigned. "Yeah," he said at last. "We were broadcasting, and then we heard a noise down in the street..."

There was coffee in the percolator. I went and poured myself a cup. As Mac described the Harmony Helpers breaking in, I stirred it slowly, keeping my back to them, shaken by how much I'd longed for Ingo in that moment. It would be almost a week now before we knew whether he was safe.

He wouldn't be lucky enough to be shot if he'd been caught.

When Mac finished, a short silence fell.

"Are you okay?" Hal asked finally, sounding stricken.

"Fine." I turned and cleared my throat. "So…what time did Ingo leave?"

Sephy's face was ashen. She tried to smile. "A little bit after you and Mac did. I'm sure he's all right."

From her expression, she wasn't sure at all. She knew as well as I did that the route he'd have taken wasn't far from where the Helpers had penetrated. I tried not to think about it.

Mac got coffee too and we moved to the table. It was covered with birth charts. Sephy cleared her throat as she moved her ephemeris. "So the second I agree to marry you, you scare me to death, is that it?" she said to Mac. "I may have to rethink this, mister."

Mac squeezed her hand, where a tiny diamond glinted. "Too late, you accepted the ring."

Sephy had finally said yes to him the month before. He'd asked her when we were all playing cards one night, and she'd jokingly complained about losing. "Hey, I'll let you win if you marry me," Mac had said.

"Okay," Sephy had replied, still studying her cards.

Hal's and my heads had jerked up. We'd stared at her and then each other. Mac had sat there looking stunned.

"You…really?" he said.

And then she'd smiled at him.

They hadn't finished the game. They'd disappeared into their bedroom for the rest of the night.

The memory flitted past. "Damn, thought I'd found a loophole," said Sephy.

Suddenly her eyes flew to the clock: a quarter to nine. She winced.

"Mac, I forgot – Jimmy was in touch. He needs to see you. Nine thirty, the usual place."

My fingers tightened around the coffee mug. Jimmy was our explosives person.

The term "poker face" had been invented for Mac. Only mild consternation crossed his features as he looked up. "Yeah? Guess I'd better hurry then."

"Will you go by the streets?" Sephy asked in a low voice.

"It's faster than the tunnels. Don't worry, I'll be careful." Mac glanced at Sephy's workload as he rose; I knew several of the charts were urgent, if the people were to be saved from Pierce before our attack.

"Amity, would you catch our glorious leader's speech and make sure everything's okay?" he said.

I stiffened, thinking of what I might have to do. *No. Please. Not tonight.* "Sure," I said, forcing a small smile.

Hal knew by now that Collie called for meetings through Pierce's speeches. He looked quickly at Mac. "I could go," he said. "I know the way, if the code to meet comes through." It still startled me slightly, how deep his voice was now.

Mac pulled on his fedora. "Thanks, pal, but your sister had better handle it."

Hal nodded reluctantly. After Mac left, he snapped on the telio. Dance music played softly. On the round screen, Kay Pierce was signing a new law in the capitol building, giggling and pursing her lips at the camera. Collie stood behind her, squeezing her shoulder. He whispered something in her ear and she laughed.

Hal's eyes turned troubled as he watched. He'd seen Collie a few times since we'd come here – brief meetings set up by Mac in the tunnels – though not for a while now. And I could guess what he was thinking.

It was becoming impossible not to wonder exactly what was going on between Collie and Kay Pierce. The rumour was that they were lovers. I wished I found it harder to believe. Yet Mac trusted him regardless.

"You've only really known Mac as a Resistance worker," Sephy had told me once. "But he was a double agent for years – he's been in similar situations. Even if Collis *is* sleeping with that woman…" She'd shrugged. "His loyalty's with us."

I hoped they were right.

"Oh, man, why can't we actually *do* something?" Hal muttered now, lightly punching his palm. "When's Collie going to come through with a plan?"

"I…guess he's working on it," I said.

Sephy's gaze flitted to mine. We'd tell Hal about the attack just before it happened, for his own safety – but not until then. Mac was adamant, and we all agreed.

At nine o'clock, the Harmony symbol appeared. After the singers' introduction faded, Pierce's voice said: "Good evening, Can-Amer. I'd like to talk tonight about destiny…"

My nails bit my palms as she went on. Would she mention it if Ingo's group had been caught? *Surely she would,* I tried to tell myself. *She wouldn't be able to resist.*

But sometimes she didn't announce arrests until the captives had been broken.

She didn't mention Ingo. None of the codes came, either. "Good," murmured Sephy when the broadcast ended.

As Hal listlessly pulled a chart towards him, I exhaled. At least I didn't have to go meet Collie and be reminded how bad my judgement had once been.

Since that night on the roof, Ingo and I had barely spent any time together. It was on purpose from my end, and I supposed from his, as well. When we did encounter each other, things seemed just the same. We smiled, even joked around a little.

Nothing was remotely the same.

I got up abruptly and went into the tiny kitchen. I'd meant to get a glass of water, but out of sight of the living room, I found myself weak with fear for him. I closed my eyes and gripped the edge of the counter, trying not to shake.

Please stay safe, I thought to Ingo. *I have to see you again.*

* * *

Two nights later, Anton drove Mac and me to a broadcasting location in his neighbourhood. I sat beside Mac, feigning calm.

My first broadcast after our near-capture had been like forcing myself back in the saddle after a bad fall. I still felt skittish, and was sick of it – I'd had more courage as a ten-year-old. Back then I'd been fearless, ready to conquer the world.

As I fiddled with the hem of my dress, suddenly I started to notice something.

"Mac, *look*." I gripped his arm. Even through the auto's window, I could see them – drawn on a signpost; chalked on a doorway; painted over a crumbling section of ancient ruins.

V. V. V.

"Holy hell," whispered Mac, straightening. From the front seat, Anton gave a short laugh. "I've counted twelve so far," he said fervently. He half-turned in his seat, grinning. "About time, huh?"

By the time we reached the location, we'd counted twenty-seven. I could hear the passion in my voice that night as I urged the city to keep on – to stand behind us.

Five more days. The attack was to happen on Friday.

On Monday, I was in the kitchen when Mac came in. "Hey, kiddo, have you seen this?"

I'd been making a cup of tea and was feeling on edge. Pierce still hadn't mentioned Ingo. If he was all right, he should be back the day after tomorrow.

I buried the thought and glanced at the piece of paper Mac was holding. Surprise lurched.

I dropped into one of our shabby kitchen chairs, reading rapidly. My fingers clenched the paper. "Is this – is this one of ours?"

"Nope," said Mac, leaning against the counter with his arms crossed. "Jimmy found it over on the East Side. Roddy says he saw a couple in London Village too. They're all over."

My own face gazed out from the poster. The photo had been taken just after my Peacefighter induction ceremony; it was the same picture that had been used in all the papers when I'd been on trial for murder.

This time the wording underneath it was very different.

V FOR VANCOUR!

On the night of September 10th, Amity Vancour, known as Wildcat, was interrupted by the arrival of Guns as she broadcast a message of hope to our occupied, terrorized city. Thousands of covert listeners heard the commotion and the calmness in Wildcat's voice as she told us that she might be about to die, but to keep fighting.

Wildcat did not die. She eluded the Guns and has since continued to broadcast. Her unflinching courage in that moment is an inspiration to us all. Amity

Vancour is only twenty years old and is willing to give her life for the cause of freedom. Can any of us be less brave and still look at ourselves in the mirror?

Follow Wildcat. Keep rebellion in your heart and don't lose hope. Pierce WILL and MUST fall.

V FOR VICTORY!

The only sounds in the small apartment were the faint ticking of the clock and the murmur of Sephy and Hal in the other room. Slowly, my eyes met Mac's.

"All those Vs we've been seeing," I murmured.

"The others have been seeing them everywhere too," Mac said. "I saw some more myself today – in the dust on autos, drawn on shop windows. There was even a broken matchstick shaped like a V left on a cafe table."

I stared down at the poster again and couldn't speak. Mac sat across from me and pulled it towards him, reading it again. His shirtsleeves were rolled up against the heat.

"Well, I guess now we know why," he said. "Amazing what having Guns busting in on you can do for your reputation."

I took a gulp of tea, my hands tight around the mug. "It's a farce though," I said harshly. "I was terrified. *You* know that."

Mac shrugged and lit a cigarette. His lips quirked. "Does it matter?"

In an undertone, he added, "Listen, kiddo, with the city on our side, we might actually stand a chance on Friday."

My bedroom in the cramped apartment was windowless, barely larger than a closet. That night I lay awake for a long time, stifled by the heat and my own thoughts. I knew Ingo couldn't possibly be back yet, but part of me craned to hear his footsteps anyway.

Staring into the darkness, I touched the tattoo they'd given me in Harmony Five, tracing its curves from memory...and seeing again Collie handing me over to Sandford Cain while the Guns' spotlights blazed. I'd thought I'd known him better than myself.

Damn you, Collie, I thought bleakly.

I knew Ingo wasn't Collie. I *knew* that. But I still wasn't sure how I could ever trust my judgement again when it came to being with someone.

That night on the roof. My chest tightened. Was I really surprised that when I'd thought I was about to be captured, Ingo was the one I'd thought of?

I scraped my fists over my hair. *Stop,* I ordered myself. This felt too complicated to deal with now. All that mattered was getting rid of Kay Pierce's regime in a few days and obliterating my father's legacy.

Later, I could figure this out.

Later, I could have a life again.

CHAPTER ELEVEN

THE TUESDAY BEFORE THE ATTACK, a group of us worked on what we hoped was the last edition of *Victory*.

Cranking ten thousand copies took hours. Hal joined us towards the end, helping to wrap batches of the dried newspapers in plain brown paper. It was after midnight by then.

"Tired?" I asked my brother. He'd been working all day with Sephy.

He shook his head. "It's good to get out and actually do something."

"You already *are* doing something."

He grimaced slightly. "Yeah. Doesn't feel like it sometimes."

Part of me wanted to tell him what was happening Friday. Conflicted, I turned away and tied another packet. He and Dwight resumed their conversation – some long-standing argument about a *Peacefighter* story thread. They were both fans of the old comic.

An hour later, the three of us were in a passage just below street level, carrying stacks of the plain brown parcels. They had to be delivered to rendezvous points around the city.

Our lanterns picked out our route. *Death to Pigs!* read faded graffiti on an old metal beam. "I wonder what the ancients had against pigs," Dwight murmured. He nudged me. "Hey, Amity, did you hear the one—"

We all froze at a volley of gunfire from above.

Hal glanced quickly at me, his face pale. I tensed at the faint sound of breaking glass – the muffled echo of more gunshots and screams.

"Sounds bad," I muttered. We were directly beneath Midtown. This time of night, all should have been quiet.

Dwight stood staring upwards, his thin form rigid. This was his neighbourhood. He lived only a few streets away.

"What's happening, do you think?" Hal whispered.

I shook my head and took a step further down the tunnel. "I don't know. Come on."

"Can we see what's going on?" Dwight blurted.

I wanted to say no, then saw the look on his face. I hesitated, my fingers tight around the packets.

"All right," I said finally.

The nearest exit was one we didn't use much. I climbed the makeshift ladder left by some long-ago explorer and slid aside a piece of board. I peeked out.

It led to ancient ruins left as a monument in a small park. What had been part of the building's peak was now a rubble-filled basement. Above, street lights shone through symmetrical triangles that were once windows.

"Clear," I whispered over my shoulder. "Be careful."

Modern cement stairs led to park level. We slipped up them and crouched behind the monument's front wall, peering out through a triangular slash.

My first dazed thought was: *Diamonds.* That was what all the broken glass in the street across from the park looked like, sparkling in the light from a burning auto.

"Holy shit," breathed Hal.

It was the Harmony Helpers again, dozens of them. They wore red-and-black uniforms and carried baseball bats and torches.

A girl swung her bat at a store window. The glass shivered, shattered. "Take that, Discordant scum!" she yelled as her comrades cheered. One had a pistol. He howled and shot out a street lamp.

Hal swallowed hard. "How…how do they know who's Discordant?"

"They don't," murmured Dwight.

The streets surrounding the park seemed huddled and fearful. *Let's get out of here,* I started to say…and then more Helpers appeared, yelling, "Just like Truce! Just like Truce!"

My stomach lurched.

They had a photo of Dad blown up on a large placard. I could see it in the street lights. It had been taken just after he became a Peacefighter – he looked young, smiling, his hair combed back just like Hal's was now.

The words read: *Truce Vancour – a traitor just like his daughter!*

"Just like Truce! Just like Truce!"

The Helpers punched the air. *Dad.* Feeling sick, I glanced at Hal. He looked bitter, his features carved in stone.

All at once more people burst from a street across the park. "*V for Victory! Down with Pierce!*"

They started hurling rocks, bricks. The Helpers stampeded towards them. The one holding the placard of our father swung it at someone's head. Suddenly there was a riot – fists flailing, people shouting.

Guns arrived, seemingly from nowhere. "Stop, Discordant scum!" Pistol shots thundered. Several people wrenched away and ran, followed by the Harmony Helpers.

With most of the Guns in pursuit, they vanished down the street. One rebel was left. He scooped something up from the ground and took off across the park.

A remaining Gun gave chase, closing in fast. The goggles of his riot helmet gave him a blank, impersonal look. "Stop!" he shouted. "Stop or I'll have to shoot!"

The rebel spun, panicked. He held a pistol.

The shot echoed through my brain. He'd gotten the

Gun at almost point-blank range. The Gun jerked backwards and went down in a sprawl.

The man raced off. Shouts from the surrounding streets drew closer. I crouched frozen, staring at the Gun's body, seeing again the sight that had greeted our arrival in New Manhattan.

Fifty people could be killed for this.

I couldn't stop to think. I clasped Dwight's arm. "Hurry – we've got to hide the body," I gasped, scrambling up. "Hal, *stay here!*"

Dwight and I sprinted out from cover towards the dark, still shape of the Gun. As we got close I slowed. I swallowed hard, then crouched and pressed my fingers against his upturned wrist.

He was dead all right. With a shiver of distaste, I grasped his still-warm arms, hating the heavy, pliant feel of them.

"Grab his legs," I said urgently to Dwight.

Dwight was trembling, but did it. Between us we dragged the Gun quickly into the monument, out of sight. Hal had half-followed us, standing on the grass uncertainly, his fists tight.

"Inside!" I cried.

Sirens howled through the neighbourhood. Dwight and I angled the body down the stairs to the basement. My hands were clammy; I glanced behind us with every step. Triangles from a ruined time fell across the floor.

We got to the dark corner and shoved aside the board.

Our lanterns still burned below. No point in being gentle, yet I couldn't bring myself to just drop the body through the hole.

I clambered down and Dwight began lowering it. The Gun slumped as if only asleep, apart from his wide-open eyes – I caught a flash of them in the faint light. I grasped the corpse by the knees, guiding it as it came down the ladder in a loose slither that made my skin crawl. Dwight followed and we laid it on the ground.

Hal came after us, pushing the board back in place. For several heartbeats I stared tautly upwards, listening. No sound of pursuers.

I turned to Hal. "Get going," I whispered urgently.

He tore his gaze from the body. "What?"

I shoved the newspapers at him. "We still have to deliver these."

"But what about—"

"Dwight and I will take care of it!"

"I'm not a child, Amity! I can help."

"I know you can! But we have to get those papers delivered."

His bitter expression was the same as when the Helpers had been shouting Dad's name. "The *newspapers?* What do they even matter? They're just more words – *words!* When are we going to—"

"In three days!" I cried. "We're attacking Pierce in three days! And we *have* to get that newspaper out – she can't suspect anything!"

Hal stared at me, his eyes wide. "Why…why didn't you tell me?"

"It wasn't my call. I shouldn't be telling you now. Just *go*, Hal."

He swallowed, glancing at the body again. "Did *you* know?" he asked Dwight.

Dwight looked up, dazed. "What? Oh. Yeah."

Hal winced. He turned away and picked up the newspapers and one of the lanterns. "I'll see you later," he said gruffly. "Be careful with…that."

"Hal…"

He left, moving away through the darkness of the tunnels.

Frustrated, I gazed after him, wishing there'd at least been time to talk about the poster of Dad. Yet what could I say? His long-ago thrown Peacefight had put John Gunnison in power. He *had* been a traitor, just like the poster said.

Dwight stood hugging himself, not looking at the shadowy body. "What…what are we doing with it?"

I swallowed. "Burying it, I guess." *It*, not *him*.

"Down here?" There wasn't much soil.

The grim thought came that we could just take the body deep below, to one of the old graveyard rooms. The idea of it slowly turning to a skeleton with the others made me feel sick.

"That section a little ways back," I said finally. "There's that old chamber off to one side – we should be able to dig a hole in there."

"With?" Dwight said faintly.

"Let's just get it there first."

The short journey seemed to take a century. Finally we got the Gun to the small chamber off the main passage. There was old graffiti on the walls and, incongruously, a modern hubcap.

Good, I thought tiredly. We could use it to dig.

We lay the Gun on the floor. Sitting down, I slumped against the wall. "You know, this night really hasn't turned out very well," I murmured. "I could use one of your jokes right about now."

Dwight didn't answer. When I looked over, he was crouched, studying the Gun, so pale that I sat up in alarm.

Before I could speak, Dwight tugged the Gun's helmet off. He sucked in his breath as if he'd been punched.

"*Dwight?*"

He started to sink back to his haunches, then fell to a sitting position, shoulders trembling. He pressed a hand against his eyes.

In a scrabble, I quickly crawled across the tiny space. Uncertainly, I touched Dwight's arm.

His voice was hoarse. "When I saw his eyes, I…I tried to tell myself that it just looks like Nate, that's all…it's just someone who looks like him…"

"You *knew* him?"

"I…he…" Dwight gulped and wiped his face. "He's the one I was involved with. Last year."

I stared at him, remembering the conversation about

Harmony Five we'd had back in July. "Did…did you know he'd become a Gun?"

Dwight shook his head, staring at Nate's face. His eyes were wet. "I didn't even know he was back in New Manhattan. He's a good person, Amity. He really is. We only broke up because of his family."

Suddenly I remembered the Gun – Nate – running after the rioter. *Stop or I'll have to shoot.* "I'll have to" didn't sound as if he'd wanted to do it. Plenty of Guns enjoyed their freedom to be cruel. But maybe for just as many, becoming a Gun seemed their only choice for survival.

The silence felt absolute.

"We still have to bury him, Dwight," I said softly "We can't…give him back to his family, or anything like that."

"I know." Dwight visibly tried to regain himself. "It's… it's okay," he got out. "Nate wouldn't have wanted anyone to die because of him. This way when he doesn't come back, they'll think he deserted." He swiped an angry wrist across his eyes. "Come on. Let's get on with it."

"Go home, Dwight," I said

He looked up in dull surprise. "What? I can't…"

"You can." My voice was harsh. "Leave. I don't want you to have to deal with this. I'll do it."

Dwight looked at Nate and shivered. I could see him imagining the realities of scraping a hole in the earth – of lowering the corpse into it and then throwing dirt over it.

"I loved him," he whispered. "I can't just leave."

The small room was on a higher level than the rest of the tunnel. I slid out of it and dropped to the uneven ground. I tugged Dwight out after me and handed him a lantern.

"Go," I said. "Believe me – this isn't a memory you want."

Dwight hesitated, looking back in at the body. "You'll, um…you'll…"

I nodded and gripped his arm.

"I'll take good care of him," I said.

Once alone with the body, I felt drained. Nate had brown hair and a mouth that looked like it had once laughed a lot.

There was dust on his eyes. I swallowed hard. I pressed my hand against the smooth chill of his skin and got his eyelids closed.

I started to reach for the hubcap, then realized something. I tensed, studying Nate's too-still features. But thinking of Dwight, there was no help for it.

I forced myself to search Nate's pockets, my fingers fumbling in one after the other. I'd searched a dead man's pockets once before: those of Russ, my team leader, back when I'd been a Peacefighter. Then I'd been acting on adrenalin and instinct. This was deliberate, as cold as Nate's body.

I didn't find much I could give to Dwight. Only a wallet; Nate didn't wear a watch. The Gemini pin on his lapel I left where it was. Dwight wouldn't want the symbol of Pierce's tyranny.

The rumble of the day's first subway train echoed up from below. Four a.m. then. As I sighed and sank back onto my heels, suddenly all of this felt overwhelming.

Dig, I ordered myself.

I'd barely started when I heard a murmuring sound. I froze, clutching the hubcap. No, I hadn't imagined it – the low rise and fall of approaching voices.

My heart leaped into my throat. I grabbed my lantern, ready to scramble away through the tunnels…and then I recognized one of the voices.

Relief and a deeper emotion coursed through me. I briefly closed my eyes.

He's back. He's safe. Thank you.

The footsteps had paused. Those approaching must have seen my light. "It's just me – Amity," I called out. My voice was hoarse. "Ingo! In here."

I dropped down to the tunnel floor just as he reached me. His face was smudged with dirt, his black curls lank.

I hugged my elbows. "I'm very glad it's you."

He gave a small, one-sided smile and set his lantern on a piece of rubble. "The feeling's mutual. I met Jimmy in the tunnels, and we thought… Wait, what's wrong? Why are you looking so—" He glanced into the chamber and his eyes widened.

We hadn't touched in almost two months, but now he gripped my arms. "Are you all right?" he said urgently.

I nodded. "It…wasn't me who did it."

Ingo exhaled. He let go of me just as Jimmy appeared behind him. He was a slim ex-thief with soft brown eyes.

"Oh, *shit*," he breathed when he saw the body.

I quickly explained. Jimmy's agitation heightened with every word. "Oh man, oh man – that's all we need, with less than three days to go! If one of the Guns saw you, we're screwed."

Ingo shrugged out of his backpack. "I'm sure Amity's aware of that," he said shortly. "Is Dwight all right?" he added to me, and then grimaced. "Stupid question. Of course he's not."

I scraped my hand down my face, remembering. "No. Not really."

Ingo didn't move. His hand clenched into a fist as he studied me. Abruptly, he turned and shifted his lantern to the chamber. He hefted himself up after it.

"So now we become gravediggers," he said in a low voice.

The soil was thankfully soft, easy to dig. Jimmy helped for a while, but then had to leave on an errand for Mac. I knew it probably had to do with the explosives, and didn't ask.

Ingo and I finished burying Nate on our own.

We scattered the excess dirt in the tunnel so there was no sign. When we were finally done and the grave was smooth I felt wrung out, far beyond my physical tiredness.

Ingo and I sat in silence beside it. I felt as if there should be words but had no idea what to say.

"Goodbye, Nate," I said finally. "Dwight says you were a good person and I believe him. I'm sorry this happened to you."

It didn't feel like enough. I glanced uncertainly at Ingo. Without my having to ask, he started speaking in Germanic. The guttural words were rhythmic, soothing.

When he'd finished, the faint buzz of traffic overhead had temporarily stilled.

"What did that mean?" I asked.

Ingo sat cross-legged, looking down. He shrugged. "Farewell, soldier. None of us knew what we were fighting for, yet you still gave your life... There's more; you get the gist. It's a poem from an old war. It seemed appropriate."

"It was. Thanks." The smoothed soil of the unmarked grave had an oddly peaceful feel now. And somehow everything felt a little easier between the two of us.

"Remember the night we met?" I said finally.

Ingo's thin lips twisted. "It's not something I'm likely to forget, Amity."

"Dancing the foxtrot with me is one of your most cherished memories?" I joked feebly. So much else had happened that night that the dancing had been the least of it.

His voice stayed deadpan. "How did you guess? I'm sure it's not one of yours though. I dance like an elephant, as you probably recall." He studied me, his almost-black eyes steady. "You're thinking about Russ."

Ingo and I had discovered his body together. I nodded, gazing at the patch of dirt where Nate lay.

"I checked his pockets, remember? And you asked me if I didn't want his watch too. Well, look." I took Nate's wallet out and showed it to him. I gave a short, shaky laugh. "I took it for Dwight. It's not much, but…"

A few months ago, Ingo would have touched my arm. I might have leaned against him just as naturally. Now he didn't move, but I could feel his sympathy.

"You did the right thing," he said. "Dwight will be glad to have it."

Remembering crouching in the cupboard, thinking that I couldn't die without seeing Ingo again, I felt on edge suddenly. I ached to touch him. And despite the sudden mental image of my arrest, of someone I'd loved becoming a stranger…I knew then that I'd lost my inner battle.

No. I couldn't deal with this now – it wasn't the time. I straightened and shoved the wallet back in my pocket, not looking at him.

"We'd better go," I said.

Ingo's dark eyes turned slightly guarded as he glanced at me. Without comment, he got up and we climbed down from the chamber, leaving the unmarked grave behind us.

"Goodbye, soldier," he said quietly as we left. "If you really were one of the good ones, I'm sorry as hell you're gone."

CHAPTER TWELVE

SEPTEMBER, 1942

KAY PIERCE STOOD LOOKING AT the dead teenager in the interrogation room. He was sprawled in a chair with his head back. He'd been strangled. A purplish bruise circled his neck. He stared pop-eyed at the ceiling.

Toby Melrose, according to his ID card. Seventeen. He'd been captured after a riot near Monument Park a few nights before – some Discordants had attacked a group of Harmony Helpers.

Had *attacked* them. Shouting "V for victory!" apparently. Kay thought of Amity Vancour's broadcasts and her lips tightened. But Collis still promised that the Resistance could be used to eliminate Cain. Though Kay couldn't keep the Guns from searching without raising suspicion, she'd taken no steps herself to find Wildcat.

With luck, the Resistance would serve them well.

The only sound was the gentle whirring of the ceiling fan. Its breeze rhythmically ruffled Toby Melrose's hair. Kay studied his lifeless form. A trace of dried foam was at the corner of his mouth.

Stupid boy.

She turned to the Gun, who stood waiting in a neat grey uniform. "Have him strung up," she said. "The sign around his neck should read *Rioter.*"

The Gun nodded, looking pale beneath his bland expression. He'd been the one ordered to carry out the garrotting.

Coward, thought Kay. She turned and left the room, heels clicking on the cement floor.

At first, Kay had been hesitant to order people killed. Now it was a dark thrill. And necessary. She'd always despised weakness; she was damned if she'd show any. Sandford Cain flashed into her mind again – still hating her, still wanting her dead.

Show weakness and you were done for.

One of the captains of the Guns stopped her as she walked towards the elevator, flanked by her bodyguards. "Madame President?"

Even now the title made her spine straighten. *She* had done this – taken advantage of Johnny's death to seize power. No one could ever take that away from her.

She turned. When she'd been Chief Astrologer, she'd

often donned a helpful expression. As Madame President, she'd learned quickly that a flat gaze worked better.

"Yes?"

The captain hesitated, glancing at her bodyguards. "Madame President, it's about your edict last night…"

"Regarding the Gun who deserted?" said Kay deliberately, and watched the captain's nervous wince with pleasure.

"With respect, Madame President, that hasn't been proven."

"Has his body been found?"

"No, but—"

"Has he checked back into base?"

The captain exhaled. "No," he said quietly.

"Then I think *you* can assume that Nate Bradley has deserted, and so *I* can assume that the Guns need more discipline," said Kay. "You'll post the notice as ordered – from now on, the families of any Guns who desert will be rounded up and sent to camps."

"Yes, Madame President," said the captain finally.

"Start with Nate Bradley's family," said Kay, and continued towards the elevator.

The sadness came from nowhere, full-force, as the elevator hummed upwards.

Dread gripped her. *No. Not this again.* Kay clutched her arms. "Take me to my chambers," she said suddenly.

One of the bodyguards glanced at her. "It's nearly time for your broadcast, Madame—"

"My chambers," she broke in. He nodded and punched in a different number. Kay stared at the buttons as each lit in turn, trying to evade the waves of grey threatening to swamp her.

On the thirty-second floor, the bodyguards walked her to the ornate double doors of her private wing. One stood with her as the other two searched the rooms.

"You're clear, Madame President," one of the searchers said finally.

"Thank you." Though sadness still weighed on her like a blanket, Kay pressed money into each of their palms. They were highly paid, but she wasn't taking chances. Sandford Cain had too many allies.

Alone in her chambers, Kay sank down shakily at her private desk and gazed around her. Everything was perfect in here, just the way she'd wanted it: the sitting room with its soft gold tones; the bedroom beyond with its tapestries and four-poster bed.

As always when this mood came, everything seemed off-kilter in some frightening way she couldn't define.

She didn't think the sadness had anything to do with Johnny – he was dead and she was glad – but memories pounded at her. She stared at some work on her desk, wanting to grab it and immerse herself in it. The effort required felt both distant and overwhelming. Finally, slowly, she crossed her arms on her desk and buried her head in them.

When Kay had first realized that John Gunnison's interest in her extended beyond her being his Chief Astrologer, she'd been thrilled. Power had always attracted her, regardless of gender – though she'd never encountered anyone, male or female, whom she'd cared to succumb to. Until she met Gunnison.

The dictator of the Central States – charismatic, compelling, the most powerful person on the planet – had lit her on fire. She'd also been scared of him: he'd held the power of life and death over her.

That, she supposed, had been part of the attraction.

She'd known it wasn't love – love was a fallacy. But she'd been wild about him. She'd longed to know what it felt like to go to bed with such power, and only partly because of what it might mean for her survival.

Kay shivered, recalling Gunnison in the months before his death, on his slide into full-on insanity.

He'd made her move into his private chambers. There'd been no escape. In bed he'd liked her to play a "dirty Discordant" who he could degrade. Or he hadn't even spoken to her, just done what he wanted, with Kay helpless to stop him. He'd ranted about "the dark mirror" – his name for Vancour. Her existence had enraged him, terrified him. Sometimes he'd seemed to mistake Kay for Vancour and had wanted to take himself out on Vancour in the basest ways possible.

In public, Kay had held her head high. She gave no hint that she was scared senseless – that Gunnison was unravelling – that she had no idea if she could survive this.

But she'd started carrying a pistol. One of the perks of being Gunnison's mistress was that she wasn't searched.

She'd first noticed Collis Reed around this time. The former Peacefighter pilot was her age, with broad shoulders and handsome, rugged features – things that had never, of themselves, pinged her radar. The golden-haired "Sandy" was a nobody.

Yet during those lonely, frightening nights, Kay had sometimes found herself thinking about Collis. When she took the trouble to dig into his past – his incarceration in Harmony Three; his history as a spy for Gunnison; his betrayal of fellow Peacefighter Amity Vancour – she'd realized why.

They were alike, she and "Sandy". They'd both been kicked around and could happily see the world go down in flames now, so long as they survived.

When Kay had seen Vancour walking towards Gunnison that day in February – when she'd had just enough time to realize that if Cain took power upon Gunnison's death, she'd either be left with nothing or have to enter a liaison with Cain – she'd seized her chance, covertly pulling the trigger on Cain in the chaos.

Moments later, as Kay had forced President Weir to sign his country away, she'd known that for a change, *she* was the powerful one. The rush of triumph had been indescribable. And when Collis was found with his bullet wound later, she'd decided that she wanted him purely because she wanted him.

Again, it wasn't love. Love was a story told in the moving-picture palaces. But what had seemed simple at first – sparing Collis because she knew she could control him – now, seven months on, felt more complicated.

Kay was starting to believe she could really trust him.

Still feeling shaky, Kay raised her head from her desk. She pulled out an astrology chart from a drawer and studied it. The date and time of the subject were written at the top: February 6th, 2.07 p.m., 1942 AC. The moment she'd taken power – the "birthdate" of her reign.

She studied it avidly. Sun in Aquarius: harmony and understanding. Yes, as far as she was concerned, this was certainly true. Rising sign Scorpio, which was her own sign. Jupiter in the sixth house, bestowing career luck. A grand trine in fire signs.

It all boded well...except for Uranus square with the mid-heaven. Uncertain – ups and downs. Not that she believed in astrology, of course. But casting charts for her own use had somehow become a habit, something she did to reassure herself.

Kay took out another chart. The only thing written at the top was *Black Moon*. Except for the military high-ups, no one but Kay had known exactly what Johnny was planning. He'd been gearing up to it for years. Finally, everything was nearly ready.

Since taking power, Kay had considered whether to go ahead. The other world leaders had made it clear they wouldn't challenge her. But people were liars. They *had* to know about her nuclear weapons – Vancour's stolen photos would have seen to that.

From spies, Kay knew the rest of the world was building up armed forces of its own.

Her spine steeled at the thought. She gazed raptly at the *Black Moon* chart. A time of unrest – great change. Scorpio ascending again: the change would work in her favour.

Black Moon. She'd do it. Soon no one, anywhere, would be a threat to her...as long as Sandford Cain could be contained.

Her private phone rang. Kay sighed, knowing what it would be. She put the charts away – her fingers lingering on *Black Moon* – and answered it. One of her aides said, "Madame President, I'm sorry to bother you, but your broadcast begins in—"

"Yes," Kay interrupted. "I'll be there."

The next morning, alone in her private dining room, Kay sat gazing at the scrambled eggs. Her reflection in their curved silver dish was worried. The eggs were fluffy, yellow-white. They still smelled warm.

Her stomach grumbled. Kay rose sharply and went to the sideboard.

Inside a drawer lay a metal box. She inspected it without

touching it. When she was satisfied that the hair from her own head that lay across the lock had not been disturbed, she placed the box on the table, then opened the Harmony symbol locket that dangled from her bracelet.

She extracted a small key and opened the box.

A packet of crackers and a few dried figs lay inside. Kay angled the box under a lamp, scrutinizing its contents. She smelled them carefully. At last she sighed and took out a cracker. She ate it staring out the window at New Manhattan while the eggs grew cold.

A knock came at the door. Kay started and turned. "Yes?" she called.

"Collis Reed, Madame President," said the maid's voice.

Kay's shoulders eased. She relocked the metal box and put it away. She sat down again and leaned back, angling a newspaper towards her. She crossed her legs at the ankles: relaxed, in control.

"Show him in," she said.

The door opened and Collis entered, carrying a briefcase. Their eyes met and held. Kay offered a hand without rising. "Collie, good morning."

His shapely mouth twisted at the nickname. She didn't usually use it. "Madame President," he said gravely as he took her hand. Kay squeezed his fingers.

"Oh, stop," she said in an undertone.

"Kay," he corrected himself. His eyes were pure blue this morning.

As Collis sat down to Kay's left, the young maid cleared

her throat and said, "Are you finished, Madame President? Would you like anything else?"

The food still sat untouched. "Wait, I'll have some of those eggs," said Collis, with a small frown at Kay. "And some fresh coffee."

Kay hesitated. Collis raised an eyebrow.

"Bring Mr Reed a plate and some coffee," Kay said finally. She hadn't touched the coffee either. She kept a small packet in a safe in her bedroom and made her own every morning. The times that Collis had shared this secret coffee, he'd never failed to tease her. In his presence, somehow her need for caution became a point of hilarity instead of fear.

The maid curtsied and withdrew.

No sooner was the door shut than Collis was on his knees beside Kay. He gripped her hands, tugging her towards him; she was reaching for him at the same time. She ran her fingers through his hair as their mouths moved together quickly, urgently. His palms stroked up and down her arms.

"Why are you here so early?" she whispered between kisses.

"Why do you think? You're not even eating."

"I can't. You know what he's capable of." Kay drew away a little, smoothing her carefully-styled curls. "Did you bring my notes?"

"Stop. Don't go into Madame President mode."

Collis drew her back to him. She didn't – couldn't –

resist. He smelled of warmth, soap, her own sheets from the night before. He'd joined her as usual after the broadcast. She'd still never let him stay an entire night. His lips pressed against her neck and she shivered.

"I won't let anything happen to you," he murmured. "Trust me. Please, trust me…"

Kay inhaled sharply at the sound of footsteps. The maid was new, not on her private payroll. She pushed Collis back towards his chair. He went reluctantly, his eyes both questioning and knowing. He kept his hand on her arm until she pulled away.

She grabbed for the newspaper and stared down at its headline: *Status meeting tomorrow; Pierce and Cain expected to discuss ongoing Discordant problem.*

The maid knocked; at Kay's command she entered. Collis had opened his briefcase, taken out some papers. Both sat impassively while she laid a place setting in front of Collis and poured coffee. She'd brought fresh scrambled eggs; she took away the cold ones.

When she was gone, Collis helped himself to a large portion of the food.

The news of Sandford Cain's plan to poison her several months ago had effectively killed any appetite Kay once had. She couldn't help wincing as Collis took a large bite of eggs and then a swig of coffee.

"See?" he said, mouth full. "They're fine." He swallowed, then leaned across and squeezed her hand. "He wouldn't do it this way, darling. Not now. Trust me."

Kay pressed a hand to her pounding temples. "I'm thinking of cancelling the meeting tomorrow," she said at last.

"You can't."

She looked up at his tone. He shook his head. "*Think*, sweetheart. He'd know you're scared. He'd use it against you. I'll be right there."

"And what will you do if it's an ambush?"

The status meeting was to be held in the new basement room. The room's very security – isolated, soundproof – made it dangerous, with Cain and his cronies in it. Kay had cronies of her own, of course. Did they outnumber Cain's? Had some gone over to his side? She could never be sure.

Something had flickered in Collis's eyes at the word *ambush*. "It won't be," he said. "If you die now, the military would never back him up – Keaton knows Cain would get rid of him in a second if he could. Cain may be power-hungry but he's not stupid."

When she didn't respond, he spooned some eggs onto her plate. The Harmony symbol swirled on an armband over his bicep. "Eat," he said softly. "Please. You hardly ate yesterday either."

Kay shrugged. "You said last night that you love how svelte I am."

"You drive me crazy and you know it. Svelte is one thing. Becoming a skeleton is another."

Kay gazed past him out the window. One of the main

execution points was only four blocks away, near Timmons Square. If she went and looked, she'd see the lamp post they used. Toby Melrose would be hanging from it by now.

She did not stop at what had to be done, and she would not be daunted by Sandford Cain.

"All right," she said quietly. "We'll go ahead with the meeting." She began to eat. The eggs tasted delicious; her stomach awoke in a rush. She devoured them quickly, washing her breakfast down with hot coffee.

"*Did* you bring my notes?" she asked, dabbing her lips with a napkin.

Collis reached for the papers he'd taken from his case. "Of course. I'm a perfect employee."

"You're perfect at a lot of things," she said, and he gave her a sideways smile.

"So I've been told."

By Amity Vancour? Kay wondered. There was no jealousy to the thought. Wildcat hadn't even known Collis. And now Vancour and the Resistance still dealt with him, with no concept of what really made him tick.

"Good," Kay murmured, as she read the notes. She started to comment, then paused, watching Collis mark something on his copy.

He'd worn reading glasses for over a month now. The sight of him in the brown horn-rimmed frames, looking so unwontedly studious, stirred something in her.

He looked up. As if reading her mind, he leaned close and kissed her, slipping a warm hand behind her neck.

"We're going to have it all, Kay – wait and see," he said in a low voice.

She'd encountered little optimism in her life. Her instinct was to find it naïve…but under no definition of the word could Collis Reed be called that. Kay thought of the Black Moon chart and gave a small smile.

"That's my plan," she said. "As long as I survive Cain."

Collis squeezed her fingers, his eyes intent. "*Trust me,*" he said. "It's all working out the way we want. Remember what I told you? We'll get rid of Cain – very soon now. I promise."

CHAPTER THIRTEEN

SEPTEMBER, 1942

AT MABEL AND ERNEST'S, the warm air stirred through the room, moved by the ceiling fan's lazy swirls. I sat on the sofa with a drink in my hands. Whiskey, no ice. There was never enough ice when all of us were here.

Mabel and Ernest had gone out for the night, leaving their home to us. The living room with its hanging beads and pretty ornaments felt crowded; all the group leaders had come for a final briefing. Still, there was barely a dozen of us.

This was it. The core army against Kay Pierce. I took a sip of my drink, trying not to think of the odds against us.

By now, the explosives would be in place.

A muted atmosphere hung over the room. People stood

in small groups, talking. A telio sat on a circular, polished table. On its screen, Kay Pierce was shaking someone's hand, dimpling widely.

I gazed at her image and thought about her dying the next day. I probably wasn't a very good person any more. All I could feel was anticipation.

Sephy came over and sat beside me. On the telio, the newsreel's narrator was exulting, "Only twenty years old, and yet she rules with charity and grace…"

"Who are Charity and Grace?" muttered Sephy. Her hair was up; somehow she looked cool and elegant despite the heat. "I swear, those two broads must be just as bad as Pierce."

I snorted out a laugh. "Is Hal okay?" I said after a pause.

Sephy nodded. "He's finishing a few last-minute charts, just in case."

Hal wasn't privy to the inner workings of the plan, though Mac had briefed him on the basics, so he'd know when to escape if need be. But Hal had begged to help somehow…and against what Mac claimed was his better judgement, he'd finally allowed it. Hal would be with me and Dwight tomorrow.

"Maybe we were wrong to try to shield him," Mac had said heavily to me. "Hell, he's already seen more than anyone twice his age should ever have to."

It scared me to think of my brother taking part, but Mac had a point – and I hardly felt objective enough to argue. I left the decision up to him.

When I tried to speak to Hal about the poster we'd seen, he'd shut me down. "I don't want to talk about it, Amity."

I'd hesitated, studying his bowed head as he worked. Finally I sat down beside him. "Look…I know that after I shot Gunnison, I wasn't really there for you. I'm trying to be now, okay?"

"Well, that's great, but I still don't want to talk about it."

"Hal…"

"Can you *leave it*, for crying out loud?" His grip on his pencil tightened, though he kept drawing the spiky astrological symbols. He spoke deliberately, enunciating every word: "Dad was a traitor. The poster's right. What else is there to say?"

I tensely watched the movement of his hand. "It doesn't have to define us."

"Yeah, like it hasn't defined you," he muttered. "Wildcat."

I couldn't reply at first. He was right. I liked to think that I'd be here doing the noble thing and fighting against Kay Pierce anyway…but would I really be, after Harmony Five?

It was all tangled up with Dad. Everything I'd done for years was tangled up with Dad.

"Well, it'll be over soon, with luck," I said stiffly.

Hal looked up then. He studied me, rolling his pencil between his fingers.

"Mac says he's the one who decided not to let me in on the plan," he said.

"That's right."

My brother's gaze was challenging. "Did you argue for me?"

"No," I said at last. I saw the hurt in his eyes and stood up then, shoving my chair back. "None of us wanted you involved in planning it," I said shortly. "And I still wish you weren't taking part now."

Mac came over and glanced at his watch. "We'll wait a little longer for Ingo," he said, and my stomach pinched. Ingo was never late. I knew he'd been replenishing a few of our old caches in the tunnels in case they were needed. Had he run into trouble?

Finally, looking at his watch again with a frown, Mac stood up and shoved a hand through his rumpled brown hair. "Okay, everyone. Let's go over it one last time…"

He described again how, at the moment of the attack, various groups of us were to take over key points of the city. Jimmy had supplied pistols, though I prayed no one would have to use them.

Meanwhile, Mac and others, also armed, would get President Weir out of house arrest and escort him through the streets on their way to the capitol building, shouting that Pierce's reign was over and Weir was back in charge.

By the time they got there, we hoped for a crowd of thousands supporting us.

We all knew our roles. Hal, Dwight and I would watch for Collie's signal from the palace, then join the group storming the telio station. I could have recited the plan in my sleep. At times I almost had, lying awake and chanting it to myself like a bedtime story.

"All right?" Mac was saying. "And remember, if it all goes haywire, try to reach the rendezvous point in the tunnels, then get the hell out of the city. Don't be a hero."

I glanced at the clock and bit my lip. A quarter past ten.

Sephy put her hand on my arm and I started. She whispered, "Don't worry, I'm sure—"

Everyone froze as three soft knocks came at the door. Pause. Two more. Mac relaxed and opened it.

Ingo came in. I exhaled softly.

"Sorry I'm late," he said, pulling off the fedora that partly hid his scar. His shoes were dirty; he'd clearly come straight from the tunnels. "There were some Guns on the prowl – I had to come back a different way."

"No problem, buddy. Glad you're okay." Mac clapped his arm. "Where were they? Nowhere near the Park Line, I hope?"

Ingo shook his head. "Over in the old Delancey sewers. We should be fine, with luck."

The meeting was basically over by then. Mac went to have a word with Jimmy. Others stood in small groups, chatting, as if no one quite wanted to leave yet. It was the Resistance's last night to ever meet this way…we hoped.

Ingo glanced around the room. Our eyes met. He hesitated, then came and sat beside me. Something both loosened and tightened in my chest.

I looked down at the remnants of my drink, swirling the amber liquid. "I was starting to worry about you," I said. "I was wondering if I should be planning another funeral."

"You can still plan it, if you like."

I smiled slightly. "Only if you plan mine too."

"Yes, what fun, a new hobby…no, on second thoughts, let's not. It's a bit morbid."

"Practical, isn't it? With what's happening tomorrow?"

"Even so." Ingo nodded at my drink. "Is there any more of that?"

The bottle was nearby. I poured more into my glass and handed it to him. Sephy had risen and gone over to Mac.

"Thanks." Ingo took a swig, then leaned his head against the back of the sofa. "It's always so strange, being here after days underground," he murmured. He'd hardly been out of the tunnels since I'd seen him; he'd been busy getting things ready.

He looked so tired. My gaze lingered on the long, angular lines of his face.

I cleared my throat. "So you got the people out safely a few days ago?" We hadn't discussed it when we'd buried Nate together.

Ingo straightened and rested his forearms on his knees. He wore grey trousers, a worn blue shirt with its sleeves partly rolled up. "Yes. A pair of schoolteachers and an old man with his two grandsons."

"Good," I said softly. There'd been discussion as to whether we should keep getting people out of the city at this point. Ingo had refused to stop, and Mac had agreed. I didn't blame him. If we failed tomorrow, those were five more people who wouldn't die.

"Are you going to drink all of that?" I asked after a pause.

"Possibly." Ingo took another sip and handed it back. "Shall I get my own tumbler?"

"No, that's okay. We've shared a lot more than this." I spoke without thinking, then caught myself. The words seemed to imply more than just using the same spoon while on the run.

In the slightly awkward pause that followed, I looked down and rolled the tumbler between my hands. "Have you heard anything more from your family?"

Ingo's voice was quiet. "No. I'd have told you. You?"

"No. And the same."

I remembered Ma's letter again. Her plea to keep Hal safe made me feel hollow, given what we were planning.

If I died tomorrow, what would I regret?

I kept my gaze on my glass. I felt as if I were standing on a cliff edge. "I suppose...I suppose that if we succeed tomorrow, you'll be catching the first ship home."

I glanced up and saw Ingo studying me, frowning a little.

"Yes, most likely," he said.

I took another quick sip. "Well, I was thinking…if we succeed, Hal and I will be going to Nova Scotia to see Ma. You could maybe come with us. And then maybe…" I trailed off.

The half-formed plan had seemed like something a friend might suggest until I'd started saying it. Now it felt momentous, if the hammering of my heart was anything to go by.

Ingo's posture stayed relaxed, but his eyes had taken on that slightly veiled look that I'd seen sometimes since that night on the roof. "And then maybe what?"

My voice came out almost curt. "Then…maybe I could go to the EA with you. If you wanted. Meet your family."

In the silence that followed, I started to take a swig of my drink and then realized my glass was empty. Ingo bent down and stretched to snag the bottle off the floor.

"Not too much," I said as he poured more into the tumbler. "Busy day tomorrow, you know."

The dark humour fell flat. Why wasn't he answering?

Ingo slowly stoppered the lid. His voice was low. "Amity…what exactly are you saying?"

The telio was playing a fast-paced rumba that reminded me of dancing with Collie, his hands on my hips as we moved. I was glad when someone snapped it off.

I shrugged and started to say something hedging.

Something like, *I'll miss you a lot when you leave, that's all,* or, *You've told me so much about them; I'd love to meet them.*

I looked down at the drink again. I didn't take a sip. "Ingo…that night up on the roof…"

I'm not sure if he heard. We both looked up suddenly as Anton appeared in front of us, holding a guitar. He handed it to Ingo. "Your nimble fingers are needed, Manfred."

Ingo had taken the guitar automatically. "My nimble fingers are tired," he said.

"Tired? On what could be your last night ever? Impossible." Anton grinned. He had longish brown hair, green eyes. "Besides, I got you something. Happy belated birthday, you ugly *scheisskopf.*" He took a bottle from a paper bag and handed it over.

When Ingo saw what it was, he laughed with real pleasure. The label pictured a peach; I saw the word *schnapps.*

"From Montemurlo, near my home village," he said to me, smiling and turning it over in his hands. "Anton and I were talking about it. *Danke,*" he said to him.

"It's your birthday?" I said in surprise.

"Last month. August 19th."

Of course – Ingo was a Leo. Once I'd had no concept of astrology. Gunnison and Pierce had taken care of that.

"Twenty-two," I said softly.

"Yes. An old man."

"Not so old."

Ingo's gaze stayed on me. His slight smile was quizzical, as if thinking of what we'd just been talking about. Anton brought out a set of bongos and started to tap out a low beat, sitting on the floor in front of us.

After a pause, Ingo looked down and began tuning the guitar, plucking at the strings. "Try it," he said to me, nodding at the schnapps.

"You have to say the right toast though," said Anton.

"Which is?" Despite having been interrupted, I was smiling too.

"*Prost*," said Ingo.

I opened the bottle; the smell of summer and ripe fruit floated out. I glanced around for a non-existent spare glass.

Ingo started to play, his long fingers coaxing out a jazzy tune. "Just swig it," he said. "We've no pride here."

I toasted him with the bottle. "*Prost*," I said, and took a sip. The schnapps was sweet and strong.

"*Prost*," Ingo echoed. Our eyes met. Impulsively, I leaned over and put the bottle to his lips as he played. He took a swig, hardly missing a chord.

"Even better than I remembered," he said to Anton with a grin.

"Anything forty proof usually is, pal," said Anton.

One of the other women started singing in a low, dreamy voice. Someone else kept time, lightly slapping their hand on the table. Mac and Sephy began to dance. She rested her head against his shoulder as he held her close.

The sudden hope in the room felt both exuberant and almost unbearable.

Please, I thought. *Let us succeed tomorrow.*

Ingo didn't look up from his playing. After a while, in an undertone, he said, "I'd dance with you, if that wouldn't put an end to the music."

My heart quickened. I pulled my knees to my chest, curling in a corner of the sofa.

"I'd like that," I said.

The corner of Ingo's mouth twisted. But his dark eyes were serious as he glanced at me. "Even though you know what I dance like?"

"Yes," I said simply.

The playing went on for a long time. I sat watching Ingo – not singing, not joining in, just gazing at his face and the movement of his wrists and fingers, listening to the music.

In a strange way, it was enough.

I realized I was faintly relieved that we'd been interrupted. I couldn't pretend that what I felt didn't still scare me. And the timing seemed wrong, somehow – unsavoury. In a matter of hours, blood would be on all of our hands.

Tomorrow, I thought. Once this was over, we could figure it out.

CHAPTER FOURTEEN

"HE SHOULD HAVE APPEARED BY NOW," murmured Hal, gazing up at the ornate bulk of the palace. We'd bought bottles of lemonade that we were too tense to drink. He tore the label from his in small, curled bits. "What do you think's taking so long?"

"I don't know," I whispered back. "Stop looking though."

We were sitting under an oak tree in Centre Park. I forced myself to lean casually back on the dry grass and cross my legs at the ankles. My dress was slightly too stylish for a late-summer day. I wore a hat with a thin black veil that I hoped would be enough to disguise me.

A Harmony flag rustled atop the nearby bandstand. An old waltz lilted – some tune that Kay Pierce hadn't banned yet. None of the gathered crowd danced. They just listened, fearful of doing something wrong.

We'd heard the explosion seven minutes ago, right on schedule. If you hadn't been listening for it, you wouldn't have known what it was. It sounded like low thunder, or construction work a few blocks away. I'd instinctively gripped Hal's hand at the noise, imagining Kay Pierce's basement meeting room.

Now, at this very instant, the other groups were carrying out their tasks. The next hour would be life or death for us all.

Where was Collie?

I tapped my lemonade bottle on the ground. Glancing down, I saw a pencilled V on one of the tree's roots. I prayed it was a good sign.

Dwight had been throwing sticks for someone's dog. He came over and crouched beside us. He'd been quieter than usual since Nate's death. He looked furtively up at the palace – at the balcony on the third floor.

"Should we just go to the telio station anyway, do you think?" he muttered.

I could see a trio of Guns wandering through the park in their short-sleeved summer uniforms. I darted a glance at the palace too. "We can't." I forced myself to take a swig of the too-tart lemonade. "We have to know what's going on first."

Dwight started to reply and then froze, his hands tight on his thighs.

"Look," he said.

More Guns had entered the park by the 59th Street entrance. The hairs at the back of my neck lifted. Coincidence? A random search for Discordants?

"Amity..." murmured Hal, staring at them.

The waltz was still playing. The Guns started fanning out. Another entrance lay behind us; I glanced at its wrought-iron gates and licked my lips.

"All right...we're going to get up and stretch. Then wander over to that ice-cream vendor near the—"

I stopped. Two figures had appeared on the palace balcony.

Two.

One was Collie, as arranged...and one was Kay Pierce.

Dwight took a quick, hissing breath. "Oh shit."

My pulse slammed against my veins. Collie had his arm around Pierce as if comforting her. Hal sat motionless, gaping upwards.

No time to wonder how things had gone wrong. I snatched up my clutch purse with cold fingers. "Quick – get out *now!*" I muttered. I rose; Hal and Dwight followed.

"Look casual," I urged. "Don't hurry." I hooked my arm through Hal's and we started for the park exit.

The music stopped.

People had started noticing Collie and Pierce; uneasy murmurs rustled through the air. Dwight strolled tensely, his hands in his denims pockets. Hal's arm in mine was like steel.

The siren that meant an announcement was imminent started wailing. We'd reached the gate. We kept on through it, then turned left, weaving our way through the passers-by. The klaxon still wailed. People were starting to stream into the park.

We reached an empty bus stop. Hal was breathing hard. Dwight kept pounding his knuckles against his palm. "Oh, holy moley, what *happened*?" he muttered. "What the hell happened?"

The wail of approaching sirens – seemingly from all directions. I gripped Hal's arms, my words tumbling over each other.

"Get to Mac's group! They'll be heading down Concord with President Weir by now. Don't run, but *hurry*! Tell him Pierce is still alive, then get down into the tunnels. You know where. *Stay safe!*"

With a visible effort, Hal steadied himself and nodded. "You too, Sis."

He set off at a brisk stride. All too soon, his dark head was swallowed by the crowd.

Dwight was pale. "What about me? The telio station?"

Jimmy's group was waiting there for us, ready to storm it and take it over. I'd been supposed to give the news to the country that Pierce and Cain were dead and President Weir was back in power. I wished frantically that I could hear what Pierce was saying.

What did it matter though? She was still alive. Maybe Cain was too.

"Yes – hurry," I said in a rush. "Get them into the tunnels, but don't draw the Guns down there, whatever you do."

He hesitated, looking pained. "Where will *you* go? The capitol building?"

"Dwight! Hurry!"

He kissed my cheek. "Be careful, doll-face," he implored, and took off.

My emotions were in knots. *Ingo,* I thought fleetingly. *Please let him have made it back into the tunnels.*

I spotted a red-and-black cab in the traffic – *Harmony Taxis,* read the sign. I flagged it. A few moments later, we were speeding uptown. Thankfully the capitol building was in Leo sector, where we were now – we wouldn't have to cross a checkpoint.

I sat in the back, fiddling with my clutch purse. "Please hurry," I said again, my voice tight. "I've got an urgent message."

Shadowcars prowled thickly in the traffic, their grey lines high and curved. The cabby's knuckles were white on the wheel. He glanced at me in the rear-view mirror.

"Something's up," he said.

It was all right to sound fearful; anyone would be. "Yes – I think they're making an announcement at the palace."

"It was the monthly status meeting today." The cabby didn't say anything else; he didn't know who I was. But he clearly thought Pierce had changed her mind about who was Discordant again – sent the Guns out in full force to clamp down.

My gaze flicked to the lamp post at Central and 42nd as we passed. No dangling body. Not for long, probably.

"Can't you go faster?" I begged.

"I'm doing my best, lady."

The capitol building used to be the city hall – an imposing structure of elongated rectangles, with broad white steps. As we reached the hill leading up to it, my heart lurched. Grey-uniformed Guns were swarming over the steps like locusts. Clubs swung as pistol fire came in staccato bursts.

At least a dozen bodies lay, unmoving.

The cabby swung to face me. "Sister, I ain't heading up into that!"

I felt punched. "No – no, turn here!" I gasped. "I have to get to Harlemtown. Hurry!"

I gave him an address several blocks from Jakov's. He refused to speed and I couldn't blame him. We wove through the traffic, my brain screaming. What had gone wrong? We'd planned everything so carefully. But Pierce was no fool; she'd guessed her attackers would try for the capitol building.

Or had been told so, by someone we'd thought we could trust.

The thought was a sliver of ice. *No. Surely not.*

Where was Hal? Had he reached Mac's group before an army of Guns appeared? I longed to fling open the cab's door and race towards Concord on foot, looking for him.

I couldn't.

We finally reached the address I'd given. I thrust some bills at the cabby and took off at a run. The shabby Harlemtown streets were quiet.

When I let myself in the deli's back door, to my relief Jakov was out front, dealing with customers. I slipped through the kitchen unseen and then raced up the dingy stairs.

From behind the door came a frantic rustling and thumping. I gave the coded knock in a rush. "It's me!" I called.

Sephy flung the door open, clutching documents. Her eyes were wild, her hair a black cloud framing her face.

"Help me!" she cried.

The telio set was on, showing the Harmony symbol. The announcer's voice was urgent:

"*Repeat! The nefarious attempt on President Pierce's life was unsuccessful, but this is still a dark day for Can-Amer...*"

Sephy was ripping up astrological charts, four or five at a time. "That file on the table! We have to destroy all of these."

I grabbed the file. "What's the news saying?" I gasped.

"Cain and all his cronies are dead. Pierce is *fine*, damn it; just fine!"

I started tearing up charts, my motions fierce, frantic. "So's Collie. We saw him in the park. He was on the balcony with Pierce."

Sephy's gaze flew to mine. "He was?"

When I nodded, she didn't answer, but her movements took on more urgency. Neither of us said it, though I knew we were both thinking it.

Had he betrayed us after all?

Sephy scooped up the tattered piles of paper and ran to the bathroom. I heard the toilet flush. The cistern refilled. She flushed it again.

She dashed back and forth, grabbing up the destroyed charts. I kept tearing, and tearing, until my fingers ached. *Why is it too hot for a fire?* I thought frantically. Smoke pouring from our chimney would be as good as sending out a beacon.

"*President Pierce urges her citizens to be strong and vigilant against the Discordant menace. If you see anything suspicious...*"

Sephy rushed back into the room just as the sirens started. She froze; our gazes clashed. I edged to the window and eased open the blinds. A Shadowcar was cruising down the street. I watched it pass, then swallowed and let the blinds fall.

"Guns attacked the group outside the capitol," I said softly. "It was a massacre. I couldn't get to them in time to warn them."

Sephy shuddered. She snatched up her ephemeris and shoved it in a shopping bag. When she spoke, her voice was under tight control.

"What about Mac? Have you seen him?"

"No," I admitted. "I sent Hal to warn his group. I don't know where Hal is now either. Or Dwight. Or—" I broke off, my temples pounding. Why hadn't I managed to say anything that mattered last night?

The small diamond on Sephy's hand glinted as she briefly gripped the table's edge. "Hopefully they're at the rendezvous point."

"Yes. Hopefully." I glanced hurriedly around the room and grabbed up my clutch purse; it had money in it. "Are we finished?"

We slipped downstairs. I could still hear Jakov in the front of the deli, and suspected he was staying away from the kitchen on purpose, to let us leave. If he'd heard the news, he'd know to destroy all traces of us.

We crept down into the cellar, with its neat shelves stacked with supplies. In a dim corner, we eased open the small door that led down further still. The earthen scent of the tunnels embraced us. We took the two hidden lanterns and started off at a jog into the darkness.

An hour later, we were deep in the old network. Normally there was no noise here. Now faint shouts echoed. *"This way! Fan out! You take the eastern route!"*

We stopped short, wincing. "This way," I muttered. We backtracked to a narrow grate in the ground. I slid it aside and we clambered down a worn ladder.

When we finally neared the rendezvous point, all was silent. The subway platform's ancient lines loomed out from the darkness, ghostly in our lantern-light.

Sephy and I edged forward. On one wall, you could still make out the station's name: *Canal Street*, in faded green and red. No lights came from its platform – not even the soft gleam of a single hooded lantern.

My neck prickled. I started to call out "Hello?" and then stopped myself. Who knew who might hear me?

From the ancient tracks, the rise up to the station platform was at least five feet. We quietly hefted ourselves up. I swallowed hard, lifting my light. *Hal*, I thought wildly. If he was all right, he should be here by now. So should Ingo – Dwight – the others.

Sephy gripped my arm suddenly. "Listen," she mouthed.

I strained my ears and stiffened: a faint crying sound was coming from nearby.

We tiptoed further across the platform and rounded the corner. Huddled halfway up a flight of stairs with a blanket and a dimmed lantern, we found them: a coiffed blonde woman and two girls. One was a teenager, the other only four or five. The younger one flinched back, her cheeks tear-stained.

I recognized the woman instantly: Gladys Weir. At the sight of me, the deposed president's wife threw the blanket aside and started down to us.

"You're Amity Vancour," she said hurriedly. "Beatrice, stop that," she added sharply to her smallest daughter.

"The monster man," sobbed the girl, and my gaze flew to her. Ingo's job had been to bring them down here to safety while Mac and the other groups attempted to reinstate President Weir.

"Yes, I am," I said shortly, still staring at the little girl. "What's happening? Do you know anything?"

Mrs Weir looked pale but composed, her red lipstick and broad-shouldered dress as perfect as if she were appearing on the telio. "Mr Jones got in touch recently to say the attack was going ahead. Then this morning, he and some others broke in past the guards – there was actually *gunfire* – and they took Arthur away as planned."

Her older daughter had risen too now – seventeen or so, as coiffed and pretty as her mother. She hefted the still-crying little girl. "Hush, now, the monster man didn't mean us any harm," she murmured.

"And another of your group, the young man with the…" Mrs Weir faltered. "With the unfortunate…"

"I know who you mean," I said tightly.

"Yes. Well, he brought us down here. He wouldn't stop pacing, and would hardly talk, though I kept trying to find out what was going on. Finally he told us to stay here, out of sight. He was going to go back to check on Mr Jones and the others, he said."

Sephy and I stared at each other. Her brown eyes were wide and startled. Ingo always did what he said he would do. Always. For him to have left his charges, something must have gone terribly wrong.

"How…how long ago was that?" asked Sephy.

Gladys Weir shook her head. "An hour?"

"More like two," put in the older daughter. She held up her wrist, showing a sleek silver watch.

My throat was sand. I drew Sephy out to the platform. "I have to go after them," I whispered. "They might need more help."

"Don't *you* get caught," said Sephy, and then we both winced, realizing what she'd implied.

"I won't." I glanced back towards Gladys Weir and her daughters and lowered my voice further.

"If anything happens, head up there, all right?" I pointed down the tunnel to a ladder running up the wall. "It leads to an old service vent. Follow it east about half a mile, then climb down to the old 6th Avenue Line. You'll come to another hiding place."

"The one with the bones?"

"That's it."

Sephy nodded and squeezed my hand. "Find Mac. Please. Bring him and the others back here safely. But if it's not safe, *you* get back here. Promise."

"I promise," I said softly.

It was a lie. Nothing was going to stop me from finding Ingo and my brother.

As I neared the surface, Guns were everywhere. Again and again I had to change my route, listening to their shouts echoing through the ancient passageways.

Finally I made it topside. The sewer's entrance led to a

dark alleyway several blocks east of Concord. As I knelt to push the cover back into place, I flinched: what I'd taken for muffled traffic was the sound of shouts.

I forced myself through to the alley's mouth – then jerked back as someone sprinted past. Peering out again, I saw Guns battling clusters of rioters, blackjacks swinging. Grey uniforms clogged the streets.

None of our group. My stomach curled. *Think.*

Hal hadn't made it this far east, or I'd have encountered him in the tunnels. He'd gone to intercept Mac on Concord. Where would he have headed, faced with all this?

Suddenly it came to me: Ernest and Mabel's. Their safe house was only seven blocks away.

I swallowed and pulled my veil over my face. I set off, keeping to the shadows at the sides of buildings as much as possible. A few times I had to break into a run to avoid a shouting crowd, or duck down a different street to evade Guns.

Finally I reached Grant Boulevard. Though I could still hear riots, the street stretched emptily before me.

I stared apprehensively. The Guns must have set up roadblocks somewhere – I'd have to hurry. Aware of how conspicuous I was about to look, I walked quickly out onto the sidewalk, head down.

The street was as abandoned as if it were a ghost from old New York. The faint sound of a telio drifted out from Stargazer's Bar. Pierce's voice was an angry wasp.

I couldn't make out the words but my muscles clenched.

How would Kay Pierce retaliate against the attempt on her life?

The safe house lay around a bend, hidden from me. I briefly raised my veil, scanning the too-quiet street. I smoothed the veil back just as a man stepped out from a doorway – middle-aged, nondescript. When I tried to pass he blocked my way and my pulse spiked.

"You're Wildcat," he whispered. Before I could respond, he gripped my hand and said, "We're all behind you – everyone I know. Keep fighting." He hunched his shoulders and hurried off.

For a moment I stared after him. Then I shook myself and kept on.

I rounded the curve and froze. In front of Ernest and Mabel's run-down brownstone were two grey, high-roofed Shadowcars.

No. I ducked into the entryway of another brownstone. When I peered out, Guns had emerged, dragging Ernest and Mabel. Mabel looked as if she'd been crying; Ernest had a bruise across one cheek.

No one else came out.

Despair filled me, along with a terrible, shaming hope. Had anyone else been there? Hal, Ingo, any of the others? My gaze flew to the parked Shadowcars. Had I arrived just too late to see who was inside?

The Guns shoved Ernest and Mabel into one. Mabel stumbled and a Gun struck her. I ducked my head away, feeling faint, remembering her stories about dancing in Paris – Ernest's kind laugh.

The sound of engines, and the sirens starting up.

Slowly, they faded.

When I looked again, trembling, the Shadowcars were gone, but they'd left a Gun on guard. He paced in front of the building, tapping a blackjack against one palm.

I stared at him, then glanced quickly behind me at the door of the brownstone. I tried the doorknob. Locked. A panel with five buttons gleamed dully on the wall of the entryway, each with a name beside it.

I buzzed one after the other. "Come on, somebody, *open* it," I muttered frantically.

No one answered. I licked my lips and watched the Gun pace. Wait him out, or try to sneak away? Suddenly my eyes widened: a small circle of red glinted from the sidewalk.

Blood, still fresh enough to be red instead of brown.

My heart thudded. I quickly scanned the sidewalk and saw another dot. Then another. They led in a loose, straggling line around the side of the building.

The Gun stood with his back to me now, gazing up the street. I didn't let myself think. I edged out from the doorway, then sprinted around the side of the house.

I was in a small yard, blocked off by a fence. Another red spot lay on the cellar's double wooden doors. I dropped to my knees beside them and knocked three times – paused – twice more.

A flurry of movement inside. "Who's there?" called a wavering voice.

I sagged. "Hal, it's me!" I hissed.

The doors swung open. I scrambled down the stairs, closing them after me. Light angled in from a single grimy window.

Hal was at the bottom of the steps. I hugged him. "Are you all right?" I gasped.

"Yeah, but…but Mac isn't," he said hoarsely. "He's been shot." He moved aside. Mac lay in the corner with Ingo crouched over him.

I rushed over. They were both in the double-breasted suits with the Harmony armband that they'd worn to enter the Weirs' house, posing as high-up Guns. Ingo had Mac's jacket off and was unbuttoning his shirt. When I crouched beside them, Ingo's dark eyes briefly met mine; I saw relief battle fear.

"What the hell are you doing here?" he said.

"Looking for you. All of you." A red stain was spreading across Mac's white shirt. He was conscious, but clearly wandering. Dry-mouthed, I gripped his hand.

"Mac, it's Amity. Can you hear me?"

He was pale as paper, sweating. "Hey, kiddo," he murmured.

"Help me," said Ingo shortly to me.

We got Mac raised up a little and Ingo pulled his shirt open, tugging it from his trousers. A bullet had ploughed into Mac's side; blood streaked across his skin from the red-black hole. A handkerchief had been pressed against it. The cloth was limp and sodden. Blood still seeped from it, far too steadily.

"You told me you hadn't been shot, you bastard," Ingo muttered to Mac. He was pulling off his own jacket now, his motions quick and frenzied.

Mac was breathing hard. "Tried to save Weir...too many of them..."

Oh no. I squeezed his fingers, trying not to show my dismay – my fear for his life. "You did fine," I said shakily. "Don't try to talk."

Hal dropped to his knees beside me, looking young, vulnerable. "I found him on Concord – it was all riots by then. Mac was hurt, and...and on the ground. I got him away and then Ingo found us – we couldn't reach the tunnels, so we came here, but..."

He trailed off, his eyes wide, fixed on Mac's wound.

"The safe house had been found," Ingo finished. He unbuttoned his own shirt and yanked it off. Beneath it he wore a thin sleeveless undershirt – just like the one he'd worn that time we'd been on the roof together. I noticed it fleetingly.

Mac had passed out. Ingo swore and felt for Mac's pulse at his throat. "*Damn* it – we need him conscious if we're getting him out of here."

"Maybe it's good," I said fervently. "He'll be in less pain, at least."

"Yes, I hope you're right...what's happening out there?"

Ingo yanked off his undershirt.

I swallowed. "Ernest and Mabel have been taken… there's a Gun on guard."

"So the plan's all gone to shit, we can assume," Ingo muttered. He bit at the undershirt's cloth, starting a tear, and then ripped it in half. "Hal told me that Pierce is still alive."

I choked out a laugh. "Yes. Cain's been killed, and all his cronies, but Pierce is fine."

"And Collis," said Ingo.

"Collie wouldn't…" Hal started, and then trailed off – clearly remembering, as I was, the sight of Collie on that balcony with his arm around Pierce.

Ingo's gaze flew grimly to mine. He didn't comment. His undershirt was a long strip by now; he wrapped it tightly around Mac's waist. "Give me yours too," he said to Hal. "Have you got anything?" he added to me.

"My slip." I stood up and wriggled out of it, staggering slightly on my weak leg. I handed it to Ingo. As I knelt beside him again he folded it in a small, satiny square and pressed it over Mac's wound. Mac groaned.

Hal handed over his own undershirt, torn into a long strip too. Ingo tied it over the square of my slip and then sank back onto his haunches and rubbed a hand over his jaw, staring at Mac.

"I think that's the best we can do," he murmured. He glanced at me. "How are the streets?"

"Bad," I admitted. "At least around Concord. And I

think they've set up roadblocks a block or two to the west – it was way too quiet there."

Ingo winced at this news. "All right," he said finally. "Centre Park. The entrance in the underpass."

"How…how will we make it that far without being caught?" asked Hal.

"Do we wait until night-time?" Ingo said to me.

I gripped my elbows. Mac was so very pale. "I think we'd better not."

"Agreed." Ingo handed Mac's jacket with its Harmony armband to Hal. "Here – welcome to being a Gun. Your sister and Mac are under arrest."

He and Hal quickly got dressed again while I crouched over Mac, stroking his damp forehead. I smoothed his unruly brown hair and thought how much I admired this man. *Mac, you've got to be okay.*

Yet despite myself, I was very aware of Ingo as he pulled on his shirt. His long, thin torso was leanly muscled. I could see the ugly, badly-healed scar on his stomach from when another miner at Harmony Five had swung a pickaxe at him, at the direction of a bored Gun.

I shoved my awareness of him away just as Hal finished getting dressed. "I'll go check upstairs – see if there's another way out." He hurtled up the inside stairs before I could respond.

"Help me put Mac's shirt back on him, all right?" said Ingo.

Mac moaned as we eased him up. Ingo somehow

managed an easy tone. "Hang on, you louse – Sephy would kill me if you died. Do you really want that on your conscience?"

We got his shirt on him. To my relief the bandage seemed to hold. "Ingo, what happened?" I said in a low voice.

For a moment Ingo didn't answer. "First, tell me something. Do you think he betrayed us?"

"I don't know," I said finally.

Ingo buttoned Mac's shirt. "I don't know either, but I know what I suspect."

From his clipped tone, dread filled me. Ingo had never warmed to Collie, though I knew he'd believed, like the rest of us, that he could be trusted.

"Tell me," I said.

He exhaled as we gently laid Mac down again. "It didn't go smoothly, getting the Weirs out. At first it seemed fine. We all looked official – they let us right in. But one of the Guns, someone high-up, seemed suspicious. He asked for the code word."

I tensed. Collie had told us this was a possibility, and that the code word changed every week. This week the code was "serene".

"So Mac gave it, telling the Gun that he'd have him reported for insubordination. And the code was wrong."

"*What?*"

Ingo bit the words out. "It was the code from last week. At the time I just thought it was bad luck – that Collis had gotten the wrong information. We had the family downstairs

203

by then and all hell broke loose. Mac tried to bluff it out and pulled his pistol. A few of the Guns were on our side, you know, and they tried to calm things down, but—"

Ingo broke off and swiped a hand over his face.

"The head Gun started firing," he said. "A few of the other Guns tackled him, but Mac must have gotten winged in the side. We got Weir and his family out; the head Gun was overpowered. The poor bastards who did it will probably all be hanged now. *Damn* it!"

He sank back onto his haunches, gazing at Mac, his expression raw with pain and anger. "And now Pierce is fine, and your charming ex is fine, but *Cain*, who we know had it in for Pierce, is dead. How convenient."

It was exactly what I'd been thinking, deep in the recesses of my mind. It hurt. I'd desperately wanted to trust Collie in this much, at least – to know that I hadn't been a complete fool to have once believed in him.

"Is 'charming ex' really necessary?" I said tightly.

"Fine, I retract it."

I started to ask what had happened when they got out onto the street, but then we both looked up as Hal clattered back down the stairs.

"We can get out the back; there's a yard," he gasped. "But we've got to go *now*. The Shadowcar's across the street again – there's three Guns talking, looking this way."

I scrambled up, recalling the blood on the sidewalk. Mac had roused slightly, looking bleary with pain. "Where are we?" he murmured.

204

"Not safe yet," said Ingo softly. He put his arm around him. "Come on, my friend – let's get you up."

Mac groaned as Ingo and Hal got him up to his feet. He stood panting, one hand pressed to his wound, head down.

"All right," he mumbled. "Fine. I'm fine."

Ingo was a foot taller than Mac. Still supporting him, Ingo yanked on his fedora, and angled it downwards, partly hiding his scar.

"Are we ready?" he said to me and Hal.

Though pale, Hal nodded. I gripped my brother's arm and glanced apprehensively up the stairs.

"Ready," I said.

CHAPTER FIFTEEN

SOMEHOW WE MADE IT the eleven blocks to Centre Park
– sometimes ducking out of sight when we saw Guns,
sometimes brazening it out as Shadowcars glided past. The
Harmony armband worked wonders.

"Not for long," muttered Ingo when I said this.
"They're sure to be looking for me and Mac already."

He had me by one arm, in case unseen Guns were
watching. Between him and Hal, Mac stumbled along as
they half-carried him. Ingo's fingers on my arm were firm,
protective.

I glanced quickly up at him. "What happened after you
got the Weirs out?" I murmured.

We'd reached the northern part of Centre Park, a good

mile from Kay Pierce's palace. This section had the zoo, and a playground. The swings hung emptily. From the streets beyond the gates, we could still hear faint yells and sirens.

Ingo started to answer – then broke off as much closer shouts came from over a small hill.

"Sounds like the Helpers," Hal muttered. His eyes met mine, briefly panicked. Ingo swore, his hand on my arm clammy suddenly. We'd nearly reached the long underpass with the tunnel entrance.

"Can you run?" he asked me, his eyes fixed on the hill.

Terror iced my spine. I pulled away and pushed him slightly, "Yes! Go – go!"

Ingo and Hal broke into a shambling run with Mac groaning between them. I ran too, ignoring the pain of my leg. Once beneath the underpass, I didn't stop. I raced for the tunnel entrance – one of several old doors set in the shadows between archways.

To my relief, the forgotten door opened as easily as always. Ingo, Hal and Mac were right behind me. Past them, through the small circle of sunshine at the underpass's end, the first of the Helpers were streaming down the hill in their red-and-black uniforms. Had they seen us?

"Hurry!" I gasped.

Ingo and Hal pushed past me, Mac sagging between them. I shut the door and groped for the hidden lanterns. I turned one on. Ingo and Hal got Mac down the stairs.

I quickly followed and handed the other lantern to Hal. Ingo gave me a level look, still supporting the semi-conscious Mac.

I think it struck us both at once how very vulnerable we were down here, with Mac so injured. This area had intersections from all over – it was probably swarming with Guns.

"This way?" said Hal, starting down the tunnel. It led roughly in the direction we wanted to go.

I exhaled, my eyes still on Ingo's. "Yes," I said. Then I glanced back at my brother. "Go ahead a little bit, will you? Not too far, but scout things out."

Hal nodded and set off, his footsteps echoing damply. This section had once been a New Manhattan sewer. Scrawled numbers on the wall must have meant something to service workers once.

Ingo and I followed. I put my arm around Mac's waist and he moaned. Even in the shadows, I was alarmed at his pallor.

"I've got him," said Ingo. "You're limping badly enough already."

"I'm all right." As we kept on, I glanced up at Ingo's profile. "What...what happened when you got President Weir out onto the street?"

Bars of light from a grille above played briefly over Ingo's face. He sighed. "I asked Mac if he was injured. He denied it, but I could tell he was – he was sweating, walking strangely. He ordered me to take President Weir's family down into the tunnels as planned. He promised me he was all right."

Ingo grimaced. "So…I took them and went. When we were under 65th Street, I let them go ahead a little bit. I thought I heard gunfire up above – fighting. I didn't tell them."

Mac and the others would have crossed 65th as they took Weir down Concord. I could hardly say it. "If they didn't even make it *that* far…"

"It had to have been only a minute or so after the explosion," said Ingo curtly. "Make of that what you will."

My thoughts reeled. I told Ingo what I'd seen at the capitol building. He cursed. "With the faulty code word, that's three for three. The lady was either tipped off, or is a very fast thinker."

His comment about my "charming ex" seemed to echo between us again.

We got Mac over a disused concrete pipe in a silence that felt weighted. "I got the Weirs down into the hiding place," Ingo said finally. "But I couldn't stay there, not knowing that Mac was injured and that the Guns had already attacked."

I nodded. Not many of the others knew all the tunnel entrances. Without that knowledge, President Weir could have been trapped in the streets above – they all could have been. I thought of Dwight and winced.

"The streets were swarming by the time I got to Concord," Ingo went on. "I tried to find President Weir, but it was chaos – it was just dumb luck that I found Hal hiding with Mac in an alleyway. Mac was a little more conscious then. He kept muttering that they didn't even get a chance to start gathering a crowd before the Guns turned up."

I bit my lip. "So you don't know what happened to President Weir?"

"No. Nothing good, I suspect."

We paused at the sound of running footsteps; Hal's lantern-light came bouncing towards us.

"I heard shouts up ahead," he panted.

Ingo and I glanced at each other over Mac's head. "The old Kemp Street sewer," Ingo said.

"Yes, then down to the 6th Avenue Line," I said quickly. "I told Sephy to go there in case of trouble."

"Good. Let's hope that's deep enough down."

As we started back, the world shuddered with a dull, thundering echo. My heart skipped as I stared at a shower of pebbles and dust pattering from a new crack in the tunnel roof.

Hal had been a bit further ahead. He spun towards us. "An *explosive*?"

Ingo's voice was clenched. "Either that, or something giving a damn good imitation."

Another boom came from below, trembling at our feet. My gaze flew to Ingo's as we both realized: Kay Pierce's tunnel experts were blocking off certain routes. We could be corralled like rats in a maze.

"*Shit*," I whispered, my grip tightening around Mac's waist.

"My thoughts exactly," gasped Ingo. "Hurry."

The way to the hiding place was a nightmare of Guns – distant shouts – the rumble of more explosions. More than once, tunnels we thought we knew the way through were closed off by new cave-ins and we had to backtrack.

Finally, there'd been only silence for a quarter of an hour. About halfway down the ancient 6th Avenue Line, we came to Ode to Bones, with its weird, intricately arranged features.

An old control room lay just opposite. Light gleamed from its depths.

"Who's there?" barked a voice. Jimmy appeared in the doorway with a rifle. His eyes widened; he rushed towards us.

"It's them!" he flung over his shoulder. "Mac's hurt!" He took Mac from me; he and Ingo lifted him.

Sephy rushed out and stopped short with a cry. "Is… is he…?"

"He's been shot. He's still alive," said Ingo as they got Mac inside and lowered him to the ground. Wordlessly, I squeezed Sephy's arm.

Mac was short but normally didn't seem it. I hated seeing how small he looked now, lying with his head falling limply to one side.

Sephy quickly crouched and gripped his hand. "Mac?"

she whispered. She stroked his brow. "Mac, hang on, sweetheart…you're going to be fine."

Mrs Weir came over, her face smudged, yet still looking in control. From her voice's steel I guessed what it was costing her.

"My husband?" she asked.

"We don't know. I'm sorry." I didn't mention what Ingo had said – that he suspected nothing good had happened to him.

Mrs Weir hesitated and looked down at Mac in the lantern light. Fresh blood was seeping through his shirt, I saw now with dread. Ingo was unbuttoning it.

"I know a little first aid," Mrs Weir said finally. "Maybe I can help."

I sat slumped against the wall, staring at Mac's prone form. Ingo was holding down his shoulders as Mrs Weir stitched his wound with a needle and thread from her sewing kit. Sephy still kneeled beside him, holding his hand.

Ingo had left a bag in the original hiding place; Sephy had brought it with her. The peach schnapps was in it. He'd brought it to celebrate with, in case we'd won.

Now we'd used it to try to anaesthetize Mac, holding his head and giving him a few large swigs. He still moaned, pale and sweating, as Mrs Weir stitched him up.

Her older daughter, Darlene, sat hugging Beatrice nearby. The child sobbed softly. I wasn't sure which scared her more: the bones visible across the tunnel, or Ingo's face. I rubbed my head, hating her tiredly – knowing I was being unfair and not caring.

Dwight was there too. He sat next to me, hugging his elbows. His cheek was badly bruised – one of his fists scraped and bloody.

"I was too late at the telio station," he muttered to me, staring at Mac. "I got there and…"

"The Guns were already there," said Jimmy shortly. "They'd attacked a few minutes before. They got Anton – Susannah – Roddy. Dwight and I barely got away."

Ingo had heard, I saw his jaw tighten at Anton's name. His dark eyes met mine.

Four for four, he didn't have to say.

Feeling numb, I gazed at the bottle of peach schnapps, recalling the summer-sweet taste of hope the night before. For months now, I'd been longing for this day – longing to put my father's actions behind me.

Now Kay Pierce would keep on.

Hal sat on my other side. I had the impression of a taut, trembling wire.

"Collie didn't betray us," he muttered to me as Jimmy and Dwight talked in low murmurs.

"I don't know, Hal."

"I'm not asking you! I'm telling you! He wouldn't." Hal beat his fist against his thigh, staring at Mac. "He wouldn't," he whispered.

Finding out about our father's betrayal had maybe been

even harder for Hal than for me. He'd been only nine when Dad died – had known him even less than I had. He'd needed him to be a hero.

Now he needed for Collie to be the man he'd thought he was too.

My temples throbbed. I stared blindly at Mac, wishing that Collis Reed had never been part of our lives.

"Something went wrong, that's all," Hal was saying in a low voice. "Maybe…maybe Pierce found out, and Collie had to pretend to be on her side, or—"

"*I don't know,* Hal," I broke in, my voice shaking. "But it's not looking great, is it? The wrong code word, Guns everywhere we were going to be! *You* figure it out."

When I saw his stricken face I hated myself.

"I'm sorry," I said finally. "We're all upset. I don't know what happened any more than you do."

Hal's throat worked. He looked away and didn't respond.

Jimmy leaned towards me. "Sephy said you saw what happened at the capitol building," he said in an undertone.

I sighed. Finally I nodded wearily, and described the scene: the Guns attacking the groups that had been waiting there; the bodies lying on the ground. Jimmy winced. He and Dwight looked at each other. Dwight's bruise was stark against his pallor. He bit a thumbnail.

"Hardly anyone's left, it sounds like," he muttered.

"And someone's been forced to talk – given Mabel and Ernest's place away." Jimmy swallowed and cracked his knuckles. "We'll have to leave the city, like Mac said. *Damnit* – what'll we do if he doesn't pull through?"

"Shh," cautioned Dwight, glancing at Sephy. She still sat holding Mac's hand as Mrs Weir worked on him.

"But what *will* we do? Mac is—" Jimmy broke off. He didn't have to finish the thought.

Mac was the heart of everything.

No. He would *not* die. I got up quickly and went over. Mrs Weir was bandaging Mac with some stitched together handkerchiefs. Ingo crouched at his head. I knelt beside Ingo, noting with trepidation how still Mac looked.

"Is he all right?" I asked.

"I'm not a doctor," Mrs Weir said tersely. "I took a first-aid course and have a needle and thread, that's all. But his pulse is steady, at least."

"Thank you." Sephy pressed Mrs Weir's arm. "I mean it. Thank you."

Ingo glanced wordlessly at me. Behind him, the display of bones gleamed in the faint light. The skulls leered, trapped in their ribcage prisons.

Mrs Weir had just finished bandaging Mac when another explosion rumbled. My chest clenched. I stood up in a rush, staring down the darkness of the tunnel.

Ingo had scrambled up too. "Where was that from, do you think?" he muttered to me.

I felt panicked. "I can't tell! Maybe—"

Another explosion. This time the ground under our feet shook.

Sephy rose slowly, eyes wide. "What…what does this mean? Are they coming?"

"They're blocking off certain routes," Ingo said. "We hoped they wouldn't make it this far down, but—"

Mrs Weir paled and looked quickly at her daughters. "Can we still get out of the city?"

"With luck." Ingo's gaze met mine. That route under the river had been so difficult to find – we'd never encountered Guns in the northern part of the Lexington Avenue Line. "But Mac can't be moved yet!" cried Sephy.

Ingo touched her arm. "He'll have to be. We'll be gentle with him."

I stood frozen, remembering the rioters shouting *V for Victory and Vancour!* And the man I'd encountered near the safe house. *We're all behind you. Everyone I know.*

Pierce would not retaliate lightly to the events of the day. How could I just leave New Manhattan to its punishment, when I'd been the one urging people to fight?

Yet what else could I do, with the Resistance shattered?

Another explosion rumbled, far too close this time. "That might be our route north gone," muttered Ingo. I could practically see his mind working. "We'll have to travel down further and then go up again—"

All at once something hit me. I looked wildly around the small, dimly-lit room. "Where's Hal?" I gasped.

Sephy's expression turned blank. "Hal? But he was just here!"

Darlene, the older Weir daughter, came over. "Are you

looking for that boy with the dark hair? He left."

"When?" Ingo said sharply.

Darlene flinched slightly, very deliberately not staring at the puckered half of his face. "Maybe twenty minutes ago? He seemed upset…" She gave a short, humourless laugh. "Well. We're *all* upset. But I just thought he was doing something he was supposed to do."

She nodded at a service ladder. "He went up there."

I stared at it. The ladder led to the eastern tunnels heading topside. Why would Hal venture out into the city now? I remembered snapping at him about Collie and felt chilled. He hadn't run off because of *that*, had he? *Hal?* Like Mac said, he was usually a steady, responsible kid.

I'll kill him, I thought. But my sudden terror whispered that I wouldn't get the chance.

Ingo drew me to one side. "Amity, we can't wait. If we still have any hope in hell of getting out of the city, it has to be now."

"I'm not leaving Hal."

"You have no idea where he is!"

"I can't leave him anyway! Don't ask me to, Ingo. You'd feel the same."

"I'm not asking! You're right! But—"

He broke off. I could guess what he was thinking. Apart from me, he was the only one who knew the tunnels well enough to have a chance of getting everyone out alive, with routes being closed off by the second.

Finally Ingo reached behind him and drew a pistol from

the back of his waistband. "Take this," he said quietly.

I did. The weapon felt heavy in my grasp.

Another explosion rumbled. The little girl started crying again. Ingo gripped my shoulders; his voice was low. "I have to leave – I don't have a choice. If you're not out of the city within *two hours* after us, I'm coming back for you."

"No – Ingo, please! Once you get out, stay safe – don't come back! Promise me."

Raw anger leaped across his angular face. "I would never make such a promise and you know it."

I couldn't answer. His hands felt hot on my shoulders as we stared at each other. The weight of what was unsaid pressed down on us.

"Ingo, I…" I licked my lips. My throat was tight.

Suddenly he seized my hand and pulled me further into the shadows. "That night on the roof," he said in a rush. "Was it because of this?" He put my hand on his scar.

I was horrified. "*No!* Ingo, no. Never." Gently, as if I could smooth the creases from his ruined skin, I stroked his cheek, close to tears suddenly.

"I don't see the scar," I whispered. "All I see is you."

Another explosion shuddered, far too close. I gave him a soft shove. "Go! *Stay safe*," I implored.

Ingo was breathing hard. "And you. Please." He hesitated, then took my hand again and kissed my palm, his lips fleetingly warm against my skin. He squeezed my fingers tightly.

Before I could respond, he turned away and half-jogged

to the others. Beatrice was still sobbing about the "monster man". Darlene was trying to soothe her.

"Let me," said Ingo hurriedly. He crouched down in front of the little girl. His voice floated back to me, suddenly gentle, hard to hear.

"I'm sorry I scare you," he said. "I don't mean to. My face is only like this because I got hurt. I'm here to keep you safe, Beatrice – I promise. But you have to be very brave and quiet now. Can you do that?"

"Please, Beatrice!" said Mrs Weir.

Hesitantly, the child nodded. Darlene scooped her up in her arms. Ingo and Jimmy got ready to move Mac, one on either side of him. *Please be all right, Mac,* I thought.

Sephy rushed over; we embraced tightly. I pressed my head against her shoulder.

"Be careful!" I whispered.

"You too. Follow us as soon as you can." She pulled away, her eyes bright, but she managed a smile. "I hope that meant what I thought, with you and Ingo."

I did too.

As she headed over to the others, I braced myself and put the pistol in my clutch purse. I grabbed the remaining lantern and started up the ladder against the wall.

"Amity, wait!" called a voice. Dwight came jogging up, his bruised face pale but set. "I'm coming with you."

I put one foot back on the ground, staring at him. "What? Why?"

His fists were tight. "Because I'm no good in the tunnels

– Ingo doesn't need me. But maybe I can help you find Hal. I know this city inside and out."

Impulsively, I lunged at him and hugged him. "*Thank you*," I gasped.

Even in the faint light, I could see his blush. "Anytime, doll-face."

Further down the tunnel, Ingo had paused, the group going on ahead. I lifted a hand to him, and saw him lift his back.

A moment later, his tall, thin form was gone, vanishing around the bend.

CHAPTER SIXTEEN

JULY, 1942

As Collis entered his office his gaze went immediately
to his desk, where a large brown envelope lay. He hesitated
just inside the doorway, eyeing it.

Frowning, he lay his briefcase on a chair and crossed to
a gold-edged mirror that hung on one wall. Behind him
he could see the buildings of New Manhattan through the
broad windows, with the giant Harmony flag that flew on
top of the Majestic in the distance. The late afternoon sun
angled in, turning his hair gold and his eyes very blue.

Collis studied himself critically. He straightened his
cuffs with short, sharp motions. His suit fitted him well –
the Leo tiepin glittered. He looked nothing like the scruffy
boy who'd grown up in poverty in Gloversdale as one of

"those Reeds". Whatever was inside the envelope couldn't touch him.

Even so, Collis glanced at his sideboard. Like his office back in the Zodiac, there was a collection of liquor bottles there.

He wavered. Finally he went over and poured himself a finger of whiskey. He could have that much. Hell, it had been months since he'd finished the painkillers, and he hadn't gotten any more. He'd barely been tempted.

Collis sat at his desk, tensely swirling the drink as he stared down at the envelope. It had arrived that morning by special messenger and he'd been avoiding it all day.

Suddenly angry, he knocked the drink back. He ripped open the envelope and pulled out the papers inside.

As he scanned the documents, he slumped. *Oh, no. Poor Goldie.* He read them again. Something in him had gone tight and hard. Why had he wanted to know this? Why hadn't he just left sleeping dogs alone?

At last he got up and went to the window. He looked out over New Manhattan, jamming his hands in his trouser pockets.

All at once he was back in Gloversdale.

Eleven years old. He'd come home from playing at Amity's one evening and found his mother, Goldie, passed out on the sofa. His father, Hank, had been sitting drinking with Collis's uncle Matt. Cigarette smoke choked the air.

Collis had stopped short in the doorway, his guts tense.

He hated it when his father was home. Hank glanced up; a solid, balding man who usually sported too-shiny suits. Just then he wore only trousers and an undershirt, his face gleaming in the summer heat.

"Well, looky who's home for a change," he drawled. He nodded at Matt. "Collis Floyd here thinks he's too good for us. Spends all his time with those rich *Van-coors*."

Uncle Matt – who was more stupid than mean – had chuckled. "That so, Collie-boy? Hey, that's not so nice. C'mon and sit with us."

"He won't," said Hank flatly. "Those *Van-coors* are better than us, isn't that right, son? Don't want to taint yourself, sitting with trash like me and Matt."

Collis longed to hightail it back out the door and make a run for it. He would have, if Goldie hadn't been lying in such an awkward-looking position. He swallowed, glancing at her slumbering form. "Is she okay?"

"Go and ask her," said Hank. He and Matt seemed to find this hilarious. Matt giggled, his large shoulders shaking.

Collis edged into the room. He went over and tried to straighten Goldie, make her more comfortable. She moaned and batted him away. "Le' me 'lone."

He jumped as his father's hand gripped the back of his neck. Hank shook him hard. "*Hey*, you little stuck-up good-for-nothing. Matt asked you to join us."

In a panic, Collis twisted from Hank like a flopping fish. He lunged across the room, banged through the ancient screen door, cleared the steps in a flying, desperate leap.

He ran.

Cutting across the twilight fields, Collis was terrified his father would follow. But Hank obviously decided it was too much trouble; when Collis reached the top of the hill and looked back, panting, he saw no sign of him.

Once he got to Amity's again, Rose, her mother, was in the warm kitchen, arranging cookies on a cooling rack. She wore a flowered house dress and her face was flushed and pretty.

"Why, Collis! I thought you'd gone home."

Collis shook his head. "No…my folks aren't there, so…" He trailed off.

"So you'll stay for dinner," finished Rose. She squeezed his shoulder. "Good. Now, here, try this." She handed him one of the cookies. "I made them different this time. What do you think?"

Amity had wandered in then, wearing cut-off coveralls and a T-shirt. Her face lit up. "Hey! I thought you left."

"Came back," he said with his mouth full, smiling.

So Amity dragged him out to the barn while Rose finished getting dinner ready, and they had a long discussion up in the hayloft about her newest passion, which was travelling through darkest Africa. She'd been reading a book about it.

Collis couldn't care less about darkest Africa. Darkest home was weighing too heavy on his mind, and he knew he'd never get to the stupid place anyway, so why waste time thinking about it? He wished she'd talk about airplanes, a passion they shared. Half the time Collis felt as if he and Amity were twins and the other half he wondered how one person could like so many things that he didn't. But he wasn't in any mood to risk quarrelling with her, so he pretended interest and they talked Africa up down and sideways until Rose called them in.

It wasn't much of a price to pay to be Amity's best friend and so welcome here. In Collis's heart, he was a Vancour... yet he knew he never could be, not really.

Because his home was that place where his dad was waiting.

Now, ten years later, Collis stood in his office staring blindly out at New Manhattan.

Well, you wanted to know, and now you do, he told himself.

The papers he'd received had been in response to a query he'd sent to the Central Records Office, asking about his parents. He had no idea why this urge had taken him. He'd lost contact with them both when he was made Discordant and sent to Harmony Three at seventeen.

He recalled, bitterly, Hank's anger at this – towards *him*, Collis, as if he'd planned it or something – and Goldie, pale and shaking from not having a drink, trying to stop the Guns from taking him and getting beaten for it. The memory was painful, confusing.

Once he'd been released from Harmony Three, he'd pretended that neither of them existed.

Collis clenched his hand shut, not wanting to see the Leo tattoo on his palm. According to the papers on his desk, Goldie – who'd had him when she was just seventeen herself and who really hadn't been that bad, apart from being a drunk – had been found Discordant soon after he had, for public intoxication. She was sent to Harmony Two and had died there.

She'd been a Pisces. Collis pictured the tattoo that would have been on her palm and felt sick.

Hank was still alive, still working at the factory in Denver, stacking boxes. The paperwork had included a photo and Collis hardly recognized him. A reply slip was clipped to the documents. *Would you like to take any action regarding the elder Mr Reed, sir?*

Collis turned back to his desk and studied the black-and-white image. Suddenly he realized that his father must have seen him on the telio – must know by now that the "stuck-up good-for-nothing" had made something of himself after all.

He couldn't stop the satisfaction that swept through him.

Actions count, not thoughts, he reminded himself harshly. He picked up a fountain pen.

No, he scrawled.

* * *

That night, making his way along the private corridor that connected his suite of rooms to Kay's, Collis felt hunted, lost. For the first time, he had no mixed feelings about being with Kay – he wanted to forget everything in that four-poster bed.

He reached Kay's door. He knocked softly.

When Kay opened it, she wore a white lacy negligee. Her hair was down around her shoulders. It suited her, softened her features. She started to say something. Collis didn't give her the chance. He put a hand on either side of her face and drew her to him almost roughly.

He'd feigned passion with her many times; tonight he wasn't pretending. He clutched her to him, letting his hands roam as their mouths moved together. *I need you, I need someone, please let me lose myself in you...*

She seemed to feel the difference. She pressed tightly against him. When they drew apart a little, she gazed at him, slightly wry, slightly vulnerable. "Collis..."

He scooped her up in his arms. "Close the door," he whispered.

The first time they'd spent the night together had been only days after their deal was made. Kay had turned up in the lavish Washington bedroom one night and slipped under the covers with him.

Collis had been asleep and had woken with a start. In the light from the open curtains he could see her features, her eyes looking very big in her pointed face, her hair loose for a change. It was longer than he would have guessed, halfway down her back.

"How's your arm?" she said, moving so that she was on top of him. Her voice sounded thick, as if she'd been crying.

"What arm?" Collis said huskily. His heart had beat rapidly: a sickening mix of automatic desire and fear. It was survival and that was all, yet he'd had no idea if he could do it.

I'll think of Amity, he decided – but when he did, all he could see was the look on her face as the Guns had taken her away. Panicked, he'd closed his eyes then and just concentrated on the physical sensations. To his surprise, he'd lost himself in them. They were a relief – a release.

The same was true tonight, except that it didn't even occur to him to think of Amity. Afterwards, Kay curled against him and he held her, for a change not comparing her slim figure to Amity's more firmly rounded one. As he drifted off he felt grateful that he'd been able to let it all go for a while.

Then the nightmare came again.

Harmony Three. A mangled corpse that came alive and accused him. This time Amity was there, being arrested again. The corpse was telling her everything, and then she was a corpse too, mangled and torn. It was all his fault. He was good for nothing; he was shit and always had been;

there would never be *anything* he could do to change any of it…

"*Collis!*"

He awoke with a start, chest heaving, and realized he'd been thrashing his head back and forth on the pillow. Kay was shaking his arm.

"You were shouting," she said.

"I…" He couldn't speak for a moment. He pressed his hand to his eyes. Kay's fingers stayed on his arm, stroking it tentatively.

"My mother died," he whispered.

"Oh," said Kay softly. With a rustle of sheets, she stretched for the bedside table. She passed him a glass of water.

"Did you like her?" she said after a pause.

The question was an odd relief. Collis propped himself on his elbow and gulped the water. He handed the glass back. "Sometimes," he said finally. "She drank too much. She was only seventeen when she had me."

"Well, I'm sorry she's dead," Kay said, her tone slightly formal.

Collis gazed at the ceiling. "Yeah."

"When did it happen?"

"Years ago. I just found out."

Kay looked as if interest were battling a wish to not share too much. They'd never really discussed their pasts.

"What about your father?" she asked at last.

"He's a bastard and he's still alive."

A bitter grimace crossed Kay's face, as if this were all too familiar. She pulled the sheet tightly around herself. "Was that what your nightmare was about?"

"No." Collis hesitated, studying her.

Kay had it in her power to close the correction camps. She'd chosen not to. "They're still needed for control," she'd said coldly when he'd brought it up. "They keep people cautious. Believe me – I've lived with that terror most of my life."

Collis hated that she was continuing Gunnison's legacy and that he had to play along. Realizing that fear was her main motivator didn't help.

Yet he knew she wouldn't judge him.

"It was about Harmony Three," he said finally. "Someone I betrayed there." Amity had asked about his nightmare too. He could never have told her. He'd dreaded seeing the look in her eyes when she found out what kind of person he was.

Kay's expression was merely expectant – curious.

Collis rubbed the back of his neck. "See…I was an informer. I betrayed other prisoners to get more food… better living conditions. And I guess I was pretty good at it. The Guns used me a lot."

Kay's small, wry smile said she'd have expected nothing less. Collis had told Mac this much too, one night in Topeka when Mac had ordered him to divulge his past. Collis hadn't gone into the details of this particular betrayal. To his relief Mac hadn't pursued it.

He cleared his throat. "Anyway, there was a prisoner with information Johnny wanted. Lester Henley. They'd put him in solitary, beaten him… Lester didn't break. So they moved me into his hut and I befriended him. He was a middle-aged guy. Sick. Lonely. I pretended I'd known his son. In a few weeks, Lester practically thought of *me* as his son."

Collis paused, lost in images that might have been filmed in the grainy black-and-white of a telio play: Harmony Three's unending greys; Lester Henley's gaunt, trusting face.

I'm not surprised you and my son were friends, Collis. You're very like him.

Kay shifted with a rustle of silken sheets. "Did you get the information?"

"Of course," said Collis bitterly. "It wasn't even that important. Just a couple of names Johnny wanted. Then I held Lester's arms behind his back while some Guns beat him to death."

A silence fell.

Kay lay on her side, considering him. "You survived. That's what counts. Sometimes that means doing things that aren't very pleasant."

He shrugged tiredly. "Yeah, I guess," he said…and fleetingly wished he could tell her his fear that the nightmare symbolized who he really was. He'd betrayed Lester. He'd betrayed Amity.

What if he betrayed the Resistance too?

"I'd have done the same," Kay added.

Collis glanced at her and smiled slightly, wondering how it was possible to despise the things Kay did, yet not despise Kay herself.

He hesitated, and then stroked a strand of her long hair back.

"I know," he said.

She sat up, hugging her knees. "In fact, I did once." Her expression was thoughtful. "There was a neighbour of mine who I thought might have reported me to the Guns. They came and tore my apartment up, and shot the client I was seeing." She shuddered, looking angry with herself for still being troubled by it. "They took me in for questioning for two days. I was terrified."

"Yeah?" Collis propped himself on his side, facing her.

"Mrs Lloyd, that was her name. I didn't know for sure whether she'd reported me, but I pretended she'd been one of my clients. They arrested her and took her away. Sandford Cain did," Kay added. "He knocked her out and dragged her right past me."

"Did you feel guilty about it?"

Collis expected Kay to just say no. She paused, considering, thinking back.

"A little, maybe," she said finally.

For several seconds there was only the ticking of the clock. "Can I ask you something?" Collis said suddenly.

Kay looked wary. "I may not answer."

"That first night we were together," he said. "Why were you crying?"

After that first time, Kay had nestled her face in the dip between his neck and shoulder. He'd felt warm wetness on his skin. When he'd asked, thinking it might be something he could use, she'd reminded him: "no strings".

"Is asking questions a string?" he'd said.

"Yes." She'd pulled away and wiped her eyes. "Talk about something else."

"Hey, just making sure it's not my technique," he'd said after a pause. He'd forced himself to kiss her. He *had* pretended she was Amity then, their lips lingering together.

It was the first time they'd kissed. It had somehow felt more intimate than what had come before.

Now Kay made a face. Her hair fell over her narrow shoulders as she traced a line on the sheet.

"I don't know," she said finally. "I just...get blue sometimes." She darted a glance at him. "That was my first kiss, you know. That night with you."

"What?"

"First kiss."

He stared at her. "But it wasn't your first time. Or was it?"

"No. But Johnny never kissed me. And he was my first." Kay looked distant for a moment, tapping a nail against her teeth. He sensed that she'd drawn a barrier around herself.

Something wistful stirred in Collis as he studied her.

Without thinking, he slipped his hand behind her warm neck and kissed her. It deepened. Her lips tasted of cherries.

Kay looked startled as they drew apart. "What was that for?"

Collis shook his head, stroking his thumb over the corner of her mouth. "Nothing."

They stared at each other. Collis let his hand fall with a sudden sinking feeling. He made a show of glancing at the gold clock that sat on the marble table. Three a.m.

"Maybe I should go," he said. "Unless I can stay?"

He always asked. She always said no. He was relieved when she shook her head this time too, though in fact he did want to stay.

The realization disturbed him. Collis got up and got dressed, trying not to look as if he were hurrying. Kay sat in the middle of the large bed watching him, her knees tucked against her chest.

When he was clothed he leaned towards her and kissed her again, because he always kissed her goodbye and it would have looked strange if he hadn't. He somehow ended up sitting on the bed again, their arms around each other as he stroked her smooth skin.

"Goodnight," he whispered.

"Goodnight," Kay echoed. She gave a small smile.

Collis left her room and slipped back out into the private corridor. Back in his own bedroom, he stood massaging his pounding head. He should hate Kay, but he didn't. Being her lover was starting to mean a lot more to him than just screwing her.

We've got to make the assassination attempt soon, Mac, he thought.

CHAPTER SEVENTEEN

SEPTEMBER, 1942

DWIGHT AND I PRESSED AGAINST the curved tunnel wall. I peered around its side.

"I think we're clear," I whispered, and we hurried on.

We'd seen no sign of Hal so far – and hardly any Guns, though unexpected cave-ins sometimes blocked our way. I suspected most were further down by now, sealing off other routes.

Thinking of Ingo and the others, the idea wasn't comforting.

Nearing the meeting place where we'd once brought President Weir, I hooded the lantern again. I looked cautiously around the corner at the tall, cavernous chamber and shock jolted through me.

A hundred feet away stood Collie.

He was clearly visible in the glow of a flashlight he'd put in a nook in the wall. He wore the same immaculate double-breasted suit he'd worn earlier on Kay Pierce's balcony. As I watched, he glanced down at his wrist.

I ducked out of sight, thoughts reeling. At my expression, Dwight frowned and checked too; he pulled back in a rush.

"What's *he*…" he whispered, and then stopped, staring at me. "He's the contact," he said slowly. "Collis Reed."

Something hardened in me; I remembered the pistol I carried. "Come on," I muttered.

Dwight hesitated. Finally he nodded.

We stepped out from around the corner. I turned the lantern up full power, shining its beam on Collie. He shielded his eyes, whirling to face us. I strode forwards, trying to minimize my limp.

"What are you doing here?" I said.

When he saw it was me, he let his arm fall. "Where's Hal?" He started towards me.

I stopped and drew my pistol from the clutch purse. "Don't come any closer," I said, my voice shaking.

He stopped, his jaw hardening. I could feel Dwight at my side, and though he was hardly the most physically imposing of people, I was glad of his presence. There was a steeliness to his thin form as he stared at Collie.

"What happened today?" I said.

After a beat, Collie nodded at my pistol. "Can you put that down? Can we talk like civilized people?"

My fingers felt cold against the metal. "I'm not feeling very civilized. Mac's been shot. The code word was wrong."

Collie's nostrils flared. Some emotion I couldn't read flickered in his eyes. "Is he all right?" he said finally.

"We don't know yet! He's still alive. The Guns were everywhere we planned on being, Collie. Want to explain?"

He stood only feet away, a statue of himself.

"No," he said quietly.

Agonized fury leaped through me. Dwight flinched as I took the safety off the pistol with a *click*. Collie didn't move.

"*Talk!*"

"You wouldn't understand."

I was shaking. "What does *that* mean? Did you tip her off?"

His voice was rough, his shoulders solid and unmoving. "Like I said…you wouldn't understand. Maybe I don't, either. Things got complicated."

"Simplify them!"

"Shoot me if you have to," he said shortly. "Where's Hal?"

Taken off-guard, I stared at him. "Hal?"

His voice rose. "Yes, Hal! Why do you think I'm here?"

"Why *are* you?" said Dwight.

"Because Hal called a meeting! Or at least I thought it was Hal. Someone on the shortwave – it sounded like him – came on and kept saying 'converge' over and over. One of my aides told me to come listen."

My blood pounded. Hal had called Collie on the wireless. Of course. He'd wanted to get answers from him.

Collie took a step closer, frowning. "What's happening, Amity? Is everyone getting out through the tunnels?"

I laughed – a harsh, brittle sound. "Do you really think I'm going to *tell* you that?"

"Fine, don't. But if they aren't, they need to. It's going to get ugly up there."

"It was ugly already," said Dwight in a low voice.

"I know that. It's going to get a hell of a lot worse." Collie glanced at his watch. "I have to go. I'm leaving the city soon. If you're shooting me, do it now."

He snagged his flashlight from the wall. His gaze rested briefly on mine, unsmiling.

"Tell Hal I came," he said.

He turned and left, his stride brisk. His light gleamed on pieces of broken machinery as he went.

I stared after him, breathing hard. For a dark moment I longed to be able to pull the trigger. I'd shot Gunnison, why couldn't I shoot *him*? Dwight hesitantly touched my arm. Finally Collie disappeared into the gloom.

Silence.

My hands felt hot. I couldn't process this yet. I shoved the pistol away. "Where was the wireless set?" I asked urgently.

"In the van." Dwight was still gazing after Collie. He gave a short shake of his head and glanced at me. "Hal saw me park it when I got to Centre Park. He knows I keep the keys over the sun visor. Can he drive? If he got topside, he might have taken it somewhere and—"

"Yes, he can drive," I broke in.

Collie had taught him. I had a sudden flash of Hal's face when he'd told me how Collie rescued him from hiding. *I'll be grateful to him for as long as I live.*

Fear winced my scalp. If he hadn't made it back here to meet with Collie, what had happened to him?

"Come on," I said hurriedly, and started to jog through the tunnel.

"Where would he have gone to broadcast, do you suppose?" whispered Dwight.

We were in a small cluster of trees just inside the Harmony Street entrance to Centre Park. Dwight had left his van nearby; it was now gone. So Hal *had* taken it.

Everything was so still – there was hardly even a breeze stirring the hot, heavy air – yet I could hear sirens everywhere in the surrounding streets. In the distance, the palace rose up above the treeline.

"He couldn't have gotten through a checkpoint," I murmured back to Dwight. "So it had to be from somewhere in this sector." That was only the park and a few blocks on either side.

"Up high, for the best transmission," murmured Dwight. He licked his lips; his eyes flicked to the highest point in Centre Park: a rocky outcrop over the lake.

Getting there would take us out into the open.

Reaching topside had been harrowing enough. The nearest entrance to Dwight's parked van was the monument of the Cataclysm ruins. I'd hated having to take Dwight back there. We'd passed Nate's unmarked grave in silence, though I'd seen Dwight swallow and touch his mother's ring.

There'd still been no sign of Hal in the tunnels. Fear was mounting in me, cold and strong. The odds were that he hadn't made it back to the monument's hidden entrance after he'd broadcasted, or he'd have met with Collie.

Neither of us mentioned what might have happened to him.

Dwight's gaze was still on the high stretch of boulders. His voice was hoarse. "Hey, Amity, what did one Resistance worker say to the other?"

My smile was just a faint lifting of lips. "Feel like doing something really stupid?"

"Hey, you've already heard it." He let out a breath and straightened, wiping his hands briskly on his denims. "Yeah. That's the one."

We brazened it out across the long stretch of grass. I had my veil down over my face — somehow I'd managed to keep hold of the small, flimsy hat through all of this. I kept hold of Dwight's arm as if we were a couple as we strode down the path.

We didn't see anyone. I kept picturing Guns hiding behind bushes, watching.

When the path entered the treeline the world became shadowy, cooler. "Should we go off the path?" I murmured.

"Holy moley, don't ask *me*...Mac's the brains of the outfit." Dwight swallowed; his pale blond hair looked damp against his forehead. "Yeah," he said finally. "Maybe."

We started making our way up the hill through the sheltering trees. The rocky outcrop was hidden from view now, but I knew it was there, looming just ahead.

I remembered my pistol and brought it out. It felt hot and heavy against my palm. Dwight gave it a sideways look. "You look pretty good as a gangster's moll, doll-face," he muttered.

"Could you knock it off with the jokes?"

"Yeah. Sorry."

We kept heading upwards. Finally a road intersected through the woods from the park's other side. Dwight touched my arm suddenly.

"Look," he said in an undertone.

His van was parked beside the road. As we left our cover I felt far too exposed, like a fly on a rock.

We peered inside the van. Dwight silently opened the door and checked the back. "The wireless set is gone," he whispered – then we both looked up sharply at the faint crackle of a handheld talkie. Voices drifted to us from somewhere down the hill, where we'd just come from.

My chest clenched in dread. Very softly, Dwight shut the van's door. His blue eyes were wide.

"This way," I murmured. We quickly crossed the road, still heading up the hill. Once in the woods again we pressed against a pair of birch trees, their lush green leaves partly shielding us.

I craned to hear approaching footsteps. None from below – but I suddenly realized how many people were in the woods nearby, rustling in different directions. More static came from above us.

Dwight swallowed, his fist tight as he bumped it against the birch's curling white bark. "Oh, wonderful, the place is crawling with them," he murmured.

I frantically scanned the hill, trying to see if there was a route up that would avoid them.

And then I saw him.

Hal was crouched behind a boulder, maybe fifty feet away. Though he still wore the Harmony armband, he could never be mistaken for a Gun. His face looked unlined, stark with fear. One hand clutched the boulder, his olive skin dark against the grey-green lichen.

He hadn't seen us. My pulse throbbed in my ears. How could we get him back to the truck with Guns all around? I nudged Dwight and nodded quickly towards Hal.

Dwight looked – and then gripped my arm hard.

A pair of Guns were walking through the woods, heading towards Hal's hiding place. One spoke into a talkie. "No, nothing yet."

The crackling response was muffled: "Here neither. He's got to be close. Keep looking."

I stood locked in horror. Hal had his cheek pressed against the boulder, his eyes screwed shut as if he hoped to make himself invisible. I couldn't take my eyes from the tightness of his fingers.

One of the Guns had a stick; he beat diffidently at the undergrowth with it as he passed. They couldn't see Hal yet, but if they kept going straight, they wouldn't miss him.

And then they'd see us too.

I thought of Harmony Five – of the severed heads on the fence. *Hal. No.*

I couldn't let them take my little brother.

My hands were trembling. I looked down at the pistol still clutched in them. I felt dizzy – unreal. Was this how I'd felt when I shot Gunnison? Slowly, I started to raise the weapon.

Dwight grabbed my wrist. I could see his chest heaving. "Amity, no…there's too many of them to get away with it. Too many people will die."

Fifty people shot for every Gun. I couldn't answer. I stared frantically at them, realizing we were all three about to be captured.

"I'll run out and distract them," I hissed. "When they take me, grab Hal and *go*, all right?"

Dwight glanced at me in alarm. "Amity, you can't!"

"Don't argue!"

Dwight was breathing hard. He looked back at Hal – at the approaching Guns. He fumbled with his finger and pressed something into my hand.

His silver ring.

"Hold this for me, okay?" he whispered. He gave me a quick, crooked grin.

Before I could react, he burst from the trees, shouting, "*Death to Guns! V for Victory and Vancour!*"

He raced at an angle through the trees, away from Hal, still shouting. His thin, gangly form crashed through the undergrowth. The Guns had already whirled around, were already after him.

Suddenly the woods were alive with shouts. Grey uniforms pounded after Dwight from all directions. A Gun sprinted right past me, so close he'd have seen me if he looked. In the distance, three different Guns had dropped to one knee, levelling their pistols and training them after Dwight. I bit my fist to keep from screaming.

Birds flew away as shots echoed like thunderclaps, one after the other.

CHAPTER EIGHTEEN

THE BLOOD BEAT IN MY ears. I didn't stop to think. I raced out from the shelter of the birches towards Hal; half-stumbled on my weak leg and regained myself.

Hal had risen slowly, gaping after Dwight. He whirled around, bright-eyed, when I reached him.

"*Come on!*" I grabbed his arm.

As we ran, I cast a frenzied glance to my left – in a dim blur, I saw Dwight's prone form. He lay on his stomach, arms akimbo, legs sprawled. His blue shirt was stained brownish-red. A Gun stood over him. Several more were approaching through the trees.

The Gun kicked Dwight's motionless body. Another shot rang out.

No. No. I kept running, the trees dimming with tears. I swiped them away, furious with myself, clutching the silver ring. Dwight did *not* die just so that I could stumble like a fool and get Hal and myself caught anyway.

Shouts came after us. "Down there!" "He's getting away!"

I still gripped the pistol; I must have dropped the purse somewhere. Hal and I reached the van and I shoved the ring onto my finger.

"Keys, where are the keys?" I gasped.

Hal slapped his pockets. For a terrible moment I thought he didn't have them, then he thrust them at me. I snatched them from him; we got in the van's cab. My hand was shaking almost too hard to get them in the ignition; I gritted my teeth. "*Focus*, damn you," I muttered to myself.

I turned the key and the engine burst into life. I wrenched the steering wheel; we lurched away from the kerb just as Guns poured down the hill after us. I floored it, quickly righting the van as we started to hurtle off-road.

In no time we were away from the wooded hill, speeding through the park. The road spun away under us in a ribbon of grey. I was panting, clenching the wheel – my gaze flicked to the rear-view mirror every few seconds.

"We can't stay on this road – we can't – they'll have put the alarm out already—"

The sound of my clenched voice startled me; I hadn't realized I was talking out loud. Hal gave a kind of sob.

When I glanced over he was sitting hunched, gripping his dark head. Relief and agony burst through me in equal measure.

"What were you *thinking*?" I cried.

"Nothing! I don't know!"

I shifted gear. "Yeah, well, your 'I don't know' just got Dwight killed."

We were heading south-east, far too close to the palace and its security. Can-Amer Avenue lay nearby. Abruptly, I spun the wheel and took us off-road. I parked with a lurch in a grove of trees next to the fence, sickly aware that our tyre tracks would show like dark ribbons through the grass. I switched off the ignition.

"Come on," I said.

Hal looked up, his face streaked with tears. "Amity…I…"

"*Hurry!*"

Sirens were approaching. The fear was cold and palpable in me. We climbed onto the van's hood and got over the fence; I staggered as I dropped to the ground. Then I stiffened: Can-Amer now had crowds lining both sides of the street. Something was going to happen and I didn't want to know what – but we had to get out of here.

We were still partially hidden by the trees. I quickly adjusted my veil and then held out the pistol to Hal. "Put this in your inside pocket, then take my arm and get us into that crowd," I whispered.

He didn't move. Panic surged; I gave him a fierce, brief shake. "Hal! Do it! And *look normal*."

He shuddered and straightened his spine. He swiped at his eyes, then took the pistol and tucked it away.

With the Harmony armband showing on his suit jacket, he took my arm. We walked down the short hill to the main street and joined the crowd. "Keep going...don't draw attention to us," I murmured.

The crowd was silent as we moved slowly through it. One woman had tears glistening on her cheeks. What was going on?

Then with a jolt of alarm, I saw Guns stationed on both sides of the street. Why hadn't I noticed before?

They stood at attention, arms behind their backs. As the sirens still droned through the park behind us, a few picked up their talkies. They started looking around, craning to see over the crowd.

My heart racketed against my ribs. "Stop," I muttered to Hal, putting my hand briefly on his. We were pressed into a dense knot of the crowd – it would have to do, for now.

A hush fell, unearthly-seeming in this busy city. Across the street a pair of frightened-looking children clutched their father's hands. The boy was holding a toy boat, as if they'd been planning to float it on the lake.

Heads started turning, peering up the street. Hal stood rigidly beside me. I saw his throat move. "What...what's going on, do you think?" he muttered out of the side of his mouth.

Just then, a figure stumbled into view down the block.

I sucked in a breath: it was a man being led by ropes. Guns yanked him from side to side, making him stumble. He had his arms tied behind his back.

The crowd was as silent as snowfall. The woman next to me bit back a sob, and I suddenly realized the figure was President Weir.

The Guns leading him were marching quick-time, their steps smartly in unison. As the deposed leader staggered closer, I felt Hal tremble. His grip on my arm tightened and I pressed close to him.

"Don't move, don't react," I whispered hoarsely.

The man who'd studied me with such troubled, intelligent hazel eyes the single time we'd met had been badly beaten. From his hunched walk, he had a broken rib. A dark, bloody bruise stained one cheek. The eye on that side was swollen shut.

A sign hung around his neck: *TRAITOR*.

As he passed, I stood stiff with terror. Part of me wanted to catch his eye – was desperate to tell him, by some nod or indication, that his family was safe, as far as I knew. The other part was weak-kneed with relief when he didn't look our way.

I'm sorry, I thought, clutching Hal's arm. He'd trusted us – to no avail. The plan that we'd all gone into with such high hopes had crumbled into dust and I still had no idea why.

What role had Collie played in its failure, exactly? What did *You wouldn't understand* mean?

My attention snapped back to the Guns. As the ones leading President Weir passed, others patrolled the crowd, peering intently at everyone. I swallowed and dropped my eyes, wishing desperately that Hal had a hat to cover his face.

The rest of the crowd seemed as nervous as I was. I could almost feel them twitching in apprehension as they wondered: what were the Guns looking for? Was anyone doing something wrong?

Or not doing something that they should?

It erupted all at once. "*Traitor!*" screamed a woman, her voice shrill and desperate. Something – a piece of fruit? – was lobbed and struck President Weir's shoulder. It left a murky stain.

Others started screaming too – "*Traitor! Traitor!*" More missiles arced through the air, pelting him.

Almost immediately, other shouts started welling up. "No! President Weir! *V for Victory!*"

At this last, the crowd surged like a wave towards the street. "V for Victory! President Weir! *Down with Pierce!*"

Instantly, the Guns started swinging their blackjacks – shots began ringing out. Next to me, a man went down, red blooming over his chest. A woman screamed as a bullet jerked her sideways, taking part of her shoulder.

Stunned, I watched her fall – saw another Gun club her with his blackjack. Everywhere I looked, the same thing was happening.

The words tore from me with no thought: "Stop! I'm

Amity Vancour – it's *me* you want!" They were lost in other shouts, though I screamed them.

"Amity! Shut up!" Hal's voice was frenzied with fear as he tugged at me.

I shook him off. The crowd jostled me as people scattered, tried to run in all directions. Pistol shots echoed every few seconds.

"*Stop!*" I cried again. "I'm—"

A sudden jolt – a cracking noise – a feeling like sharp pressure on my head. I sank to my knees. In a dazed blur I saw the Gun who'd hit me stride away into the crowd, still swinging his blackjack. "*Get back, Discordant scum!*"

Almost seamlessly, I was lying on the ground – feet were stampeding all around me. I stared at them, weirdly disconnected, watching how they moved – noticing people's shoes.

I became aware of Hal pulling at my arm. "Hurry! *Come on!*"

Pain thunderclapped through me as he got me to my feet and I cried out. It was as if my skull had been cleaved with an axe. We started staggering away through the mob. I felt my little brother's arm around me – I gasped and put my hand to my head.

Warmth. Redness.

The world swam in and out of focus. Dimly, I became aware that my head was on Hal's shoulder – that the streets had become quieter.

"Keep going, keep going," muttered Hal, and I had a

sudden, distant memory of flying a plane with my leg shot – of Ingo's hands on my injured thigh as he said the same thing. Had that really happened?

The half-memory faded. We were in a building. What building? I didn't know. I was lying on the ground again. Hal's voice came, distant and urgent at the same time:

"I don't know how long we're safe here. I…I'd better…"

Black.

President Weir was executed on one of the few days of these long, hot months where rain finally broke through, changing the humid blanket that hung over the city to a warm drizzle. A crowd of thousands was forced to watch – to cheer when he dropped. Anyone seen not cheering was shot. Guns posted in the crowd made sure of it.

As President Weir's body hung, gently twirling, people cried through their "cheers" – those with umbrellas thankful that their true expressions were shielded. Some people didn't cheer anyway, staring stoically at the gallows, and were killed. When the sombre crowd was finally allowed to depart, dozens of bullet-ridden bodies lay on the ground.

That's what I heard afterwards.

The first I knew about it was when I opened my eyes and squinted painfully at my surroundings. I was in what seemed to be a small storage room. There were dusty boxes stacked against one wall. I lay on a piece of cloth – I only knew that because I was clutching it with one hand. Something small was digging into my back.

Hal sat nearby, elbows on his knees and his head in his hands, his fingers raking up through his dark hair.

I stared at him blearily, my head throbbing. "Where are we?" I asked, but nothing came out. I cleared my throat and tried again.

At my first noise, Hal's head had come up with a jerk. He scrambled to my side. "Amity! Are you okay?"

I tried to sit up and the world tilted – my skull felt like a knife was stabbing into it. I fell back again, gasping. "Is there any water?" I whispered.

He had a soda bottle filled with some. He put his arm around me and helped me drink it. I licked my lips. "Thanks," I murmured.

I wanted to close my eyes again but didn't. I gazed up at the ceiling. It was corrugated metal. It was all starting to come back, the thoughts pounding at me like my headache: the assassination attempt going so wrong; Mac being shot; Dwight's death.

Ingo.

My memory stopped with watching President Weir being dragged through the streets. "What…what happened to my head?" I got out.

Hal put the bottle aside. "You were hit. A Gun got you with his blackjack." His voice was husky; he wasn't meeting my eyes. His own were red-rimmed. Wearily, I remembered telling him that Dwight's death had been his fault.

I wanted to tell him that I'd been too harsh with him – that things hadn't been that simple. The words felt slippery, hard to grab hold of. I struggled to focus. "How long have I been out?"

"Over a day. I mean – you came to a couple of times, briefly. I helped you out back to the…the outhouse – but…I guess you don't remember."

I tried to shake my head and winced. "Where are we?"

"The storage shed at Stargazer's Bar." Hal swiped a hand over his face. "The owner knows we're here, but he's not doing anything to help us. Well, that's what he says – he's been throwing out plenty of good food since he saw me. But if Guns so much as look at him sideways, he says, he's turning us in. I think he'll do it too."

I saw Hal's throat move. He looked down. "I can't really blame him," he whispered.

I struggled to sit up again. The shed swam but this time I managed it, propped on one hand. I'd been lying on Hal's jacket; I saw now the small object pressing against my spine was one of his buttons. I gazed at the silver ring on my finger.

Dwight, going down in a storm of bullets. My eyes pricked at the memory.

"Hal, what were you doing?" I said raggedly. "Why… why did you signal to meet Collie?"

My brother looked up, startled. "How did you know?"

"Dwight and I saw him in the tunnels. He got your message. He came."

Hal stared at his hands. He clenched them and choked out a laugh. "It sounds so stupid now…I had to know. I had to know whether *he* betrayed us too."

Too. Like our father did. I'd known that had to be the reason.

An ache beat through my head. All I wanted was to lie down again and close my eyes. "I don't think he did," I said.

I hadn't realized that I thought this until I said it. Hal gave me a quick look.

"I don't know what happened," I said into the silence. "He just said that I wouldn't understand. But he came when he got your message. Why would he do that if he'd betrayed us?"

"That's it? He said you wouldn't understand? Well, *that* was sure worth Dwight dying over, wasn't it? Oh hell…" My brother shuddered and swiped a hand over his mouth.

"Hal…listen. I was wrong. It wasn't your—"

"Skip it!" His voice was rough. "Please. For the love of everything. Skip it."

I swallowed, feeling nauseous and strange. It took too much effort to argue. "All right," I said faintly.

Hal rose in a quick scramble. He went over to a small, grimy window. Standing sheltered in the shadows, he peered out. His stance was rigid – I could see the hard line of his shoulders, his spine – and I realized in a startled flash that he was going to be a much bigger man physically than Dad. He was like a puppy with large paws that he'd someday grow into.

The thoughts felt woozy, disjointed. I sank to the ground again, gasping with pain.

"President Weir was executed," said Hal.

My eyes flew open. Hal stood with his fists jammed into his trouser pockets, still looking out the window. When I didn't respond, he glanced back at me. "Things are…bad, Amity."

"How do you know?" I whispered. "About President Weir?"

Hal nodded towards the shed's door. "I can hear the bar's telio from here; they've got the windows open. Pierce…Pierce broadcast it. Live."

I couldn't speak. The man who I'd met that hot spring day months ago had been decent and honest; you could tell that. Can-Amer would have been in good hands with him, as he tore down Gunnison and Pierce's rotten infrastructure and replaced it with something better, something fair and full of hope.

How had it all gone so wrong?

I didn't know I was crying until Hal crouched hurriedly beside me and said, "Amity…oh, shit, *please* don't! I shouldn't have told you."

I still gazed at the ceiling, though its corrugated lines had blurred into smoothness. Hal said things were bad. Collie had said they'd be bad too.

Dread crawled over me. I started to ask how bad exactly

– what was going on? But my skull throbbed then, so sharply that I gasped, stomach lurching. I felt clammy and cold all at once.

"Hal – I think – the outhouse…" I got out.

He helped me up; I cried out in pain. Minutes later, I gripped the wooden toilet seat, tasting acrid bile. When there was nothing left to throw up, I slumped against the outhouse wall, the world going in and out of focus.

I hadn't asked, I realized dimly. I still didn't know what else my entreaties to fight had brought down on this city.

When Hal came in to get me, I tried to speak but the effort was too much. He got me across the backyard – a closed-off, dusty space. The bar's grimy bricks swayed in my vision. He was right; the faint sound of a telio was floating out, though the words sounded distorted and strange.

The next thing I knew, I was lying on the storage shed floor again, shuddering. Everything slipped away once more – and part of me was relieved that I still didn't know.

CHAPTER NINETEEN

WHEN I NEXT WOKE UP, it was dark outside. After a confused moment, I knew where I was. I sat up gingerly. To my relief the headache didn't stab me this time.

"Hal?" I whispered.

No answer.

"*Hal?*"

Silence. I staggered quickly to my feet. As my eyes adjusted to the faint glow of a street light coming in through the window, I saw with trepidation that I was alone.

Had he gone to the outhouse? I went to the window, gripping the sill as I tried to spot him in the shadowy yard. Stargazer's Bar was going full blast. I could hear voices, and the brassy beat of swing music.

Even from here it all seemed muted – false – as if people were only out to be seen to be living as normal. I stared at the lit windows.

What was happening to the city?

The door opened. I jumped, whirling towards it. My shoulders relaxed as Hal appeared; he stopped short at the sight of me, then shut the door behind him.

"You're up," he said hurriedly. He crouched on the floor and put some things down. "Here – I've got food."

My stomach both rumbled and felt sick at this news. *I'm not hungry*, I started to say – but knew I should eat. I sank to the floor beside him.

The food was roast chicken and soggy Belgian fries, cold to the touch – yet wrapped in clean wax paper.

"See? It was lying right on top of the garbage in the trash can. I think he's doing it on purpose, to help us out," said Hal, tearing off a piece of breast meat. Then he looked at me. "Um – you remember me telling you that, right? About the bar's owner?"

The recollection came, vaguely. Much more vivid was what Hal had said about President Weir. My stomach recoiled. I put down the Belgian fry I'd been about to eat. In the half-gloom I could see the worried lines of my brother's face.

"Sis?"

"What's happening in the city?"

Hal picked listlessly at the chicken. "Eat something first," he said finally.

"No. Tell me."

He sighed and pushed the food away. "Amity…"

"Please," I said softly. "I've got to know."

He hesitated. "It's really not good."

"Yes, I'd somehow gathered that."

"All *right*. Um…well, Pierce knows you were behind the assassination attempt. Or at least, that the Resistance was. But it's you she's talking about on the telio. She's telling everyone that you're a madwoman – that you want to blow up the whole city. I mean, I'm sure no one *believes* it, but that's what she's saying."

He stopped. I waited. When nothing else came, I stared at him. This was no worse than Pierce had already been saying about me for months.

"And?" I said.

Hal's throat moved. "Listen, can we just…leave it at that, until you've eaten? You haven't eaten in two days, pretty much. You've got to—"

"*Tell me!*"

He jumped and glanced worriedly at the window. "All right! Well, you know how…how for every Gun who dies…" He trailed off.

I went cold. "Go on."

When my brother spoke again, I could hardly hear him. "She's executing people. She's taken over Gunnison Square Garden to do it. She says that…that fifty people will die every hour until you turn yourself in."

My lips felt numb as I stared at his shadowy shape.

"How long has she…"

"Over seven hours now."

My mind reeled. Seven times fifty was…

"No," I whispered.

Three hundred and fifty people. I tried to stand up. I was trembling too hard. With a gasp I hunched over, clutching my head. My wound throbbed. I barely noticed.

Hal put his hand on my arm. "Amity?" He sounded young, frightened.

There was only one thing I could do. The realization came with crystal clarity. I might end up in Harmony Five again, or just be shot.

I still had no choice.

I managed to get to my feet, bracing myself against the wall. Hal rose too; his hand tightened on my arm as if he didn't know whether to help me or just hang on.

"Amity—"

"Stay here, Hal." My voice was faint but steely. "Don't move from this spot for a while, all right? Then later, try the tunnels again."

"No!" He grabbed me as I started towards the door. "What are you planning on doing?"

"It doesn't matter."

"Of course it matters!" His voice rose, panicked. "What…are you going to give yourself up? Get executed too? How the hell will *that* help? Pierce'll still be in power! She'll still—"

"*No!*"

My voice rang out in the small shed. Hal fell silent, staring at me.

"No," I repeated, more softly. I rubbed my aching head. The fear was ice in my stomach. "I'm going to try to fight."

Hal's eyes widened. "Really?" he said hoarsely.

I choked out a laugh and let my hand fall. "Yes. Really. What else can I do?"

"Then I'm fighting too."

"No, Hal."

"You can't stop me!"

"I told Ma I'd keep you safe!"

He shoved away from me. "Well, too bad! I'm almost sixteen! What are you going to do, lock me in? Holy hell, do you really think I'd just *stay* here while you go off and risk your life?"

I stared at him. He was taut – his eyes bright.

"Screw you, Amity," he whispered. "Those Helpers were shouting my father's name too."

Terminus Station lay half a mile north of Gunnison Square Garden. Hal and I hid in an alleyway across from it, watching late-night commuters exit through its grand pillars and stream down the stairs – all seeming cowed, heads down. There was barely any traffic.

The sound of a telio wafted out from an open window above. I felt bile rise at Kay Pierce's too-familiar voice:

"Well, New Manhattan, you've got your wonderful

hero Wildcat to thank for this. Until she gives herself up, the cleansing will continue. This is a direct result of the attempt on my life and the cold-blooded murder of Sandford Cain and many of my staff. Innocent people died then, and they're dying now."

My nails gouged at my palms. Hal gave me a quick sideways look. "It's not your fault. Don't believe her."

"I don't," I whispered shakily. "But I hate her."

Pierce's voice went on: "We have twenty-two more minutes until the next people die because of Wildcat, and so I think we should get to know them. What's your name, Miss?"

"H-Hester Carey."

"How old are you, Hester?"

"Seventeen."

"Tell us about yourself."

"I…I don't know what to…" A small sob, and then silence.

Whoever was inside the building snapped the telio off. I hadn't realized how rigid I'd been until I sagged slightly. I scanned the street, searching frantically for something I could use.

I found it.

"Go into that bar, Hal, okay?" I whispered to him. I told him what I needed; comprehension flickered in his eyes. He strode quickly off.

A few moments later he was back. He pressed the small packet that I'd asked for into my hand. "How are you going to do it?" he muttered, frowning towards the Gun who stood on guard at the front of the station.

I hesitated, hating what I'd have to ask him to do. We'd brought the pistol; it was tucked in his jacket's inside pocket.

"Go keep an eye on the Gun," I said finally. "If he tries anything…" The words refused to come. Hal wasn't even sixteen.

He looked pale but nodded. "Don't worry. I won't cock it up."

I glanced tensely at him. "Can you shoot?"

"BB gun back on the farm, remember? Collie taught me." Hal grimaced, as if sorry he'd mentioned him. He shifted the pistol from his jacket's inner pocket to its outer one without looking at me.

His face was so much like our father's – so much like my own. Knowing what would happen if this didn't work, I longed for some fine, perfect words to come.

None did. I cleared my throat and squeezed my brother's arm hard. "Hal, listen…about Dwight…"

"Skip it," he said softly. He gave me a small, twisted smile. "Good luck, Sis." He glanced both ways and then crossed the street. A few moments later, I saw him take up position outside the station, lounging casually as if meeting someone.

The crowd coursing down the station steps had increased – maybe a few trains had arrived at the same time. I stared at the steady flow.

Now or never.

Nearby a Harmony flag hung in front of an astrologer's shop. Its swirl of blood and darkness was clear under the street lights.

I stepped from the alleyway. I went to the shop. The flag was on a short pole, attached to a bracket. I got it free with cold hands and crossed the street.

Stay safe. Please, Ingo had said to me. Was he even still alive?

I couldn't think of it now. My weak leg trembled as I clambered up onto an auto. I stood on its smooth roof. My throat was dry, but the words burst out of me.

"I'm Amity Vancour!" I shouted. "Listen to me! *I'm Wildcat!*"

Commuters on the stairs stopped in their tracks, gaping. In a blur I saw that Hal was now at the Gun's side. *Don't die,* I thought fervently, and raised my voice, calling:

"Have you been listening to your telios? Do you know the news? Do you?"

I saw a few furtive nods.

"Kay Pierce has executed over three hundred people today!" I yelled. "More will be killed in twenty minutes! If it would make it stop, I'd turn myself in, but it'll *never* stop, not until she's gone! It's time to fight!"

The scene was dreamlike. Was it really me standing on this auto? The crowd looked on edge. More people exiting from the station pushed forward, listening avidly.

I felt hot, unreal. I took the packet of matches Hal had gotten for me. With a small scraping noise, I lit one and touched it to the flag's corner.

The flag began to burn.

Adrenalin pulsed through me – fear – a wild, pagan excitement. I held the flag aloft, feeling its heat as the fire grew.

"*V for Victory!*" I yelled.

The crowd shouted, surging forward. At first I thought they were about to attack me. Then I heard the cries of "Wildcat!" "V for Vancour!"

I started down from the auto. Its height defeated me and I almost slipped. Immediately, several dozen hands were outstretched, carrying me to the ground.

At the warmth of their touch, I shivered. People were going to die. I knew that.

But people were already dying.

Some of them slipped away into the night. It didn't matter. As we streamed down the street, others rushed to join us. Many of them grabbed up flags too – touched them to mine to set them ablaze.

"Down with Pierce!"

"Freedom for New Manhattan!"

"*V for Victory!*"

With every cross-street we passed, I kept expecting Guns to appear. Where were the ones posted to this area?

But thinking of the firing squad at the Garden, I had a terrible feeling that I knew.

A man hefted a trash can through an astrologer's shop window. The harsh sound of breaking glass, then cheers. Someone else clambered in through the gaping window and emerged with piles of astrology books, posters, birth charts. They were set on fire too.

Maybe I should have stopped it. I didn't. I felt like doing the same.

Hal, I thought in sudden fear. Had my brother gotten away from the Gun?

I craned to look backwards. People were punching the air, street lights and flames giving their faces a frenzied glow. It was impossible to tell if Hal was among them.

"Vancour!"

The shout came clearly. Something about it jogged a memory. Glancing back again, I saw a solid set of shoulders bulldozering towards me. They belonged to a muscular man with a broad, open face and tousled brown hair.

"*Hey, Vancour!*" he bellowed again, cupping his hands around his mouth. He was grinning. "How the hell d'you join the Resistance in this town?"

Harlan?

As people passed me I stopped, staring, recognizing my former Peacefighting teammate. When he reached me, he scooped me into a hug. I gasped and clung to him.

"Harlan! But how—"

"Good to see you, Amity," he said gruffly. Back on the

Western Seaboard base, we'd bantered in the locker room; caroused in speaks with other pilots; played poker together, drinking his terrible rotgut liquor.

As we let go of each other Harlan's face was grim, but alive with adrenalin.

"'Bout time for this," he said. "Vera's here too, further back."

"What are you *doing* here?"

"I live here! Me and Vera both."

No time for questions; we'd almost reached a checkpoint. As shouts rang around us, I said hurriedly, "Listen, would you do me a favour? I can't see my brother, Hal – he looks like me. Can you see it—"

"Got it." Harlan gripped my arm, then ducked back into the crowd. A moment later I wondered if I'd dreamed him.

People were grabbing up makeshift weapons: clubs, bricks, rocks. The humid night pressed down as I battled through the crowd to reach the front. Whatever was going to happen, I couldn't be so craven as to let others face it first...though the part of me that still lived in Harmony Five wanted to be.

My flag had burned to almost nothing. People grinned as they recognized me, patted me on the back. I heard "V for Vancour!" over and over. Their trust scared me. *You could all die,* I wanted to say.

They already knew. No one could live in this city and *not* know.

We rounded the corner onto 7th Avenue. Ahead was the checkpoint for Cancer sector. The pair of Guns guarding it backed away from us, looking young, stunned. One spoke frantically into his talkie. The other raised his pistol with a shaking hand.

Before he could start to fire, dozens of people charged them, screaming, throwing rocks and bricks. The Guns broke and ran. We poured through the checkpoint like a river. People were burning their Harmony IDs, holding them aloft.

Gunnison Square Garden used to be called Henderson Square Garden. It was a large covered stadium that once housed boxing matches, ice skating extravaganzas, concerts. It rose up on its own, from a broad parking lot. A row of Harmony flags flew in its courtyard.

As we neared it, a volley of rifle fire echoed. It went on and on.

The twenty-two minutes had passed.

I'd stopped with a gasp at the first shots. *Hester Carey*, I thought dully.

My chest was heaving. I started to run without realizing it, still holding the charred flagpole. Others were faster. They charged past me, shouting, clutching flags that still burned. The night turned jostling, flame-edged. Scraps of burning fabric drifted through the air.

This was where the rest of the Guns were. Dozens of them waited for us in a grey-clad line outside the stadium, their black boots gleaming in the approaching flames.

As we neared, one shouted an order. They all dropped to one knee. They levelled their rifles and started firing.

The night exploded into chaos. The echo as each chamber went off pounded at my ears, battling with my pulse. Rage and terror rushed through me, white-hot and white-cold.

People started falling in front of me – screams – I had to scramble over a man's body. I kept going, frantic. Some of the Guns were still firing. Others had been swallowed up by the attacking crowd.

Hundreds of us stampeded through the double doors into the Garden. Our shouts echoed around the lobby area with its empty concession stands. Ahead was the main section of the stadium.

Its broad space was bordered by thousands of empty seats rising towards the ceiling. As we burst in, a crowd of people stood on a raised platform at its centre, hands tied – apparently those scheduled to die next. A gleaming wireless set sat nearby.

The floor glistened with fresh blood. A mop lay abandoned. Guns had been carrying out dozens of bodies. As we appeared they dropped them, scrambling off the platform towards us as Pierce screamed frantically, "Get them! Get them!"

Our eyes met. I saw her fear. Then her bodyguards hustled her away.

No! Suddenly I was enveloped in a frenzy of swinging fists – clubs. Rifle fire battered at my ears. With a cry,

I wielded the flagpole as a baton, swinging it at the back of a Gun's legs.

Someone slammed into me. I staggered on my weak leg and fell. Panting, I scrambled up again. *Where was Pierce?* I snatched up a fallen rifle and raced after her.

I skirted the battle's edge. Pierce's bodyguards had taken her through a door. I lunged through it into a long corridor with another door at its end. Suddenly it was eerily silent, with only the sound of my pounding footsteps.

I burst through the second door out into the rear parking lot. Sirens pulsed, growing nearer. Pierce's long limousine was already a dot across the asphalt. I took a few futile, running steps, but it pulled onto the main road and sped off, the Harmony flags fluttering on its hood.

Gone.

"Oh, you bitch," I whispered raggedly. "You cowardly bitch."

I realized then how close the sirens were. I swallowed, took a step backwards, and then ducked into the stadium. I ran back down the corridor and met Harlan heading towards me. A scrape stained his cheek. "Saw you come through here," he called.

"She's gone!" I cried as I passed him.

"What?"

"She got away – more Guns are coming!"

He swore. When we re-entered the main stadium I stopped short at the scene. It was over. A strange hush hung over everything.

Bodies lay sprawled on the floor. People stood in small, frightened clusters. Four others held rifles on at least a dozen Guns. A few people had started freeing the prisoners.

The faint sound of someone crying. It woke me up. *All these people.* There had to be over three hundred in here.

I gripped Harlan's arm. "Hal?" I gasped.

"He's fine – he's over there with Vera." Harlan gave a small smile. "Hell of a kid brother you've got, Vancour. Says he threatened the Gun with a pistol, then smashed the guy's talkie and got away through the crowd."

Relief swelled. "Start getting people out," I implored. "Don't let anyone panic. But get them out of here, fast, before the Guns arrive and they're trapped."

"On it."

I raced for the platform – pounded up its stairs. Spatters of fresh blood stained the floor. On a table to one side, the wireless set was still on.

I slid into the chair that Kay Pierce must have recently vacated. The wireless wasn't a field one like I'd always used for my broadcasts; black cords snaked off it to a control panel.

How long until someone cut the power?

I hit the mic's *talk* button and leaned forward.

"This is Amity Vancour, the voice of the Resistance. We've taken Gunnison Square Garden…correction, *Henderson* Square Garden, and have stopped the executions. I repeat, a group of us have taken Henderson Square

Garden. The next fifty captives who were due to be shot have been released."

As I spoke I swivelled in the chair, watching. With Harlan and Vera directing them – I recognized my old roommate as if I'd seen her only yesterday – a long line hurried towards the doors, the able helping the wounded.

"The time has come, New Manhattan," I said roughly. "I can't stress the dangers enough, but I implore you to fight. Kay Pierce cannot continue. We must do whatever it takes to bring her down."

A dozen or so people lingered, listening. Their expressions were solemn, but had a hard exuberance.

My brother was one.

My throat felt dry as I met his eyes. "I just saw her limo heading away from the Garden down 8th, probably going to the palace. Fight her, New Manhattan! There's strength in numbers. Please, I beg you, make this end."

Suddenly I realized something was wrong.

Those leaving had passed through the doors into the lobby area but I could still see their shadows – a shifting, anxious-looking mass. Harlan came sprinting back, all muscle and speed.

I spoke on, watching worriedly as he barrelled past the platform and through the doors that led to the rear entrance.

"Oh, shit," I heard someone mutter. "Is it the Guns?"

Several people pelted for the main doors. Hal's eyes met mine again, wide and startled. Then Harlan was back, veering towards me. He ignored the stairs leading to the platform and vaulted onto it. I quickly let go of the *talk* button.

"We're surrounded," he panted. "There's troops already gathering out there – front and back."

Fear stabbed me. I recalled the sirens – how close they'd been. I thrust the mic towards Hal. "Here – keep talking."

His voice croaked. "Me?"

"Hurry!"

He hesitated and then hefted himself onto the platform. I squeezed his shoulder as he sat down. "Just press that button."

"What'll I say?"

"Tell them what's happening!"

As I clambered off the platform, I heard him say, "This…this is Halcyon Vancour. I'm Amity Vancour's brother. Troops have surrounded the building…"

A moment later, I was pressing through the crowd clustered in the lobby – face after face looking panicked, mutters rising in a pulsing buzz. "Miss Vancour!" gasped a woman, clutching my arm. "Miss Vancour, what's going to happen to us?"

"I don't know," I murmured.

Near the front I stopped short. I gazed out. In the street lamps' glow I could see troops crouched in position at the edge of the parking lot, rifles trained on the doors.

The captured Guns were being held to one side of the lobby. I went over. "Will they attack?" I said in a tight voice.

Their leader scanned me coldly. "Obviously."

"But she wants you taken alive if possible," said another – a young-looking man with blond hair. "We were under strict—"

"*Quiet,*" hissed his superior.

Harlan had followed and stood beside me. I was breathing hard, acting on instinct.

"Let them go," I said abruptly to one of the men holding the Guns captive. He hesitated, then nodded. Motioning with the rifle, he beckoned the Guns out the front door. They exited in a line, hands clasped over their heads.

The young blond one hung back. His eyes were red-rimmed. "Listen, plenty of us hate this too," he blurted. "We're local. Those…those were our friends and neighbours she was making us kill."

My temples pounded. This was all supposed to have been finished by now, with Hal and me on our way to Nova Scotia and our father's legacy over for ever.

"You don't have to go back to them," I said.

He blanched. "No, I…I can't," he whispered. "But I mean it – plenty of Guns have had enough."

His motions heavy, he joined the others, hands up. I watched him grow smaller in the street lights with the troops beyond.

Yes, Pierce wanted me taken alive – so that she could kill me herself. But if I surrendered, there'd be no clemency for the rest. She'd execute everyone here.

I felt numb. Everyone stood silently, hundreds of worried eyes watching me. Vera appeared at my side. My former roommate was small and cherry-blonde. She squeezed my arm.

"Fancy meeting you here," she said hoarsely.

With a hollow laugh, I gripped her hand. From outside, a voice boomed from a megaphone: "Give yourself up, Wildcat! You're under arrest! Come peaceably and there'll be no further trouble!"

"Ha," whispered Vera.

Suddenly a spotlight swept the darkened lobby. "Back!" Harlan yelped.

We rushed inside the main area. A woman was limping; I put my arm around her. We shut the doors behind us and I put my hands to my head, trying frantically to think.

"How many rifles do we have in here?" I murmured to Vera and Harlan.

"I've seen maybe a few dozen," said Vera.

"And plenty of ammo," added Harlan. "I don't think she was expecting you to surrender anytime soon, Vancour." He studied me grimly. "Do we defend?"

I stared at the ragged clusters of people, some of them wounded; at the bodies that still lay on the floor, Guns and civilians both. Everything seemed too bright – hyper-real.

"I don't think we've got much choice," I said softly.

* * *

As the megaphone echoed outside, we gathered all the weapons together and found out who could shoot. We posted people around the upper rim of the stadium, where broad windows looking out to the parking lot encircled the highest seats.

One of the women was a doctor. A few others knew first aid. We found a medical kit in the stadium office and they got to work on the wounded.

Seventy-two bodies lay motionless, cool to the touch. Fifty were the executed who'd been discarded by the Guns. We carried them all into a back room and gently rested them there – men, women, old, young, black, white.

One, a tall, lanky girl with hazel eyes, had been shot twice in the chest. Her neat powder-blue blouse was darkened with blood.

Somehow I knew. I checked her ID card and an aching anger filled me.

"I'm sorry, Hester," I whispered.

Close to hand near the platform were mops, buckets, bleach – Kay Pierce apparently didn't like the sight of blood.

A few of our number cleaned up the mess.

When I finally went over to my brother, I felt wrung out. He sat hunched in front of the mic, talking so intently that he didn't notice me.

"…I can hear the megaphone still going. We've got snipers in place. If they want a fight, I guess we'll give them one. Maybe…maybe these people we saved will only get a few more hours of life, but...well, hell, I'd rather go down fighting than be shot on the wireless by Kay Pierce."

My chest clenched. A few people stood listening at the platform's edge; others sat on the floor nearby. All eyes were locked on my brother.

"And, yeah, what you've probably heard is true – everything that's happening now is because of our dad. That's why Amity and I are fighting it so hard. It's pretty personal for us." Hal hesitated, playing with the mic's wire.

"But it's personal for everyone now, I guess," he said. "You all must have friends or family who've been taken away. Listen, I...I had a friend killed just the other day. He let himself be shot down to save me and my sister. His name was Dwight Perkins. He was eighteen years old." Hal's fist was tight. "Pierce has *got* to be defeated. We have to do whatever it takes."

I propped myself against the table, watching him. He saw me then and hastily said, "More in a second." He lifted his thumb from the *talk* button and raised his eyebrows at me, his expression tight.

I touched his shoulder. I couldn't express all that I was feeling. I cleared my throat and said in an undertone, "Listen...depending on when the Guns attack, the shooters might need to take shifts. Can you relieve one if we need you to?"

Hal studied me. After a pause, he whispered, "We're not getting out of here, are we, Amity?"

"You want the truth?"

His level gaze was my answer.

I looked around us at the three hundred or so people.

"Probably not," I said roughly. "Don't spread that around. As long as we're alive, there's hope."

Chapter Twenty

September, 1942

"It's a very simple order," Kay said, her voice low and too-controlled.

The technician on the other end of the phone sounded miserable with fear. "I'm deeply sorry, Madame President. The electrician says that there's a problem with the grid."

From the gleaming wireless set on a table came a young man's voice: "But it's personal for everyone now, I guess. You all must have friends or family who've been…"

"*A problem with the grid?* What does *that* mean?" Kay wanted to pace; the phone's short cord kept her tethered. She rapped a pen on her desk. Several aides stood nearby, their faces anxious.

"He…says he's trying. But that it may take some time."

"That is *not* good enough," hissed Kay.

"I can only apologize, Madame—"

Kay propped a hand on the desk and leaned forward as if the man were in front of her. She enunciated every syllable. "I don't care about your apology. Find someone who can cut that power off *now*, or I'll have you arrested."

She slammed down the phone and glared at the wireless set, which had thankfully gone silent for the moment.

"Leave me alone," she said to her aides.

They left the room. She could see them all trying to hide their relief that they were being released.

When the door closed, Kay went to her window and peered out. The lights of the night-time city were spread out before her – including the low, arcing shape of Gunnison Square Garden to the south. She studied it, her lips thin.

The wireless came alive once more. Kay started, turning towards it.

Vancour's voice again – low, slightly throaty, sounding both exhausted and passionate: "This is Amity Vancour. To repeat, myself and a group of rebels have taken over *Henderson* Square Garden, where the executions were being held. We've released the next batch of prisoners and have cleared away the bodies. There were seventy-two of them. Pierce has no regard for human life. Please, New Manhattan, *fight* her! She must be there in her palace right—"

Kay had been standing, wide-eyed, clutching her elbows with white fingers. Suddenly, trembling, she leaped for the wireless set. She snapped it off and the hated voice thankfully went silent.

Vancour and the Resistance had done just what she and Collis had needed on Friday, getting rid of Cain and his allies. Who could have foreseen what followed, especially with the New Manhattan Resistance shattered? Kay shuddered, recalling the mob bursting into Gunnison Square Garden. She'd imagined being torn limb from limb and had felt queasy with fear.

How dare they? she thought. Yet deep down there was a tiny flower of knowledge that you could only push people so far before they snapped.

She buried it irritably as she looked out the window again. What had she been meant to do? There'd been an assassination attempt on her life – her Special Investigation officer and a dozen high up officials had been murdered. Wildcat had been behind it and the whole city knew it. To let it go without a firm show of control would have left her open for revolt.

But now it seemed she might have one anyway.

Her ride back to the palace had turned nightmarish as they'd neared their destination. Out of nowhere, another mob had descended on the limo – shouting at her, rocking it. Kay hadn't been able to hold in a shriek, clutching the seat. Distorted faces had pressed up against the glass, screaming obscenities.

Guns beat the crowd back. Kay's limo had gotten through safely. In the secure silence of the palace's underground parking garage, she'd sat pressing a handkerchief to her mouth.

"Are you all right, Madame President?" one of her bodyguards had asked.

"Fine," she'd said shortly, and forced herself to move.

And now there were more mobs out there. Below she could see torches snaking through the streets. Wildcat was ordering them to attack and they were *doing* it.

The phone crouched on the desk, black and shining. Kay grabbed the receiver, with the intention of calling the field phone of the Guns stationed outside the Garden.

But no – the commander already had his orders. Kay wasn't going to change them. The prize would be worth it.

She made a different call instead. At the end of it, she was convinced that the electrician was stalling – deliberately letting Wildcat's broadcast play for longer.

"Have him shot," she said in a low voice. "Find someone else who'll do it. *Now.*" She hung up.

Pierce has no regard for human life. Kay choked out a small laugh as she stared out at the torches. Yes, and what exactly was so wonderful about human life? Any fool could mate, have babies, bring more squalling children into the world.

To survive, that was the smart thing. To triumph, even better.

Collis, she thought, rubbing one of her rings. She wanted him badly. He'd left for the far north days ago, on an errand for her. He was the only one she trusted to do it.

Looking back, Kay realized that on some level she'd known what Collis was telling her when he'd promised so intensely that they *would* get rid of Cain, and soon. Even so, the meeting in the secure basement room had been nerve-wracking.

Though the chamber was lavish, there was no getting away from the fact that they were underground, far from listening ears. Apart from Collis, the ten other people in there were all, Kay suspected, in Cain's secret employ, though several pretended allegiance to her.

The very blandness of Cain's features made them more menacing. His near-colourless eyes were extremely polite as he said, "I'm afraid, Madame President, that you don't grasp my point."

"I grasp it." Kay kept her spine straight. "I don't need a Chief Astrologer, Mr Cain. I'm an expert on these matters myself, as you may recall." Collis had sat to her right. Kay had been glad of his presence.

Cain's gold signet ring showed the glyph for Cancer the crab. He rubbed its stylized claws with a slow thumb. "The role is needed," he said "You've taken on far too much, Madame President."

One of his colleagues added, "Yes, particularly for one so…inexperienced."

Young, he meant. Kay was just shy of twenty-one. Feigning unconcern, she took a sip of coffee, glad that Cain had drunk from the same pot first so that she could.

"This topic is closed," she said, and knew she'd just

earned more sleepless nights when she saw the look Cain exchanged with a few of his cronies.

Sandford Cain inclined his head in a parody of acquiescence. "As you wish, of course, dear Madame President."

Collis leaned back in his seat, big and solid, his body language relaxed, though she sensed tension from him. "Mr Cain, if I recall, the item on the agenda is—"

A knock came.

Cain frowned. The room went silent.

The guard at the door held a quick, whispered consultation with the palace messenger who'd knocked. The guard came over to Kay.

He whispered in her ear. "My apologies, Madame President, but this just came in over the wireless. They need an immediate response." He handed her a slip of paper. Its message was in code.

Kay's brow furrowed; from the first symbol, she saw that this was to do with international relations. "Please continue without me for a few minutes," she said to the room at large. "Mr Reed, you'll take notes for me, won't you?"

Collis started to say something and stopped. He nodded. "Yes, of course."

Kay left the room.

She strode some way along the empty hallway and then turned a corner, heading for a quiet stairwell. When she reached it, she looked carefully in both directions, before extracting the key for the code from her charm bracelet.

She quickly deciphered the message. It was short and to the point. There was a question asked at the end.

It felt as if the breath had been knocked from her. Kay slumped against the wall, thoughts reeling. As if the difficulties *within* her regime weren't thorny enough.

A secure phone that went through a private switchboard was on the wall nearby. Kay went to it and reached General Keaton. Her side of the conversation took place in low, urgent murmurs.

"Don't worry, Madame President," Keaton soothed. "This won't hold us back. Our troops will take care of it."

After Kay hung up, she tried to compose herself, realizing suddenly how run-down she was. She'd been running on caffeine and nerves for months.

She started back to the meeting room. Collis had just come out. He spotted her and headed her way, almost jogging. Relief rushed through her, yet when he reached her she said, "I told you to wait, Collis."

He gripped her arms. "Kay, listen," he said quickly. "What I've been promising...this is it. The Resistance have been planning an attack." He glanced at his watch. "In seven minutes, a bomb will go off in that room. I was just about to get you out when the messenger came."

Kay caught her breath. "Have you stalled Cain?" she gasped. "Will they stay in there?"

Collis looked oddly defeated now. "Yeah," he said. "I've...just passed out copies of the Discordant report.

I pretended to be annoyed that you were gone for so long, and Cain asked me to go check on you. I think he and his cronies want to discuss their next move."

He rubbed the tops of her arms with his thumbs, gazing down at her almost angrily. His voice was husky as he said, "I care about you, you know. I've tried not to."

Kay's immediate response – to say, *I care about you too* – alarmed her. She squelched the thought and pulled him further down the corridor. Glancing back at the meeting room, she felt grim satisfaction.

"Tell me the whole plan," she said.

Six minutes later, Kay had made several phone calls, directing troops of Guns to various points around the city. Then, unable to help herself, she drifted back down the carpeted corridor, gazing avidly at the closed meeting room doors.

"Not too close." Collis was pale.

She slid her hand slowly up his firm chest without looking at him. "Don't ruin it," she murmured.

Collis licked his lips and glanced at his watch again – showed her the second hand sweeping up it.

When it reached twelve, thunder roared in her ears and trembled up through her feet. Kay gave a laughing yelp and almost fell, clutching Collis, who steadied them both. There was a pattering noise – thuds of masonry against carpet.

The excitement was almost unbearable. She pushed Collis against the wall and they kissed fiercely. Kay shivered, wanting him. She pulled away abruptly and ran to the meeting room.

Where it had been, there was now a mess of concrete and rubble. The doors and the clock that had hung over them lay a dozen yards down the hallway. Dust rose in a choking cloud. The guard lay against the wall, clearly dead.

It was beautiful.

A whirlwind of events had occurred after that: herself on the phone, barking more orders; security workers streaming onto the scene, yelling and heaving at the rubble – "Is anyone alive in there?" "Shout if you can hear us!"; appearing on the palace balcony with Collis to announce that a strike had been made against Harmony and that she *would* retaliate.

Satisfying reports had started trickling in: Weir had been captured. Resistance members had been arrested at a telio station; the capitol building; parading down Concord – everywhere Collis had told her. Vancour hadn't been captured yet but she would be. Guns had entered the tunnels and were busy searching.

Though the hour was a triumph for Kay, fear still lurked. Cain's death would make little difference if the matter she'd discussed with Keaton wasn't resolved.

The first chance she had, she'd drawn Collis into her private office and locked the door.

"Something's happened," she said.

Collis was unsmiling as he studied her. Kay had the sense that the seriousness of the morning's events had only just hit him.

"Go on," he said.

"It's the reason I was called out of the meeting." She explained the new threat, and told him also about Black Moon.

There was a pause. Collis's small smile was rueful. "We really *will* have it all, won't we?"

"If we can overcome this." Kay gripped his arm. "You'll have to go out there. Will you? You're the only one I can trust."

"You know I will," he said quietly, linking their fingers together. "I'll do whatever I can."

Before Collis had left, something had happened between them that Kay hadn't expected – something that she'd never have imagined herself doing. It had been impetuous, though she wasn't sorry she'd done it.

Collis was gone and she wanted him here. But she'd spent most of her life alone. She'd cope.

Yet standing there at her window, gazing out at the torches that still wove through the night, she remembered the mob that had burst into the Garden and was frightened.

The tanks, she thought in sudden panic. If she needed outside help, how long would it take for the tanks Gunnison had had built to be transported to New Manhattan along with more troops? The army was currently guarding certain key points out west. She couldn't call many of them back, not with what was happening out there.

But she might have to. She bit a fingernail.

Kay started as a knock came. She straightened. "Yes?"

One of her bodyguards opened the door. "Madame President, rioters are trying to break into the palace. We think we should move you to a more secure room."

She stared at him, her thoughts skittering. "But there's no chance of them getting *in*!" she cried.

It was half-question, half-prayer. Ten minutes later, she was in a chamber on the second floor. There were no windows. Her bodyguards stood poised at its entrance, pistols drawn.

I am not afraid. I refuse to be.

"Do whatever it takes to control the city," Kay said into the phone to the Head Gun. "Is Vancour still broadcasting?"

At the answer, her spine felt hot. "Go to the electric company," she said in a low voice. "If you have to shoot someone every thirty seconds, I don't care. But *find an electrician who'll turn it off*."

She banged the phone down and sank into the chair, rubbing her temples.

Yet thinking of Vancour, barricaded in the inescapable Garden with hardly any food, a hard joy came. They'd confirmed that her group was armed. Was Vancour expecting a big battle where she could kill lots of Guns and

be a hero? Well, she'd soon be brought to her knees –
humiliated – shown to the world as a defeated coward.

"No going down in a blaze of glory for *you*, Wildcat,"
Kay muttered. "Let's see how much your followers love
you when this is over."

When this was over.

A thought came – pressing, unavoidable. Kay checked
the desk's drawers and was relieved to find an ephemeris
and blank astrology charts.

Black Moon, she wrote at the top of one.

She began to cast the chart. She almost knew it by
heart; only infrequently did she have to flip the ephemeris
open to check a planetary position.

The room felt too-silent. The chart grew under her
pencil, an elaborate interplay of spiky glyphs, exact
notations, connecting lines.

In her mind's eye Kay saw an image of a mushroom
cloud blossoming against an eclipsed moon. She took
power from it – let it brace her spine.

"See?" she murmured. "Strength. A time of great
change. They will *not* beat me."

Somewhere below, there might be a mob breaking in.
The quick, steady scratching of Kay's pencil didn't slow.

Chapter Twenty-one

September, 1942

I EXPECTED THE ELECTRICITY to be cut off at any moment. It didn't happen.

About half an hour after we'd first seen them, some of the Guns tried to storm the place. The snipers we'd posted opened fire. One reported later that at the first rifle shots, the Guns had fallen back – and that he could see fires in the distance near the palace, as if further riots were going on.

It was around nine o'clock when I'd started broadcasting. Incredibly, it was almost three a.m. before the electricity went out, plunging the broad space into darkness.

My voice had gone croaky: "...we've been seeing fires across the city, so we think riots are going on. Target the palace. We *must* bring down Pierce—"

Startled gasps as everything went black.

I swallowed hard, looking up from the darkened console. The whole time I'd been broadcasting, I'd expected another attack. It hadn't come. I thought I'd almost prefer to get it over with.

Ambient light from the city angled in through the broad windows circling the Garden. The people were shadowy shapes on the floor. Many had been huddled talking. Now an apprehensive silence fell.

A group had searched the office while I broadcast and found flashlights. Vera handed me one. "You've got to say something to everyone," she whispered.

I knew with a sinking feeling she was right. Slowly, I stood up and shone the flashlight on myself. It cast the rest of the world into blackness.

"All right, I…I won't sugar-coat this," I said, lifting my voice. "You all know we're surrounded. If we try to leave, they'll just shoot us down as we exit the doors."

Silence. The air felt heavy. "But when they attack us here, we'll fight," I said. "Some of us might get away then. Or, if we're lucky, there'll be enough unrest in the city that Guns will be drawn from their posts, and we can try battling our way out."

Lowering the light, I caught a few nervous nods. They all seemed to be hanging on my every word.

I exhaled. "So, for now, I guess we just…wait. And be watchful."

Though it was so late, few slept. A woman had a portable transistor radio and kept twiddling the dial, hoping to pick up a broadcast. So far there was only static.

People passed the flashlights around to take shadowy trips to the restrooms and water fountains. Someone else found the concessions storeroom and passed out candy bars and liquorice sticks.

"A few of us have been looking around," Harlan whispered to me. "You'd better come and see this."

I went with him to the cellar: a large, boxlike space with an industrial boiler. In the flashlight's beams, the boiler looked like a prehistoric beast.

Harlan showed me a dusty-looking metal door.

"I think it leads to the tunnels." He shot me a glance. "The Resistance used them, right? Please tell me those damn things really exist, and weren't just rumours."

The sudden hope felt painful. "They exist, all right."

We creaked the door open and started down. The stairs had the tunnels' familiar, musty scent, but you could only go down ten of them before rubble blocked the way.

"Maybe we could dig it out – what do you think?" said Harlan.

I stared at the debris, going over my mental map. "We could try."

"You're not hopeful."

"No. But we'll try anyway." Reluctantly, I added, "I

doubt we can clear it before an attack comes, though. The cave-ins in this area are pretty bad – we never found a route that led here."

"All right," said Harlan finally. "Good to know."

"It is?"

"Sure. It's like poker. You want to figure out the other guy's hand, if you can. When it comes to the tunnels, sounds like the Guns' isn't shit-hot either."

I sighed, remembering what had been happening when Ingo and the others left. "Unfortunately, they've got explosives," I said.

Harlan winced at this. We closed the door and started back across the cellar. "Well, it still beats truck-driving, I guess," he said.

I smiled faintly. "Is that what you've been doing?"

"Yeah, can you feature it? I've been going stir-crazy. Me and Vera both – she's been driving a cab. Damn thing is, she makes more than me. Everyone gives her tips 'cause she's cute."

As if realizing the odd normality of the conversation, Harlan grimaced and shoved a hand through his hair.

"Ah, what the hell," he muttered.

I didn't want word to get around about the caved-in tunnel. It seemed worse for people to hope if nothing came of it. I quietly spoke to a few burly guys I'd noticed earlier – steady-seeming types. They agreed to start trying to dig it out and to keep quiet. Harlan said he'd help too.

We found a pair of coal shovels and a wheelbarrow in

the cellar. Along with the flashlights, we were lucky to have that much.

The passage was too narrow for more than two workers at once. Harlan was on the second shift…if there'd be one. I glanced warily at the snipers still poised above. Hal was up there too, now.

Meanwhile, Harlan, Vera and I sat and talked in the shadows. Having them both here felt surreal. So did the fact that they were apparently a couple. Harlan had had a crush on Vera back on the base; I'd never thought she might return his feelings.

The last time they'd seen me, we'd flown into battle together when Gunnison attacked the Western Seaboard. Though it wasn't my favourite subject, I told them briefly what had happened since – my arrest, Harmony Five, joining the Resistance.

"I'm very glad you made it," said Vera, touching my arm. She'd gone pale even from my glossed-over description of Harmony Five.

"And glad you wasted Gunnison," added Harlan.

"It didn't make much difference," I pointed out bitterly.

"Glad you did it anyway."

I learned that they'd been in New Manhattan over a year now; ever since the Western Seaboard base had been decommissioned. Appalachia had still been free then.

"We tried to leave when Pierce took over, but we were denied," said Vera. I could very faintly see her freckles in the glow from the street lamps. "We didn't push it.

We were afraid they'd rethink having cleared us in the first place."

"It was that bastard Collie who cleared us," said Harlan sourly. "You know he was there when they decommissioned the base?" he said to me. "In a Gun's uniform. The other guy sent three dozen people off to die and he just stood there."

Explaining that "the other guy" had been Mac, the Resistance leader I'd told them about, felt beyond me just then.

"Yeah," I said finally. "I heard he was there."

They went on. Later, when my broadcasts had started, they'd both begun drawing Vs everywhere, passing the newspapers on, doing whatever they could.

"Been trying to find you for months, Vancour." Harlan nudged me with his foot. "You secretive Resistance-types don't exactly advertise how to join you."

I had to smile. "No. Mac is pretty careful about who can join. He's been Resistance for years; he was a double agent under Gunnison. He's an amazing man."

"Where is he now?" asked Vera. She wore her wavy hair tied back with a scarf.

I had my arms around my knees; my grip tightened. "He was shot trying to get President Weir out of house arrest," I said softly. "He's still alive...or was the last time I saw him. Most of the Resistance was arrested or killed."

I looked down at my hands and cleared my throat. "Ingo...someone I know...left a few days ago to try to get Mac and some others out of the city through the tunnels."

Vera was studying me quizzically. Harlan gave a slow nod.

"So…we're kind of it, then," he said.

"Yeah," I said. "We're kind of it."

Harlan lay propped on his side. In the silence that followed he shifted and pulled out a hip flask.

"Here," he said, handing it over to me. "Just the thing to wash down liquorice and candy bars."

I took the flask, amused despite everything. "You just happened to have this on you when you heard the shouts and came out to join us?"

"Yup."

"You carry it with you at all times?"

"Yup."

"And why not, in this city?" muttered Vera.

"See? My true love understands," said Harlan. "Are you having any of that, or not, Vancour? 'Cause I've got better uses for it than watching you sit there holding it."

I took a swig. The welcome warmth burned through me. My muscles loosened a little and I sighed. I passed it to Vera.

"Maybe I should have been carrying a flask too, all these months," I said.

Hal joined us then, looking weary. It was almost dawn; someone had relieved him at his post.

"What's happening?" I asked quickly.

"Still there," said Hal. "Even more than we thought. They're all armed."

Vera and I glanced at each other. Harlan swore softly. If Kay Pierce's plan was to drive me crazy with waiting, it was working.

After a pause, Vera took a sip from the flask. She offered it to Hal. He hesitated and took it. He winced slightly at the taste, then had another sip and handed it to Harlan.

"Is this what Peacefighters did?" he said finally. "Sat around drinking whiskey?"

"Damn straight," said Harlan. "If you'd made it, you could have joined our poker game." He took a swig and capped the flask; he put it away again. His voice turned deliberately light. "Hey, Vancour, tell him about the time you lost your actual shirt and had to sit there in your brassiere."

Hal snorted with surprised laughter and darted me a look. "Seriously?"

"*Harlan.*" I kicked him. "I just…got into a kind of stand-off situation and was out of credits," I said to Hal. "They'd all seen me in my brassiere a thousand times anyway." The mixed-sex changing rooms had allowed no privacy.

Vera was snickering. "I knew I was missing out, not joining the poker game. If I'd realized we could bet our *clothes…*"

"I'd have stacked the deck so that you lost every time," said Harlan.

"Cheat."

"Justified."

Hal's cheeks were a little red. "You didn't play?" he asked Vera.

"No," she said, settling against Harlan. "I was far more refined. I was probably off dancing and drinking gin somewhere."

My brother nodded slowly. "So...the safety of our country was in the hands of a bunch of poker-playing, gin-drinking alcoholics, basically."

"The boy catches on quick," Harlan intoned.

Hal fell asleep, lying on the floor with one arm under his head. Harlan followed not long after, his head in Vera's lap. I sat leaning against the bleachers, unable to relax.

"How did this happen?" I murmured, gazing at the sleeping people – the snipers crouched against the windows rimming the stadium's ceiling.

Vera smiled sadly. "I guess it didn't go quite to plan. But you've put something in motion, Amity. Maybe it'll all work out."

I didn't see how it could, but hoped she was right. Then I looked at her.

"So...you and Harlan?"

Her expression turned gentle as she looked down at him. "Things on base were...well, pretty awful after the Western Seaboard fell. But people started talking more. You know?"

I nodded, remembering all too well the customary reserve on base. When someone could die any day, you didn't let yourself grow too close.

"So I got to know him better. And he wasn't at all like I'd assumed. He's so solid, Amity. A good person. And he really thinks about things, you know…he just doesn't always let on."

Vera gently brushed back a strand of Harlan's hair as he slept. "It's funny how some people aren't really who they seem to be, isn't it?"

She realized what she'd said and winced. Our eyes met.

"Yeah," I said. "Funny." I was glad Hal was asleep. I sighed and tipped my head back against the bleachers.

"Collie joined the Resistance," I said, my voice low. "He helped us plan the attack on Pierce."

Vera's eyes widened. "Tell me," she whispered.

I told her all of it, including Collie's betrayal of me, which I'd avoided before. When I finished, she said slowly, "You know, we couldn't believe it when he turned up on base in that uniform."

I hesitated. "The other Gun was Mac."

Vera's face slackened. "Your *Resistance* leader?"

"He was expected to arrest a lot more people. He risked his life to only send so few away."

I couldn't tell what Vera was thinking. "Was Collie with the Resistance too then?" she said at last. When I told her he wasn't, she hesitated. "Well…do you think he had anything to do with the attack going so wrong?"

Our voices were hushed. By now, most people had gone to sleep. I could see their shadowy forms – hear the rhythmic sound of breathing. A few others still talked in faint murmurs. The large space somehow felt drawn-in, intimate.

I slowly shook my head, remembering the encounter with Collie in the tunnels. "It's strange, but I don't think so. Mac trusted him, and...I suppose I do too, at least when it comes to the Resistance."

"Are you still in love with him?"

"No."

"So...is there anyone else?" When I didn't answer, Vera traced a circle on Harlan's shoulder. "Over a year is a long time," she pointed out.

I fiddled with the silver ring Dwight had given me. "I hope there's someone else."

"Ingo?"

I glanced up. "How did you—"

"The look on your face when you said his name before. Who is he?"

I exhaled and raked my hair back with both hands. "His name is Ingo Manfred," I said finally. "He was a Peacefighter for the European Alliance."

"Go on."

"He's Germanic...has dark, curly hair...plays guitar. His family owns a vineyard near the Med." My voice had grown gentle. I thought as I spoke, choosing each word carefully. "He's incredibly honest. Straightforward. And funny –

303

he makes me laugh even when I don't want to."

"Is he handsome?" Vera had her elbows propped on Harlan's muscular shoulder, as if I was telling her a bedtime story.

I pictured Ingo's tall, lean form. "*I* think so," I said softly. "You probably wouldn't. He has a—" I swiped my hand down one side of my face. "A bad burn scar. All down here. When people first see him, they flinch. He never shows that it bothers him, but it must."

"He sounds very brave."

"He is, but he'd say something sarcastic if you told him that."

"And very contrary." Vera smiled. "You know, I can definitely see this."

I told her about how I'd first met Ingo in The Ivy Room – our escape from Harmony Five together, our work in the Resistance. Vera listened quietly.

"When we were on the run, there was this one time…" I swallowed. "The Guns were after us, and I was injured… and I was so scared, Vera. I wanted to die rather than go back. Ingo promised that he'd do it. That he'd kill us both if he had to; he wouldn't let either of us be taken. And I knew I could trust him. I was able to let myself pass out then, against his shoulder. I could hear the Guns coming, but I wasn't scared any more."

I looked down, playing with a fold of my dress. "That's the way it always is with him. I know that I can trust him with…anything."

A silence fell. Vera looked as if she understood more than I'd said.

"Oh, Amity..." she murmured.

That night on the roof flashed back, taunting me. I pressed my fingers hard against my temples.

Vera squeezed my arm. Neither of us spoke again for some time.

CHAPTER TWENTY-TWO

JULY, 1942

THE WIRE MESH OF THE rooftop pigeon hutch gleamed in the moonlight.

Inside a dozen shadowy shapes were roosting. As I waited for Ingo to come up, I opened the door and took out Harold, my favourite. He stirred with a rustle. His small body was warm, alert with life.

Still trying to forget the execution I'd seen earlier, I stood stroking the bird's smooth feathers, feeling his heartbeat against my palm and gazing out at the buildings of Harlemtown. This late, they were mostly dark. Though the New Manhattan lights drowned out almost everything, a few stars shone through here and there. The moon was tipped on its edge – a white boat sailing across the sky.

My chest eased a little. I thought of flying a Firedove above the clouds – the way the moonlight stroked across their tips to make a weird, silvery landscape.

"You'd love it, I bet," I murmured to Harold. "Do you ever fly that high?" He trilled in response, pushing at my fingers with his beak. I fed him a bit of seed, then kissed his head.

"Your new man?" said Ingo's voice from the doorway.

I glanced over. "How did you guess?"

Ingo shut the door to the roof behind him and came over. He'd taken a shower and wore beige trousers and a soft-looking white shirt. Its sleeves were rolled up, showing his forearms.

He stood beside me and stroked Harold's head with a knuckle. His hair was still damp. "Which one is this?"

"Harold, of course. Don't you recognize him? I think you've hurt his feelings."

Ingo inclined his head. "*Bitte entschuldigen Sie vielmals, Harold. Harold?*" he added.

"A distinguished name for a distinguished bird." I put him back on his perch and latched the door.

Ingo draped his arm across the top of the hutch. "So are you going to tell me what's wrong?" he said quietly.

I grimaced, seeing again what had happened and not wanting to go into it, not even with him. Finally I glanced at him and tried to smile. "Want to sit down?"

He raised his good eyebrow.

I nudged him. "Come on."

It was still hot even though it was so late. We dragged the wooden deckchairs next to each other. I wore a sleeveless blue dress, slightly too large, so comfortable it was like a nightgown.

"We should just sleep up here," I said, stretching out. "It's funny. I used to not be able to sleep unless I had a soft bed."

Ingo lay on his back with one arm under his head, gazing up at the sky. His angular features were clear in the dim light. "Yes, me too...we've a lot to thank Harmony Five for, I guess." His voice held a tinge of bitterness.

His shirt was unbuttoned; it lay open over a thin undershirt that showed the sharp lines of his collarbones. I found myself studying him, and then we both started to speak at the same time.

"You first," he said, turning his head towards me.

I propped myself on my side. "Any more news from your family?"

"No, nothing more since the first letter," Ingo said. "You?"

I shook my head. Ingo's gaze was still on me. Before he could ask again what was wrong. I said, "Show me the photo again?"

His dry smile said he knew I was stalling. He sat up and fished in his back pocket for his wallet. I shifted over to his deckchair. We sat side by side on its edge as he took the photo out and angled it towards me.

The black-and-white image his mother had sent showed a table set up under a tree, beside a house made of mellow, worn-looking stone. Rolling hills covered with vineyards rose in the background.

His family – his parents, his older brother and his younger sister – sat at the food-laden table, holding up glasses of wine in a toast to the photographer. You could tell the photo had been taken especially to send to Ingo.

"You look just like your father," I said.

Ingo's father had a patrician air to him – a long, serious face with a faint twinkle in his dark eyes.

Ingo lifted a shoulder. "I used to. Not with the scarred mug."

"No, you still do." I pointed to the house. "Which was your room?"

He tapped the photo. "This one. I had to share with Erich for years, and then I begged to have the attic. I liked the quiet, and the view." He smiled slightly. "I used to stare out at the vineyard – study the way the vines were trained. Draw sketches. Wonder if we could do it better."

"The way the vines are trained?"

"Yes, look." He indicated a tiny vine. "No, I guess you can't really see. But the vines have to be trained against something. We weave the branches against posts; it's been done that way in our region for centuries. But you lose some of the grapes. We grow pinot noir, mostly; it's delicate. I wondered if we wouldn't have a better yield if we spaced the vines out more, trained them lengthwise. When I was twelve I showed Dad one of my sketches and he started laughing – said he'd raised an anarchist."

I grinned. Ingo went on. "He took me into his library and showed me books about the different methods. The one I'd thought of is called trellising. I asked him why we didn't do it, and he said over his dead body. But he still gave me a couple of rows and let me try. Every year when I came home from school, I'd spend all summer out there." He smiled, rubbing his jaw. "I finally yielded a few mature bottles when I was sixteen. Dad served them at a party and when people complimented it, he laughed and said, 'Thank Ingo. He'll change this whole damn place when he gets the chance.'"

"He's very proud of you," I said quietly.

"I know. He's proud of all of us. But I suppose I'm the one most like him." Ingo studied the photo, tapping it lightly against his fingers.

"One day," he muttered.

Though I knew what it meant to him, sadness touched me at the thought of his going back there. I realized I was looking at Ingo, not the photo.

I cleared my throat. "I'd like to meet them all someday."

"Yes…I'd like you to. Very much." He hesitated and then looked at me, his dark gaze steady.

Suddenly I was aware of how close we were sitting. Neither of us moved. As we looked at each other, my heart unaccountably beat a little faster. Nervous for some reason, I looked over at the pigeon coop.

Ingo straightened and put the photo away. He rubbed

the back of his neck. Finally his mouth twisted in a crooked smile.

"All right, so we've established that neither of us has heard anything new. We'll skip the platitudes about how we're sure everyone is fine. Now what's wrong?"

When I didn't answer, he said softly, "You don't always have to be so strong, you know."

I felt very conscious of him beside me. "You of all people should know that I'm not always anything of the sort," I said finally.

The same hand that rested beside mine had once held a shard of twisted metal to my throat. I'd held a piece of glass to his. Abruptly, I recalled crouching together, shaking with fear, ready to die rather than be taken by Guns. More recently, I'd cried in Ingo's arms when everything had caved in on me.

From the look on his face, he was remembering it all too. "Amity...tell me."

"There...was an execution today," I said at last. "I was at Ernest and Mabel's...we could see it from the window."

Ingo shifted so that he was facing me. He went still, listening.

I described how we'd been working on *Victory* when we'd heard the shouts and sirens – how we'd seen the shaven-headed woman dragged out and shoved on top of a Shadowcar. How a Gun had read out her crimes, then put a noose around her neck.

"She was...arrested for aiding Discordants." The words

felt thick in my throat. "They hanged her from the lamp post. They didn't give her any last words, but…just before she dropped, she yelled, 'V for Vancour!'"

The distant rattle of an elevated train went past. It faded to silence.

Ingo touched my shoulder, his hand warm on my skin. "Why the hell didn't you tell me, instead of letting me babble about the vineyard?"

I gave a shaky laugh. "I liked hearing it. It made things seem more normal. As normal as they ever get here."

He slowly let his fingers fall. "Are you all right?"

I rubbed my forehead. "You know what?" I said finally. "When it happened, I was just glad that Hal was *here*, at the deli, safe. That woman died thinking about my broadcasts…and Wildcat sat watching, terrified, glad that it wasn't her and her little brother who'd been caught."

"You're allowed to be afraid."

"People think I'm so brave, though! It's a *joke*. Every time I see a Gun in that uniform, I remember Harmony Five and I…" My throat closed.

"Amity. I'm scared every day too – don't you know that?" Ingo's voice was low. "Harmony Five isn't some place you can just forget about."

No. It wasn't. I saw in a sudden flash a platform with a crescent moon behind it. A terrified girl being shot for a crime I knew she didn't commit. When her body had fallen to the ground, I'd scrambled with the others, fighting to wrest the boots from her still-warm legs.

I felt lost in that other time, seeing it all so vividly. "You want the truth?" I said. "I don't even know who I am any more. I've killed two people."

"You didn't kill Melody."

"Please don't split hairs."

"I'm not. I'm telling you the truth."

"I stood there and watched her die, Ingo! For a pair of boots!"

"I'd have done the same, probably," he said. "I was in that place too, remember? I know."

"Yes? And what about Gunnison? I walked right up to a man and shot him, and I hardly even remember it!" I laughed shakily, shoving my hair back. "If I were captured…I don't even know what I would do. Apparently when my back's to the wall, I might do *anything* – murder, betrayal. Who knows?"

To my surprise, Ingo gripped my hand. "All right, listen to me. I know you, even if you don't. And I did plenty in that shithole that I'm not proud of, either. Do you trust *me*?"

"Of course I do," I whispered.

"Fine, so trust me now. You would die before you betrayed Hal, or Sephy, or Mac, or me, or anyone else in the Resistance." He squeezed my fingers hard, his dark eyes intent. "I'd bet my own life on it."

I let out a long breath, holding onto his hand. Ingo hesitated, then smoothed a strand of hair from my cheek. "It's not actually necessary that you be superhuman, you know," he said. "An ordinary human will do."

Something eased in me. I gave a small smile.

"Please don't bet your own life," I said finally. "You might lose."

I leaned forward until my forehead touched his chest. I felt him stroke my hair. His head dropped down to mine.

"No," he whispered against my ear. "I don't think I would." He gently caressed the back of my neck.

I closed my eyes, savouring his warmth. The moments passed in the rattle of another elevated train; his heartbeat through his thin undershirt. I shifted so that I was pressed against him, and Ingo put his other arm around me, drawing me close.

I could stay like this with you for ever.

The thought was so natural that at first I wasn't aware of it. I slipped my own arms around him – explored the long line of his spine through his shirt.

My blood quickened as I realized what I'd thought… and that I wanted to touch skin instead of cloth.

I felt Ingo swallow. I was hyper-aware of his lips still beside my ear. His heart was pounding too. His hand slowly travelled up my arm, his palm warm against my skin.

The air had turned electric. I wanted whatever was going to come next.

In confusion, I pulled away.

We stared at each other.

I tried to speak. The words felt too tangled. *No,* I thought fearfully. *I can't fall in love with you.*

Ingo looked just as rocked. "Amity…" he said softly, starting to reach for me.

I hugged my elbows and blurted, "Ingo, whatever that was…I can't do it."

One of the pigeons cooed. I gazed tensely towards the hutch, seeing with sickening clarity my arrest – someone I'd loved becoming a stranger.

"I'll probably feel like a fool in a minute," Ingo said in a low voice. "But why? I thought…" He stopped.

Because I can't lose you, too.

"I just…need you to be my friend, all right?" I'd sounded curt. I hadn't meant to.

I was desperate to fill the silence that followed but didn't trust myself to speak again. Ingo sank back. Something faded in his dark eyes as he studied me.

He looked away and swiped roughly at his scar, as if it bothered him.

"Friendship it is," he said. "I apologize. It won't happen again."

Chapter Twenty-three

September, 1942

I MANAGED TO SLEEP A LITTLE. When I woke up, it was daylight but still felt early. Vera and Harlan were asleep nearby; she lay curled against his chest like a kitten.

I sat up. Hal was gone. When I scanned the top of the stadium, I saw him crouched in position with the snipers again.

No attack yet.

In the morning light, the stadium gleamed, its every inch bright and modern. You'd never have guessed the slaughter that had happened here...apart from the people. They looked like refugees. Many were still asleep on the floor; others sat in the bleachers, talking in huddled groups.

I tried not to think about the bodies we'd left in one of the offices.

Vera stirred then, and looked blearily around her. "I thought I'd dreamed it," she murmured.

"No. We're still here," I said.

Soon everyone was up, eating junk food breakfasts in tense clusters. I prowled restlessly, checking often out the upper windows. As Hal said, more Guns were out there than we'd thought. I'd expect them to attack at first light, but they seemed to be waiting for something.

The drone of sirens was continuous. Around nine o'clock we heard a faint chanting. It slowly coalesced into words: *Down with Pierce! V for Victory! Down with Pierce!*

Gunshots. The chanting stopped. More sirens. Through the high-up windows, we could see that something seemed to be happening around the palace. The night before, we'd seen flames. Now plumes of smoke curled against the blue sky.

Still no news. The woman who'd brought the transistor wireless kept trying it. Only static and dance music came from its curlicue speakers.

Harlan and the others worked on digging out the tunnel. I went down to check several times. Each time, in the light from the flashlights, it seemed as if the pile of rocks and rubble had barely shifted.

"Feels like it too," grunted Harlan when I said this. He had his shirt off, trundling the full wheelbarrow across the cellar. As he tipped it out beside the coal pile, the tattoo of the scantily-clad woman on his bicep rippled. He accepted the water I handed him.

"But what the hell – it's better than just waiting for them to make their move," he added. He toasted me with the water. "You throw a hell of a party, Vancour."

The hours dragged past. Around noon, I went and found Hal, who, after a brief nap, was taking another shift with the snipers posted around the top of the Garden. The heat was bad enough down below; up here it was choking.

The atmosphere was grim, watchful. The Guns encircling us seemed etched on my brain: a faintly shifting line at the edge of the parking lot as a few of them milled around, talking – yet always with several dozen of them holding rifles on our doors.

Come on, get it over with already, I thought. It felt like when I'd been Peacefighting, scanning the clouds for an opponent who refused to appear.

I gazed beyond them towards the palace. The smoke we'd thought we'd seen earlier was gone. An eerie stillness seemed to have fallen over the city. I could hardly see any traffic.

What the hell was happening?

I sighed and glanced back at Hal. He swiped his wrist tiredly across his eyes. There were purplish smudges under them, and faint, boyish fuzz on his jaw.

"How are you?" I asked.

"Just dandy," he said without looking at me. "I'm

keeping an eye on a horde of attacking Guns with my sister. What could be more fun?"

I smiled faintly at the echo of what I'd once said to him back home in Sacrament, when we'd waited for Ma and he'd asked if I was okay.

Oh, I'm just dandy. I'm sitting on a park bench evading Guns with my brother – what could be more fun?

Hours later, we'd put him into hiding.

Remembering how much I'd wanted to protect him that day, I cleared my throat. "You know…what happened to Dwight really wasn't your fault."

He stiffened. "Don't give me that."

"It wasn't."

"Right, so whose fault was it?"

"It doesn't always work that way. It's just…what happened." When he didn't respond, I gently reached for his rifle and lowered it.

His jaw went hard, but to my surprise, he didn't resist. He leaned against the wall with his head back, gazing at the ceiling. "I don't want to talk about this," he said. "Can we drop it, please?"

"All right," I said quietly. "But I want you to have something." I pulled the silver ring from my finger and put it onto one of his. "Dwight gave it to me just before he died. It was his mother's."

It fit Hal's right middle finger. He stared down at it and then looked quickly up at me. "Why…why would you give this to me?"

I shrugged. "Because I think you should have it."

Abruptly, his eyes were red-rimmed. "Are you crazy? Why should *I* have it? It's my fault he's dead!"

"*No.* It isn't."

His throat worked. "I never…*ever* would have gone to signal Collie, if – if I'd known…" He gave a heaving gasp and squeezed his eyes shut. He jammed his fists against them, shuddering.

"I'm sorry," he choked out. "Amity, I'm so fucking sorry."

I put my arm around him, not knowing what to say. It was like holding stone. I rubbed his shoulder, my heart aching for him.

"I know you are," I said at last. "Dwight died to save us. If we survive this somehow, just…prove him right, okay?" I rested my head against his.

We sat like that for several minutes. Finally Hal pulled away. His cheeks were damp. Still looking down, he touched the ring.

"Yeah," he said. "Okay."

Silence curled around us. From nearby came the faint sound of the next sniper along shifting position. Hal leaned back, his face still moist. He wiped his eyes.

"Amity…why did he do it?" he said woodenly.

"Dwight?"

"No. Dad."

I tensed and stared down at the tiny figures moving about in the arena below. "I already told you what Madeline said."

"She hardly said *anything*. Just that it was a mistake and he did it for the money. I don't believe that. Do you?"

I sighed. "I guess I do," I admitted. "I don't think there was any big reason, Hal. He was young. He wasn't that much older than me. It just…happened."

Hal fell silent, rubbing his forehead. In profile, he looked more like Dad than ever.

"I wrote to Ma a while back," he said.

"Okay," I said, confused by the change of subject. Then I realized it wasn't one. "You mean about Dad?"

"Yeah. I just…thought she might know what really happened."

The stifling heat pressed down. The thought of our mother receiving such a letter felt both very distant and far too close.

"What did you say?" My tone was stilted.

He made a face and nudged an old candy wrapper on the floor. "That Madeline told you Dad had done it for the money, and because she asked him to. That I wanted to hear Ma's side."

"Hal, it's just…there are some things that I don't know if Ma knew."

"You mean that Dad and Madeline were having an affair?"

I looked at him in surprise. He shrugged.

"Figured it out," he said tiredly. He pushed his hair back and gave a short laugh. "Yeah, I wasn't really thinking when I gave Ingo that letter. I just felt…I don't know."

Neither of us spoke for a few moments. What would Ma think when she got Hal's letter? I wasn't even sure whether she'd known about Dad's thrown Peacefight before it came out during my trial – though she must have known *something* was amiss, all those years. Mustn't she? We'd always had more money than most Peacefighting families. Dad had been so clearly riddled with guilt for almost my whole childhood.

Hal looked down, running his thumb over the silver ring. Finally he said, "Amity, listen…I know you've been trying to apologize for not being there for me, or whatever, after you shot Gunnison…"

I went still.

He sighed. "I kind of get it now," he said softly. "I didn't mean to keep shutting you down. It just…felt really hard for a while."

My throat was tight. "I know. It's okay." I kissed his cheek and stood up. "And, Hal, don't worry about the letter. You had a right to ask Ma for answers."

But glancing down at the waiting Guns again, I doubted we'd get to hear her response.

It grew close to evening. In the ladies' restroom, I attempted a quick sponge bath. My clothes felt sticky on my back. I'd been wearing the same too-formal dress for days now. My face looked unfamiliar in the mirror – there was still a purpling bruise over one eye, and a cut through one of my eyebrows from the Gun's blackjack.

Vera joined me and washed her hands. "People are wondering if it's even going to happen today," she said, her voice thin. "They're scared that Pierce is planning something really terrible for us, and that's why the Guns are waiting."

"I hate how likely that sounds," I muttered.

I'd found some other clothes in the stadium's lost-and-found box: a plain green dress and sandals that almost fit. I pulled them on, and saw Vera's eyes widen at my old bullet wound.

She started to say something else. We both looked up, startled, at the sound of shouts.

"Listen! Everybody listen!"

We raced back into the main area. The woman with the transistor stood on the platform, holding it up over her head.

Kay Pierce's voice blared tinnily, trembling with emotion: "…V for Victory? Well, *I* say V for Villainy! V for Violence! Vancour's a dangerous criminal, New Manhattan, but she's too craven to hold out for long. Don't worry, this unrest will soon be over! I've left the city and am speaking to you from somewhere in Connecticut, where I'm…I'm currently on a prearranged tour. But as soon—"

Sudden cheers drowned out the rest. Unexpectedly, my spirits soared. As the room erupted I gave a wild, whooping laugh, cheering as loud as anyone. Vera grabbed me and we jumped up and down together.

"Prearranged my ass!" shouted a man.

"Wildcat! Wildcat!" someone started chanting. Others took it up, punching the air in unison.

I grinned, for once not even hating the nickname. Just then it didn't matter that if Kay Pierce was gone, New Manhattan couldn't reach her. She was on the run.

People quietened, shushing each other, as she kept talking: "…as soon as the tour is over, when I'll be joined by my new husband, Collis Reed, who's currently away on business. Mr Reed will, of course, have a vital role in my regime, and I know that Can-Amer wishes us all happiness. Goodnight."

Static. I stood stunned, wondering if I'd heard right. Collie had *married* her?

The mood in the Garden hadn't been dampened. "So Reed actually married the witch," laughed someone. "Poor slob."

"Ah, he's as bad as she is," said someone else.

Hardly anyone knew about my history with Collie. Hal had just come down from taking a shift with the snipers. We stared at each other. My brother snorted, looking bitter.

"Still think he didn't betray us?" he said.

"I don't know," I said finally.

After the first surprise, I felt oddly detached at the news of Collie marrying someone else – and *Kay Pierce*, of all people. The sudden flash of memory – Collie whispering, "Hey, if you ever marry anyone, it's going to be me" –

brought only a distant sadness, as if hearing about someone I'd once known. It was Hal I felt worried about.

For myself, all I thought was, *Collie, I hope to hell you know what you're doing.*

We started picking up underground broadcasts soon after that, as if people felt emboldened by Pierce fleeing the city.

A jubilant male voice floated from the speakers: "…and people near the Garden report that the stand-off continues. Vancour's still in there now, with a group of armed rebels! The executions have stopped!"

Excited murmurs. People sat hugging their knees, listening avidly.

"There's been no further announcement from Pierce," the voice went on. "In Aquarius sector, Guns have been thin on the ground – we've only had three arrests today, even though astrology shops have been destroyed up and down my street. The V sign is everywhere."

A shaky, exuberant laugh. "We've been hearing lots of sirens, though. Smoke was seen over by the palace earlier – it seems pretty clear why Pierce went on a 'tour'. And people here in Aquarius have been burning their ID cards. I saw a Gun strike a man for doing it, but he *didn't arrest him* – and there were at least ten other people doing the same thing in plain view!"

I stood greedily drinking in the first news we'd had in over a day. Exultation and apprehension beat through me.

New Manhattan sounded on the verge of exploding.

But Pierce wasn't even here.

The voice was still speaking a quarter of an hour later – far longer than Mac and I had ever dared. The Guns obviously weren't bothering to police illegal broadcasts – or other things either, if the announcer was right.

What did that mean? They were being kept too busy elsewhere in the city? Or that, like the Gun here had told me, Pierce had lost support with her mass executions?

If I were her, I'd bring in outside forces, I thought.

My arms prickled at the memory of her troops and tanks on the streets of the Western Seaboard. If I'd thought of it, surely the nimble-brained Pierce had.

Unfortunately, the Guns outside the Garden were loyal enough. Every time I'd seen them today, they'd looked purposeful, alert. The sight was nerve-wracking – they still didn't seem to be gearing up for an attack.

And then my chill deepened as it hit me. *She's too craven to hold out for long,* Pierce had said.

"Hold out." She knew we were armed, short of food. Why allow me to get taken in a heroic battle that the public might get wind of, when she could just let us rot in here?

She wasn't going to attack at all. She planned to wait us out.

CHAPTER TWENTY-FOUR

"STILL ONLY ONE CANDY BAR EACH?" asked the woman as I handed it to her.

"Yes," I said shortly. "I'm sorry."

Vera shot me a sympathetic glance. Another day had passed. Realizing there was no end in sight, I'd had to lock the concessions supply room and start rationing the food. Even with us all on a single candy bar and a handful of peanuts a day, we'd run out in a week.

As I looked down the long line of people waiting for their share, I was suddenly propelled back to Harmony Five — how we'd all trembled with hunger as we'd watched a Gun ladle out our thin broth.

Except now I was the Gun.

My stomach lurched. I forcibly regained myself and handed the next person in line their ration.

After the unknown broadcaster had finished exulting about the unrest in the city, he'd said, "Wildcat, if you're listening – New Manhattan is behind you!"

Static. I'd remained standing, my thoughts whirling. The sunset had shone through the stadium's high windows, casting the woman in silhouette as she still held up her transistor.

She'd turned it off and clambered to the floor. She was smiling, her cheeks damp.

"Wildcat – Miss Vancour – we're all behind you too," she said hoarsely.

Even then, I'd known it wasn't totally true. People were scared. But there was applause – a few cheers.

There were no cheers now. Everybody realized we were under siege. I'd announced that we were trying to dig out through a caved-in tunnel, though had to admit success was far from certain.

"If I give myself up, she'd still execute everyone here," I said. "You can leave if you want – I'm not stopping anyone. But I don't think she'd be merciful. The tunnel's probably our only real hope."

My clenched fists likely hadn't gone unnoticed. A real hope...but such a slim one.

A sea of apprehensive faces had stared back at me. No one left.

* * *

Another day passed in a haze of dense heat – of our snipers still guarding us, and the Guns still waiting. Some had cameras, I saw now. I gazed bitterly at the boxy instruments. Of course: Pierce wanted to record my surrender.

The diggers had rapidly become heroes in my eyes. They worked tirelessly. About fifteen feet of the cave-in had been cleared now, the work lit by flashlights. I'd held half the batteries back and was parcelling them out like a miser. We could do without flashlights up above. Not down there. I watched their progress closely, sick with hope, praying it wasn't one of the cave-ins that lasted hundreds of feet.

Three days on, most people seemed in shock, as if wondering how the hell they'd gotten into this. Following me in the heat of the moment had been one thing; this was another.

Almost as bad as the constant tension and the hunger, was the boredom. As the hours dragged, squabbles broke out often. I found playing cards in the concessions storeroom and passed them out.

"Yup, you sure throw a great party," drawled Harlan.

I managed a thin smile. "Hey, you ain't seen nothin' yet."

Even with all of that, things still weren't too bad…though I didn't realize that until the morning of the fourth day.

That's when they turned the water off.

When a woman came to tell me the toilets weren't working, a cold foreboding swept me. Vera and I had been counting the remaining candy bars. We locked up the office and raced for the ladies'.

"Please, please," I muttered a few moments later, standing in the shadowy, tiled room. I tried flushing first one toilet, then another. The tanks gurgled uselessly.

"No!" I darted to the sinks. Vera was already trying them, her face pale. I twisted a tap. No water. I twisted the next one. No water. Next one. Nothing. I tried every sink, my panic rising.

At the last silent, stilled tap, I slammed my fist against the sink. "Damn it! You *bastards*!"

Shuddering, I leaned against the cool porcelain and put my head in my hands. "You bastards," I whispered again.

Vera touched my arm. She didn't speak.

I let my hands fall. Our gazes met. Vera's eyes were round and scared – mirrors of my own.

"I…I guess we have to go tell people this now," she said.

"Yeah," I said finally.

The non-flushing toilets quickly became unusable. We found all the containers that the Garden owned – buckets, popcorn kettles, a vat for boiling hot dogs in – and put these in the restrooms instead. Within hours the rooms turned fetid.

People had been drinking the soda and beer all along.

I'd allowed it, because the beer cheered them up. Why, *why* couldn't I have seen this move coming? Now there were far too few bottles of each left – hardly even enough for everyone to have a single bottle of beer and another soda.

I kept the beer back for now; it would make people thirstier. We doled the soda out in the smallest cups the stadium had. Groups gathered up in the bleachers, whispering. Sometimes I caught snippets of conversation:

"I thought she had a *plan* when I followed her. She's Wildcat!"

"Is this really her best strategy? Damned if we do, damned if we don't?"

"Yeah, the tunnels don't sound very hopeful. At least she freed the captives, I guess."

"Wonderful, now they can die of thirst instead…"

Down from one of his shifts, Hal murmured to me, "Things are getting bad, Sis. I can hear people talking—"

"Yes, I know!" I snapped. I squeezed my temples. "Sorry," I said. "Sorry."

The weather stayed unseasonably hot. I had to give the diggers extra soda rations or they couldn't have kept going.

Harlan and I stood in the cellar's shadowy main stairwell. He drained his soda ration in a single gulp and jerked his sweat-stained head upwards. "What's happening in the city? Can you tell?"

"Riots might still be going on," I said. "We can see smoke from the east side, and Hal said he heard more chanting earlier. But all *our* Guns are still right there outside."

Harlan's expression was as stony as I felt. He started to respond, then we both fell silent as a faint, low rumble came from somewhere below.

"Explosives," I murmured. I stood listening hard. "Remember, I told you the Guns have them?"

We exchanged a glance. "Trying to get in here through the tunnels, do you think?" said Harlan.

I frowned. "Maybe."

The Guns didn't know we were trying to dig our way out. If Pierce was tired of waiting, perhaps they hoped to stream in and grab us, without us having a chance to make a stand.

Harlan gave a hard smile. "Well, they're in for a surprise if they try anything." He was right; defending a single narrow tunnel entrance would be child's play.

"Let's hope they do," I said flatly. "We could use help digging it out."

I longed for more news from the outside – so much that when the woman's transistor had finally died, I'd been tempted to give her some of the precious batteries. But digging out the cave-in, if we could manage it, was more important.

Other explosions came occasionally. Thankfully, up on the main level you hardly noticed. All I needed was more panic.

Soon it seemed as if swallowing too-hard against a dry throat had always been our reality. On the evening of the fifth day, a small group decided to leave. I didn't try to stop them.

As we watched from the windows above, they waved white flags made from torn shirts and ventured out the front door – over a dozen, mostly older people. One was a woman who'd said she was a librarian. Another a man who'd been injured in the battle. His arm was still in a sling.

They were all shot down.

The deaths left the Garden stunned and cowed. To my shame, I took advantage of people's fear and cut their soda ration even smaller, knowing they were less likely to grumble just then – trying desperately to make it last a little longer.

My own fear was a cold snake choking my insides. We were nearly out of food now too. *I can't let them down,* I kept thinking. *There must be something I haven't thought of.*

"Maybe we *should* just forget the tunnel and storm out – take our chances," I whispered to Hal the next morning. I was up beside one of the windows with him as he crouched on guard duty. I gazed down at the Guns with helpless loathing.

Hal swiped his grimy face across his shirtsleeve and glanced quickly at me. "You don't mean that."

"I don't know. Maybe I do."

My brother's eyes flashed. "No," he said. "Too many people would die. The rest would just be hanged later." When I didn't answer, he added, "You told me yourself… as long as we're alive, there's hope."

I pressed my head against the warm glass. My five-days-ago self seemed hopelessly naïve to me now…and I'd never thought I could be naïve ever again, after Collie and Harmony Five.

A dozen pairs of work gloves lay in a supply closet that smelled of bleach. I took a pair myself and doled out the rest. Vera took one, and Harlan, and the others who'd volunteered: a young mechanic; a schoolteacher; a few more.

"We'll all take turns," said Vera.

I shook my head, surveying the different groups scattered across the bleachers. "People are already muttering about me," I said in an undertone. "I can't let them see me sitting back while others do this."

Harlan and Vera glanced at each other. At this point, we all knew what a knife-edge things teetered on in here. Finally Harlan gruffly clasped my shoulder.

"Come on then, Vancour," he said. "That shit's not going anywhere on its own."

The smell that assaulted us in the toilets brought back my shed in Harmony Five, with its constantly-overflowing chamber pot. The improvised commodes were heavy, awkward. It was impossible to carry them up the stairs that cut through the bleachers without sloshing some of their contents.

With our snipers covering us, we awkwardly angled each container out of a broken window and emptied it in fetid streams that stained the wall and plopped onto the parking lot below.

Part of the window sill exploded in a bullet's whine, wood and mortar shattering outwards. A piece hit me on the wrist and I yelped, almost dropping my side of the popcorn kettle.

Our snipers responded immediately. No more bullets came, but raucous shouts and laughter drifted up: "Filthy Discordant animals!"

"We're trying *not* to be filthy, if they haven't noticed," muttered Vera. Her damp hair clung to her neck.

Shaken, I put the empty cauldron down. It half-fell, landing with a clatter. Harlan pressed my shoulder when I reached for another, pushing me down onto a bleacher. I sank onto it wearily, rubbing my wrist.

The images of Harmony Five were very strong now, except I wasn't always sure where in the parallels I stood. Was I the one rationing food, ordering people what to do? Or the one cowering in fear?

How could I be both?

Finally we carried the containers back down the long stairs and cleaned them out the best we could, dousing them with bleach and wiping them down with scraps of newspaper.

"Does it still beat truck-driving?" I asked Harlan.

He grimaced. "I'm not even gonna answer that."

Once we were done, the eight of us shared a single bottle of warm beer in the kitchen. *Seventy-two left,* I thought automatically. It sounded like so many. It was nothing.

"At least people won't piss as much, when they're not getting enough to drink," said Harlan wearily.

"They're already starting to use the containers again," said Vera. "There's a line outside both restrooms."

It struck all of us as darkly humorous, for some reason. I snorted, pressing my hands to my temples.

"We should ration *that* too," said Joe, one of the diggers who'd taken a break to help us. "One piss a day. No arguments."

"Why stop there?" I said with a faint smile. My tongue felt fuzzy, aching for water. "We'll say you can only go if it's your star sign's turn. And if it's more than the regulation amount, we'll—"

"Oh, don't!" moaned Vera with a tired chuckle. "We'll have to start calling you Madame Pierce."

We went back out into the main area. The group dispersed, our helpers heading off towards the bleachers. Harlan stretched and started to say something – then frowned, squinting towards the cellar entrance.

"Think something's up," he murmured.

The mood tensed abruptly. I glanced over and saw another of the diggers, standing in the cellar doorway scanning the stadium. He saw us and started over.

Vera, Harlan and I met him halfway. "We've heard Guns on the other side of the cave-in," he said in a low voice. "We think they've almost made it through."

I caught my breath. My eyes flew to Harlan's and Vera's. "A way out," she whispered.

My thoughts raced. How many Guns would there be? A dozen? Two dozen? "We have to defeat them – we have to get into that tunnel," I said. "We *have* to."

"We'll fucking defeat them," said Harlan grimly.

I quickly scanned the top of the stadium, where the snipers crouched. We had to get weapons down here – and fast – but if people realized there was a danger, I could have a panic on my hands.

Without taking my eyes from the snipers I said, "Can you three go and bring half of them down here? Say that… we need to service the rifles."

Vera licked her lips. "Will anyone fall for that?"

"I don't know! Maybe some people. Just…keep it looking casual, all right? But *hurry.*"

Ten minutes later, an armed group, including Harlan, had gone down the concrete stairs and headed to the tunnel entrance, their flashlights hooded. Hal, Vera and I stood just inside the cellar, craning to hear. Hal still held his rifle, his jaw tense.

The dull scrape of rock against rock came from the

tunnel. At a direction from Harlan, the group rushed through the doorway leading to it. Two hung back, shining flashlights over the scene.

"*Stop right there!*" boomed Harlan.

Shouts – the sound of a scuffle. I sprinted forward, Vera and Hal right behind me. At the top of the tunnel stairs, I stopped short. Two of the snipers had a man pinned up against the rough, earthen wall, his hands in the air.

Harlan's cheek was bruised; his rifle lay on the ground. He had a second man in a half nelson. The other snipers covered the struggling captive. His grey suit with its Harmony armband was rumpled and torn – he was taller than Harlan, but thinner, with dark curls.

"Go on – shoot me – do you think I give a shit?" he gasped out between gritted teeth.

I felt faint suddenly.

"Harlan, let him go!" I cried. I lunged down the stairs – rushed over just as Harlan slowly released him. The others lowered their rifles uncertainly.

Ingo.

CHAPTER TWENTY-FIVE

INGO STOOD BREATHING HARD, massaging his neck, his dark eyes still fierce. In the flashlight's glow his scar looked like some strange half-mask.

The surge of joy and relief left me weak. Ingo. Alive. I remembered him gripping my arms, saying, *I will come back for you.* The warmth of his lips on my palm.

I gripped my elbows tightly. I was close to tears.

"I told you not to come back into the city," I whispered.

Ingo's gaze hadn't left mine. "Yes, I know you did," he said softly.

A draught whispered in from the narrow tunnel. I swallowed and tried to regain myself. "We've – we've been hearing explosions for days. We thought the Guns were trying to blast their way through to us."

"Maybe they were," said Ingo. "Maybe they closed themselves off by mistake, somehow. But we were able to get through."

I couldn't stop staring at him. "How did you know where to find us?"

"You're infamous on the airwaves these days, Wildcat. Or didn't you know?"

For once, there was no humour in his tone. His eyes were hooded with exhaustion – his features drawn. I glanced belatedly at Harlan.

"It's okay, he's Resistance," I said. I looked at the man Ingo had brought with him and cleared my throat. "Who…?"

He had round glasses and an intelligent face. With a glance at the snipers, he stepped forward. "I'm Jean Buzet, Miss Vancour. From World United."

His English wasn't nearly as good as Ingo's. It took me a beat to decipher "United". He held out his hand and I shook it automatically. It added to the sense of unreality.

"What's World United?" I said.

"It's a new organization," he told me. "A league of allies against Can-Amer. All fifty-nine countries have joined."

"Amity, it's what we've all been hoping for," Ingo said. "The world's finally ready to act."

* * *

We moved into the cellar's main space. As the snipers slipped back upstairs, I gazed after them. It was just starting to really hit me: *we could escape.*

"Ingo, we've got over three hundred people in here," I said in a quick undertone. "We've *got* to start getting them out. The Guns have turned the water off. Things have been…bad."

Mr Buzet had overheard. "Let us talk first," he urged me. "Ten minutes."

"What about?"

"There's a reason I brought him here," said Ingo. From his expression, whatever the reason was, he wasn't crazy about it.

When they learned there was a way out, people would go berserk. I glanced at Harlan and Vera. Hal, who'd hung back, stood behind them. He caught my eye and shrugged.

"Ten minutes," I said finally.

Mr Buzet looked relieved. "Good. Thank you." Then he hesitated. "You say there is no water? Is there a restroom?"

Unreasonable irritation hit me. I told him where it was. He climbed the stairs and headed off across the stadium. I hoped no one would realize that he'd only just appeared.

Hal still held his rifle, pointing it towards the ground. He nodded at Ingo. "Hi," he said. "Holy moley, are we ever glad to see you."

Ingo's mouth twisted dryly. "You look like you've gotten a year older in a week."

"Yeah," said Hal. "I guess this kind of thing will do that to you."

I exhaled. "Ingo, this is Harlan Taylor and Vera Kelly. We were Peacefighters together. Ingo was a Peacefighter too," I added.

"Sorry about before, buddy." Harlan offered a large hand. "We're on the same side, looks like. Least, we are now. Who'd you fight for?"

"European Alliance," said Ingo after a pause. They shook. "And forget it. I'd have pulled a rifle on you too."

"Yeah, I bet. You guys were always hell up in the air."

Vera held out her hand. "I've heard a lot about you." At her quick, knowing glance, my ears heated.

"And you," said Ingo as they shook. "You and Amity were roommates, yes?"

Vera gave a small smile. "In a different lifetime."

Ingo snorted and raked a hand through his hair. His tone turned flat. "Yes," he said. "A lot of things happened in a different lifetime."

We sat in a cluster at the bottom of the stairs, where it was lighter. Ingo's gaze went over me. "When did you last have water?"

"Over two days ago. We've been drinking beer and soda, but—"

He had a canteen over one shoulder; I hadn't noticed it. He handed it over. "Here. It's from one of our old caches; it's almost full."

Suddenly I was almost shuddering, I wanted it so badly. I uncapped the canteen and took a gulp, then another. The water was too warm and tasted metallic. It was wonderful.

I forced myself to stop and handed it to Hal, who took some and then passed it to Vera. As Harlan took a swig, I glanced up the stairs, wondering if I could ration some out to those most in need without causing a riot. I decided I couldn't, and rubbed my forehead wearily.

As Ingo recapped the canteen, I said, "So you got everyone out safely?"

"Yes, in the end."

"How's Mac?" I asked softly.

"Alive. Apart from that, not well, the last I saw him."

I winced, thinking of the dank underground river – the narrow crawl spaces. "But the railroad will help him and Sephy get to Nova Scotia?"

"Yes. Not immediately though. He needs medical care first." Ingo frowned and looked down, bouncing a fist on his thigh.

"Where'd the World United guy come from?" Harlan asked.

"From the European Alliance, originally," said Ingo. "I'll let him explain. But he needed to get into the city somehow, and the railroad knew that…I'd be going back in."

I glanced at him, wondering at his slight hesitancy. He cleared his throat. "So you've been busy," he said to me.

"Wildcat on the rampage," drawled Harlan.

Ingo gave a faint smile. "She often is." He was still

343

studying me. "I'm very glad you're all right," he added quietly.

"The feeling's mutual," I murmured.

Our gazes stayed locked. It was the wrong time, yet my body didn't seem to know that. Recalling again his lips on my palm, warmth fluttered through me. Ingo was the first to look away.

When Jean Buzet returned, he frowned at Hal. "Should the boy stay? There are things I need to explain which are quite sensitive."

Hal raised an eyebrow, his chin lifting.

"My brother stays," I said.

My tone didn't harbour any arguments. Jean Buzet inclined his head. "Of course, Miss Vancour."

He undid the first few buttons of his shirt and drew out a large brown envelope. He opened it and slid out three crumpled, much-handled photographs. He handed them to me.

I went still as I recognized them: the photos that Ingo and I had found while on the run from Harmony Five. We'd come across a factory; when we'd stolen a plane from its tiny airport, these had been on a bulletin board.

The glossy black-and-white images showed a mushroom cloud – a graph titled *Bomb blast effects on a typical city of ten million people* – two fat, swollen bombs lying side by side.

"Holy hell…they're real," Harlan whispered, taking them from me.

"Didn't you know that?" I said. "We published similar ones in *Victory*."

Vera looked dazed too. "Yes, but…I guess we hoped the Resistance was just making them up to scare us into action."

"No, they're very real," said Ingo. "We saw the factory."

His eyes met mine…and I knew he was remembering, like me, how I'd gotten shot as we stole the plane – his hands pressed over my wound as I took off.

It was the first time Hal had seen these photos. His face hardened. Neither of us had to say it: our father had been indirectly responsible. He handed the crumpled images back.

"Our man Grady took these to the European Alliance earlier this year," I told Harlan and Vera. I glanced at Mr Buzet. "He said the world was too afraid to act."

"Yes, correct." Mr Buzet adjusted his glasses with a quick, practised motion. "That was a ruse, in case your Mr Grady was captured. When we received the photos – and by 'we', I mean the EA, Africa, and Russo-China we met secretly and then brought other nations on board. Then we sent our own people into Can-Amer to verify this information."

He tapped one of the photos. "We've had spies in this country for months. We've seen this factory for ourselves now: Atomic Harmony Devices. It was difficult to find, but we did it. And we've seen other factories."

The whole time he spoke, there was a slight lag as I

worked out what he was saying. Now all of us got it at the same time.

"There are *more* bomb factories?" I gasped. Vera's eyes were wide.

"No, no. That is the only one for nuclear bombs. But…" Mr Buzet frowned; he turned to Ingo and said something in rapid Euro. Ingo responded. He sat unmoving, with his head tipped back against the wall.

Mr Buzet continued: "There are also many foundries, you call them, and factories for the making of tanks, airplanes, and so on."

My voice had gone steely with fear. "They're still in production now?"

"Oh yes. Every day. *Night* and day."

"But she's already *got* Can-Amer," said Vera blankly.

Then we all realized.

"And ships," went on Mr Buzet. "For troops. And others with the big…the platforms, for planes to take off from."

"Ships that can carry planes?" echoed Hal.

"Yes. To the EA, presumably." Ingo's tone was bitter. "When I decided to fight, part of me thought I was just being stupidly noble. Getting involved in a mess that wasn't mine."

"It's all our mess, looks like," muttered Harlan.

"Yes – everyone's," said Mr Buzet. He sketched a map in the dust on the floor. "This is Can-Amer, yes? To the west, there are factories all along here. People are forced to work in them – forced to keep quiet."

His finger traced a line that stretched in a Y from Alaska and the Yukon, then down the coastline of what used to be the Western Seaboard – the home country of four of us in the room. Mr Buzet's finger passed through Sacrament, and I saw Hal wince. A lot of his friends were still there.

"Then over here…" Mr Buzet drew an arc around New Manhattan Island, expanding several hundred miles in each direction. "There are many more factories," he said. "These are mainly the tanks, and the planes. She is gearing up for something big."

"Well, ain't *that* just peachy," muttered Harlan. "Oh, man – *why* couldn't the bitch have tripped when she was running out of here?"

I was asking myself the same thing. I stared at the arc drawn so precisely in the dusty floor.

"Now then, the bomb factory – did you know that these are the *only* nuclear bombs she has?" Mr Buzet tapped the photo showing the two bombs.

"Really?" I glanced at Ingo and saw that he'd already been told this. Two was bad enough, but it was a relief – all of us in the Resistance had imagined dozens.

"Yes, only two, though she is trying to build more. It is a difficult process, it takes much time. But with only two bombs, all of us in World United have decided to take the risk and fight. We can't let her create more and take over the world. We've already attacked to the west."

My head jerked up. "You have?"

"Yes. While our spies gathered information, World

United built planes and troops of our own. In fact, many of us – fifty countries – started over a year ago, with the news of Gunnison's…activities. Now we've come in across the Bering Strait, here."

He drew a short, determined line at the upper part of Alaska. "She was not expecting it. We have troops stationed in hiding in many remote places now. They are attacking her factories there as we speak. And yesterday, troops came up through the Mexican desert and are attacking her holdings along the lower west coast."

It was as if the sun had just come out, yet suddenly I was close to tears. For months, the Resistance had been so alone on this island with Kay Pierce. I pressed my hand to my mouth, and felt Ingo's gaze on me. Vera squeezed my arm, her eyes bright.

"Finally," I whispered. My eyes met Ingo's. There was an emotion in their dark depths that I didn't understand, but he gave a small smile.

"Finally," he echoed.

"Oh, *hell* yeah," said Harlan, grinning. "Go on, Mr Boo-zay, tell us more good news."

A precise smile flickered across Mr Buzet's face. "That is all the good news for now. The rest is…" He frowned and turned to Ingo again; another brief consultation in Euro. "Is *potential* good news," he finished. "Miss Vancour, we need your help."

"*My* help?"

"Yes! We need New Manhattan Island. There are vital

factories along the east coast. We need a place where we can house troops, have an airport. And to our luck, it is the perfect time. The island is already in a state of unrest. We heard this on the wireless before we entered the tunnels."

"Unless things have calmed down?" Ingo said to me.

I shook my head. "We're still surrounded here. And we keep hearing sirens and seeing smoke sometimes." I explained about the executions. There was silence as I described the blood on the platform.

"She lost some support from the Guns with that move," I said quietly. "They're all local – too many people died. Pierce fled the city days ago," I added with grim triumph.

Ingo's lips twisted faintly. "I would too, with Wildcat telling everyone to attack me. You're quite formidable, my friend."

Our eyes met again. I tore my gaze away as Mr Buzet went on:

"Outside New Manhattan, from what we can tell, there is not this division – the military is firmly on her side." He drew a dusty map of the city and tapped the region of the Garden.

"This stadium is near the ports," he said. "We have ships with troops waiting out at sea. What we need is a distraction – some way of bringing the Guns to *this* end of the island" – another tap – "the very northern part. Then our troops can attack with a clear route to the airport. Once we take that, it is all but done. We clean up the rest of the Guns, including any in the tunnels, we destroy the bridges and – *voila!*"

"Destroy the bridges?" echoed Vera.

"Yes. We will not make it easy for Kay Pierce to retake New Manhattan. Supplies, food, will come in from the EA. We will use air strikes against her factories."

Another sweep of his finger, obliterating the Xs in a semicircle around the eastern coast. "A few months, maybe," he said. "If we can only take New Manhattan, we *will* destroy her. This region is vital to her war effort."

He turned to me, pleading. "Miss Vancour, you are the only one who can give us the distraction we need. To put the fine point on it, *you* are Wildcat! *You're* the one who has roused the city to this fury!"

Ingo had been sitting silently. Now he stirred, his expression sharpening to annoyance. "Kay Pierce may have had a little more to do with the city's fury than Amity. It's funny what hanging people on street corners will do."

"Yes, yes, of course! I just meant…"

"Skip it," I said tiredly. I gazed at the rubbed-out Xs. "So…our side's been making bombs too," I said after a pause.

Mr Buzet's tone turned clipped. "Yes. Very unfortunate, but necessary. Pierce will attack; we have no doubt. Even if she were gone, General Keaton and others agree with her goals. We cannot stop them without weapons of our own. It is the only way."

Sadness stirred. He was right; it was all too far gone now.

Even putting Weir in charge might not have helped – from the sounds of it, we'd have had a military coup anyway.

I kept studying the finger-drawn map, envisioning the northern part of the island – what was there. What I needed to do seemed coldly obvious to me.

Yet to cause this sort of distraction meant using people who trusted me. Some would surely die in the process of diverting the Guns' attention. The fact that I'd risk my own life hardly made it better.

I vow to preserve the sanctity of life…

A faint, bitter smile pulled at my mouth. Finally I swallowed back my feelings and looked at Ingo. "What are the tunnels like now? How hard is it going to be to get everyone out of here?"

He shook his head. "The routes are all different – the cave-ins have changed everything."

"They wouldn't have to go very far. Maybe to the 5th Street entrance, if we still have it." Just far enough so that they could slip away without the Guns realizing we were leaving.

Ingo considered. "Yes, that route is the same, pretty much. It's just hard going, is all – rubble everywhere, and unstable as hell."

"It'll have to do." I had a flash of thankfulness that we'd saved half the batteries for the flashlights. I turned to Hal. "Could you get them out as soon as it starts getting dark?" I glanced at Harlan and Vera. "He'll need help to organize everyone and start taking them out."

"Yeah, I can do it," Hal said. I squeezed his shoulder hard.

"Got it," said Harlan, and Vera nodded.

"Dare I ask what *you'll* be doing?" said Ingo after a pause.

I pressed a hand to my throbbing temples. I wanted Ingo to be safe…to be able to go home and see his family again.

But it was too late. He was already here.

Finally I straightened and gazed at his half-ruined face. The dearness of it – of what he meant to me – pierced me and made my voice curt.

"I need your help." I cleared my throat and glanced at Hal. "And some of the snipers, if they'll come."

CHAPTER TWENTY-SIX

SEPTEMBER, 1942

THE TRAIN MOVED THROUGH THE DAWN. Though Collis had a first-class sleeper compartment, he'd spent the night in the easy chair by the window, gazing out at the darkness. Now, as the first bars of sunlight lit the landscape, he shifted uneasily.

It was all so familiar: the long vistas; those barren snowy mountains; even the hawks circling overhead.

Collis's compartment was a medley of stainless steel and curved lines. The bed had a mint resting on the pillow, left by a maid. A silver bowl on the table held fresh fruit.

The last time he'd journeyed to this region, he'd been in a cattle car, crammed in with dozens of others.

Collis looked down and fiddled with the plain gold

band on his finger. For a long time, he'd thought he'd never get married, because what could he offer Amity Vancour? But when he *had* imagined marriage, it had always been to her.

Yet he wasn't sorry about the marriage he'd actually made.

It had been on the spur of the moment. He and Kay had been in his chambers at the palace, hurriedly going over the plans for him to come out here. He'd felt grim from the events of the day. Betraying the Resistance hadn't come at an easy personal price, no matter the reasons. Then he'd seen the look on Kay's face.

She'd gripped her arms in that half-wry, half-vulnerable way she had. She shrugged as if in explanation.

"I'll miss you," she said.

She'd never said anything to indicate that she truly cared about him, though he thought he'd seen it in her eyes. It hadn't even been a decision. Collis had dropped the shirt he was folding and gotten down on one knee on the plush carpet.

"Marry me, then," he said.

"What?"

He'd taken her hand. Unaccountably, his heart was pounding. "*Marry me.* I love you, Kay. I didn't want to, but I do."

She'd given a small smile and slowly kneeled beside him. "Collis, we're both old enough to know better. There's no such thing as love."

He took her face in his hands. He wanted to say, *Do you have any idea at all what I've done today?*

"What is it that I feel then?" he asked hoarsely.

"I don't know. Compatibility? I told you, we're very much alike."

And Collis knew it was true. Probably truer now than when she'd first told him that. He stroked the corner of her mouth with his thumb. "Fine, so I'm compatible with you and you're compatible with me. Is that a yes?"

A strange expression had crossed her face. "We are, aren't we?" she said.

She rose, leaving him kneeling there. She paced across the room. Finally she turned, staring at him. "You really want to marry me?"

"Yes," he said.

"Why? Your job's quite secure — you must know that."

"Forget my *job*. We're two of a kind. No one else will ever understand us the way we do each other." In a low voice, Collis added, "And besides, maybe I want to stop getting kicked out of your bed in the middle of the night. Know what it's like to wake up with you."

Kay came slowly back to him. She crouched beside him again, slim and neat in her blue skirt and jacket. She traced the shape of his broken nose — drew a line down to his mouth.

"It could be good politically," she said. "We'd make quite a team."

Collis had to laugh: his first proposal and this was the reaction. "Is that all?"

"No," Kay said finally.

The expression in her blue eyes had twisted something inside of him. She leaned forward and kissed him, her lips brushing lightly against his. He slipped his hand behind her neck, holding her to him.

"All right," she said when they pulled apart. She cleared her throat. "Yes. I'll marry you."

As it happened, he'd gotten on a train less than an hour after he and Kay had said their vows, so he still had no idea what it was like to wake up with her. But he knew what it was like to talk to her – to be accepted – to not see his own guilt in her eyes.

The train sped across a plain. Collis gazed unseeingly at a herd of grazing elk, hoping like hell that Mac and the others were all right. He hadn't meant for Mac to get shot. The guy was his best friend, or had been.

Maybe Mac would understand.

He grimaced. Like with Kay, he could be himself with Mac…except that around Mac, he was constantly striving to be better. Constantly aware of how far he still had to go.

Sometimes a fellow got sick of never measuring up.

Finally the train slowed. In the distance, Collis could see the munitions factory, its tall chimneys grey against the blue sky. Somewhere behind the spread of trees to the east, he knew Harmony Two sprawled. Its workers laboured in the factory.

He'd already showered and packed. He glanced in the mirror and combed his hair, and then hunched into a jacket; it would be cold outside.

How well he knew it.

Collis shuddered to be so near a camp again, but hid his anxiety. He grabbed his case and made his way down the train's narrow corridor, with its patterned carpet and gleaming wood panelling. There weren't many others aboard – just a few camp officials who greeted him warmly.

When the train had stopped and Collis stepped onto the platform, two men were waiting for him. "Ah, Mr Reed!" exclaimed one. They hurried over; hands were shaken all around. "We're so glad you could make it. The situation is worrying, to say the least."

Collis tried to forget the barbed-wire fences that lay out of sight. But forgetting them was impossible and his voice was brusque. "Don't worry, we'll get defences in place," he said. "If the troops make it this far, we'll be prepared."

As they started off towards the auto, he added, "Can you put a call through to Atomic Harmony Devices for me? I need to set up a meeting with them as soon as possible."

Chapter Twenty-seven

September, 1942

THE TUNNELS WERE IN AS CHAOTIC a state as Ingo had said. He got us to the north side of the city through them anyway.

At exactly six thirteen that evening, an armed group of us entered the Majestic Building – the tallest skyscraper in New Manhattan. High overhead, the giant Harmony flag flew from its iconic needle.

Ingo and the six snipers who'd come were dressed as high-up Guns; from the people back in the Garden, we'd cobbled together grey business suits. The dead Guns in the office had provided the Harmony armbands.

My spine felt slick with fear. I had a small handbag from one of the women; I gripped it tightly. Just as we entered the Majestic's marble and mahogany lobby, I muttered to Ingo, "Are you sure I can't convince you to go back to the tunnels?"

He didn't look at me. His fingers were tense on my arm. "I'm not even going to dignify that with an answer."

Even with the rebellion sweeping the city, nobody dared stop a group of armed high-up Guns. They pushed aside the elevator girl and shoved me on board.

NMB – New Manhattan Broadcasting – was on the top floor. We got inside in a flurry of shouting, with the "Guns" barking that they'd captured Wildcat – that I was going to give an on-air confession.

"She goes on *now*," snarled one of the snipers, slapping his hand on an executive's desk. She flinched and shot me a fearful look. I could see her sorrow that Wildcat had been caught.

"Yes… yes, of course," she said.

Five minutes later, I was in the studio.

The large space had a desk sitting incongruously at its centre. Two shiny black telio cameras – huge, ungainly things on spindly legs – crouched nearby. A woman with a Virgo brooch had been reading the news. She stopped short as we advanced.

A few of our number hustled her aside. "We're commandeering this station! We've got Wildcat. She's making an announcement."

"Do it," a quavering voice ordered. "I've just had a phone call. Keep rolling."

"You're up," muttered Ingo. His fingers slowly left my arm. "Good luck."

I gave a nervous nod and started forward. In the sudden silence, people stood gaping at me.

As if in a dream, I slid behind the vacated desk.

The lights were so bright that I couldn't see anyone's faces; just a pool of darkness, black as the tunnels. One of the cameras had a steady red light. I fixed my gaze on it.

I hadn't planned what I'd say, but somehow the words were there. "I'm Amity Vancour, the voice of the Resistance." I managed a smile. "I guess the face of the Resistance too, now that you can see me. For the past six days myself and a group of rebels have occupied Henderson Square Garden. Now I'm in the Majestic."

It hit me again, forcibly: I was urging people to fight a battle that I doubted they could win, just to cause a distraction.

Ingo would understand exactly how I felt. Knowing he was somewhere out there in the darkness steadied me.

"We're taking this building," I said levelly. "We need to take the whole northern part of the island – the uppermost sections of Capricorn and Pisces. It's vital for the Resistance. Help us! If you've been fighting, this is where to do it."

As I spoke, a stirring came from the shadows beyond the desk. "What the hell…" I heard someone murmur. Someone else gave a gasp that sounded joyful and quickly stifled it.

A grease pencil lay on the desk. There was a backdrop

behind me – a giant photo of New Manhattan. I took the pencil and rose. In the utter silence of the room, I scrawled a V over the city in broad, harsh strokes.

Please, World United, don't let us down.

I turned back to the cameras. I clenched the desk and leaned forward. "V for Victory," I said, emotion thickening my voice. "*Fight* – with everything you have!"

As if coming out of a trance, the director yelped, "Cut! Get the cameras off! Somebody call security, *now*!"

The lights came on. Suddenly everything was hustle, motion. Our group quickly surrounded the set, rifles aloft. "Don't move! Nobody move!"

Ingo came sprinting over. I snatched up the handbag and lunged from the desk. He grabbed my arm, hurrying me along.

Our group rushed out the doors, holding rifles on the studio until the last moment. I caught a mix of stunned and exultant expressions. Several people were crying. Some made covert V signs at me.

As we left, I glimpsed a woman racing to a wall phone.

We made it back out to the elevator. The door to the stairwell was beside it. As planned, half of us took the steps. We were on the top floor – a hundred and two floors up.

But there was a short flight of stairs that led up further still.

"What do you think?" I hissed to Ingo, staring tensely up them.

We'd discussed this – had agreed it was insane, but might be worth a try. Ingo gave me a terrible grin, breathing hard. "Might as well. Let's be fools to the last hurrah."

We pelted up the stairs. The three remaining snipers, as arranged, started racing downwards. With luck, at least some of us would make it out and could rally people from the ground.

The door at the top was locked. "Can you pick it?" asked Ingo hurriedly.

I shook my head. "I don't have anything."

"Stand back."

I took a shaky step or two backwards, and he levelled his rifle at the doorknob. He shot. We didn't wait to see if anyone would come running. Ingo wrenched the door open, and we rushed through.

We were on the roof. The wind had picked up; New Manhattan lay below us, spread out in a golden sunset – so beautiful, despite everything. The famous needle of the Majestic Building spiked above, with the giant Harmony flag stirring in the breeze.

Ingo and I climbed up to the needle's base using a series of metal ladders and found the flag chain. We rattled it downwards. The giant flag made a snapping noise like the sail of a tall ship as it dropped. Its red-and-black swirls were taller than I was.

Before we'd left, Harlan had given me his hip flask. "Take it, Vancour – you might need it more than me," he'd said.

I drew it from the handbag and hurriedly uncapped it. The peaty odour of whiskey floated out. "What is it you say again?"

Ingo knew what I meant. For the first time since I'd seen him again, his smile looked real.

"*Prost*," he said.

I toasted him with the flask and took a quick swig. "*Prost*."

I handed it to him and he did the same, echoing the toast back. Then he poured the rest of the whiskey over the flag in great, sweeping arcs. "*Prost* to you too, you bastard…long may you burn."

The matches I'd brought caught instantly. In seconds, the grey corner of the flag was blazing. As heat poured from it, I felt fierce and giddy at the same time.

"Back up you go," I said to the flag.

It was heavy, but with both of us working the chain we hoisted it again. I knew we should run, try to escape the building – yet for a few snatched seconds we just gazed at our handiwork in awe.

The flames had devoured a small corner already. The blaze was eerily bright against the sunset-streaked sky. Sparks and scraps of burning cloth floated on the wind.

Ingo gave a soft, unbelieving noise. "If this doesn't get every Gun in the city over here, nothing will."

"I almost don't care," I murmured. "It's the most beautiful thing I've ever seen."

* * *

Minutes later, we were running down the stairwell.

The concrete silence cloaked us – the only sound was our footsteps as we spiralled down, down, down. If it hadn't been for a sign on each landing – *97th floor, 92nd floor, 88th floor* – I'd have lost count.

Just past the eighty-third floor, we stopped abruptly. A cry escaped me.

The three snipers who'd gone before us lay sprawled on the stairs. One was Joe, who'd helped empty the makeshift chamber pots. Blood glistened on the concrete floor. There was a streaked red handprint on the wall.

I gaped numbly at them. Then we both started, staring upwards.

The clang of a metal door closing above. A second later came the echo of heavy boots heading down.

Five floors above us? Ten?

I was trembling. We sidestepped the bodies. Ingo's hand was briefly firm under my elbow. We kept rushing down, as silently and quickly as we could, staying close against the wall.

I gripped Ingo's arm suddenly. We froze, chests heaving. "…*on fire*," said a hushed female voice from below. "My boyfriend called me – he said you can see it for miles!"

"You can see riots starting already out the window."

"Are you going to fight?"

The pounding footsteps drew closer. Ingo and I kept going, hurtling one more flight, two, before we reached the speakers – a woman and two men.

They'd gone quiet as they heard us approach. When we came into view the woman's hand flew to her mouth. The men straightened slowly, staring. I realized what we must look like – me with my still-bruised face; Ingo with his scar and gripping his rifle.

"Wildcat?" whispered the woman.

Then they heard the footsteps behind us and flinched. "Can you help?" said Ingo in an urgent undertone.

"We don't want to endanger you," I added. "But—"

One of the men took a step backwards. He was as big as Harlan, with slicked-back hair. "Hey, listen, I don't want any trouble…"

Fire sparked in the woman's eyes. She opened the stairwell door and motioned us in.

"Hurry," she whispered, glancing quickly upwards. "You can take the service elevator. I know where the key is."

Out on the street, the traffic had stopped.

The service entrance led out to an alleyway. A few cigarette butts lay on the ground – some only half-smoked, still glowing.

As Ingo and I emerged from the alley, we saw long lines of autos, their chrome fenders glinting in the sunset. Horns echoed. Shouts churned the air. From somewhere I heard breaking glass.

My emotions were in chaos. I had set this in motion. Now I had to see it through.

Ingo looked as if he knew what I was thinking. He'd been carrying my veiled hat in his inner jacket pocket; he handed it over.

"Come on," he said quietly. "We're too close here to see it – we need to get a few blocks away."

I realized what he meant. I braced myself and nodded. On the street, we joined a tide of people heading north like I'd told them. Some were punching the air, yelling: "*V for Victory! V for Vancour!*"

"*Come and get us, Guns!*" shouted someone else.

Once we got a few streets away, people stood in thick clusters, staring raptly upwards. Some were even perched on the roofs of their autos.

The last scrap of the Harmony flag was still burning.

The flames had already devoured the blood-and-night swirl. Now there was only a long, thin line of grey material left against the Majestic's famous needle, fire consuming it, like a lit matchstick against the sunset.

"Oh, my word, if that ain't just the prettiest sight I've ever seen," murmured a man next to me. He had his hat off, clutched against his chest.

"You're all crazy!" cried an old woman, her voice cracking. "She's brought the Guns right down on us! She's brought 'em right down on us!"

I stared silently up at the still-lit flag, knowing that she was right.

Finally the last of it sizzled and died. Smoke rose up in a beacon. Triumphant cheers rose up. Exultation was on almost every face around me. The horn-honking had faded. There was only this moment, this street, with hundreds of people gazing upwards.

In a soft voice, someone started to sing: *Oh, Appalachia… my Appalachia…* Others joined in, growing louder, their voices carrying in the twilight. The national anthem of the annexed country had been forbidden by death under Kay Pierce's rule.

I heard my own national anthem, that of the Western Seaboard, coming from my lips in a low murmur. My fists were tight.

Most people *were* sane. Most people *were* good. They just wanted quiet, happy lives. They didn't want Kay Pierce's regime to continue. They didn't want what my father had made possible to continue. That was worth fighting for, wasn't it?

It has to be, I thought. *Please.*

Beside me, Ingo was softly singing too — a song in his harsh-sounding native Germanic, which sounded less harsh to me the more I heard him speak it. The song had a quiet lilt — less like a national anthem and more like a lullaby.

Slowly, people went silent. An unearthly hush fell.

I swallowed, studying Ingo. "What was that?" I asked softly.

At first I thought he hadn't heard. He still stood looking upwards, his face expressionless.

"Something my father used to sing to us," he said finally.

I started to respond, then my head jerked up at a crunching, mechanical noise. The rock crusher at Harmony Five came back in a rush of memory. I stared down the street...and my veins iced.

In the distance, a long line of tanks was heading towards us in a rolling wave. They came right over the parked autos, crushing them like tin cans.

I watched dumbly. Back at the Garden, I'd thought that if I were Kay Pierce, I'd bring in outside troops.

Now they'd arrived.

Suddenly, screams filled the air. A roar of fear and rage rose from the crowd. Some people started hurriedly snatching things out of their autos and running off into the side streets.

Others raced towards the tanks, their faces distorted with fury. "*Yeah, come on, you bastards!*" shouted the man who'd said what a pretty sight the burning flag was.

The old woman stood yelling, unmoving in the tide of people, her face frantic. "I told you! I told you! She's brought 'em down on us! She's brought 'em right down!"

Ingo and I moved hastily against the side of a building. He still held his rifle; his long fingers were white as he gripped it. He gave me a wolfish grin that was more like a baring of teeth.

"Well, I'd say that we've caused a pretty big fucking distraction. If World United can't take the airport *now*, they'll never be able to."

I nodded, breathing hard. The grating, crumpling noise

was louder now, battling the sound of screams. The line of tanks looked endless, gleaming away down the long avenue.

"I made this happen," I whispered. "On purpose." I flashed Ingo a quick look and tried to smile. My voice was ragged. "Let's just hope Mr Buzet wasn't full of hot air, right?"

Ingo didn't respond, but the expression on the good half of his face changed as he gazed down at me. Something flickered in his almost-black eyes that made my heart twist. He looked abruptly away and cocked his rifle.

I started to say his name – to put my hand on his arm. I stopped in confused despair. Not now, not like this.

Ingo straightened and studied the oncoming tanks. "I won't insult you by trying to protect you," he said quietly. "Ready to fight?"

I nodded, fear and regret coursing through me. At the same time came a surge of adrenalin that I knew well from Peacefighting. Gazing at the tanks, I slowly pulled off my hat with its covering veil. I tossed it to the ground.

From the handbag, I took out my pistol.

"Ready," I said softly.

CHAPTER TWENTY-EIGHT

WHEN WE WERE A BLOCK away from the first tank, it fired into the oncoming crowd. The explosion took out part of the sidewalk – people were thrown through a department store window as the ground under our feet trembled. Smoke billowed upwards. A woman lay motionless, her eyes open as she lay in a display of household goods.

No. No. I kept running towards the tank, aware of Ingo beside me. We weren't the only ones with weapons. I saw dozens clutching hunting rifles, and pistols that they might have once used for target practice.

The only time I'd ever shot a weapon at someone was the dreamlike moment I'd killed Gunnison. The pistol felt cold in my grip.

I vow to preserve the sanctity of life...

The Peacefighting vow jolted through my brain along with my running footsteps. I gritted my teeth. I ducked into a shop doorway and fired on the first tank, trying for the thin slot of a window. I shot again, and again.

Another missile whined away from the tank. It exploded in a mess of auto parts and people. The street shuddered; I cried out and staggered. Something landed at my feet: a hand. I saw a gold ring on it.

Incredibly, few people stopped. Some of them swarmed the first tank, crawling over it like ants; a man yanked open its hood. The driver inside must have had a pistol – the man staggered and fell back, rolling down the tank's steep shell.

Others climbed onto the tank too, shouting. Smoke billowed past. When I could see again, a second man had reached the hood. He had a two-by-four and appeared to be bludgeoning the driver. Another tank fired; an auto blew up nearby. Its fender slammed into the crowd in front of me.

Panic beat through me; fury; adrenalin. *We have to win. We have to defeat them.* I fought to reach a tank myself.

Suddenly Ingo grabbed my arm. He pointed down a side street, shouting something I couldn't hear.

Troops were approaching – hundreds of them jogging towards us.

"Fall back!" I shouted frantically, waving my arm.

My words fell in a slight lull; some people heard and

joined us. We raced across the street, weaving between parked autos, crouching behind them and firing as the troops spread out into the melee.

The next few hours passed in a blur. When my pistol was empty of cartridges, I grabbed up a fallen rifle. The night-time streets were lit with the throb of neon signs – with burning autos and the flash of artillery fire.

Somehow Ingo and I kept sight of each other. Even when we weren't side by side, I kept an awareness of him. Once I thought I'd lost him – then I spotted him half a block away, shooting over a half-flattened taxicab. As if realizing he'd momentarily lost me too, he looked around and our eyes met.

I went to join him, dashing between bursts of bullets. The sidewalk was buckled and torn. I slumped beside him, panting. The ruined taxicab had been number 55, I saw disjointedly.

"How's your leg?" Ingo asked without looking at me.

"Sore. A cane wouldn't be too practical right now though."

"Lean on me if you need to." He shot again.

All too soon, I'd run out of ammunition. The adrenalin abandoned me too, just when I needed it most, leaving me with only fear and a trembling resolve. By midnight, the Shadowcars had arrived – seemingly hundreds of them, clogging the already-filled streets.

Guns strode into the crowd, attacking people with blackjacks, shoving them into the backs of vans. Some of the Guns went down, but as the night went on it seemed like a smaller and smaller number. Grey uniforms were everywhere.

Worse, they had some sort of hand-held explosives they were throwing: small black things, dimpled like pineapples. Some new device of Kay Pierce's – maybe one that she was producing in those factories of hers. Explosions rumbled through the night, brilliant orange against the shadows.

We're losing, I thought in despair.

Jean Buzet had been going to make his way to the docks and radio the waiting ships once the Guns were drawn to the northern tip of the island. That should have been hours ago.

"Where the hell's World United?" I gasped out to Ingo. "Why aren't we hearing bridges being blown up?"

Ingo shook his head. We were crouching behind a restaurant at that point, peering out from behind a row of trash cans. He'd run out of ammo too by then.

"I wish I fucking knew," he said, his thin form rigid. "Jean seemed to know what he was talking about. That's the only consolation I have at this point."

He was almost trembling. His shadowy figure swiped a fist over his jaw. I shot a glance at him. *What's wrong?* I almost asked. I bit the words back; they were ridiculous. What *wasn't* wrong?

Another explosion came from close by, lighting the trash cans orange. In the brief glow, we saw a group of Guns approaching at a jog. Ingo swore and grabbed my arm.

We scurried down another alleyway. I longed for a friendly tunnel entrance to appear, but there were none this far north.

Ingo and I and a small group of others kept having to retreat, back and back – until finally we found ourselves in Little France, a quiet, village-like neighbourhood on the island's very northern tip.

The houses here were small, made of thick grey stone. Ingo had said once that it reminded him of his home village near Florence. Most of its residents had been found Discordant – many of the houses were vacant, their windows like empty eyes.

We couldn't tell if the Guns were purposefully following us, or just securing the sector. "Much further and we'll be trapped," I whispered to Ingo. My pulse was slamming against my throat. Little France had an ancient wall around it, too high to climb.

"I think we may be already," said Ingo, glancing furtively over his shoulder. "*Shit.* More of them. Quick, in here."

He started for an archway that led to a courtyard. We both ducked back, scrambling, as pistol fire broke out. The group that had been loosely travelling with us had darted in a different direction. The Guns had opened fire on them.

"Run," I panted. "We've no choice."

Ingo grabbed my hand and we pounded through the archway. The world bucked as an explosion came from right behind us, briefly illuminating the buildings ahead.

We went sprawling. I yelped as I hit the cobblestones. Another explosion came, from in front of us this time. I covered my head as rubble pattered around us.

Darkness fell again, along with an eerie deceptive silence – back there in the shadows, the Guns weren't far away. I sat up hastily, struggling to see in the gloom. Ingo lay prone a few feet away.

He wasn't moving.

My heart seemed to stop. I scrambled over. "Ingo! *Ingo!*" I gripped his shoulder, shook it. "Please, please…"

He stirred. "I'm all right – just banged my head," he mumbled.

The relief was overwhelming. He staggered as I helped him to his feet.

A metallic *clink* came from nearby. The dimpled shape looked innocuous against the shadows as it rolled to a stop beside a bakery.

"Hurry!" Ingo gasped.

With our arms around each other's shoulders, we half-lurched, half-dived into the nearest stone cottage. Its windows had been blown out. Rubble lay everywhere; dust clogged the air. The bakery went with a dull, violent *whumpf* – the glow briefly lit the square as debris rained down.

Another explosion thundered. I held back a cry as we were flung against a wall.

Ingo grabbed me, wrapped his arms around me tightly. The world rocked again; part of the ceiling collapsed with a groaning wrench. The sound of cascading rocks and rubble roared in our ears.

Ingo's head was ducked against mine – our hearts beat wildly together.

As silence settled, for a confused moment I thought we'd died, and were in some dark, dusty afterlife.

Then footsteps came in a rhythmic tread that sounded both bored and determined.

"Will you stop wasting those?" said a voice.

"Hey, new toy…hope we'll still get to use them, once we get the scum under control."

A blast rumbled from the opposite end of the square, as if the Gun had whirled and flung another device. A whooping laugh.

"You moron," said the first voice.

I flinched as light erupted in the cottage. A bright spotlight shone in, illuminating the worn stone wall at the back. A blackened painting of a seascape hung on it, I saw wildly.

The spotlight started to move.

Ingo and I were near the front wall. The light glided slowly towards us, showing rubble, broken chairs, fallen ceiling beams. As it angled through a deep-set window, a dark shadow was cast over our corner. We cringed into it.

Trembling, I pressed my face against Ingo's neck. His arms tightened around me as his pulse drummed. I could smell his sweat, with the clean, spicy scent of his skin just underneath.

"No shard of glass this time." His mouth moved against my ear, the words barely audible.

"No," I murmured back. The thought came – confused, inarticulate – that it didn't matter, as long as Ingo was here.

The light licked at the edge of our shadowy corner. It vanished, then swept the opposite wall.

"Anything?"

"Not sure. Thought I saw someone running through the square before."

I kept motionless, my blood pounding.

Ingo's lips stayed on my ear. His breathing ruffled against me: harsh, too-fast. Even through the fear, my heart quickened as his mouth moved slightly – an almost-kiss, tentative against my earlobe.

Had I only imagined it? As the thought flickered past, my mouth moved of its own accord, pressing against his neck in return.

He shivered. We both froze as the footsteps came closer, pausing only a few feet away. Ingo's hand found the back of my neck; he pressed me protectively against him. I tried not to breathe. I slipped my arms tightly around his waist.

The light briefly whipped around the cottage again.

"Well?"

"Nah, don't think so – it's all collapsed."

"Thanks to me."

"Yeah, yeah."

The footsteps moved away.

I was shaking, my mouth still against Ingo's neck. This

was insane. I didn't care. I pressed my lips to his skin again, lingeringly, feeling the beat of his pulse – the same place where I'd once held a shard of glass.

It was as if another explosion had gone off. Ingo buried his hands in my hair and lifted my head. When our mouths met, it was wild, fierce, hungry.

I shuddered and wrapped my arms around his neck, stretching up to meet him as we kissed silently, frantically – felt his arms around me, one hand still buried in my hair, the other roaming my spine, clutching me to him.

We jerked apart as the voices floated back. Breathing hard, Ingo held my head to his chest – poised, listening.

"Okay, let's check the next square. This whole section's walled anyway; we've got it sealed off. If we've missed someone, we'll get them at daybreak."

A laugh. "Yeah, let the vermin sweat. I heard we're not even going to take 'em in – we're just doing a mass hanging tomorrow. Give them something to think about instead of that fucking flag."

The footsteps faded, taking with them the dim glow of the flashlights.

Darkness. Silence. I was sickened by what I had wrought. The image of a mass hanging flashed into my mind. *No.* I couldn't think about it.

But if this was my last night, I knew what I wanted.

Ingo's long fingers stroked through my hair again, bringing my head back to his. I was already craning towards him.

Our kisses were even more frantic than before. His lips

were warm, slightly rough. I could feel the crinkled mass of his scar to one side, the dryness of his mouth there. I didn't care.

Ingo.

I ran my fingers again and again through his chaotic curls. Still kissing me, he dipped his knees and rose – his hands stroked up the backs of my thighs, under my dress, gripped my buttocks.

I felt drunk. I pushed his jacket off his shoulders.

"Here," I gasped.

I pulled him to the uneven floor with me. He cleared it of rubble with a swipe of his arm and then drew me back to him, our mouths hardly leaving each other.

I wanted his clothes off but didn't want to take the time. I tugged his shirt from his trousers ran my palms over the long smoothness of his back. The feel of his skin was breathtaking.

Almost roughly, Ingo rolled on top of me. His body was lean and firm; the warm weight of him felt just as I'd imagined so many times. He kissed my mouth, my cheeks, my neck.

"Amity...Amity..." he murmured. One hand caressed my breast. I caught my breath and held it in place, my fingers linking with his as our hands circled together.

Knowing the Guns could return any second heightened everything – like flying combat. Shivering, I reached for his belt buckle. Ingo raised himself up and helped me, fumbling with his flies. I stroked him, and he gasped out loud.

He touched my cheek in the darkness. "Are you sure?" he whispered hoarsely.

I felt electric, every nerve ending alive. I kept caressing him, feeling his hardness, the vulnerable silkiness of his skin. I turned my head and kissed his fingers.

"Yes – yes," I muttered back. "Ingo, please… I want you…"

He moved quickly, adjusting me. I lifted my hips as he tugged my underwear free. Neither of us undressed more than that. I gasped as he entered me.

It was over in minutes. The feel of him as we moved together – his back flexing under my clenching hands – *Ingo…oh, Ingo…*

From somewhere distant, I heard myself cry out as he jerked against me a final time – held himself there, shuddering.

I swallowed in the sudden silence, dazed. We were both breathing hard. Though Ingo had stopped moving, his muscles stayed taut.

For a long moment, neither of us stirred. Emotion robbed me of speech. I touched the good side of his face in the darkness, gently exploring its long planes and angles. I knew it so well that I didn't have to see him to picture every dip, every curve.

Finally Ingo withdrew. I heard him adjust himself – the sound of him doing up his flies. Without a word, he pulled me tightly into his arms. He pressed his lips against my temple and then kept his head against mine, his body still tense. He was shivering.

"Here," I murmured. I shifted, pulling his jacket over us, and rubbed my hands over his arms.

"I'm not cold," he whispered. "I just…" He trailed off.

I thought I understood. I unbuttoned his shirt and slipped my arms around his waist; pressed myself against his bare chest. He clutched me to him.

Neither of us spoke. Soft chest hairs tickled my cheek. I stroked his back, gradually starting to feel drowsy, despite everything. A deep sense of rightness filled me. It was like that time on the deli roof, only now there was no fear.

Slowly, I felt Ingo relax a little too. His breathing became regular, gently stirring my hair. His arms were warm around me.

We fell asleep that way, with the distant sound of explosions still thudding.

Chapter Twenty-nine

I JOLTED AWAKE WITH THE confused sense of thunder — a low, fierce rumbling that shuddered the walls of the stone cottage.

The stone cottage.

It all came back, feeling like a dream. As the thunder faded I sat up slowly, Ingo's jacket sliding off me onto the dusty floor.

Ingo stood at the broken window with his back to me. A greyish dawn lit the room. His back looked straight and stiff. His fist tapped the sill.

Still feeling disoriented, I watched its movement. I started to speak and then gasped as another drumming of thunder came, so close that it sounded like we were inside it.

Then I realized there was no rain.

The bridges. I scrambled up and went to Ingo's side, gripping the stone sill and craning to peer towards the river.

"World United?" I gasped.

He nodded, gazing in the same direction. "Must be. That's two of the bridges now."

I let out a quick, ragged breath. "Oh, thank you," I whispered. "Thank you." I had no idea who I was even thanking. One of the old gods, perhaps, that the world used to believe in.

"And listen," said Ingo quietly.

I strained to hear, leaning out the window into the pre-dawn. Auto horns honking — cheers. Distantly, a burst of gunfire came too. A victorious firing-off, or some of the Guns still hanging on?

It almost didn't matter. World United were liberating the island. We were no longer alone here, battling this regime by ourselves. I gave a short, weak laugh, slumping against the sill.

"So Mr Buzet wasn't full of hot air after all," I said.

Ingo cleared his throat. "No. I didn't think he was."

A silence fell. Ingo's shirt hung open over his chest. Remembering unbuttoning it the night before, heat swept me — that feeling of rightness again.

Pressing close, I hugged his slim waist and kissed his collarbone. "We've got a lot to celebrate this morning," I murmured, lifting my face to his.

Ingo went very still. For a moment I thought he was going to touch my hair. Then he turned away and swiped a hand over his jaw.

"Amity…"

All at once my breath felt painfully suspended. "What?"

There was a long pause. Finally he exhaled and rubbed his eyes. "I can't do this right now," he said softly.

"Do what?"

"This. Us. I'm sorry."

My mouth had gone dry. "What do you mean?"

Ingo let his hand fall. His tone was hoarse. "Can we talk about this tomorrow, please?"

"No, we'll talk about it right now! Ingo, what—"

"I just…I need some time to process this, all right? Please – can I have that?"

Prickly heat swept my cheeks. I stared at him. "You wish we hadn't," I whispered.

He ran a fist over his mouth and didn't respond.

"You do, don't you?"

"It's not that simple."

I grabbed his arm. "Answer me!"

Ingo pulled away; his voice rose. "*Tomorrow,* Amity! For fuck's sake, give me a little breathing space—"

"Oh, sorry if I'm crowding you! You made love to me! We had sex – right there! And now…what? It was all a mistake?"

"I don't know!" Ingo slumped against the sill, massaging his temples. "I don't know. Oh, hell…"

In the long silence that followed, another distant explosion came – the Gunnison Memorial Bridge, maybe.

"'I don't know' isn't good enough, Ingo." I felt choked with tears, with anger. "Come on, you're a smart guy. You can do better than that."

"Amity—"

"Tell me! What's going on?"

He stiffened. "What's going on is that I need some time, and you seem hell-bent not to give me any!"

I was shaking. "Sorry, pal – you don't get *time* after what happened last night!"

He straightened quickly and gripped my arms. "Fine, you want me to say things I'll regret? *Yes*, it was a mistake! I've been awake for hours wishing I could forget it ever happened! Happy now?"

I shoved away from him, my pulse crashing in my ears. We stared at each other.

"You asshole," I whispered.

Ingo gave a hollow laugh and pinched the bridge of his nose hard. "True," he said. He stood motionless in the dawn glow.

"I'm sorry I've let you down," he said tightly. "Believe me, you're not the only one. I need you to be my friend, all right?"

I need you to be my friend.

It was what I'd said to him that night on the roof. Was this some kind of joke? Some way of getting back at me? But Ingo wouldn't do that.

I'd never have believed that he'd sleep with me and then want to forget it ever happened either.

I couldn't speak. I felt punched. I went to the corner where we'd lain the night before. I could see marks in the dust from our feet, and from where my hand had gripped at nothing, flexing over and over. Remembering how right it had felt – both at the time and lying in his arms afterwards – my chest ached.

Somehow I'd done it again.

The ghost of Collie hovered. No – I refused to cry. I grabbed up Ingo's jacket from the floor. I went back and shoved it at him.

"You may not get to forget it," I said curtly. "We didn't use a proph. I'll let you know if I'm pregnant."

Ingo tensed; he shut his eyes. Then he pulled on his jacket with mechanical motions. "So I was an idiot in more ways than one," he muttered. "Yes. Tell me if you are."

Having to travel through the city with Ingo that morning was a mix of pain and euphoria.

As we learned later, the World United troops had taken the airport and the southern half of the island by midnight – just about the time that the Shadowcars had started arriving in upper Pisces in such force.

Almost every Gun on the island was in Capricorn and Pisces by then. The other ten sectors were liberated by the WU troops easily. By the time Ingo and I were standing at the cottage window in Little France, listening to the bridges being blown up, people at the southern end of the island were popping champagne on street corners while skirmishes still took place only blocks away.

Some of the remaining Guns started trying to leave the city, given orders to retreat by panicked superiors. Others were told to stay, to keep fighting. For hours, battles continued in the last two occupied sectors as World United's troops defeated Pierce's. She'd had twenty tanks altogether. The WU had mortar launchers specially designed to fight them.

Ingo and I got out of Pisces that morning along with thousands of others – the checkpoint leading into Aquarius was now controlled by WU troops. The sign with the water bearer on it had been torn down. A new sign was up: *This way to the free zones of New Manhattan!*

The WU troops wore new blue uniforms. As we passed through, they held out buckets for everyone to discard their Harmony IDs in. A grinning soldier handed out candy to the children.

Despite everything, my heart was singing in that moment. Finally, others were here to help us take care of this. Finally, Kay Pierce's regime was on its way out.

The soldier holding the bucket recognized me and excitedly called his superior over – a woman with gleaming blonde hair.

"Miss Vancour!" She drew Ingo and me over to one side. "You have made it," she said fervently, shaking my hand.

Sidonie Durand, said her name tag. "Congratulations. Burning that giant Harmony flag? Genius!"

I thought of the snipers from our group who'd died in the stairwell. I managed a thin smile.

"Thanks," I said.

"Were you in the Resistance too?" Sidonie asked Ingo brightly, and it startled me to hear the past tense. So many months of struggling, planning. So many deaths. And now it was over with.

"Yes. Ingo Manfred," said Ingo. His expression was drawn. We'd hardly spoken since leaving Little France.

Sidonie shook his hand, hardly flinching at his scar. She smiled at me. "So I suppose you want to know the way to the billeted accommodations, yes?"

At my furrowed brow, she explained, "We've taken over the old Grand Hotel, on Bridge Street. It's the nearest to the airport; our pilots will need lodgings. I heard you were one of the best, Miss Vancour. Were you a pilot too, Mr Manfred?"

"Tier Two," he said after a pause. "European Alliance."

"*C'est magnifique!* There are many of the old EA gang here, so you wouldn't be alone. You'll both be joining us?" Sidonie glanced hopefully from Ingo to me. "We need everyone we can get – Pierce won't waste time trying to get this island back."

No, I almost said. After all that had happened, did I really want to keep fighting? Yet thinking of the gathering pilots, somehow a different answer came out.

"Yes, I'll join," I said softly.

Ingo's eyes were bitter. "I will too," he said finally. "I might as well."

I could hardly look at him. The confused cocktail of pain and anger was too much.

I cleared my throat. "Could you possibly help me find my brother?" I asked Sidonie. "And some friends of mine?"

A few phone calls later, I learned to my relief that Hal was already at the Grand, along with Harlan and Vera – they'd gotten everyone out of Henderson Square Garden safely.

"Would you like a lift?" suggested Sidonie. "I've got the best jeep that the WU offers, right here at your service."

I stood gazing down the recently-liberated street. "You go," I said to Ingo. "I'm going to walk for a little bit."

He drew me to one side, dropping his hand from my arm almost immediately.

"Amity…" he started.

I'd tensed at his touch. "I mean it. I want to be alone," I said quietly. "And, Ingo…I think it's best if we stay away from each other for a while."

He stood motionless. Finally he looked away and gave a soft snort.

"Fine," he said. "I understand."

As I walked through the New Manhattan streets there were impromptu parties on almost every block I passed.

The morning was dawning cooler than usual, giving a fresh tinge to the day. People had brought tables outside, and phono players. I had three glasses of champagne before I'd even reached Sagittarius sector – people kept pushing them into my hand.

Music soared through the air – scratchy, beloved discs that had been kept hidden during Kay Pierce's reign. Despite everything, I relished it. I laughed as a man grabbed me to dance a few turns of a once-forbidden jitterbug, then left me for another partner.

People were gleefully tearing down anything to do with astrology. In Aquarius I saw a water-bearer statue toppled from a fountain as a crowd cheered. The astrology shops looked abandoned, their windows broken; one street was roasting frankfurters over a bonfire of astrology books. In what used to be Sagittarius, a restaurant owner tore down a sign saying *Archer's Delight*.

"It's Frank's Place again!" he shouted, throwing his arms towards the sky.

When I got tired of walking, I took the subway the rest of the way to the Grand.

Here, too, people had been busy – the old signs admonishing people to watch out for Discordants and to listen to Pierce's nightly talk were gone, except for one that had a moustache and horns drawn on her image. They suited her.

I hoped she was scared, wherever she was. I hoped she felt hunted.

When I went up the stairs leading from the subway station to Bridge Street, a flower vendor was giving out free roses. "A pretty flower for a pretty lady," he said with a bow.

I took it with a smile. Yellow — my favourite colour.

The airport bloomed incongruously here, on the tip of the island, but the Grand was still a fine old hotel, only a short walk from its complex. Holding the flower, I jogged across the street when the light changed and entered the hotel's gold swinging doors. People wearing WU uniforms were clustered outside, smoking. They parted when I approached.

"Hey, aren't you…" started one, and then fell silent.

Inside, the hotel was lavish, with red velvet sofas and gilt-patterned walls. Even so, it had a bustling, military air now: a World United desk had been set up near the front of the lobby. A sign read, *Check in here, THEN get your room key!*

I went over. The uniformed man behind the desk looked up. His eyes widened behind his glasses as he took me in: the torn, dirty dress; my smudged arms and face. I was still holding the rose.

There had been a giant zodiac wheel painted on the wall. Decorators were already whitewashing it out. My throat suddenly felt tight. I lay the rose gently down on the desk.

"Pilot Amity Vancour, checking in," I said.

The man gave a slow nod, his eyes never leaving mine. "Welcome, Wildcat."

PART TWO

OCTOBER 1942

CHAPTER THIRTY

"*SCRAMBLE!*"

The shout echoed up and down the hallway. I'd already tumbled out of bed at the first sirens.

"*No,*" I muttered as I yanked on my flight suit. Kay Pierce's bombers would *not* destroy more of this city.

Doors were slamming all over. I wrestled my boots on and raced out of my room without turning off the lights.

Other pilots were running down the opulent hallway too. Some had wet hair, as if they'd just taken showers. Though we were on the fifth floor, none of us waited for the elevator – too slow. We streamed down the concrete service stairs, our footsteps thundering.

As I burst out into the pre-dawn air, I caught sight of

Vera ahead of me. We fell into pace together, jogging the few hundred yards to the airport entrance.

"Where's Harlan?" I panted out. Searchlights were already sweeping the sky, eerily bright against this blacked-out section of the city.

"Not sure – he'd gotten a poker game together. I don't know what floor it was on." Vera glanced over her shoulder at the dark form of the Grand.

Harlan hadn't asked me to join the game, but I wasn't really surprised; he'd asked me a dozen times already these past weeks and I'd always said no. I couldn't even say why I didn't want to. Maybe it all felt too tangled up with my previous life back on the Western Seaboard base, when I'd been so sure Collie was the one – so oblivious to the fact that I hardly knew him.

My capacity for misjudging men wasn't something I wanted to think about.

Jeeps waited at the airport gates, engines already running. We piled into one with several other pilots. The driver barrelled us across the long stretch of pavement. The Firedoves supplied by World United waited in long rows, noses pointed towards the sky as if aching to leap into it. Fitters swarmed over the planes, readying them, warming the engines.

It had been less than a month since New Manhattan's liberation. It was impossible to believe. Surely we'd been billeted here for ever; fighting here for ever. After I'd checked in that first day, I'd only managed a few hours of familiarizing myself with the new planes before the attacks had started. Kay Pierce hadn't let up since.

I'd learned that same day that my brother had become a fitter.

"*What?*" I'd said, staring at him.

"I've signed up," Hal had repeated. We'd been standing on the edge of the airfield, me in my new flight suit and Hal looking unfamiliar in the blue jumpsuit that all the fitters wore.

"How?" I demanded, fear for him sharpening my voice. "You're only fifteen!"

He shrugged, lifting his voice as a Dove touched down nearby, all power and speed. "You can sign contracts at fifteen in the EA, and those are the laws the WU is operating under."

When I didn't answer, he said levelly, "I grew up around planes too, you know. I still remember the preflight sequence. I'm not going to just go home to Ma, with all this going on."

You could die. I didn't say it. He wasn't an idiot; he knew. Behind us, the Dove's engine came to a stop. Finally I sighed.

"All right," I said. "But *you* get to be the one to write to Ma and tell her this."

When I'd signed up myself, I'd expected people to be like they were on the old Peacefighting base: friendly, but with a distance. Instead there was a real, deep camaraderie from the start. Friendships were formed quickly. Maybe it came from fighting an actual enemy, rather than for an ideal. I already felt as if I'd known some of the other pilots for years.

Hal seemed to feel the same. In between battles I sometimes saw him with a group of fitters and younger pilots, hanging out together in a corner of the bar, all of them obviously close.

I'd rarely seen my brother laugh this past year. Now there was a giddy, hyped-up feel in the air, despite the tiredness, the too-frequent deaths from bombing raids and pilots getting shot down.

It felt like you had to grab life while you could.

As we approached the airfield, Vera sat tapping her red-painted nails on her thigh. "There he is," she said suddenly as our jeep slowed.

At first I thought she meant Ingo, and my heart pinched. But when I followed her gaze, I saw Harlan standing by his plane, putting on his helmet.

Vera shook her head. "Hard to know whether I wish he was back at the hotel, or up in combat."

The Grand was always a potential target for bombing. I shrugged. "Well, he'd be cursing a blue streak if he hadn't gotten to one of the planes in time to go up."

"True. And Harlan in a bad mood is a grumpy man indeed."

Our jeep lurched to a halt. We jumped out and headed over to him.

"Those damn sirens interrupted my poker game!" Harlan shouted with a grin over the roar of the Firedoves. He murmured something in Vera's ear and they kissed briefly; then he swung himself up into his plane, his big form nimble.

When I reached my own plane, I clambered onto the wing. The new World United emblem was on each one: an image of the earth with a dove guarding it, wings outstretched.

As I climbed into my cockpit, I glanced around the airfield, at all the rows and rows of planes. Propeller after propeller erupted into whirling fury. The planes in front were already starting to taxi, getting into position in long lines.

My gaze snagged on a tall, thin pilot pulling on a helmet a few rows over.

I looked quickly away and slid into my cockpit.

The sirens changed to short, fierce blasts. The enemy planes were close now. Tess, our squadron leader – a former Peacefighter like all of us, and the highest-ranking Tier One here – jogged down the lines, shouting, "Don't get distracted by the Scorpions! Go for the bombers!"

I waved to show I'd heard and then my focus narrowed to the familiar black control panel. Undercarriage down, flaps up, mixture control to rich. The engine was already grumbling, the cockpit vibrating around me. I gave the primer pump a few quick strokes.

Hal appeared. He hopped onto the wing and helped

strap me in, his dark hair mussed. In the last four weeks his motions had become deft.

"Ready?" he said, raising his voice over the engine.

I nodded and pulled on my goggles. "Thanks, Hal."

He shouted down, "*Chocks away!* Give 'em hell, Sis," he added, briefly clasping my shoulder, and then he slid down the wing and was gone, another blue-suited figure running away across the dawn-tinged airfield.

I slid the hood shut. The Dove wobbled from side to side as I taxied into position. It was a MK12. It climbed faster than my old MK9 and had a higher top speed, but personally I thought we'd lost something on the overall manoeuvrability. I wasn't alone – WU pilots argued the MK12's pros and cons late into the night sometimes. Half loved the newer version and half of us longed for the old ones.

I reached the runway. The plane ahead of me took off, growing smaller in the sky; I counted five and hit the throttle. My Dove's vibrations shook through me; my hand stayed steady as I travelled down the grey river of runway. As it became a blur I drew back the stick and the Dove and I lifted into the sky.

The buildings of New Manhattan swam into view below. They shrunk and angled to one side as I banked, circling for height.

More planes took off after me, over a hundred of us altogether. The old Western Seaboard base had been busy like this sometimes, when everyone's scheduled fights had come up around the same time – but we'd all been heading off in different directions, to fight single opponents.

Now I could see the enemy planes approaching from behind the Statue of Freedom – three bombers up high like bloated birds, and swarms of Scorpions protecting them, a shifting mass against the sunrise. Kay Pierce's air force had the red-and-black Harmony swirl on each wing, with a spiky scorpion at its centre.

I wondered how long it would take before she put her Scorpio sun-sign on every Harmony symbol.

I was in a mile-tall vortex of planes, all of us fighting for height. *Don't get distracted by the Scorpions.* Tess was right – but you still had to get past them alive, and protect your comrades if you could.

One moment I was surrounded only by other Doves. Then a shadow crossed over me: the first bomber was above.

The horizon lifted as I roared higher, Gs tugging at my stomach. A red-and-black swirl flashed in my mirrors. I darted away, keeping my eye on the bomber. Higher – higher. Three more Scorps appeared and I fired on them, pulled back – got a few rounds in on the bomber before I had to swoop away.

Checking your mirrors had never been more vital. My blood pulsed as I tried to keep watch on all positions at once. We'd never realized how easy we had it as Peacefighters, battling only one other plane. Even with cloud cover, you knew they could only come at you from one direction at a time.

A Scorp on my tail – another coming at me from starboard. A Dove sliced past and got the starboard Scorp. The world tumbled as I barrel-rolled and came at the remaining one from behind. *Damn.* Another Scorp. New Manhattan swung back and forth as I tried to evade it and go for the bomber again.

The Scorp was still right behind me. "*Bastard,*" I muttered, my skin prickling with heat. I'd quickly learned how different it was, fighting someone I really thought of as an enemy. Peacefighter pilots had shared a mutual bond. In a strange sense, we'd all been on the same side: the fight for peace.

No more. I might respect these pilots for their skills, but I burned to bring them down. Even worse was the knowledge that some of *them* might have been Peacefighters.

Cloud cover. I dived into it and then banked sharp starboard, trying to lose the Scorp.

Risky, risky, my internal voice chanted as the mist howled past. Far too easy to have a full-on collision in these conditions. Somehow my fingers stayed light on the stick, though sweat slicked my spine.

I burst out of the cloud. No Scorp. The bomber glided below like a whale; further below still was the swirling mass of the dogfight. *Yes!* I dived straight at the bomber – concentrated on getting its fuselage in my crosshairs.

Before I could fire, the Scorp was back, and had brought a friend. I rolled sideways as bullets raked my port wing.

Damn. I dived, tensely watching my engine. No flames erupted – good.

Black spirals as several planes went down, smoke curling darkly over the city. I winced as one of ours crashed on the streets below, hoping the pilot had managed to bail; that no civilians had been hurt. When those sirens went off, they were meant to take cover.

The thought flitted past. I saw a Scorp about to fire on a Dove and got in there first, scattering bullets over the Scorp, my thumb working overtime on the firing button. My weak leg twinged from jamming on the left rudder; I ignored it and screamed upwards after another bomber. Its Scorps were tardy, fending off other Doves.

"All alone? My, what a pity," I muttered.

I chased it over the northern part of the city, ducking in and out of the clouds. I swore as I saw its hatches open – saw bombs tumble out in a terrible slow motion. Gritting my teeth, I dived right at the bomber. I got over it and let loose, then pulled out.

A fireball erupted, blowing a hole in its broad side. At the same instant, puffs of explosions began to scatter up from the streets below.

The damaged bomber was still flying – I could actually see the crew inside. One appeared to be injured; the others were clustered around him. The pilot was looking over her shoulder, shouting something. I hesitated, cruising beside them – glimpsed their panicked faces as they saw me.

I started to fire again…then set my jaw and abruptly peeled away.

Less than an hour after I'd taken off, I landed, out of ammo and low on fuel.

"Check the port wing," I said hurriedly as the fitter – not Hal this time – helped me from the cockpit.

"Will do, Wildcat," he said with a freckled grin.

They all called me Wildcat. I'd decided not to mind, though deep down the label given to me by the press would always sting.

As usual, the adrenalin had left me shaky, too abuzz to stand still. Above, the battle still raged. I paced as I watched it, longing to be back up there.

Several other pilots had landed. One came over – a young English guy with thick russet hair. Despite his obvious weariness, his eyes had laugh-crinkles at their corners.

He put his hand out. "Hello, I'm Percy Allen. I'm a friend of your brother's."

"Amity," I said as we shook. I recalled then that I'd seen him with Hal sometimes this past month, occasionally just the two of them sitting talking at a table.

Percy seemed about to say something, then apparently changed his mind. "Tough up there today. How'd you do?"

"A bomber and a couple of Scorps."

He whistled. "You got a bomber?"

I grimaced, remembering my hesitation. "I didn't down it," I admitted. "But it won't be bothering us again anytime soon. You?"

"A Scorp. It got my fuel tank though. If I hadn't been almost empty…" Percy shrugged.

The fitter brought us strong, hot coffee and toast. I gulped them down, still keeping an eye on the battle, and then the fitter pronounced my refuelled plane ready to go again – the port wing would hold.

"Good luck," I said to Percy. "Don't die." It was the kind of not-quite-a-joke that we always said.

He grinned tiredly. "No, it's too pretty a day to die. And I've got plans later that I'd rather like to keep."

I swung myself back into the cockpit; at the all-clear I taxied into position and took off again. Moments later I'd caught up with the battle and plunged back into its swirling mass.

I fought and landed, fought and landed – four more times that day. Kay Pierce seemed to have a relentless supply of bombers; her Scorps were even worse. I'd learned to hate that spiky scorpion shape almost as much as the Harmony symbol that framed it.

By four o'clock that afternoon, I was in the small cafe near the airfield, resting with my head back against the booth. A meal that I was too jumpy to eat lay in front of me.

Harlan slid in across from me, looking at least ten years older than he was. *Did I look like that too?* I wondered.

"Pretty hot up there today," he said. "Thought I was going to eat dirt once. You eating that?"

"Feel free."

He drew my plate towards him and started to eat. "Only two bombing hits so far though," he went on, his mouth full. "We held the rest of 'em off."

Vera appeared with a tray and sat beside Harlan. She sagged briefly against him, then straightened with a sigh. "We're going out tonight, if the bombing doesn't start up again," she said to me. "There's a place in Midtown that I've heard about."

"Oh no, not one of your terrible music places," said Harlan with a good-natured groan. He shifted to put his arm around her and she nestled in.

"No. One of my *good* music places. Want to come, Amity?"

I nodded without lifting my head from the back of the booth. I'd learned quickly these past few weeks that after a day of full-on combat, sleep wouldn't come until I'd done something, anything, to expend the pent-up energy.

"Anyway, it's damn good to be flying again, even on days like this," went on Harlan. "And, man, these new planes? They are the *business*."

I smiled slightly. "Tell me you're not an MK12 person."

"Um, yes. Have you noticed how much faster they are than the 9s?"

"Twenty-two miles per hour, and have *you* noticed the lack of control on the turns?"

He smirked. "Only if you can't handle the power, girlie."

"Fuck. Off."

Harlan laughed and scraped the fork across the plate, scooping up some baked beans. Outside, another Dove landed. They were coming in fast and furious now – the bombers had all departed or been brought down; the Scorps were heading home.

Where had they come from this time? Rhode Island? Boston? Pierce seemed to have airbases everywhere now.

We fell silent as the medics' truck careered to a halt beside a just-landed plane. I didn't want to watch, but found my gaze lingering anyway as the fitters got the cockpit open.

They lifted out a pilot. I could see her blood from here. I winced.

Vera sighed. When she spoke again her voice was bright, deliberate. "You know what planes *I* liked?"

She glanced at herself in a small compact, rearranged a curl, and then snapped it shut again. "The old Moths. Remember them? My mother took me up in one once, and I was hooked. Forget power. They were just... *elegant.*"

"Which Moth?" said Harlan.

She wrinkled her nose at him. "The Gossamer," she and I said in unison. If you were talking elegant Moths, there was only one.

"The Goss? Wait, you mean the *biplane*? With, like, sheets instead of wings?"

Vera flapped a hand at him. "Some people just don't appreciate beauty."

Harlan gave her a private smile. "Oh, I do."

Tess stopped by our table. "Good work today, all of you." She was tall and straight, a former Peacefighter for Alaska. Her slightly detached, no-nonsense manner was the opposite of Russ, my old team leader. I liked her though. Her blue eyes were very direct. You could trust her.

Tess studied me, her gaze suddenly narrowed. "When's the last time you had a day off, Vancour?"

I shrugged tiredly. "A day off? What's that, sir?" Like the Guns at Harmony Five, all female officers here were "sir". By now, I'd almost stopped making the association every time I said it.

She smiled slightly. "Don't be a smart-ass. Take tomorrow off unless I tell you otherwise. You two as well," she added to Harlan and Vera. "I want you all flying a sortie on Wednesday. We're going to go for one of Pierce's little secrets."

A smile grew across my face. So far, I'd only been defending this island. I'd been longing to go out on the offensive and start obliterating those munitions factories.

"Understood, sir," I said gravely.

After Tess left our table, Harlan held up his water glass. Vera and I clinked ours against it. "Until we can toast with something stronger," he said. "Because *that* is the best damn news I've heard all day."

"All *week*," I said fervently.

"Might even make up for whatever music you're planning to subject me to," Harlan added to Vera.

"You'll like it," said Vera.

"You always say that."

"Well, *Amity* likes my taste in music, anyway," said Vera.

I started to respond, and then stopped – Ingo had just walked into the canteen.

His eyes briefly met mine. He gave the faintest of nods. He went to the line and leaned over the counter. I saw the server's expression stiffen at his scar as he spoke to her. A few moments later he carried a tray over to a table of EA pilots.

As I studied his dark, curly head, I felt empty. If Ingo were really the man I'd thought he was, he'd bite the bullet and ask me if I were pregnant. He wouldn't just wait for me to tell him.

I wasn't, as it happened. I'd found out two days before, after several weeks of tensely imagining what I might do if my period didn't arrive. The relief when it had was tempered with an emotion I couldn't quite express.

Regret, in a strange way, that the worry was over…and with it, the last connection I'd ever need to have with what had happened between Ingo and me.

CHAPTER THIRTY-ONE

VERA TOOK US TO A non-blackout section up in the West Side. The streets pulsed with neon lights and noise.

I tipped my head back as we walked, drinking it in. There was a looseness, a giddiness in the air, even with the near-daily bombings and the rationing that controlled people's lives now. The WU was shipping in supplies to the island as promised, but they weren't inexhaustible, and things like sugar and butter were already in short supply.

No one seemed to care. People took pride in being inventive in their cooking and finding ways around it. Being free from Pierce's rule made everything a lark. Who cared if you had to use lard instead of butter?

Ground troops were being shipped in too. I kept seeing WU uniforms on the streets. The rumour was that we were planning a big push soon, to start snatching back more eastern cities.

"This is it," said Vera.

Carl's Roadhouse, read a flashing blue sign up ahead.

Harlan brightened. "Roadhouse? You mean, cold beer and decent music?"

"Don't say I never did anything for you," said Vera with a grin.

Carl's was smoky and loud inside, with red shades over the lights and a decadent air that suited me fine just then. Two hours later, I was jitterbugging on the crowded dance floor with an African soldier whose name I hadn't caught – telio-star handsome, with melting brown eyes.

His palm was sweaty as he grabbed my hand and spun me, our legs working overtime to the drumming beat. I knew I'd pay for this in the morning with my weak thigh, but didn't care.

Finally, laughing, I collapsed at the table where Harlan sat smoking. He grinned and slid a fresh beer towards me. I gulped down half of it at once.

Cold, sharp, delicious. I'd lost count how many I'd had. The adrenalin from dancing was keeping me from getting too drunk, though I'd reached that happy stage where everyone I looked at seemed as if they must be wonderful people. I wanted to go talk to all of them.

"There is nothing better than beer," I said, leaning

forward. "Nothing on the whole, wide planet. Did you know that, Harlan?"

"I always suspected, it must be said."

Vera was still on the dance floor. Some guy was attempting that move with her where you spin the girl around your legs, stepping over her as you go. She was shrieking with laughter. Harlan shook his head, watching with a smile.

I nodded over to her. "You don't mind?"

"What, her dancing with someone else?" Harlan blew a stream of smoke towards the ceiling. "Nah. I'm no dancer. But I like the music and I like watching her. If I tried it, I'd just drop her on her head."

I'd have guessed he'd be jealous. I sat studying his blunt, handsome features, thinking of all those nights we'd played poker together – how little I apparently knew him, for all that.

It seemed to be a theme. I looked down, my good mood fading, and pushed the beer glass around its ring of condensation.

As if guessing what I was thinking, Harlan leaned back in his seat. His voice turned deliberately casual. "So come on, Wildcat, spill… What's the story with you and Manfred?"

I shrugged, wondering what Vera had told him. "No story. We're friends, that's all."

"He's a hell of a pilot."

"I know."

"Be kind of crappy if he got himself killed."

"What?"

At the alarm in my tone, Harlan glanced over. "You haven't noticed? Vancour, the guy flies like he's got a death wish. He saved my ass the other day, but I'm still in shock that he didn't annihilate himself."

"We all do that," I said. "Take risks to try to save each other."

"Not like this. He flew right at the Scorp that was on my tail like he wanted to crash into it. If the Scorp hadn't gotten away, he would have. He just kept firing. He didn't pull out."

A chill swept me. When I didn't answer, Harlan slowly stubbed out his cigarette in the ashtray. "I tried to thank him afterwards, in the locker room. You know what he said?"

"What?" I said faintly.

"He said, 'Don't bother. It's not like it mattered to me.'"

"He was kidding."

"No, he fucking was not."

I started to answer and stopped. "That's...not Ingo," I said finally.

"Thin guy, face like it's half-melting? About six-three?"

"Stop it. I mean, he can be acerbic, but—"

"Knock it off with the ten-dollar words. Give me the nickel version."

"He can be sarcastic," I said. "But he's kind, Harlan. He's a good guy."

Harlan studied me in the dim, smoky light. "We thought Collie was a good guy too," he said.

My voice shook. I hated that I was having to defend Ingo – hated it even more that I'd been having the same thoughts. "That's unfair."

"Is it?"

"Yes." Despite everything, the answer came immediately.

I fell into a tangled silence, staring at the quickly-shifting dancers. All I could see of Vera through the crowd was a flick of her green skirt. I thought of the weight of Ingo's body on mine – the way he'd shivered afterwards and clutched me to him so tightly.

Confusion throbbed. I drained my beer. "You know what? This evening isn't helping to take my mind off things any more," I said.

"Fine, I'll shut up," said Harlan.

He did, too. He started talking about the MK12 again. I fell into the argument gratefully.

We were just at the point where we were scrawling diagrams on paper napkins when Vera half-danced back to our table and dropped into Harlan's lap.

She squealed as he stood up suddenly with her in his arms. He kissed her and put her down in the chair.

"More beer," he said, and set off for the bar. He turned, pointing at me while he walked backwards. "You're still wrong!" he called.

Vera smiled after him, then studied one of the drawings. She shook her head. "I have no idea which side of the debate this is meant to show. How much have you had?"

I started to say something joking. For some reason it died on my lips. I hesitated and looked down, rubbing at a faint spot on my dress.

The music changed from swing to boogie-woogie and the crowd whooped in approval. On the bandstand the pianist's hands were pounding the keys.

"What is it?" asked Vera, watching me.

I gave up pretending that I cared about the spot and cleared my throat. "Vera, have you ever slept with someone, and then…everything changes?"

Comprehension flowered over her face. She touched my arm. "You and Ingo?" she whispered.

The words felt lodged in my chest, hard to get out. "Last month. I thought…I was so sure we both felt the same way. And then the next morning, he said it had been a mistake. We've hardly spoken since."

"Oh, Amity…" Vera breathed.

I hated the pity in her eyes – hated that my own were suddenly prickling. I forced a shrug. "I'll live. I just wish I hadn't been such an idiot."

"Some men are like that," she said after a pause. "The second they get you in bed, forget it. But…" She trailed off.

"What?"

Vera traced a finger over the tablecloth. "Well, I hardly know him. But you two have been through so much

415

together… I don't know. It seems strange." She studied me. "How was it?"

I gave a bitter laugh. "Wonderful."

"Too bad," she sighed. "At least if he was lousy in bed…"

"Anything but. Unfortunately." I scraped my hair back. "It just…it felt so right. I don't understand how I could have felt that way unless he did too."

"I don't know." From Vera's doubtful expression, it was eminently possible.

I miss him all the time – every minute. I barely managed not to say it. Holy hell, how much *had* I had?

I made a face, irritated with myself. Forget Ingo. I was here to have a good time. "I'm going to go dance some more," I said.

Before Vera could respond, I pushed my chair back and stood up. Harlan was just returning with more beers.

As he put them down, warning sirens split the air.

I sucked in a breath, taking a pointless step backwards as I stared at the ceiling. Vera jumped up, her eyes wide.

"Oh no," she gasped.

The lights came on as the music stopped mid-bar. Suddenly the air throbbed with urgency. The musicians hastily started packing up. All around us, people were grabbing their things and rushing for the door.

Harlan shoved the beers onto the table, slopping them in his hurry. Then he snatched a glass back up and gulped most of it down at once.

"Come on," he said, reaching for Vera. He took my arm too, and we wrestled our way from the club, Harlan using his broad shoulders for leverage.

Outside, we paused briefly with the crowd streaming around us, watching the spotlights sweep overhead. I could hear the heavy approaching drone of bombers. Lights started going off all over the city, patches of buildings going dark.

"Not again," I muttered as I frantically searched the sky. "How many bombers does she *have*?"

"Too many. *Damn* it," said Harlan. We were at least five miles from the base.

"We're off anyway, remember?" said Vera. But her face was tight with the same frustration. You couldn't be a fighter pilot and not want to get up there when you heard that noise.

The whine of an incoming bomb. Fear spiked. As we ran for the nearest shelter, I staggered, paying now for my dancing, and Harlan put his arm around me, helping me along.

Air raid wardens wearing miners' hats had appeared. "This way!" called one, beckoning people to the stairway for the 72nd Street subway station.

Just as we reached it, the world pitched sideways and I screamed, slamming against the wrought-iron railing. A drugstore a few buildings down erupted in a burst of brick and glass. Panting, I ducked my head as rubble pattered around us. Shouts filled the night.

"*Medic! Medic!*"

"Someone's hurt!"

"Hang on, sir! We'll get someone there as soon as—"

Another incoming whine. A hand gripped my arm. "Come on!" said Harlan, and then he was hustling both Vera and me down the stairs, practically carrying us.

Down, down. The lights were on once we got below ground, though they were fizzing and flickering, giving the scene a nightmarish, slow-motion quality as the streams of people running down the stairs with us went in and out of view.

Finally we reached the lowest platform. I sank thankfully onto the cool tiled floor. Harlan and Vera sat next to me. The small space was crowded with people, some in their nightclothes. A little boy wearing a bathrobe clutched a stuffed tiger. Above, the bombs still distantly rumbled.

Vera pressed against Harlan. "Must be nice to be so big and strong," she said shakily.

"Not big and strong enough," he said, scowling upwards towards the invisible bombers.

Suddenly I noticed a cut on Vera's cheek. "Are you okay?" I asked, leaning over Harlan and touching her arm.

"I…" She pressed a hand to her face and gave an uncertain laugh at her reddened fingers. "Fine. I think. Oh, I hate Kay Pierce. I hate her so much." There was a reedy note to her voice – Vera, who was as unflappable as they came.

Harlan drew out a handkerchief and dabbed at her

wound, his large hand gentle. "Hey, you're all right, sweetheart," he murmured. "You're all right."

He seemed unnerved himself suddenly. He pulled her onto his lap and held her close, burying his head against her neck. He whispered something and she nodded, her eyes shut tightly.

I swallowed and turned my head, gripping my elbows. Some of the air raid volunteers were passing around sandwiches, hot coffee. I wondered if they kept the coffee ready at all times, or if they made it specially as soon as they heard the sirens. *No, dear, I can't go to the shelter just yet – the coffee hasn't brewed.*

I was going crazy. I managed a smile and accepted a cup. It was strong, surprisingly good. I sipped it from the tin cup slowly, then sighed and leaned against the tiled wall, listening to the rumble of the bombs.

Pierce had taken us by surprise this time, all right – she didn't usually attack twice in one day.

I flinched as the lights went out. Everyone gasped. As the darkness pressed down, the floor rumbled with an explosion from above and the little boy started to cry.

A moment later the lights flickered and came on again. I released an unsteady breath and gazed down into the blackness of the subway tunnel. And despite myself, I remembered those weeks spent exploring the ancient network with Ingo.

Where was he now? At the Grand, or up in the air?

I hugged myself. Up above, the bombs kept falling.

CHAPTER THIRTY-TWO

"MISS?"

Someone was shaking my shoulder. I blinked. A blanket had been draped over me at some point and I clutched drowsily at it.

One of the wardens was there, holding a flashlight. "The all-clear siren just went," he said. "You can go home now."

I nodded. I sat up stiffly and stretched. Harlan and Vera were asleep too and I nudged them.

"Hey," I said. "It's over."

Ten minutes later, we were making our way up the stairs with the others – a long, trudging line of us in creased clothes. The coffee-and-sandwich ladies carried empty urns.

An odd normality had descended back over everything. It wasn't the first air raid everyone had been through – I suspected it wouldn't be the last. People talked in undertones of prosaic things. I heard a woman fretting that her dishes had been unwashed when the sirens began.

"We still have a day off, don't we?" said Vera drowsily. She carried her heels in one hand.

Harlan nodded, his thick hair tousled. "Breakfast somewhere," he said. "Then sleep. My room."

Officially, pilots weren't supposed to share unless they were married. Unofficially, Vera was in Harlan's room every night, or he was in hers. I started to say something, then my eyes widened – a familiar dark head was a little way ahead of us, moving upwards.

What was *he* doing here?

"Listen, I'll see you both back at the base," I said, frowning. I started to jog up the stairs. "Thanks for the night out," I flung over my shoulder.

"Hal!" I called as I caught up with my brother. He turned, his eyes widening. For a second he looked older than usual, so that I thought fleetingly that I'd accosted a stranger.

Then he smiled tiredly. "Hey, Sis."

We fell into step together. He was wearing nice trousers – a sports jacket.

"What are you doing here?" I said in confusion. "I thought you were back on base."

He shrugged. "Had the night off."

"So where did you go?"

"Dancing."

"*Dancing?* Since when?"

The tips of his ears were reddening. "I like dancing," he said defensively.

"I didn't even know you could."

"It's not exactly difficult."

"And anyway, dancing with who? You mean you were in a club?" We'd just emerged into the grey light of pre-dawn. I stopped short, the questions fading as we took in the street.

Several buildings had taken hits. Bricks and broken glass were everywhere. A film of dust lay over the parked autos. The dull scrape of concrete against concrete came as workers cleared the debris.

"Shit," whispered Hal. "You think she was trying for the water tower over on Peterson?"

"Maybe," I said grimly. "Or maybe she's just trying to flatten morale."

I felt shaken. We started walking again, making our way down the rubble-lined street. Remembering the shouts for medics the night before, I stopped the first warden we saw.

"Was anyone hurt?" I asked urgently.

"Yes, a few injuries – no deaths though. Lucky, given the state of this." He nodded at the street, distracted but kind. "Don't you worry, miss – our pilots are the best. They'll keep protecting this island, no matter what."

I nodded, aware of Hal's sudden, privately amused glance at me. "Thank you," I said. "That makes me feel a lot better."

"I don't think her plan to destroy morale is exactly working," Hal said as we continued down the street.

He was right: people looked tired, but were going to work as usual. A bookstore had taken a blast – hardcover volumes lay all over the sidewalk. Passers-by were picking them up and neatly stacking them back inside the front window.

Pride stirred in me. For the first time, I realized how deeply I'd put down roots in New Manhattan. You couldn't keep these people down, not for long. Kay Pierce hadn't been able to do it with her executions, and she couldn't do it with her bombings either.

Hal and I turned onto Ridgemont, where we could catch a bus. Suddenly the buildings all looked normal, as if nothing had happened.

I glanced at my brother. "So you didn't answer my questions," I said after a pause.

"I was hoping you'd forget about them. Ma."

"No such luck. Were you in a club? And who did you go with?"

He looked exasperated. "*Yes*, I was in a club. And I was out on a date, all right? If you must know."

My lips lifted in a surprised smile. "Really?"

"Yes, really."

"Was it your first date?"

"No."

"*No?*"

He rolled his eyes and jammed his hands in his trouser pockets. "Will you just drop it, already, for Pete's sake?"

I halted in my tracks, suddenly spotting something. Before Hal could stop me, I tugged his shirt collar down. A fading hickey was on his neck. He jerked away. "Hey! Get *off*."

"Halcyon…Vancour!" I gasped. I grinned. "Do I need to give you a lecture about always using a proph?" It would be rich coming from me, but I didn't tell him that.

His cheeks were blazing now. "Oh, holy hell, please don't."

"Are you going to tell me who it is?" Something in his expression made me add, "He? She?"

Hal rubbed the back of his neck. "He." His eyebrows drew together as he glanced at me. "Do you mind?"

I slowly shook my head. "No. Of course not." I was surprised but not shocked. On some level, maybe I'd already known.

We reached the bus stop. After a pause, I nudged him. "So who is he?"

"A pilot."

A memory stirred: the pilot I'd talked to earlier. He'd said he had plans he wanted to keep. "That friend of yours from England?"

My brother gave me a startled glance. "Yeah, Percy. How'd you know?"

"I met him earlier; he came over and said hello. He's good-looking," I added. "How long have you two...?"

Hal gazed up the street as if longing for the bus. "About a week," he said grudgingly. Then he looked at me and hesitated. "I really like him, Amity. I can talk to him – you know?"

"Talking's good. I bet getting the hickey was nice too."

"You are such a jerk." But he snorted out a laugh. He leaned against the side of the bus stop and looked down, playing with his cuffs. "I've liked him since I first met him," he admitted finally. "Doing his straps up was...kind of embarrassing."

I stifled my grin. "I bet." Doing a pilot's straps meant a lot of contact near the groin region. "So how old is he?"

"Eighteen. Barely."

"So he's more than two years older."

"Good for you – you can subtract sixteen from eighteen."

"You're not sixteen yet."

"Almost."

The bus's high, curved lines loomed into view then. We showed our WU passes as we climbed on board – as staff we got free travel around the city.

Hal and I took a seat. "So where's Percy now?" I asked as the bus started down the street with a lurch.

"On base. He had an early call. I stayed out with some friends a little longer – then the sirens went."

Thinking of the wildness of Carl's Roadhouse, I grimaced slightly. "Okay…I have to do the Ma bit now."

Hal slapped his hat against his hand. "You already *have* been, for crying out loud."

"Look, I haven't asked you this before, but…you're not even sixteen. Are you drinking?"

For the first time, real anger flickered across Hal's face as he studied me. "I've been doing a man's job, if you haven't noticed."

"I've noticed, and you didn't answer the question."

"Yes, I have a drink sometimes. Back off, Amity. You did a lot worse at my age, so don't pull the 'it's illegal' crap."

"Hal—"

His voice was low. "I could die any day and you know it. No one cares that I'm fifteen when I'm out there working on the planes and dodging bombs. Are you seriously going to tell me that I can't go out and have a few beers with my friends?"

The bus stopped. Some people got off; others got on. We trundled away from the kerb again.

"Okay," I said.

Hal looked at me, his brow furrowed. "Okay what?"

"Okay. You're right."

He smiled slightly, looking down at his hands.

"Thanks," he said.

The bus travelled through Timmons Square. In the pale dawn, the famous theatre district looked slightly seedy, like the aftermath of a drunken party. I started to say something else, then noticed Hal's expression. He was gazing down at Dwight's silver ring, his fist tight.

"What?" I said.

His voice was stilted. "You know, um…when I went and called Collie on the wireless…I know that was really bad judgement."

I went still. He looked up, his eyes pained. "I think maybe I felt like you did when you shot Gunnison," he said roughly. "I never understood it before, how you always said it was like a dream. But I just…lost it. I didn't care. It was like I was outside of myself, watching."

He sighed. "Anyway…I know it was a stupid thing to do. And that Dwight…what happened to Dwight…" He faltered. "You told me it wasn't my fault," he said finally. "But we both know it wouldn't have happened otherwise."

I hesitated. "Were you and Dwight…?"

"No," said Hal softly, playing with the ring. "But he knew about me. We talked a few times."

After a pause, I said, "Listen, Mac always thought you were one of the steadiest kids he ever met – you know that, right? He'd never have let you work for the Resistance otherwise."

Hal looked quickly at me, his face vulnerable. "Yeah?"

"Yeah. And you're right; you're doing a man's job now. Doing it well." *Dad would be proud,* I wanted to say, except that mentioning Dad that way was still too hard for us both.

Hal exhaled and let his hand fall from the ring. "Thanks."

A few blocks passed. Skirting Centre Park, Kay Pierce's abandoned palace came into view, now the headquarters for World United.

Hal said, "I heard back from Ma."

I glanced at him – then realized he meant in response to the letter he'd written about Dad.

Apprehension touched me. "What did she say?"

"Here, see for yourself."

He dug a hand into an inside jacket pocket and pulled out a letter. I recognized Ma's curly handwriting. The mail service was still irregular. The phone service was even worse; you could only make calls within New Manhattan.

I stalled for a second, studying the envelope: *Halcyon Vancour, c/o World United, Free Zone New Manhattan.*

Then I lifted the flap and pulled out thin sheets of paper.

Dear Hal,

It was so good to hear from you and know that you're safe and well, and of course I was as thrilled as the rest of the world about the liberation of New Manhattan. I still can't help worrying about you, we hear about those terrible bombings, but I know you're a sensible young man and of course your sister is there too, which eases my mind greatly.

I'm very sorry not to have responded to you sooner. I started to so many times, but was uncertain whether a letter would reach you in your previous circumstances and there were things I didn't want to commit to paper if that were the case. I must say that I still feel somewhat the same, even though New Manhattan is Free again.

My darling Halcyon, I think that for now I will just say to you that your father was a good man, but flawed. As we all are. I loved him very much and never stopped, no matter what he did. When I see you in person again, I will try to explain more. In my mind, he was never completely to blame.

Please write again and tell me all about what you're doing. Amity says in her letters that you're a very good fitter and that the pilots depend on them...

It went on from there. I stared at the third paragraph. *In my mind, he was never completely to blame.* What exactly was Ma talking about? Dad throwing the civil war fight? His affair with Madeline? Both, neither?

Hal gazed out the bus window, his chin on his fist. "So *that* clears everything up just dandy, huh?" he said gloomily.

I made a face and refolded the letter, curious despite myself as to what Ma could have to say...and hating the flutter of hope that came with the wondering. I wished that Hal had never mentioned any of it to her.

"Yeah. Crystal," I said finally.

CHAPTER THIRTY-THREE

KAY STOOD IN JOHN GUNNISON'S old office at the Zodiac and gazed out at the mild autumn day.

She'd never thought to find herself in Topeka again, much less Johnny's old domain. She wouldn't have come back here, but Kansas had no important factories and was too far from World United to be in danger.

World United. Kay's fingernails bit at her elbows.

When she'd fled New Manhattan, Kay had at first planned only to stay away until Vancour was captured and things cooled down. The news that had come instead stunned her.

She'd been in a hotel in Baltimore and had sunk slowly onto the bed, clutching the phone's black receiver to her ear as the Head Gun frantically reported World United's attack on New Manhattan.

No, thought Kay, dazed. This could not be happening. "Fight!" she'd shouted. "You've got to hold it!"

Less than two days later, New Manhattan had been "liberated".

The thought of her lost capital city sent hot needles pricking across her skin. The unexpected fighting force that had only recently attacked her holdings in Alaska and along the south-west coast now had a beachhead to the east too.

"We'll get the WU out of there, don't worry," Keaton's crackling voice on the long-distance line had said grimly. He was currently out west, battling World United's other troops. "That island's vital."

Airports in key surrounding cities – Baltimore, Boston, Philly – were quickly made into bases. The Can-Amer air force had been gearing up for months, preparing for Black Moon. Now Kay's planes were battling above her own soil. Liaising with Keaton, she'd been orchestrating attacks on New Manhattan for weeks.

But World United's air force was already ensconced there, along with the gathering troops. Though Kay had ordered almost daily bombing raids for nearly a month, the WU pilots had so far managed to hold the city. They were skilled, the best of the best – former Peacefighters, no doubt. Kay thought of Amity Vancour and wanted to throw something.

At first the WU pilots had merely fended off her strikes against the island. Then more planes had arrived from the EA and they'd begun attacking her eastern holdings. For the past ten days, the whole region had become too unstable for Kay to remain in. Bombing raids – signalled by singing sirens and the terrifying whistling of incoming missiles – had come frequently, targeting munitions factories, railroads, shipyards.

She pressed her forehead against the glass and watched a bus glide down Zodiac Avenue. Here in Topeka, two thousand miles away, it was as if there was no war at all.

She hated being back in this place.

Deliberately, Kay straightened and turned, taking in the ornate office with its heavy wooden desk and gilt murals. Her office now. She'd have thought herself a coward if she'd used any other.

Strange to recall how much she used to love coming in here and giving Johnny her reports, back when she'd first been appointed Chief Astrologer and had strode down the Zodiac's corridors in her high heels, on top of the world.

One mural showed a golden archer, half-man, half-horse, shooting an arrow upwards. Kay's muscles hardened. All at once she saw again Gunnison standing against that wall, a solid man with blond hair greying at the temples. *I bet you've done this a lot, haven't you, Kiki?*

From his grip on the back of her neck as he pushed her downwards, it hadn't been a choice. Someone could have walked in any second. She'd found it exciting. The most powerful person in the world, and he couldn't wait to have her.

That's what she'd told herself anyway.

Kay shivered and then hated herself. Moving suddenly, she grabbed up the phone. She dialled. When a voice answered, she said, "I want painters up here. Now." A pause; she tapped her fingers on the desk. "I don't care! *Any* colour."

When the painters – two men in white jumpsuits – arrived, she took a paint can from them. *Devon Cream*. She chipped a fingernail prising open the lid.

"Madame President, we'll do that! And we haven't put down drop cloths yet…"

She ignored them. They fell silent as she grabbed a paintbrush and swirled it in the can. Paint dripping onto the carpet (*good!*) she slapped the brush against the wall, obliterating the centaur's tail. Another wild stroke, and part of his back vanished. She kept on and on, her motions frenzied, craning on tiptoes to reach the archer's bow. The painters watched mutely, not daring to comment.

When she'd finished, faint gold markings still showed through. Something had been exorcised all the same. *Take that, Johnny.*

Kay let the still-dripping paintbrush fall to the floor.

"Black," she said. "I want this whole wall black. And then a golden Scorpio mural. With stars."

* * *

"We have to do it," Kay said into the phone against her right ear. She had a receiver to each one, carrying on a double conversation. Keaton's voice – once so reassuring and confident – was starting to sound hounded.

"We're trying, Madame President. We've lost dozens of bombers; even more Scorpions. We're training new pilots as fast as we can, but—"

"Black Moon won't be compromised, will it?"

Silence from the other end.

"It can't be," Kay whispered. Her gaze flicked to the new mural. The scorpion's spiky tail glinted, yet in her mind's eye she could still see the archer…and Johnny standing there.

No. She was the powerful one now. Kay saw again the mental image of a mushroom cloud against a darkened moon and steeled herself from it.

"Madame President—"

"*Listen to me,*" Kay interrupted. "We are launching a nuclear strike against the European Alliance. The bomb will drop on Florence during the February lunar eclipse. And then our ground troops will move in. We'll take the EA. From there, Africa. From there – you know the plan! Black Moon *will* go ahead."

Keaton said levelly, "If you give me the order when the time comes, I'll do it, Madame President. But it's vital that we defend our own soil. From our intelligence reports, they very likely realize that we only have two nuclear devices at present—"

"*I know!*"

"So if we use one before their troops are defeated, they'll redouble their efforts – do anything to destroy you! Madame President, we *must* reclaim New Manhattan and protect our holdings to the north."

Kay squeezed the phone receiver to her ear with her shoulder and slid open her desk drawer.

She pulled out a copy of the Black Moon chart. Her eyes flicked over it.

She collected herself and spoke into the other receiver. "Benedict, did you hear some of that? General Keaton needs more planes as soon as possible."

The new voice was static-y. "We're putting a rush job on the new factories, Madame President. But those three we've lost in the Western Quarter have hurt us. And their troops are still advancing."

"Stop them!"

"We're trying."

We're trying had become Kay's least favourite words. "Liaise with my husband about fortifying the holdings to the far north," she said. "Mr Reed is authorized to act on my behalf."

"I have been, Madame President. Mr Reed has been most helpful – a true benefit to our Harmonic society."

After Kay hung up both receivers, she studied the chart again, gently touching the spiky M that was Scorpio in the ascendant. There was nothing to astrology, of course, not really. But it was comforting anyway.

Fate didn't help people who sat back and waited for it, though. Keaton was right: they had to get New Manhattan back. Without that crucial toehold, the WU's eastern forces would fall.

As Kay put the chart away, she wondered what Collis had learned from Atomic Harmony Devices. Thinking of the nuclear weapons factory buried deep in the Yukon, she shut the drawer sharply.

Please, let him have good news, she thought.

"Wait for me. I'm going out," Kay told her bodyguards a few days later. They'd just reached her private rooms. The two men nodded and posted themselves outside the double panelled doors.

As Kay entered the suite, she relaxed a little. In this matter, she'd faltered. She could not – would not – set foot ever again in Johnny's private chambers. She'd chosen instead the most lavish suite in the Scorpio dome and refused to chide herself for it.

She got changed quickly, ignoring the dozens of expensive, tailored outfits in her closet and choosing instead a plain skirt and sweater, like a credit-an-hour secretary might wear.

Looking in the mirror, she carefully unpinned her curls. She combed out her hair, then tied a scarf over it and reached for a pair of sunglasses.

A knock came. Kay looked apprehensively towards the

front room; her schedule was supposed to be clear. She hurried to open the door.

"What—" she started, and then broke off, surprise and an odd buoyancy rushing through her.

Collis stood there. He raised a wry eyebrow.

One of her bodyguards said, "Sorry, Madame President. We weren't sure whether—"

"Mr Reed doesn't need your permission to enter," Kay said.

She ushered Collis in and closed the door. He'd clearly come straight from travelling – he wore rumpled chinos, a creased blue shirt. He put his suitcase down. It was the first time she'd seen him since the day they'd gotten married.

"Hello, Mrs Reed," he said softly. He tossed his jacket aside and drew her to him. He bent his head to hers.

With no thought, Kay pressed close, twining her arms around his neck. When the kiss ended, she gazed at him with her hands on his chest, frowning. She'd missed him, yet now that he was here she felt flustered somehow; irritated with herself because of it.

"I'm keeping my own name," she said.

Collis gave a small smile. "Fine." He kissed her again. It felt like giving in to let herself enjoy it so much.

When he drew back, he started to say something, then looked her up and down. His mouth quirked. "What's this?" He tugged lightly at the scarf.

She'd forgotten her outfit. Her chin jutted up as her neck heated. "I was going out."

"Like that? Madame President?"

She pulled away. "What's the news from Atomic Harmony Devices, Collis?"

He sighed, his faint teasing air fading. "It's detailed. Basically, the answer is 'not yet'."

"You're sure they're not fobbing you off?"

"Yes. I'm sorry."

Kay wanted to swear, to kick something. She walked briskly to the bedroom. But when she picked up her sunglasses, she just stood playing with them, looking down. Collis followed.

If he laughs, I'll kill him. "I go out sometimes," she said curtly. "Like this, so no one can recognize me. I just... like to walk, when I'm feeling blue. Look at places I used to know."

He didn't laugh. His changeable eyes met hers in the mirror – forest green in the sunlight angling in from the window. The understanding in them reassured her a little.

"It's silly," she said.

"No, it's not."

Collis glanced down at his travel-creased clothes – much more casual than what he usually wore. He pulled off his tie and undid his collar button; rolled up his shirtsleeves. He took a pair of sunglasses from his upper shirt pocket, then mussed his always-immaculate hair.

"What do you think?" he said.

* * *

As Collis told her what he'd found out, they walked down a busy Topeka street with the bodyguards following half a block behind.

"They can't make any more bombs faster than they're already doing it." Collis had his hands in his trouser pockets, his fedora pulled low.

Almost two years ago, as a black market astrologer, Kay had walked this same street after being released from her arrest, terrified that she might still receive a death sentence. The memory flitted past.

"But they have everything they need," she said tightly.

"Not quite. They need more yellowcake."

"I thought they had whole storehouses full!"

"They still need more."

Collis explained what he'd learned as they skirted the edge of Pierce Park: yellowcake, made from the raw uranium ore mined at Harmony Five, needed to be treated still further to extract the metal needed to make a nuclear bomb.

"It's not an efficient process, apparently," he said. "Just getting a small amount of uranium takes tons of yellowcake. The two bombs they've got now were years in the making."

"I can't wait *years*."

"No. But it'll be another few months, at least."

They'd reached the graceful arch that was the Bradford Bridge. They stopped halfway across it, leaning against the railing. The wind sang in the wires above, barely audible over the traffic.

Kay tapped the railing. "What if I make the mine increase production?"

Collis shook his head. "It's already working to full capacity. The ore isn't a very high grade – it's why the ancients didn't bother with it." He contemplated the Kansas River glumly. "Too bad that the Western Seaboard mine depleted so quickly."

Before they'd destroyed themselves, the ancients had mined almost all the world's uranium. The discovery of traces of the mineral in a dusty Western Seaboard town had been why Johnny seized that region. But there, too, the ancients had plundered the mine before him. The Harmony Five mine was the only one Kay had.

"Anyway," said Collis finally. "The scientists say it'll be summer before they have enough for another device."

"Not in time for Black Moon in February then," Kay muttered. She'd been hoping to take World United, so certain that she only had two bombs, by surprise.

Fine; it didn't matter. A time of power – great change. When the time came, she'd give the order…and Keaton would carry it out.

She glanced at Collis. "I need you to keep liaising up in that area."

"Yes, fine."

"Are we moving the bombs?" No one was certain if World United knew the facility's location.

"No. I discussed it with Keaton – the place is a natural fortress, with all the mountains around it. Even if they know the location, we're better off leaving them there." Collis grimaced. "It's a good thing – I'm not even sure where else would be safer, with everything going on."

Kay's glared at the tumbling water. "We *have* to get New Manhattan back," she muttered.

"We will." Collis turned and leaned his back against the railing. He hesitated, then put his hand over hers.

"Hey," he said.

Kay looked up, wary at his change of tone – even warier at the flutter that went through her because of it.

"You, um…said you'd miss me," he said. "Did you?"

Kay glanced down at her plain gold wedding ring, still unfamiliar. Why had she married Collis? She wasn't entirely sure, except that she'd been so taken aback by his proposal and had also known instinctively that marriage meant more to him than to her. He might betray a lover, but not a wife.

"We're one now," he'd whispered after the Justice of the Peace had pronounced them wed. Kay was certain she hadn't mistaken the depth of emotion in his eyes as they kissed.

"One," she'd agreed huskily.

Now, as Collis's question hung in the air, Kay rubbed her ring with the side of her pinkie finger. *Yes,* she wanted to say. She'd missed him in her bed at night; missed talking things over with him during the day; missed their secret, warm-between-the-sheets conversations. She'd looked forward to his regular letters and phone calls.

I still want to know what it's like to wake up with you, he'd written in the last one.

She shrugged, not looking at him. "Maybe a little," she said.

That night, for the first time, Collis didn't slip into her room in the late hours. He unpacked his suitcase and hung his clothes in the walk-in closet. He took a shower and brushed his teeth in her bathroom.

Their bathroom now, Kay supposed. She could have insisted on him having his own rooms, but found she had no desire to. This didn't alarm her as much as she thought it probably should have.

She sat in bed hugging her knees, watching him get ready. "Do you always do that when you brush your teeth?"

He glanced at her through the open bathroom door. "What?" he mumbled.

She motioned. "That…thing."

Collis was easing himself up and down on his toes. He spat out his toothpaste, rinsed his mouth and grinned. "No," he said. "Calf stretches. They're kind of sore, after the long flight."

When he finally slipped between the sheets, wearing his boxers, it felt strange – him coming to bed to sleep, as well as for whatever else happened.

Collis seemed to sense it. He lay on his elbow, facing her. Very gently, he touched her hair.

"I like it like this," he said. "Down your back."

"I know. But it's not very stylish."

He shrugged his toned shoulders. There was a pause; she could hear the creaking of crickets from outside.

"I guess this is kind of our wedding night," Collis said.

It hadn't occurred to Kay. She smiled slightly. "I guess it is." Then she remembered: "But we can't do very much. I've got my monthly."

"That's okay. I'm just happy that you're not going to throw me out of bed tonight." His lips twisted. "You're not, are you?"

"No. You're my husband." Though she'd said it partly to gauge his reaction, Kay was surprised at the look that flickered in his eyes – and how it tugged at her.

When she'd fled New Manhattan, she'd taken some of Collis's files. Going through them, she'd found one containing information about his parents. She'd been far more fascinated by this than it warranted. She'd gazed at the images of Clara "Goldie" and Henry "Hank" Reed for a long time, searching for Collis in their eyes, the lines of their jaws.

He looked like his mother.

From nowhere, Kay heard herself say, "I'm going ahead with Black Moon. No matter what."

"I know," Collis said quietly.

At his tone, she glanced sharply at him. "How did you know?"

He shrugged.

"Tell me."

"Because Johnny was going to," Collis said finally.

Kay stiffened. As their gazes locked, she realized Collis had guessed how vulnerable Johnny had made her feel… and that now she had to beat the memory of him at his own game, so that she could look at herself in the mirror without seeing fear.

She lifted her chin. "Do you agree? About Black Moon?"

"Does it matter?"

"No. But tell me."

Collis sounded disturbed but resigned. "Well, it goes beyond Johnny now, doesn't it? I guess it's like you said when I told you about my nightmare. Some things aren't pleasant. But you've got to do them if you want to survive."

"Yes," Kay murmured. *Survive.* If she showed the world she was afraid, they'd destroy her. They were already trying to.

Collis lay studying her, his mouth and jaw resolute. "I'm with you," he said roughly. "Whatever you do."

The sense of not being in control of herself bothered her. Yet Kay gave in to her impulse and stroked his arm – felt its firm warmth.

A silence grew.

He took her hand and played with her fingers. "I hope I don't wake you up tonight."

Kay felt her eyebrows rise. "I thought you were over the nightmare."

Collis cleared his throat. "No. I'm still having it." He glanced at her and gave a rueful smile. "You haven't asked me if I missed you."

For some reason the comment relaxed her. She smiled and stretched out on her side, propping her head on her hand. "Do you want me to ask?"

"You don't have to. I'll tell you." Collis looked troubled as he touched her hair again, tracing a strand down its length.

"Yes," he said. "I did."

CHAPTER THIRTY-FOUR

THE WESTERN SEABOARD'S LOCKER ROOM had been run-down around the edges and all its pilots had come from the same small country. The World United locker room was sleek and new and echoed with dozens of languages.

Somehow it felt just the same.

Early Wednesday morning – still the middle of the night – I got dressed in there for the sortie Tess had promised us. A few other pilots were around too, preparing for reconnaissance missions.

Just like back in the Western Seaboard, Vera and I had lockers close to each other. Harlan's was across the aisle. The tattoo on his bicep flexed as he pulled on his shirt.

"Yep, looks like you've lost your touch, Vancour," he

said sadly. He winked at Vera. "Time was, you could out-bluff anyone."

I rolled my eyes. I'd finally given in and joined his poker game earlier that night, to kill time. It hadn't seemed worth going to bed for just a few hours.

"*One* hand," I said with a grin. "You call my bluff for one lousy hand, and—"

All at once Vera nudged me. I looked up and tensed.

Ingo was heading towards me.

He had on only a pair of trousers. His skin and hair were damp, as if he'd just showered. His dark eyes stayed on me as he approached, and suddenly I was very conscious that I was standing there in my brassiere. I jerked my chin up, meeting his gaze.

Ingo came right up to me, ignoring Harlan and Vera, who'd gone silent. The good side of his angular face looked tired.

"Can I talk to you, please?" he said.

I wavered, and then nodded. We went to the end of the long row, where no one else was present. I was a lot more aware of his body than I wanted to be, and hated myself for it.

"It's been a month," said Ingo.

"Yes?" I said stiffly.

His expression turned bitter. "You're not going to make it easy for me, are you?"

"I don't know what you mean."

"Of course you do. Just tell me, Amity. Are you pregnant?"

I stared at him, remembering my thought of only two days before: that if Ingo was the man I'd thought he was, he wouldn't wait for me to tell him this. He'd ask me himself.

"No," I said slowly. "I'm not."

"You're certain?"

I nodded, and he exhaled and closed his eyes briefly. "All right," he said. He rubbed his forehead. "Thank you."

"What would you have done if I was?" The words came from nowhere.

Ingo snorted and let his hand fall. Fleetingly, he seemed as vulnerable as Hal when I'd told him about Mac's high regard for him.

"Do we really need to waste time on hypotheticals?" he said.

"I'm curious. Tell me."

Anger and something else flashed in Ingo's eyes. "Stop, Amity," he said in an undertone. "We've been too much to each other to do this."

Aren't we still? I couldn't say it. I gripped my elbows hard. After a pause, I said, "Harlan tells me you've been flying like a maniac."

"Harlan's been talking too much." Ingo glanced behind me. "You've got a sortie to fly." He hesitated, studying me. He beat a fist against his thigh, over and over.

"Be careful, please," he said.

He turned and walked away.

Pain, I realized belatedly. That had been the other

448

emotion in his eyes. An answering ache came from within me. I gazed after his retreating figure.

I started as Vera touched my arm.

"Hey. We've got to hurry," she said.

I nodded and tried to shake it all away. "Yeah," I murmured. "Yeah."

We flew through the night. I kept my gaze locked on my control panel, watching the line of the artificial horizon – adjusting the Dove in relation to it. Looking out into darkness was too disorienting; you could be flying right towards the ground and not even know it.

Above and below me, cruising at different altitudes, were Harlan and Vera. Beneath us was the bomber we were protecting.

Just before sunrise, I banked west. The horizon tilted sideways. The others did the same, our wings all saluting in unison.

Out of the gloom it swam into view: a boxy grey factory in the middle of a patch of woods.

It made weapons, ammunition. I could see a couple of tanks on a flatbed truck, looking like toys of the ancients.

Our bomber opened its hatch. The dark, elliptical shapes tumbled downwards. Seconds later, the factory was exploding in a series of fireballs that touched something elemental in me, each more satisfying than the last.

"Soon, Dad," I murmured, my fingers tense on the stick.

* * *

We were twenty miles outside of New Manhattan again when my radio crackled into life: *"Scorps and bombers sighted, incoming! Repeat, Scorps and bombers..."*

I swore. Glancing across at Harlan and Vera in their planes, we traded frustrated looks. When the city slid into view, there was a dark, shifting cloud of planes above it.

We got our bomber down safely, with other Doves coming to our aid. The fitters came racing to refuel our planes and we took off again.

It was one of the bad attacks. It went on and on, with new Scorps arriving regularly. The world spun and plunged around me, my engine screaming as I worked the firing button. I'd been up all night but was shuddering with adrenalin.

The third time I landed to refuel, I taxied to a stop just as the medics lifted a pilot from his plane. I winced automatically...and then saw that it was Harlan.

No. With suddenly clammy hands, I fumbled my straps undone. I shoved my hood back and scrambled down from my wing – raced across the asphalt.

The medics had him on a stretcher, hustling him towards the ambulance. Harlan lay motionless, his flight suit soggy with blood. My mind numbed at the sight of it.

"Will he be okay?" I gasped out, jogging along beside the medics.

"Don't know how he even landed the damn thing," said

one of them in a rush. "He's been hit through the chest and stomach – hang on, big fella, we're getting you to the hospital!"

They loaded Harlan into the truck. I stood frozen. As its doors closed I glimpsed his large, prone form, his head turned limply to one side.

The doors slammed shut. The truck peeled away, sirens blasting. All around me were shouts, fitters clambering over planes, the roar of engines.

I realized my eyes were stinging and swiped my hand angrily over them.

"Don't you dare die, Taylor," I muttered.

A fitter appeared. "Wildcat! Your plane's ready!" For a second I just stood there. Then I let out a shaky breath and glanced up at the ongoing battle.

I headed back to my plane.

When Tess finally told me I could stay down it was twilight. I went straight to the hospital and found Vera in the waiting room, sitting hunched over on one of the worn wooden chairs. She was still in her flying gear too, one hand pressed to her mouth.

As I sat down beside her, she started. Her face crumpled when she saw me.

"They're not sure," she whispered against her fingers. "He's lost so much blood…they're operating now, but they don't know whether…" She didn't finish.

My throat closed. I took her other hand.

"He's strong," I said, squeezing her fingers hard. "He's a fighter."

Two hours dragged past. Finally a doctor appeared. Jerome Washington, read his name tag.

"He's alive," he said without preamble.

Vera gasped in relief, clutching my hand – and then seemed to notice, as I had, the gravity of the doctor's expression.

"Go on," I whispered.

Dr Washington sat on the coffee table in front of us.

"I'm afraid it's still touch and go," he said gently. "The next few days are crucial. On its own, he'd survive the chest wound. It's the stomach wound that…" He grimaced and looked down, tapping his fingers together.

"If septicaemia sets in, we'll do whatever we can," he said.

Tess gave Vera a few days' compassionate leave. She barely left Harlan's side. Three days later, he was still feverish and unconscious…but alive.

I went whenever I could between the air raids that still hammered the island. I hated feeling so helpless, waiting there with Vera as she sat stroking his forehead with a damp cloth.

"I'm here," she kept murmuring. "I'm right here."

In the quiet of the hospital, there was too much time

to think. As I gazed at Harlan's flushed face, I couldn't stop remembering my locker room encounter with Ingo – the pain in his dark eyes.

Other memories were coming back too.

The night of the battle, before we'd ended up in the abandoned cottage, that same look had been in Ingo's eyes. In fact, now that I thought of it, he'd been off-kilter ever since he returned through the tunnels to the Garden.

Confusion and unease stirred. The way Ingo had clutched me to him so tightly after we made love, as if he was drowning and I was a life raft. And then the next morning…

I can't do this right now, he'd said.

Why "right now"? What had been going on?

Recalling what else he'd said – *I've been awake for hours wishing I could forget it ever happened* – the familiar hurt stabbed. I locked away thoughts of Ingo and brought Vera endless cups of terrible hospital coffee.

The afternoon of the third day, Harlan regained consciousness. I'd just pulled a chair beside Vera's at his bedside; I caught my breath as his blue eyes came blearily open.

"Vera?" he whispered.

She was smiling through her tears. "Hello, you big lug." She caressed his hair back.

"Feel awful," Harlan mumbled. His gaze fell woozily on me. He squinted. "Vancour? What the hell…? Is this a party?"

"His fever breaking is a very good sign," Dr Washington said, relief clear in his voice as he, Vera and I stood in the hospital corridor. "Mr Taylor's still got a long recovery ahead…but we can be hopeful now that he won't die of blood poisoning."

After the doctor left a few minutes later, Vera sagged against the wall, briefly covering her face.

"I thought I'd lost him," she murmured. She gave me a shaky grin. "He's going to be a terrible patient, you know. He'll *hate* being bedridden."

Dr Washington had explained that Harlan would be sent to a World United convalescence home in Nova Scotia. He might be there for some time.

I squeezed her arm. "Tell him it wouldn't have happened in a MK9," I said after a pause, and to my relief she laughed.

"I will not," she said. "He'd bust his sutures."

That night I somehow found myself standing in front of Ingo's room at the Grand.

I started to knock and then stopped. I wavered, torn. Finally I grimaced and let my hand fall.

As I turned away, the next door down opened and another pilot came out. "You looking for Manfred? He's not there."

"Oh." I glanced back at Ingo's door and hesitated. "Do you know where he is?"

The pilot headed past me towards the elevator. "Walking, probably," he said over his shoulder. "That guy's like a ghost – spends more time walking the streets than sleeping."

Through the window at the end of the hallway, New Manhattan lay spread out for as far as I could see. Since when had Ingo been restless, unable to sleep? The sense of trepidation that had begun in the hospital room grew.

"Thanks," I said softly, though the pilot was already gone.

Ingo's an adult. If something's wrong, he can tell me. Irritated with myself, I went down to the hotel bar. It was thick with cigarette smoke and blue uniforms. A woman sang on the stage as a small band played. "*When the swallows…come back…to Capistrano…*"

Hal and Percy were there. It was the first time I'd encountered them out together since Hal had told me they were seeing each other. Hal saw me and waved me over.

"Hey," he said when I reached their table. "How's Harlan?"

I smiled, remembering. "It looks like he's going to be all right."

"Well, I'd say that calls for a celebratory round," said Percy with a grin. He stood up. "What'll you have?"

I suspected they'd chosen the tucked-away table for privacy. "That's okay. I'll leave you two alone."

"Don't be daft. Wine? Champagne? Come on, let me treat Hal's sister."

I laughed. "All right, you've talked me into it. Red wine, thanks."

"Same again?" Percy said to Hal, touching his shoulder.

"Yeah, thanks." Hal's eyes followed Percy as he went to the bar.

"He's nice," I said, sitting down. "You've got good taste."

Hal looked shy and buoyant at the same time. "Well, of course."

Percy laughed a lot. He turned out to be one of those naturally ebullient people who genuinely enjoy life. He asked lots of questions, though tactfully stayed away from my infamy as Wildcat.

"So you always wanted to be a pilot?" he asked cheerfully.

"Yes, though not necessarily a Peacefighter," I said. "But flying – yes, always."

"Like Hal then," said Percy. "He's put in for training."

I glanced at my brother. "Really?"

He looked amused. "Thanks, big mouth," he said to Percy, who winked at him. "I can't start until I'm sixteen," he added to me, "but yeah."

I sighed, thinking of Harlan. "Why am I not surprised?"

"It does have the flavour of the inevitable," said Percy. He touched his beer glass to Hal's. "You'll be bloody brilliant," he said. "But I'll hate to lose a good fitter."

"'Bloody'," said Hal, shaking his head with a grin.

"Damned. Extremely. Extraordinarily. Any better? *You* knew what I meant," Percy added to me.

I laughed, liking him – liking both of them together. "Hal's just being contrary."

Hal raised an eyebrow. "*You're* accusing *me* of contrariness?"

"You have your moments," I told him. "Do I really need to start dragging out childhood memories?"

"That's okay," said Hal hastily. "Percy believes you. Don't you, Percy?"

"No, Percy would very much like to hear them, actually." Percy leaned forward.

"Vancour code of silence," said Hal to me.

I had another sip of wine and took pity on my brother. "All right, he's invoked the Vancour code. Just take my word for it."

"Forewarned is forearmed," said Percy. He raised his glass. "To contrary Vancours!"

We clinked glasses. The music soared. All around us, pilots who'd been in battle hours previously were dancing, drinking...grabbing every second of life they could.

I told myself that I wasn't thinking of Ingo at all.

CHAPTER THIRTY-FIVE

THE SIRENS WRENCHED ME FROM bed at dawn. This time it was just a quick bombing raid. When I landed it was barely seven a.m. and the skies were already clearing of planes.

Coffee and breakfast, I thought, climbing down from my wing – though I hardly needed caffeine, with the adrenalin still pulsing through me.

As I headed towards the cafe, I saw Ingo standing near the office doors, his helmet under one arm. He was looking down at something.

My steps slowed. I studied him, as torn as the night before. I still hadn't decided whether to go over when Ingo abruptly wheeled away with a piece of paper clenched in one hand.

He headed for the hangars.

I glimpsed his tormented expression and my heart clenched. I stared after him as he disappeared into the hangar's darkness, almost running.

Suddenly it felt as if I were waking up.

I hadn't been mistaken about the kind of man Ingo was – he'd asked me straight out if I were pregnant. I didn't really think I'd been mistaken about his feelings for me, either.

And for the man I knew to have acted the way Ingo had that morning in Little France…

"Oh, holy hell, I'm an idiot," I whispered.

I dropped my helmet and sprinted across the tarmac. When I reached the hangar, I ducked inside its large, shadowy space. It was empty of planes now, empty of people.

Except for one. Ingo sat against a corrugated wall, his elbows propped on his knees. His hands clutched his head, raking his curls back. His shoulders were heaving. I could hear his sobs.

I reached him and sank to my knees. I touched his shoulder – and then, trembling, wrapped my arms around him and pressed close, resting my cheek on his head.

"Shh," I murmured, stroking his back. "Ingo…shh…"

The minutes passed as he cried. A truck drove past outside. At last Ingo straightened a little and pulled away. He massaged his eyes but didn't look up.

"Who?" I asked, hugging myself.

His throat worked. "My father."

"What…what happened?"

Ingo still had his hand over his eyes. "He had cancer. There wasn't anything they could do."

I thought of the photo taken outside their house, his family holding up their wine glasses. Ingo's father, so like his younger son.

"I'm sorry," I whispered.

He let his hand fall. His cheeks were damp.

"He was asking for me before he died," he said thickly.

I hesitated. "How…how do you know?"

"There was a letter for me when I got Mac and the others out of the city. Lena said to get home if I could – that he was dying – asking for me. The doctor said he couldn't last more than a few more days."

Ingo gave a short, ugly laugh. "The letter was two weeks old when I got it."

I gripped his arms tightly. "You couldn't have made it home in time anyway! Don't blame yourself."

The hangar felt vast, quiet. Finally Ingo said, "When I got back into the city…I knew he must already be gone. But I kept thinking maybe he wasn't. Maybe he was still asking for me. Maybe even while…" He trailed off.

Even while he'd been having sex with me in Little France. My heart ached. *Oh, Ingo.* No wonder he'd wanted to forget it had ever happened.

His jaw was stone. "Then walking to the checkpoint… I just knew. Dad had died and I wasn't there."

"But this is the first you've heard for sure?" I cursed the uncertain mail service; the lack of phones.

"Yes. I was right; he's been dead for…oh, *fuck*." Ingo slammed his fist against the floor. "Fuck," he whispered again, gripping his head.

My throat was tight as I wrapped my arms around him again. I pressed my cheek against the side of his head. "Don't," I murmured hoarsely, caressing his back. I kissed his hair. "Ingo, please…please, don't do this to yourself."

He went still. I could hear his breathing. Then his muscles turned to steel and he pulled away.

"*Stop*, Amity. I don't need your pity."

"*This isn't pity!*" I cried. "I'm in love with you!"

Ingo stared at me, his dark eyes startled. I realized I was crying. "I'm in love with you, you idiot," I got out. "Don't you know that?"

Before he could answer, the sirens split the air again. *No!*

"*Scramble!*" someone shouted from outside. We lunged to our feet. Our footsteps echoed as we raced from the hangar.

The planes stood in long lines, waiting. An explosion went off nearby, rocking the airfield. Ingo and I sprinted for our Doves.

They weren't far from each other. As we started to separate, he clutched my arms. "Be careful!"

"And you! Forget about everything! *Concentrate*." I was terrified that he'd be too distracted to fly well.

461

His eyes were still red. "It was the not knowing," he said. "Now I know." He hesitated, then squeezed my hand. Our fingers interlocked.

"Thank you," he said.

We took off into a seething sky.

That battle kicked off three solid days of fighting as Kay Pierce blasted New Manhattan Island. By evening on the second day I'd flown and landed more times than I could remember and it wasn't over yet.

When I landed around twilight, Tess grabbed me. "Night-fliers, I need night-fliers!" she gasped. She shoved coordinates into my hand. "We think we've found her new airbase."

I raced for a fresh plane and took off with a few others. The coordinates were only an hour away.

We found the base – it was awash with people. My heart gave a fierce leap when I saw half a dozen bombers. I peeled away and went low, strafing the airfield. People had thought the humming noise was from their own planes and now they ran, shouting, or dropped to the ground with their hands over their heads.

"Get out – leave – it's your *planes* we want," I muttered. The airfield angled as I pulled up. Our own bomber was overhead; I'd barely cleared the field when I saw the missiles tumbling down.

As people raced from the field, their bombers began to

burst into flames. *Yes.* The exhilaration felt hard within me. The tarmac leaped and buckled, then went dark as the airbase lights went out in a sweeping fizzle.

I tore my gaze from the treacherous night sky and looked only at my control panel. Compass point thirty-two degrees east. Altitude fifteen thousand.

"Trust the instruments," I murmured. It was what Russ always used to say. He was the best team leader I'd ever had, even if he *had* turned out to be taking bribes.

When I got back, I tumbled into bed exhausted. Four hours later, it was dawn and I was back in a plane again.

Around three o'clock that afternoon, we hit a lull.

I returned to my room and slept. When I woke up, it was after six. I lay without moving for a minute, gazing out at the sunset against the New Manhattan skyline. I felt tense with anticipation.

Finally I got up and took a shower. I put on the same black strapless dress that I'd worn when I'd gone out with Harlan and Vera.

It hugged me in all the right places, then flared out down to my knees. I swallowed, studying myself in the mirror. My hair fell sleekly to my shoulders. I pinned some of it up, creating two waves that softly framed my face. I stroked on some lipstick.

When I went down to the hotel bar, it was busy but not heaving for a change. A lot of the pilots had wanted to get away from the airfield. I'd heard a group talking about taking the subway up to Harlemtown.

I was glad.

I sat at a table to one side. The singer wasn't there that night, but a small band was playing. When the waiter came over I ordered a glass of wine and then sat fiddling with it.

I looked up just as Ingo walked in.

I went still, the wine glass forgotten. He was wearing grey trousers, a green-flecked sports jacket. His eyes met mine across the crowd and he headed over, weaving his way through the room.

When he reached my table neither of us had taken our eyes from the other. The expression on his half-scarred face was serious, unsmiling.

He held out a hand. "Dance with me?" he asked softly.

I was already rising.

We'd danced once before, a lifetime ago. Then, moving with him on the dance floor had just felt comfortable, no tensions between us. Now I shivered as he drew me close, his left hand holding my right. I rested my head on his shoulder, my heart beating hard.

His own head was slightly bowed, his cheek against my hair. We moved to the music: a low, hypnotic tune with horns and clarinets that I didn't know the name of but knew I'd never forget. I closed my eyes.

Ingo's lips moved against my ear. "I'm sorry."

"No," I murmured back. "I should have given you time. I should have known something was wrong."

"I was being an ass; how could you?"

"Because I know you." I pulled back a little and studied him. "I'm sorry too," I said. "I forgot that I do. I thought…" It was hard to say. I rubbed my thumb across his shoulder, my throat tight.

"I confused you with Collie," I said.

The lights had dimmed. As we moved to the music, other couples were dark, intimate shapes around us. Ingo held our clasped hands tightly against his chest.

"I couldn't tell you then," he said finally. "I could hardly think about it without going crazy. I hated myself that morning for…for having been with you, for enjoying it, when Dad…"

"Stop." I put my hand over his lips.

He exhaled. As he pulled me close again the music changed to a slow tango.

We kept dancing the same steps as before. I wrapped my arms around his neck. I could feel his heart pounding, and the warmth of his skin through his shirt, and I felt short of breath.

Ingo was caressing my side, his hand moving slowly up and down. "I've been trying to figure it out, you know," he murmured.

"What?"

"Why I didn't realize the moment we met how beautiful you are. I must have been spectacularly stupid."

"Me too," I got out.

He pulled back. His good eyebrow rose. "I don't need a platitude, my friend," he said quietly.

"It isn't one."

"Amity, when we met, I still looked normal. It wasn't unheard of for women to find me attractive. I didn't make small children cry."

"Then, you were just…some guy. Now you're…" I trailed off. I touched his scar, gently exploring the ruined skin. "Everything," I whispered.

Ingo's throat moved. He put his hand over mine. "I love you too," he said. His voice was rough. "You know that, don't you? I've been in love with you for a long time."

"I know." I was trembling, electricity sweeping through me. We danced in silence, holding each other close. The music and the electricity built and built, until I couldn't stand it any more.

"Come to my room," I murmured in his ear.

His lips were against my cheek. "Mine is closer," he whispered huskily.

"Mine's more private."

"Yours," he said.

He put his arm around my shoulders. We left the dance floor, weaving through the still-moving couples. Behind us, the plaintive, dramatic chords of the tango wailed.

We started kissing in the elevator as the small chamber hummed upwards. One of the pins in my hair came out as Ingo stroked his hands through it, our mouths moving together, the two of us pressed tightly up against the wall. When the door slid open I almost didn't notice. Then I stepped away, dazed, and grabbed his hand.

"Hurry," I said.

My room was at the end of the hallway. The room next door was always empty; the pilot billeted there lived with his girlfriend. Ingo kissed my neck as I fumbled in my clutch purse for my key. I found it and tried to put it in the lock. I gasped as his lips slid across my skin.

"You were faster as a lock-picker," Ingo muttered.

"It's your own fault...holy hell, why isn't this working?"

"Give me that." He was smiling. He plucked the key from my hands and opened the door; we got inside.

I snapped on the light. In the silence that followed I swallowed, gazing at him. I moved close and gently pushed the jacket from his shoulders. Ingo shrugged out of it and tossed it onto the armchair. Then he took the other pins from my hair, easing them out one by one and putting them on the dresser.

I stood motionless, taking in the familiar angles of his face. His left jaw was freshly shaved. His eyes looked very dark.

Ingo pulled the last pin free. I rose on my tiptoes and slipped my hand behind his neck. He pulled me to him as we kissed lightly, our lips sipping at each other, then more deeply. I played with his crisp curls, teasing my fingers through them.

"I'm better prepared this time," Ingo whispered against my mouth.

I grinned. "Me too."

I could feel him grinning as well. His hands glided down my spine.

"Let's try going slowly for a change," he said.

I stood at my window gazing at the dawn. New Manhattan lay spread out below me, its buildings tipped with rose and gold. In the distance I could see the river – a thin, gleaming cord.

It all looked so beautiful.

A rustle came from the bed. I shivered, smiling, as Ingo slipped his arms around me from behind. I pressed against his bare chest's wiry warmth and he kissed my temple.

"I didn't think you were awake yet," I said.

His muscles flexed as he yawned. "You left. I felt bereft."

I smiled. I turned in his arms and leaned back, studying him.

Ingo's mouth twisted. "You look happy," he said softly. He touched my face.

"There's a reason for that." I turned my head and kissed his hand. "Don't go back to your room."

"I wasn't planning on it."

"No…I mean, stay here in mine from now on."

He smiled. "Am I allowed to go and get my clothes?"

I wrapped my arms around his neck. "Yes, but not yet. And I don't want you wearing them very often."

Ingo tickled my cheek with a strand of hair. "How nice it is when two people want the same thing."

"Isn't it?" I said.

Part Three

April 1943 – August 1943

CHAPTER THIRTY-SIX

APRIL, 1943

As COLLIS DROVE, THE DIRT ROAD seemed to dim. The jeep lurched violently and he started, hands clenching the wheel. Pothole – hadn't even seen it. He grimaced and grabbed the flask on the empty passenger seat. Keeping his eyes on the road, he unscrewed it and took a swig of lukewarm coffee.

Stay on your toes, Reed, he ordered himself, shifting gears as he started up a hill. He'd been up for over thirty hours. It would be just his stupid luck to get so close to the place and then die by crashing the jeep.

He'd been out in the Yukon for several weeks this time, touring the factories that Kay still held and inspecting the defences against World United – who now controlled

Alaska and part of the western Yukon and had spent the winter consolidating their forces just as Kay had. Even after so many months of journeys to the region, it had taken this long to ditch his driver without suspicion and arrange his schedule so that three free days had been secretly built into it.

The spring day was cold and drizzly, the barren mountains lost in the haze. Collis knew from the map that he must be in their territory by now, though there'd been no marker in the desolate landscape.

Finally he reached a chain-link fence stretching across the road. A sign read: *No admittance.* The pair of soldiers guarding it had heard him coming. They waited, wearing blue uniforms and holding rifles.

Collis stopped the jeep. He steeled himself and then swung open the door. He approached the soldiers with his hands over his head.

"I'm Collis Reed," he said. "I surrender."

They questioned him for over five hours. Collis was desperately aware of the clock – it had taken him over a day to get here, and he needed almost the same time again to get to his next meeting and not be suspected. Over and over, he repeated his story to the two World United officials.

"Let's have it again, Mr Reed," said one, a woman named Sergeant DeBacca. Her pointed face reminded him disconcertingly of Kay. "I'm not sure I'm quite grasping your story yet."

Collis rubbed his eyes. "I'm with the Resistance," he said, his voice scratchy with tiredness. "I helped organize the assassination attempt that killed Sandford Cain. I have information that's vital for you, if you want to take Atomic Harmony Devices. And you need to, as soon as you can. She's still making nukes."

"Are you trying to *sell* us this information, Mr Reed?" sneered the man – Foster, thin and rangy. "My, I'm sure your wife would be distressed."

The mention of Kay brought a confusing mix of emotions. Collis's tone stayed level. "No. I'm giving it to you."

"How do we know the info's good? This could be a trap."

The conversation had been circling for hours. Collis longed for a drink. "Look, *someone* in the WU must know who Mac Jones is. He was a double agent under Gunnison. In the Resistance he went by Vince Griffin. If you can just—"

"I've never heard of Mac Jones," broke in DeBacca flatly.

"His man Grady was the one who delivered the photos of nuclear weapons to the EA in the first place! Get in touch with Grady. He knows I'm Resistance."

After another hour of this, DeBacca and Foster withdrew. Through the glass door of the office where they'd been questioning him, Collis saw them talking. Finally DeBacca picked up a phone and started to dial.

There followed several phone conversations that he couldn't hear. DeBacca wrote something down. More silent discussions. Another phone call. To Collis's surprise, he dozed a little, his head slumped on his arms on the desk. He awoke with a start: someone jostling his shoulder.

"Here," said Sergeant DeBacca curtly, handing him a phone.

His thoughts still bleary, Collis took the receiver. "Hello?"

There was a pause. "Hello, Collis," said Mac's voice finally.

Collis sat bolt upright, his heart hammering. "Mac! Oh, holy hell, I'm glad they got hold of you. Listen—"

"Cut it." Mac's voice was cold. "I want you to tell me in two sentences why you betrayed us, and don't try to bullshit me and tell me you didn't. Then you can explain exactly why the WU shouldn't take you hostage and use you as leverage against Pierce, which they're thinking about – though I doubt she cares if you live or die."

That's not true, Collis thought automatically. He squeezed the bridge of his nose.

"I can tell you in one sentence," he said.

After he'd realized back in July that he was starting to care for Kay, Collis had been desperate to arrange the assassination attempt while he still felt capable of doing it.

476

Even as it was, he'd felt like the lowest kind of shit. Kay was as harsh a dictator as Gunnison, yet on a personal level – the two of them alone together – Collis liked her. In an odd way, he could be himself around her. She was his lover and he was plotting to kill her, and what did *that* make him?

Around that time, a conversation with Kay had revealed that, on some level, she believed in astrology. Collis had always assumed that she thought it was garbage, that she only used it for her own ends. But lying in his arms one night, talking through their days, she'd mentioned drowsily that she'd cast a chart for herself that afternoon.

"Yeah? What for?" Collis had asked, keeping his voice relaxed.

She'd seemed to wake up a little then, and had given an embarrassed grimace. "Just habit, I guess."

She cast charts for herself. *That* was interesting. And, to Collis's relief, he wasn't so far gone yet that he'd let this information slide. It took time to manage it, but one afternoon he quickly searched Kay's private desk.

Most of the charts he found were simply her casting the fortune of her reign, over and over. The others were for something labelled only *Black Moon*. Collis checked: two lunar eclipses were coming up in the next year. Collis knew enough astrology to realize with a quick check of her ephemeris that the chart was for the earlier eclipse.

Why had Kay cast a chart for it?

It took weeks before a conversation with her had

naturally turned to the night sky. When it had, Collis had said, "Hey, aren't there a couple of lunar eclipses next year?" From her reaction – a private smile, an affirmation and then a change of subject – he suspected that yes, something was happening. He still had no idea what.

Did it matter? If she died, whatever she was plotting wouldn't happen. But Collis couldn't shake the feeling that he needed to know.

Mac had wanted a few more months to raise support in the city before they made the assassination attempt. Collis had told himself that was good – he could find out what was going on. But as the weeks passed, part of Collis became scared that if they postponed the attack too long, he wouldn't be able to go through with it.

Finally, no more the wiser, Collis realized it was now or never. Whatever this thing was between himself and Kay Pierce, it was growing daily. Despite everything, he couldn't deny the ease and closeness he felt when it was just the two of them. His emotions could *not* interfere with what had to happen.

He'd told Mac they had to set a date for the plan: a meeting that Kay had already arranged with Cain and the council in mid-September.

In the days leading up to the attempt, he'd thrown himself into the role he played with Kay with such passionate abandon that it was as if on some level he wanted it to be true. He wasn't sure he'd be able to live with himself afterwards. Part of him considered dully whether he'd just stay in the meeting room when the time came.

Knowing himself, he doubted it.

Sitting at the conference table beside Kay on the day, Collis had felt cold and sick, wondering if he could go through with it. Remembering the night before – holding Kay in his arms, talking softly with her – part of him wanted to tip her off, and he hated himself for it.

Mac trusts me, he kept telling himself. The man he wanted to be was the man Mac trusted. That was all he had to hold onto.

When Kay was called from the room, it was as if the fates had decided to play a cruel trick and take the matter out of his hands. For several stunned minutes, Collis hadn't been able to react. Then he'd taken advantage of Cain's grumbling to pass out the report that was on the agenda and go after her.

He hadn't seen her in the corridor. He'd walked towards the stairwell, his footsteps muffled by the carpet.

And he'd heard what she was saying on the secure phone line.

Dazed, he'd listened for a few moments, and then softly returned the way he'd come. In his mind's eye was the image of a mushroom cloud blooming against an eclipsed moon.

Oh, holy hell – so *this* was what Black Moon meant.

Only one solution came. It sickened him; it meant betraying the Resistance just like his nightmare had taunted that he would. And what if he only thought this was the right thing to do because of his own messed-up feelings?

But the plan that ticked through his mind was still the only way Collis could see to prevent what he'd overheard.

He'd waited. When Kay appeared around the corner, he'd pretended that he'd just come out of the room. And he'd told her that, just as he'd promised, the plan was in place to do away with Cain.

Collis summed up what he'd overheard from Kay in a single sentence.

There was a long silence on the other end of the phone.

Finally Mac blew out a breath. "Aw, shit, buddy-boy," he murmured.

Collis's shoulders sagged at the softening of Mac's tone. "I didn't know what else to do," he said gruffly. "I thought if she stayed alive, we'd have a chance, at least. I don't have any influence over Keaton."

"Yeah, I get you. Aw, shit, pal…all right, tell me everything," said Mac.

Collis did, starting from learning about Kay's Black Moon charts up until when he'd had to grass on the Resistance. "The first nuke's supposed to take out Florence," he said. "Then she's going to send ground troops in…" He went on, outlining Kay's plan.

When he'd finished, Mac still sounded stunned.

"Well, that explains it," he said. "I'll tell you, Collis, at first I thought I'd been taken in like no man ever had."

Collis winced. "Amity said you were shot. I didn't know about the code word being wrong, I swear it."

"Pierce fed you wrong info sometimes," said Mac.

"What?"

"Yeah. Unless you were lying to me, which I don't think now you were. After the first few bits you gave me, I was always careful about using anything. Half the time it was bogus. I was hoping like hell we wouldn't have to use the code."

Collis realized he wasn't surprised. "She knew I was meeting with you," he said. "When I first woke up after I shot myself, she knew I'd let Amity go. I had to make a deal with her."

"Yeah, I figured."

Collis had thought Mac might have guessed; the confirmation was a relief. "I'm sorry," he said hoarsely. "There were times I had to give her stuff about the Resistance. I always tried to…protect what needed protecting." The words sounded feeble.

"Collis, believe me, I know how these things work," said Mac levelly. "It's lousy, but you were in a hell of a position. I've been there."

"Mac…" Collis glanced at DeBacca, who had withdrawn from the office but still stood outside. He wanted to admit that he'd gotten in too deep. His proposal to Kay had been pure instinct, an act…yet it meant more to him than it should that she'd married him. When he was with her in that lavish suite in the Zodiac, their marriage didn't feel like a sham.

"What is it?" said Mac.

Collis choked out a laugh and massaged his temples. "How are you?" he said instead. "How's Sephy?"

"I'm fine. So's my wife."

Collis straightened with a grin. It was the first time he'd smiled in what felt like months. "Hey, really?"

"Yeah, you're not the only one to take the plunge into wedded bliss. Pal."

Collis stared down at his wedding ring and closed his hand into a fist. "Things...got complicated," he said.

He'd said something similar to Amity, when he'd played his part to the hilt in the tunnels, in case she was later captured. His tone then had been very different.

"Again: I've been there," said Mac quietly. "I'm not judging you, buddy."

No, Mac never had. Collis had always been the one to do that. Yet as Mac's words echoed on the crackling, long-distance line, he realized that he hadn't needed to hear Mac say it.

For a change, he wasn't judging himself, either.

Collis straightened, frowning; the thought seemed fragile. *I'm not in the business of absolution,* Mac had told him once.

His actions counted, not his thoughts. Maybe that was really true. No matter what crap his recurring nightmare about Harmony Three kept telling him…he was here now, risking his life.

Feeling slightly dazed, Collis cleared his throat. "Okay, so…this is what I've got," he said. And he explained the information he had about the defences, and what it was that World United needed to do.

CHAPTER THIRTY-SEVEN

APRIL, 1943

"HOW'D YOU DO, WILDCAT?" asked the fitter as he helped me down from my wing.

I pushed up my goggles and glanced at the sky. The Scorps had all been taken out or were heading home. A few dispersing spirals of black smoke drifted against the clouds.

"Took a hit on the wing," I told the fitter. "Is Ingo Manfred down?"

"Landed about ten minutes ago."

I relaxed a little. "Thanks." It was my second time down that day. I started tiredly towards the cafe in the spring sunshine.

A few months, Jean Buzet had said when we first started. It seemed hopelessly naïve now.

World United had expanded its eastern holdings. In November, troops based here and protected by our planes had taken New Jersey to the south and lands to the north as far as Boston.

The attacks over New Manhattan had died down over the winter – we suspected Kay Pierce was gearing up for an even bigger initiative. We'd spent our free time flying sorties, acting on illicit intelligence to try to find the new munitions factories that we knew must exist.

Some we'd found. Others we clearly hadn't. And now things were heating up again – three raids already this week. Both sides were digging in for the long haul.

New Manhattan kept on, despite the renewed pounding it was taking, and the rationing that had tightened everyone's belts. The parks felt sedate these days. There were few children left in the city. The WU had been ferrying them out to places where it was still safe: Nova Scotia, the EA.

The phone service was better and Ingo had spoken to his family by now, on a crackling international line. I'd been there with him, in the hotel's small comms room, and though I couldn't understand what he was saying I'd heard the emotion in his voice.

Finally he said in English, "Mama, Amity's here." He'd written to his family about me. His gaze went to me and he smiled. "Yes…very." Then he laughed. "Lena's grabbing the phone," he said. "She wants to talk to you."

"Hello?" I said into the heavy black receiver.

A voice that was lively even from so far away crackled through the line. "Amity? I'm Lena. I've heard so much about you!"

"I've heard a lot about you too." Smiling, I reached for Ingo's hand; our fingers interlocked. "I have to thank you, actually," I said. "When Ingo and I first got to know each other, he told me the code phrase you use to keep him in line. It's come in useful a few times."

She and Ingo laughed at the same time.

"I like you," Lena said.

During the phone call, Ingo's mother had told him the terms of his father's will. He'd left Ingo the power of decision on the house and vineyard, with the understanding – or the hope – that Ingo would someday be running it. Both Erich and Lena agreed that the place should rightfully be his. Ingo's mother was staying on to keep it going for him, though she hoped to retire to nearby Florence someday. Meanwhile, Erich and Lena were helping all they could.

I knew Ingo worried about his mother – she and his father had adored each other. But he was here, signed up like the rest of us, and could do nothing about it. And these past six months together, Ingo and I had snatched every experience we could.

Between sorties this quiet winter, we'd explored New Manhattan – seeing shows, going to clubs and museums. Growing up in a small town, the museums were a new world for me and I was crazy about them. *Whole buildings* dedicated to the most obscure pieces of knowledge. We'd wander slowly through them, reading the placards aloud to each other.

One rainy winter afternoon, Ingo took me to an art museum. I'd hesitated – looking at paintings?

"There's that exhibition on steam machinery at the York," I hedged.

Ingo had grinned. "You'll like this."

I'd loved it. The exhibition was called "Flight" – paintings of airplanes and the sky. One painting – a pure blue sky with cirrus clouds – had caught me and I'd gazed at it for a long time.

"It reminds me of the first time I ever flew," I murmured, and Ingo glanced at me in surprise and put his arm around me.

"I was just thinking that," he said.

A few times we'd taken one of the ferries across to New Jersey with a borrowed auto and gone hiking there, or braved the cold beaches. I was amazed that Ingo didn't know how to skip stones; we spent a whole afternoon at it until he got the knack. Another time he brought a soccer ball – the only sport he liked, he said – and taught me to pass and kick in a park.

"You're a natural!" he'd shouted as I scored a goal. Later we'd had a chilly picnic with a bottle of wine and ended up making love in the woods on the dry, cold leaves. I'd lain in his arms afterwards, smiling, and pretended that there was no war.

Now, as we all too often hurtled up into the skies again to the sounds of screaming sirens and gunfire, those days seemed like a dream.

We never talked about the future.

As I neared the airport cafe, I heard a whoop and saw Percy bounding towards me, his russet hair gleaming in the sunshine.

"Have you heard?" he called.

My heart skipped. He was practically dancing across the pavement. "What, what?"

He propelled me into a hug and kissed my cheek. "We've only bloody gone and taken Pierce's nuclear weapons factory, that's all!" he shouted, gripping my arms.

"We *have*?" I stared at him – then whooped for joy too. We raced for the cafe. I could see a group of pilots and fitters, blue uniforms and grey ones, gathered around the telio.

We burst inside, pushing through the glass door. Silence. Everyone sat riveted around the small screen. The mood was deflated, like a party that had suddenly been broken up. I stood in confusion, wondering if Percy had gotten it wrong.

The grin slid from Percy's face as we saw what was on the screen.

Harmony Five.

Shock punched me in the stomach. There were the gates we'd marched through every day, when Guns had waited on snowmobiles to force us to the mine. The severed heads that had perched amongst the barbed wire were gone. World United jeeps drove through in a steady stream.

Loaded in each one were skeletal people in rags.

Their faces. Their eyes. Their terrible thinness.

I felt Percy hesitantly touch my arm. Across the room, Hal sat in front of the telio, slowly rubbing a fist across his mouth. He looked over at me, his eyes anguished and too-bright.

Dimly, I became aware of the announcer's voice saying, "*The free world is horrified and stunned to learn that the rumours of Can-Amer's infamous correction camps are all too true. Their liberation has now been completed, but the images will remain for ever…*"

The camera moved to the inside of the camp. I saw my old hut, and the platform that Melody's body had fallen from, and thought I might faint.

Suddenly Ingo was there, his features drawn. He put his arm around me. "Come on," he whispered.

We watched the rest of the footage in our room.

I perched on the bed, feeling like stone, unable to take my eyes from the telio. Ingo sat tense and silent too, his arm tight around my shoulders as I pressed against him. The cameras showed it all.

We stared at images of the moving-picture screen where the films of Gunnison had played day and night…the solitary confinement cells with their stained walls... the now-abandoned food truck.

There were no Guns in sight; the announcer said that they'd fled, leaving the prisoners, as they'd heard news of the other camps being liberated. At footage of prisoners pressing against the fence as the WU soldiers first arrived, I swallowed hard, scanning their gaunt, dazed faces. It had been well over a year since Ingo and I escaped – a lifetime in there.

I didn't see a single person I knew.

The images went on and on. Finally I couldn't bear it any more. I buried my head against Ingo's neck, shuddering.

Without a word, he pulled briefly away to snap the telio off. "I don't know what the hell to feel," he murmured.

"Let's go to bed," I said raggedly. "Please."

It was only seven o'clock. He gently eased my clothes off. I did the same for him. We got under the covers and held each other. I traced the long, twisted scar on Ingo's abdomen. It rose up from his skin like a worm.

My throat clenched, remembering the day he'd gotten it – the sight of him emerging from the mine at Harmony Five, hunched over and in pain. Ingo took my hand and looked down at my Aries tattoo. He brushed his thumb over it.

Neither of us had to say it: we wouldn't be together without that place. The emotions were tangled, contradictory.

Finally Ingo cleared his throat. "You know...when I

490

realized how I felt about you…it was sometime during those first few weeks mapping the tunnels. You were measuring a passage and you said something, made some joking comment, and I looked over and thought…when did she become so beautiful to me?"

Exploring my tattoo again, he gave the ghost of a laugh. "Then it hit me. I was stunned. Looking back over everything…I realized I'd been in love with you for months."

I closed my fingers around his. "The same for me, with you," I got out. "I think even from back when we were in hiding together."

Ingo's almost-black eyes met mine. He lowered his head, stroking his hand through my hair. At first the kiss stayed soft, our lips teasing each other – then I moaned and hooked my leg over his waist.

We'd had nights of fire and passion. This was tender – gentle. I didn't realize I was crying until Ingo paused to kiss the tears from my cheeks, his curls brushing my face.

"Do you want me to stop?" he whispered.

"No…no." Our hands found each other; squeezed hard. He half-rolled and sat up, taking me with him; my legs wrapped around his waist. The final shudder made me cry out, clinging to him.

Ingo's lean form stayed curled around me. He stroked my back. I closed my eyes and held him tightly, my face still damp…seeing again the images from Harmony Five; knowing he was too.

"We're alive," he murmured hoarsely.

* * *

That week, I avidly devoured newspapers with screaming headlines: *Pierce Loses Nuclear Weapons!* Just like the liberation of the camps, WU soldiers had taken her bomb factory in a perfectly-orchestrated offensive. Then they'd destroyed the main buildings and their materials so that they could never be used again.

Sitting with Hal in the cafe, the two of us read the passage over and over. "Holy hell, I can't believe it," Hal said.

Still staring at the story, I pushed my hands through my hair and gave a shaky laugh. "They're really gone. For ever."

Hal looked as dazed as I felt. He took a swig of his coffee and glanced down, playing with the mug. "I still want to know why Dad did it though," he said finally.

Sympathy stirred. I'd been thinking of our father too — the man who'd put all of this in motion. We hadn't heard anything else from Ma on the subject.

"I know," I said.

Hal had on flying gear; he'd turned sixteen in February and was training to be a pilot in his spare time. Part of me hoped he never made it, though I wouldn't have told him that on pain of death. Having *two* people I loved in the air during battles…I could barely think of it.

But gazing at the news story, I still felt something in me ease. The worst part of our father's legacy was gone.

All around us, New Manhattan had erupted in celebration at the news. The war couldn't last much longer now, everyone said to each other. Though Kay Pierce kept fighting, it was only a matter of time.

"I just wish it would end before Harlan gets back," muttered Vera. We were in the locker room. I glanced at her, and she gave a small, troubled smile. "He'll be here next week, with luck."

I slowly closed my locker door. Harlan had had complications from his wound – a secondary infection had set in, and for a while around January things had looked bad for him again. Vera had managed to go up to Nova Scotia twice to see him. For the last few months he'd been solidly on the mend. I knew from his infrequent letters how stir-crazy he'd been going.

But two weeks after taking Pierce's bomb factory, the air raid sirens were starting to blare with regularity again. We'd had two pilot deaths already this week.

I touched Vera's arm. "It'll be good to see him," I said finally.

"I'm telling you, Vancour, your mother's a saint," Harlan said.

He'd arrived on a transport plane just in time for the worst fighting we'd seen since the previous November. Vera had been terrified at him going up; he hadn't flown in months.

No time for retraining. He'd just had to get up there.

Now, a week later, we were in the lobby of the Grand with Ingo, waiting for Vera. We'd had seven raids in five days. This was the first time that we'd been able to sign out to go someplace even just in the pilots' radius, and despite my weariness I felt hyped-up; giddy with the release of it.

Hal lounged against one of the columns; he was meeting Percy in the hotel bar soon. He and I exchanged a slight smile at Harlan's comment. I'd written to tell Ma that Harlan would be in Nova Scotia, and she'd promised to visit him.

"'Saint' might be a little strong," Hal said.

"I'm glad to hear it. Growing up with a saint sounds exhausting," said Ingo.

"Saint," repeated Harlan firmly. "Twice a week, like clockwork. And she brought *cookies*." Reverence tinged his tone.

"She makes good cookies," I admitted.

Harlan was a little thinner now, not quite as burly, but essentially the same old Harlan. "And I've got a surprise for Vera too," he drawled, running his hand over his brown hair. He smirked at me. "Your mother may just have given me a few dance lessons."

Hal grinned; he'd seen Vera on the dance floor. "Not *jitterbugging*."

"Nah, I wasn't a well man. But I can cut a mean foxtrot."

"Maybe your mother would give *me* a few lessons," said Ingo to me. He had on his green-flecked sports jacket; a crisp white shirt.

I smiled. "I can give you any lessons you need."

"Why does that sound dirty?" demanded Harlan.

"On that note..." Hal glanced at his watch and straightened. "See you later. Don't do anything I wouldn't do."

"That gives us plenty of leeway," I called after him.

"Yeah, look who's talking," he threw back.

When Vera stepped out of the elevator, she wore a bright red dress and lipstick to match. "Now, *that* was worth waiting for," said Harlan as she reached us.

"Why, thank you, kind sir." She took his arm.

Outside, the afternoon sun painted the buildings golden. Vera said, "All right, Ingo, where are we going?" The two of them conferred as we headed down the sidewalk – they were both real jazz aficionados, and kept track of who was playing at what club.

Harlan took my arm, holding me back a little. "Glad I was wrong about the guy," he said in a low voice, nodding towards Ingo. Once this past week, still buzzing with adrenalin from a raid, the four of us had sat up drinking and talking, with Ingo playing the second-hand guitar he'd bought in London Village.

I smiled as I studied the line of Ingo's shoulders. "Me too," I said.

As we entered the club, Harlan said casually, "So what kind of place is this?"

"Jazz in the basement, dancing up on the second floor," said Ingo, just as casual.

Harlan put his hands in his trouser pockets and rocked back on his heels. "Hey, let's go upstairs," he said. "I feel like taking a turn or two on the dance floor."

Vera had been rooting for something in her clutch purse; her head jerked up. A smile bloomed across her face. "Really?"

Ingo and I went to check out the jazz, leaving Vera doing a slow number with Harlan. As raucous chords blared in the dark, smoky room, I tried to persuade Ingo to go kick the guitar player off and take over.

"Seriously," I said, lifting my voice as we sat close together at the tiny table. "You're much better."

"You're great for my ego, you know." Ingo grinned and kissed me. "Even if you're tone-deaf."

"I'm not."

"Hum middle C for me, please."

"See? You know these things." I jokingly jostled his arm. "Come on. We can take him."

"'The Jazz Revolt'," mused Ingo. "No, that's awful. Wait – 'The Great Guitar Skirmish'."

"Yes! Or—"

We both looked up as a woman appeared at our table:

middle-aged, carrying a cocktail. She leaned down.

"My dear, I just want to say how brave you are," she said, her mouth close to my ear to be heard. "It must have been so difficult when he had his accident."

I stared blankly and then got the implication: I must have been with Ingo before his face was burned. I couldn't have fallen for him otherwise.

"It was difficult for my boyfriend, not me," I said deliberately. "I barely knew him then."

She glanced doubtfully at the right half of Ingo's face. "Well...you're very brave anyway." She patted my hand and kept on towards the bar.

"Have I told you how much I love your bravery?" said Ingo after a pause.

"Stupid woman," I muttered.

My fist was tight. Ingo had his forearms propped on the table. He ducked his head and kissed my clenched fingers. He started to say something else; we both started as the lights came on. All at once the room looked shabby, too smoky.

"Oh no," I breathed. The music stopped. We could hear the bleating of sirens from outside. The bar echoed with scraping chairs as people started jumping up.

Ingo grabbed my hand and we battled our way out. We found Harlan and Vera in the lobby; a minute later we were all outside. Traffic had stopped. A crowd swelled at the subway entrance as people streamed into the depths.

We broke into a run, Vera and I hastily yanking off our

heels. As the four of us pelted down the sidewalk, a warden shouted, "Get in the shelter!"

"We're pilots!" I called back, and the warden waved us on.

"Run faster, in that case!" he yelled, and even with the drone of approaching engines, it was still funny.

"My father always told me I shouldn't be a pilot," called out Vera, her eyes laughing. "You know what? I should have been a race-car driver!"

"You still could!" bellowed Harlan. "I'll come to your meets and—"

The world lurched with a roar. I screamed as I was hurled to the ground; a second later I felt Ingo on top of me, shielding me with his body. The patter of flying debris – screams. I lay breathing hard, smelling Ingo's aftershave.

When he sat up, a piece of dusty brick slid from his back. "Are you all right?" he asked urgently.

I was bruised and sore. It didn't matter. "Yes, but you're bleeding!" I touched his forehead.

Ingo swiped his hand impatiently over the wound. "I'm fine." He glanced quickly at the sky as we scrambled up. We could see the battle raging now – Tess would need all hands on deck.

The bombed building had been a stationers' shop; pens and paper littered the road. Ingo cupped his hands to his mouth. "Harlan!" he called over the sirens and the whine of planes. "Vera!"

I saw a familiar big form sprawled in the rubble. "There!" I gasped.

We raced over. My heart felt caged in my throat. "Harlan!" I cried, falling to my knees beside him.

He slowly sat up. Rubble fell from his jacket. I started to smile in relief...and then I saw.

Vera.

She lay without moving, her eyes open. Harlan had shielded her as Ingo had shielded me. From the look of the wound at her temple, it had already been too late.

"No," I whispered, and felt Ingo grip my arm.

"Vera," said Harlan, touching her. "*Vera?*" He shook her shoulders lightly. Her head fell to one side, dust and blood in her carefully-arranged hair.

"*Medic!*" shouted Harlan.

Kneeling too, Ingo felt for her pulse. He was pale as he gently let go of Vera's wrist. "It's too late. I'm sorry."

"We need a goddamn medic!" Harlan bellowed, twisting to look behind him.

I couldn't stop staring at Vera's eyes. So blue. "Harlan... she's gone."

"*No, she fucking is not!*" Harlan roared at me. "Get back to base! Both of you! Get out of here and fight! *Medic!*"

Another explosion. I cringed and glanced upwards at the swirling battle – dozens of Scorps and Doves both.

Two wardens and a medic rushed over. "You people need to get in the shelter!"

"We're pilots," said Ingo faintly, standing up.

"Get to base or get in the shelter!"

"Somebody help her!" Harlan was shouting. "Can't you

see she...she..." Suddenly he faltered. He half-fell back onto the rubble and covered his eyes with one hand as his shoulders heaved. The wardens helped him up. The medic crouched briefly over Vera.

I felt dizzy. Ingo stood statue-still, his fists helpless at his sides. We looked at each other.

Overhead, our planes were needed.

"We'd better go," I whispered.

CHAPTER THIRTY-EIGHT

I COULDN'T THINK ABOUT IT. Couldn't. When we reached the airfield, it was pulsing with action – fitters scrambling over Doves, pilots racing towards their planes. Engines started up, one after the other, the propellers bursting into life.

We couldn't take the time to change. Still in my dress and tattered stockings, I sprinted for my plane. Hal was in the cockpit, starting it up. He climbed down in a flurry of blue jumpsuit. "Where the hell's your flight gear?"

"No time," I said curtly.

My helmet was in the Dove. Another fitter rushed up with a parachute and helped me strap it on. Up in the air, I lost sight of Ingo's plane. The Scorps were on us almost immediately, their spiky symbols taunting. The bomber they protected cruised above.

I wanted to annihilate it. Gs tugged at me as I fought for height. A Scorp appeared in my mirrors; I stomped on the right rudder and the skyscrapers spun. The island's southern tip jutted out into the bay as the bomber tried to reach the docks.

"No, you will not get our ships," I muttered. The Scorp was still after me. *Fine, you first.* I darted into the clouds, banked hard, and came out above it. The Scorp swung back and forth in the crosshairs, my cockpit vibrating around me.

I fired and pulled out. My pulse spiked with hard joy as flames erupted across the Scorp's fuselage. It went spinning down into the bay, black smoke curling. Others were already on the bomber and it was going high – higher – retreating.

Even when the Scorps were just departing dots and the bomber had been chased away, I wanted to stay in the sky. If I landed, I'd have to think of Vera.

Finally I brought my Dove in, my chest made of lead beneath my straps. As I landed, the Dove ahead of me was just trundling to a halt. Relief filled me as I glimpsed the "91" on its tail: the last two digits of Ingo's call number.

I came to a stop and switched off. The propellers slowly stilled. In the sudden silence I undid my straps and slid open my hood. My weak leg gave a twinge as I dropped down onto the wing – slippery under my torn stockings

– and glanced towards Ingo's plane.

The Scorp screamed out of nowhere – flying low, strafing everything in its path. Bullet fire whistled and thudded.

I gave a yelp; my feet shot out from under me. I slammed against the wing and then hit the ground – scrambled under my Dove just as the Scorp passed over again, its shadow like an attacking hawk. Holes peppered across my plane in staccato whines.

Shouts – the roar of the engine, fading now.

Had he gotten my fuel tank? I lunged out from under my Dove and ran until I was clear. *Ingo*. Panicked, I jogged to a stop and looked towards his plane. A dark-haired figure emerged from beneath the wing.

The "91" Dove exploded in a fireball of noise and colour.

"*No!*" I screamed. I started running, my skirt churning around my legs as shrapnel pattered to the ground. The heat from the blast slapped me and with a cry I had to stop, shielding my face. The figure had been thrown clear.

Not Ingo. Hal.

I jerked into motion again, ignoring the heat. I dropped to my knees beside him. "Hal…Hal…"

My brother lay sprawled, eyes closed, a rough scrape on his face. His legs were raw meat and blood. A white stripe gleamed through the right one and it hit me that the stripe was bone and the world swam.

So much blood. The coppery smell gagged at my throat.

I frantically tried to put my hands over the wounds but the wounds were everywhere.

"Hal! Hang on!" I gasped. "*Please.*"

I was shuddering. My hands were slick and red. He didn't move. He wasn't moving. I heard a low keening and realized it was me.

"Amity!" Ingo appeared, panting, just ahead of the medics.

He crouched hastily and felt for Hal's pulse, then gripped my arms. "He's alive. He's alive."

The medics hefted Hal onto a stretcher, too fast to be gentle. He came half-conscious and screamed, his face a terrible ashen colour. In a confused rush I jogged along beside them, clutching Hal's hand. I told him it would be all right, just fine, don't worry. There was no room for me in the ambulance because there were other wounded too, and I struggled to go in, shouting at them.

Ingo wrapped his arms tightly around me. His voice was hoarse. "Amity…shh…shh…"

The ambulance drove away. The airfield felt deathly silent. As Ingo still held me I collapsed, crying, against his chest. He stroked my hair and then helped me upright.

"Come on, we have to get to the hospital," he whispered.

We sat in the waiting room and I stared down at the cold cup of coffee that I hadn't been able to drink. I'd washed the blood off my hands but could still see it.

I put the coffee down and it blurred in my vision. "He has to be all right," I murmured.

Ingo looked as pale and drawn as I felt. He put his arm around me without speaking. I leaned against him, my throat tight and aching. First Vera, and now…

"I think I could do with a platitude for a change," I said finally.

Ingo was silent for a long moment. "I hope he'll be fine," he said. "He's young and healthy and in good hands."

"I want more than hope."

"I can't give you that. But I think the odds are on his side." Ingo gently rubbed my shoulder, his lips against my hair. "I've never lied to you, my friend," he whispered. "I'm not starting now."

Our fingers found each other and linked tightly together. Though part of me just wanted comfort, the fact that Ingo remained exactly who I knew him to be gave strength on its own.

"I thought it was you at first," I admitted.

He straightened a little, looking down at me, his dark eyes concerned.

I swallowed. "The…plane's call letters. I thought they were yours."

"No, it wasn't my plane," Ingo said, and I nodded. At some point in the confusion I'd glimpsed the wrong call letters with the same final digits lying in the wreckage.

I thought again of the fact that we'd never spoken of the future. Not once, in over six months together. If we both lived it felt inevitable that we'd share one…but saying this out loud seemed like tempting fate.

I shut my eyes and pressed close to him. He held me.

Neither of us moved again until a doctor appeared and told us what they'd done to Hal.

Through the covers of his hospital bed, I could see the shape of my brother's left leg, bulky with bandages. His right ended mid-thigh. Below that, the covers lay flat.

"I was hoping we could at least save the knee," the doctor had said heavily when he'd come to speak to us. "It was just too damaged. There was nothing left to work with."

He's alive, I reminded myself harshly. Nothing else should have mattered…but I had a sudden memory of him walking across the airfield laughing with Percy, and my head felt as if it might split in two.

He was barely sixteen.

The hospital room was silent. Hal was still sleeping; so was his roommate. I pulled a chair close to my brother's bedside. I forced myself to look at the flat sheet. I would not let on to Hal, ever, how much it horrified and saddened me.

Finally I exhaled and lay my forehead on my hands, the sheets crisp against my fingers. Ingo had gone to get fresh clothes for us; we still wore our outfits from the club. As long as things remained quiet, we'd stay here.

"Amity?" murmured Hal.

I sat up quickly and wiped my cheeks. I clenched his hand. "I'm here."

My brother's gaze was slightly glassy from painkillers. His voice sounded thick, as if he'd been drinking.

"They took it off, didn't they?" he whispered. "I heard them talking...in the ambulance..."

I stroked his damp hair back. "Yes," I said levelly. "But you're going to be fine. Having two legs is overrated anyway."

He closed his eyes tightly. His throat worked. "Percy?" he said finally.

"Ingo's gone back to base. He'll tell him. He'll probably bring him back here."

"No."

When I didn't respond, Hal looked at me again. "I don't want him to see."

"Hal, he—"

"*Please.*"

"Okay," I soothed. I rubbed his arm. "Okay."

Hal stared up at the ceiling. His eyes were wet. When he spoke again I could hardly hear him. "I want to go home."

I wondered how cogent he was. He hadn't really had a "home" since he'd lived in Sacrament.

"You mean back to base?" I said.

Hal slowly shook his head. "No. Home with Ma. I don't want to stay here." He looked over at his roommate then

— a guy with a leg up in traction, bandages covering his face. He shuddered.

"Please, Amity," he whispered hoarsely.

"Okay," I said.

He looked at me. His face had the same tight look as when he was a child and struggling not to cry. "You mean it?"

"Yes. As soon as you can travel." I had no idea how I'd get him to Nova Scotia but I'd do it or die trying. I gripped his hand. "Try to rest now."

After he'd finally drifted off again, I went out into the silent hospital corridor. The only other person was the night nurse, doing paperwork at her desk. I leaned against the wall and massaged my pounding head.

I looked up as the elevator opened. Ingo and Percy stepped out. Percy looked wide-eyed, keyed-up.

My spirits sank. I went over and explained as tactfully as I could that Hal was asleep and that he didn't want to see Percy. Tact has never been my strong point. I could hear myself getting it wrong, bumbling the words.

"He's still pretty doped up," I finished. "Maybe later he'll feel differently."

"I'll stay," Percy said faintly.

I didn't argue. Percy went over to the waiting area and sat down. He rested his head on his fingertips.

Ingo put his arms around me. I pressed close, shutting my eyes.

"Hal wants to go home," I murmured against his neck.

Ingo drew back. "Where does he mean?"

"Nova Scotia. I promised I'd get him there. I'm not sure how I'll manage it, but I have to." New fighting had broken out north of Boston recently. Ships hadn't sailed near Nova Scotia in weeks.

Ingo nodded and squeezed my fingers. He kissed them. "We'll do it," he said. "Don't worry."

I let out a breath. Ingo had never lied to me. He wasn't starting now. I wrapped my arms tightly around him and he stroked my back. The only noise was the night nurse, shuffling her papers.

CHAPTER THIRTY-NINE

MAY, 1943

I HARDLY LEFT HAL'S SIDE at the hospital, returning to flying only when the fighting was heavy and they couldn't do without every hand.

Three weeks after his amputation, my brother hadn't changed his mind about going home. He hadn't changed his mind about not seeing Percy, either. Every time I saw Percy on base he looked devastated – but it was Hal's decision to make. I didn't have it in me to lecture him.

Vera's funeral had been a sombre affair. It had been all wrong, every dignified chord of it. We should have been drinking gin and dancing the jitterbug. But Harlan had been too flattened to plan anything different – at the service he stood stiff and red-eyed in a suit – and I'd been too distracted by Hal. I'd worn a dark dress and stared bleakly at her casket, thinking, *I'm so sorry, Vera. I wish I'd arranged something special for you.*

On April 16th, I'd had a birthday. I'd forgotten about it until Ingo gave me a small book of prints from the exhibition we'd especially liked.

"Thank you," I whispered, paging through it. I paused at the print of the painting of high, airy cirrus clouds – it had reminded us both of the first time we ever flew.

"We'll celebrate properly later," Ingo said softly, and I nodded.

Meanwhile, Ingo had gone to Tess – the straightest of straight arrows – and somehow convinced her to let us take one of the long-distance sortie planes, signing us out on an unofficial "mission".

"Be back in five days or it's my ass," Tess said gruffly when Hal was well enough to travel. Then she squeezed my shoulder. "I hope he'll be okay."

So did I.

"He's sleeping – Lorna is going to sit with him for a while," said Ma, coming back into the living room where Ingo and I waited. Lorna was the nurse that Ma had hired.

"Good, he needs the rest," I said. It had been a ten-hour flight – we'd had to take a long, curving route over the safety of international water. Even after sharing the piloting, Ingo and I were tired too.

Ma sat down across from us in a faded armchair, carefully arranging her skirt. Through the window behind her I could see a street of slightly shabby houses, with a glittering that might have been the ocean in the distance.

Ma was living in a boarding house in Provincetown, Nova Scotia. She no longer had any of the antique furniture or other nice things that she'd had when Hal and I were growing up; it had all been left behind when Collie rescued her and Hal from the Western Seaboard.

I'd never cared much about our belongings – Ma's apartment had been so crammed full of things you could hardly breathe – but it felt strange that they were gone. So much of our family history had been there.

If it bothered Ma, she didn't show it. I'd learned these last few years that she had a core of strength. When Hal was made Discordant, she'd had a plan in place to hide him. When I'd cabled her the news of his injury, she'd cabled back, *He's alive. All that matters. Bring him home.*

Even so, I'd worried on Hal's behalf that she might burst into tears when she saw him – cling and sob and make things even worse. My brother's moods had swung wildly this past month, ranging from fury to despair to grim humour. The only way to handle him, I'd found, was to go along with the humour and not give in to the rest of it.

But to my surprise, our mother – who sometimes seemed to view herself as the centre of a great drama – had hugged Hal hard when we got his wheelchair off the plane, but stayed nearly dry-eyed.

"Why, I guess you'll do anything to get home, won't you?" she'd laughed shakily, dabbing at her eyes, and Hal had snorted, looking pale and drained.

"Yeah. Guess I must have been pretty desperate."

The relief had been enormous. Ma and I had hugged too, there on the airport tarmac. I'd felt tears threaten as the smell of her perfume had mixed with the fresh, salty air, my love for her sudden and unexpected in its power.

When I'd introduced Ingo, she'd hardly flinched as they shook hands. I'd warned her of his scar in a letter that I'd prayed would reach her in time, wanting to spare him her reaction. I'd written to her already about Ingo and me, of course, though hadn't gone into much detail – just the basics about his family, and that he used to be a Peacefighter too. She hadn't asked for more.

In retrospect, I should have realized this wasn't a good sign.

Now, with Hal settled and the excitement over, I sat in this strange living room filled with unfamiliar, rented furniture beside a man who was very definitely not Collis Reed…and my sociable mother suddenly appeared to have nothing to say.

"I want to thank you, Mr Manfred, for helping my daughter get Hal here," she said finally.

He cleared his throat. "Please, call me Ingo." He'd confessed his slight nervousness to me. His own family was so important to him – he wanted to make a good impression.

Suddenly I noticed a childhood photo of myself and Collie on Ma's mantelpiece. Tucked into the side of the frame was a cut-out newspaper photo of Collie now, smiling, looking handsome in a suit.

I stared at it. Why hadn't she taken that *down*?

"Ingo," repeated Ma, as if tasting it. "Such a funny name."

"Not where he's from, Ma," I said automatically.

She'd wanted me to marry Collie. She'd been overjoyed when we got together. She loved him like a son – maybe with a special protectiveness, because he'd needed a mother so badly.

I looked sideways at the photo again. She *had* to know he was married to Kay Pierce, didn't she?

"Is that right, Ingo?" Ma said finally, her voice too formal. "Is it a common name where you're from?"

Ingo shook his curly head. "Not really. It's a little old-fashioned now. It was my grandfather's name."

My lips tugged upwards as I glanced at him. "I didn't know that."

"Man of mystery," he said.

"And I believe Amity said you have two siblings?" said Ma.

"Yes, a brother and sister. Erich and Angelina. I'm the middle one."

I could see Ma's not-quite-hidden reaction to the guttural "*ch*" sound of "Erich".

"How nice," she said.

Silence.

"Ma, is there any coffee, or…?" I asked at last, desperate to banish the quiet. I felt awkward, out of place. In our apartment in Sacrament, I'd have helped myself.

Ma jumped up in a relieved flurry. "Oh, of course! I'm so sorry, I'm not thinking."

"Understandable," said Ingo, propping his forearms on his knees.

Ma had a hot plate and kettle hidden away in a cupboard. I watched her put water on to boil with a faint sadness. It was all such a far cry from what she'd once had.

"Ingo, do you take coffee?" asked Ma, bringing out a tin canister. "Or…" She hesitated, somehow managing to hint at a myriad of guttural-sounding beverages that she'd never heard of.

"Coffee's fine. Thank you."

"You speak very good English," said Ma, measuring coffee into the percolator, and Ingo and I exchanged a private smile, remembering when I'd once said the same to him.

"His mother's from New Manhattan," I said. "He went to school there."

"I was sorry to hear about your father, Ingo…how did he and your mother meet?" asked Ma. I winced slightly at the mention of Ingo's dad, but was curious – it had never occurred to me to ask.

"She went to art school in Florence," said Ingo.

"But she's a musician," I said in surprise.

"Yes. Her youthful rebellion, she says. Everyone expected her to be a musician, so she wanted to try something else." Ingo looked down, fiddling briefly with a cuff. "My father says…said…that she reneged on the deal when she went back to music. He was expecting paintings all over the house. Thank you," he added to Ma as she handed us our drinks.

We were on the sofa, close but not touching. He wore grey trousers, a green shirt, his sports jacket. I knew he'd brought the jacket along especially to wear when he met Ma.

"So your mother's been happy at the vineyard?" asked Ma, settling down again with her own cup.

"Very happy, I think." Ingo's tone became soft, slightly stilted. I knew he was thinking of his mother's grief.

I touched his thigh. Ma looked at my hand and then away again, her lips thinning. For a moment I was confused, and then it hit me. I stared at her, amazed.

Despite everything, she'd still hoped that Collie and I would get back together.

"And I suppose you think Amity would be happy there too?" she said to Ingo.

"Ma!"

Her shrug was overly casual. "You two are obviously quite serious."

"We haven't discussed it," I said, my cheeks flaming.

"Well, I can't imagine why not."

Because every day might be our last and it's tempting fate. I didn't say it.

Ingo had gone still. Finally he put his coffee down and said, "No, we haven't discussed it. But if we both live… then I very much hope that Amity will feel she could be happy there."

My heart skipped. I looked at him.

Ma had winced at "if we both live", but regained herself. "You couldn't move here?"

"Not easily, no."

"I wouldn't want him to," I said. "It's his heritage, Ma. It means more to him than anything."

"Not quite," said Ingo quietly. He glanced at me. "If Amity wasn't happy…I could work something else out. But it would take time."

"I would never let you sell it," I said in a fierce undertone. "Never."

Ingo's expression deepened. As we studied each other, it felt as if more had been said.

"What about your face?" Ma asked suddenly.

My blood heated; my attention snapped back to her. "What about it?" I said before Ingo could speak.

Her gaze travelled across his scar's wrinkled skin; the drooping eye; the partial eyebrow. Though she didn't then look at Collie's photo, she might as well have.

"It's just such a shame, to be so terribly scarred at twenty-two," she said stiffly. "Can't anything be done? Surgery?"

"Ma, this is none of your business!"

Ingo put his hand over mine; our fingers linked together.

"No, I'm afraid I'm stuck with being only half a telio star," he said levelly. "The World United doctors I saw weren't hopeful. Even if something could be done, I doubt I could afford it."

"But the vineyard," protested Ma.

"It's not large. Some years are a struggle."

"Oh," said Ma, managing to weigh the small word with meaning.

"Are you finished?" I said. "Can we talk about something else?"

"Why, of course, darling." Ma gave a forced laugh. "But honestly, I would have thought you'd had enough struggle by now."

With an effort, I bit back my response. I thought of how enthusiastic she'd be if this were Collie, and wondered bitterly if she knew why we were no longer together.

Ingo still held my hand. He looked down at it, playing with my fingers. In a low voice, he said, "Mrs Vancour... I'm in love with your daughter. For some reason, she loves me, too. If we're lucky enough to have a future, she won't starve. If we have children someday, they won't starve, either."

My throat closed. I squeezed his fingers hard.

"You want children, then?" said Ma after a pause.

His soft sound was almost a laugh. "At the moment, I just want us both to survive. But if the time comes, I'd prefer to discuss that with Amity before I do with you."

"Of course," said Ma coolly. As if she couldn't help

herself, she did glance at Collie's photo then. He'd always jollied her along, flirted with her. When we were kids, I'd sometimes wondered which of us he'd been coming over to see, me or my mother.

Ingo had seen her look. In the stilted silence that followed, he checked his watch. "I...think maybe I'll go take a shower before dinner."

Ma had told us that the boarding house served it at seven. He got up from the sofa and leaned down to quickly kiss my cheek. "Thank you for the coffee, Mrs Vancour," he said to Ma.

"I'll be up in a minute," I said, and Ingo nodded. The two of us were staying in a room on the top floor, which another resident had left vacant for a few weeks.

After he left, I sat staring at my mother, who looked unrepentant. "How *could* you?" I burst out. "You made him feel...you didn't even tell him to call you Rose!"

"I hardly know him."

"But *I* know him! Don't you understand, Ma? I love him."

She gathered up the cups and went to rinse them out at a small sink. "Come help me with these," she said. I gritted my teeth and did so, drying them with a dishcloth. When I'd finished the last one, Ma said, "Are you sure you don't want to sleep down here?"

"What? No, of course not."

"You're not married, Amity. It's not nice."

"You didn't care when I shared a room with Collie."

"I've known Collis from the time he was seven."

"Yes, and look how well *that* turned out," I couldn't help snapping. I leaned against the sink and pressed my fingers to my forehead. "Ma, you do realize he's *married to Kay Pierce*, don't you?"

"Well, I'm sure that's not what he wanted!"

"Do you know?" I said softly. "What he did to me? Did he tell you?"

Collie had driven Hal and Ma across the country after rescuing them – I knew that on that journey he'd told Hal, at least.

Ma sagged a little. She sank down into the armchair. "Yes," she said heavily. "He told me. He thinks it was his fault that you were…sent to that place."

"It *was* his fault."

Ma frowned, looking worried. "I had the impression that maybe he was just being very hard on himself. Maybe you misinterpreted things, Amity. You must know how much he's always loved you."

My mother regularly rewrote history, but this still felt like a slap across the face. "No," I said sharply. "I did not misinterpret anything. He told the Guns to take me away and they did."

Ma let out a long breath. "Poor Collis," she murmured.

My emotions were a frayed, trembling rope. "Poor *Collis*?" I cried. "Do you know what it was like in there? Didn't you see the footage?"

To my surprise, my mother's eyes filled. She took my

hand. "Poor you too," she whispered. "I didn't mean otherwise, darling. It killed me to know you were in there."

I exhaled and sank onto the arm of the chair. We sat in silence for several long moments. "Ma...you have to understand," I said. "It's been over with Collie for a long time. I'm in love with Ingo. That's been true for a long time too."

"That face," murmured Ma.

"What does it *matter*?"

"In an ideal world, it wouldn't." Ma hesitated, looking pained. "I like him," she said.

I stared at her.

"I do," said Ma. "He's intelligent, well-spoken; he obviously comes from a nice family..." She sighed, as if she'd been saying the opposite. I could almost see her trying to reconcile herself to a man in my life who wasn't Collie.

"He'll be good to you," she said finally. "I can tell."

I was tempted to ask about Dad then – to find out what Ma had alluded to in her letter to Hal. I felt too drained to pursue it. I kissed Ma's cheek. "See you at dinner," I said.

When I reached the bedroom on the top floor, Ingo was slumped on the bed wearing only his trousers, his fingers buried in his dark curls. He didn't look up as I closed the door.

"Well, that went well," he said.

I went and crouched on the floor in front of him. I rubbed his knees. "She likes you," I said.

He laughed.

"No, I'm not kidding. She told me."

Ingo's eyebrows rose. He pulled me onto the bed and I straddled him. "She thinks you're intelligent and well-spoken." I kissed his neck – nibbled it lightly. "She says you'll be good to me," I murmured.

His good eyebrow was still high. He caressed my thighs. The feel of his hands on my skin undid me and I pushed him back onto the bed. We landed in a tangle and I laughed.

"All right, I think my powers of observation have completely failed me," Ingo said. "What would it have been like if she *didn't* like me?"

"It wouldn't have mattered." I smoothed his hair back. "I'm so sorry," I added. "I should have guessed that she'd…"

"Stop." He slid his hand behind my neck and kissed me. "If you meet my family, you'll have three of them firing questions at you."

If. I understood. I did the same thing. Part of me was glad that Ma had forced the issue of our future out into the open…though I was scared that the depth of my feelings might jinx it all, just as much as saying *when* instead of *if*.

* * *

What remained of Hal's right leg was slightly elevated, its bandages pristine. They had to be changed twice a day. I could look at it now without wincing.

I sat beside him on the bed the next morning, careful not to jostle him. "How's it going?" I asked.

"Peachy," Hal said.

"What's Lorna like?" I'd met the nurse Ma had hired only briefly.

He shrugged. He was sitting propped up against the pillows.

"Nice? Not nice? Any of the above?"

"Okay, I guess."

"Hey, you've got a view," I said, noticing. There was a street, and then beyond it, hills. The sound of seagulls squabbling drifted in.

He didn't look. "Mmm. Yeah."

"This seems like a pretty good place. Ingo and I met everyone last night. Some of the boarders aren't much older than you."

"Great. I can make new friends."

I sighed. "Are you still glad you came?" I said after a pause.

Hal seemed to rouse a little. He rubbed his forehead.

"Yeah," he said, his voice rough. "I couldn't stand being at the base hospital so close to where…people…had known me before. Or so close to base, when I can't work on the planes any more."

I studied a vase of flowers on the bedside table. Casually,

I said, "You know, once the war's over, maybe you could still be a pilot someday."

The air felt charged suddenly. Hal shot me a dark look. "With one leg?"

"You'll have a prosthetic."

"My fucking *knee's* gone, have you forgotten? How would I push down on the rudder?"

I ignored his anger and shrugged. "I was talking with the doctor before we left New Manhattan. It's not impossible, depending on what type of prosthetic you'll have. And how much exercise you do to build up the muscles left in your thigh."

Hal didn't answer. His mouth was tight, his expression half-resentful. I sensed that now wasn't the time to push it – that I should just let the idea germinate a while.

"Did Ma talk to you?" I said at last.

He knew what I meant. The tension defused. He sighed and plucked at his sheets.

"Yeah," he said.

CHAPTER FORTY

AFTER DINNER THE NIGHT BEFORE, Ma had said that she wanted to speak to me privately. Somehow, from her expression, I'd known it was going to be about Dad. A sickening mix of dread and hope had rushed through me.

"Yes, of course," I said stiffly.

Ingo guessed too – his eyes had been concerned as they met mine. He remained in the communal parlour, talking with another pilot who was staying there. Ma and I went back to her rented living room, with its cheap knick-knacks that seemed to have little to do with her.

Hal was asleep. I perched awkwardly on the sofa. I didn't think I was going to learn anything that would help, but the hope that I might felt devastating.

"I know you and Hal have questions," Ma said, looking down at her hands. "I don't really know where to begin."

"Did you know Dad threw the Tier One fight?" I blurted.

Ma sighed. Finally she rose. She went to the same cabinet where the kettle and hotplate hid and took out a bottle of sherry. She poured us each a small glass and sat down again.

She swirled her drink, gazing down at it as if mesmerized.

"Yes," she said in a small voice.

I stared at her. I'd always assumed that she hadn't – couldn't – have known.

Ma cleared her throat. "Let me back up. I met Truce when I was seventeen. He was nineteen and a Peacefighter and I thought he was the handsomest, most charming man on the planet. I loved how he never took anything seriously."

My forehead creased. My father had joked around at times, but he'd taken plenty of things seriously. My childhood was filled with memories of him intently telling me stories of our ancestors, who'd fought so hard to bring peace to the world.

"That…doesn't sound like him," I said.

"You never really knew your grandmother on his side," Ma said. "I wish you had. You can't understand Truce unless you understand her."

In a disconnected flash, I wondered if the same was true of me. Could I be understood without understanding my mother?

I shifted on the sofa, my heart pounding. "Tell me," I said.

Ma did. She explained how she used to go visit Pacifica Vancour with Tru. His mother was a former Peacefighter herself and formidable. Ma – "Silly little Rose Petrie", as she described herself – had felt nervous and inadequate around her.

"I was sure she'd tell Truce that he shouldn't waste his time on me," she said. "And of course she did. She couldn't have done me a bigger favour."

At my quizzical expression, Ma said, "Tru resented his mother terribly. He always had."

I nodded slowly. He'd never told me that, but I could see it. The night before he died, when I'd come across him drunk in the kitchen, he'd sounded so bitter about her.

"She was a domineering woman," said Ma. "Tru was the life of the party, but then we'd get to Pacifica's and he'd go silent. He never wanted to be a Peacefighter," she added.

I stared at her. "But…"

"Pacifica bullied him into it. None of the ideals meant much to him, back then. He loved the flying, but…" She shrugged helplessly.

I fell silent, stunned, remembering how much pressure Dad had put on *me* to become a Peacefighter.

"Did you know about Madeline then?" I said finally. Madeline had been a Peacefighter for Can-Amer with Dad. According to her, she and Dad had been seeing each other too at that point – had been in love.

Ma's expression tightened. "I met her a few times. I could tell that they were...involved."

Surprise stirred. "You knew even before you got married?"

She slowly nodded. "But you have to understand, Amity. Truce was such a good-looking man – so charming. Any woman would have wanted him."

Though she was defending Dad, in a way, I could see old anger and hurt on her face. She looked down. "So... then I got pregnant," she said. "And I made sure Pacifica knew about it."

Ma had known, she said, that if a grandchild was involved, Pacifica would make Dad do the right thing. And that Dad wouldn't stand up to her, because he never did when it was something important.

"You mean you got pregnant on purpose?" I whispered.

"Not on *purpose* exactly," she said weakly. "But, well, I suppose part of me thought that I wouldn't really mind if..." She trailed off.

You're not married, Amity. It's not nice. I took a gulp of sherry, even though I didn't like sweet drinks.

Ma said that Dad had thrown himself into marriage at first, as if it were a game. He'd finished his Peacefighting term and then Pacifica had deeded him her grandfather's farm in Gloversdale and he and Ma had started fixing up the rambling old house.

But he still kept seeing Madeline, even after I was born. Ma decided to ignore it, to believe his claim that they were just friends.

"He said...that he needed someone he could really talk to," she confessed softly.

I winced. Madeline used to *visit* us – spend weeks during the summer months with us. How could either of them have done that to Ma?

She looked up and saw my face. "Your father loved me, Amity. But I suppose after we'd been married awhile..." She studied her sherry. She sounded tired as she said, "We were very different people."

I thought of our house in Gloversdale, on the edge of town and surrounded by fields and woods. It had never occurred to me that my childhood spent romping outside might have come at a time of loneliness for Ma. She had just always been there, doing things for us.

"And I think...Tru resented me, on some level," confessed Ma. "He loved you, but I don't think he wanted to get married so young. And then Pacifica died when you were three and left most of her money to charity, and we started to run into financial problems with the house, and..." She sighed.

Distant memories were surfacing. In them, our house in Gloversdale seemed huge, the furniture tall. Angry voices – slamming doors. Hal had been born around that time.

I remembered standing on my tiptoes to peer down at this strange new being in its bassinet, so small and olive-skinned – resenting him, thinking that all the upset must be his fault.

"I didn't behave very well for a long time," Ma said softly. "I nagged Tru about money and told him that we didn't have enough for you kids, and that he was a failure who couldn't even keep a house going. I was angry about Madeline, but I just went on and on at him…" She lapsed into silence.

I gripped my drink, thinking of how jovial they'd always been with each other when I was older. Even back then, it had seemed oddly false.

Then when I was six, the civil war Peacefight had come around. Would Can-Amer stay one country, or divide into two, with John Gunnison ruling the more prosperous one?

By that time, Madeline had left Peacefighting as well; she'd been involved in Senator Gunnison's campaign. Dad, though retired from Peacefighting, had still trained new pilots.

Ma said he'd come home one day and told her that they wanted an experienced pilot to fly the civil war fight on the "remain united" side, and that he'd agreed to do it.

"The way he said it…I knew something was up, but I couldn't imagine what," Ma whispered. "It was as if…he were blaming me, or defensive, or defiant of what I might think… I don't know."

When we'd listened to the civil war Peacefight on the

telio, I hadn't known it was Dad flying. No one had. Pilots were always anonymous.

Ma hadn't breathed a word. But as she'd listened to the announcer's blow-by-blow description, she'd wondered. One of Dad's favourite fight moves was to go into a tight, fast turn and hold the plane a knife-edge from stalling.

This time he'd stalled. He'd been shot down.

Her voice was hoarse as she described Dad coming home the next day. He'd tossed an envelope onto the kitchen table, his gaze hard and challenging.

"Never talk to me about money again," he'd said. He'd turned and left the room.

Half a million credits were in the envelope.

"I guessed then," whispered Ma. "I was horrified. I tried to forget all about it. I put some of the money in the bank and I spent some of it on you and Hal and then I started fixing up the house. Truce and I never spoke of it, not once."

"Why did you stay together?" I burst out in agony.

Ma shook her head helplessly. "It may not sound like it, but we did love each other. I knew he'd never leave me for Madeline."

She wiped her eyes. "Besides, he was crazy about you kids – you know that, Amity. We just pretended everything was fine. Sometimes it felt like things really were. But deep down…it was always broken after that."

"I know," I got out, remembering the man who'd told me fervent bedtime stories about the importance of

Peacefighting – who'd been too hilarious at times – who'd drunk in secret.

I cleared my throat. "Madeline...Madeline said she was the only person in Dad's life who knew."

"Maybe the only one he talked to," said Ma wearily. "But he knew I knew."

She stared at her glass. "Actually, it's not quite true that we never spoke of it," she said. "One night years later, he came to bed and he'd been drinking, and he said, 'You know how you betray a nation, Rosie? Just keep thinking, *Eye on the prize...eye on the prize.*'"

She gave a shaky laugh and pushed her hair back. "I was a coward. I pretended I was asleep and hadn't heard him."

Eye on the prize. I felt like a statue.

"I didn't know until your trial that Madeline was the one who asked him to do it," Ma said. "But I always suspected. It felt very...pointed. As if he'd been trying to hurt me."

She looked down. "That's why...I said in my letter to Hal...that I never thought he was completely to blame. I have to be to blame too, don't you see? I manoeuvred him into marrying me when I knew he'd never have done it otherwise, and then I goaded him about money for years. I was cruel about it. I belittled him whenever I could."

My heart felt too tight to keep beating. *He was cruel to you too,* I thought.

"It was no excuse for what he did," I whispered.

"No," said Ma. "But maybe it's an explanation."

* * *

The next day, Hal plucked at his bedclothes.

"I hate everything Ma told me," he said. "But at least Dad didn't just do it because Madeline batted her eyelashes at him. Not that I think the reasons he *did* do it were great, but…"

"I know what you mean," I said. Ma was right. You couldn't understand our father without understanding where he'd come from. Not an excuse, but an explanation.

It meant something to have at least that, after so long.

After talking to Ma, I'd told Ingo everything in the privacy of our room. And lying in his arms, I realized that what Dad had done still hurt, but distantly – part of my past rather than my present.

"It's strange," Ingo had said. "I think it would help me to know all of that, even without any real answers. Does it you?"

I'd nodded, staring at the ceiling. "There were so many secrets. I always had Dad on a pedestal. Now I know how flawed he was. Ma too. Their marriage was…" I trailed off, sadness washing over me.

"I think they were both in a lot of pain," I said finally. I turned towards Ingo, taking him in. "Remember the day before we came into New Manhattan? I told you that I couldn't be happy until everything Dad had put into place was gone."

Ingo smoothed a strand of my hair back. "I remember very well."

"I was wrong." I whispered. I kissed his chest. "I just need for all of this to be over with, so that we can hold on to what we have."

Now I moved to Hal's window and looked out. The hills had seagulls perched on them like white handkerchiefs scattered by the wind. I saw my brother reflected in the glass behind me.

"Use 'Eye on the prize'," I said.

Hal looked startled. "Huh?"

I turned and nodded at the stump of his leg. "Ma told you what Dad said, right? Turn it around…make something good come of it. 'Eye on the prize'. Your prize is flying, if you work your muscles enough."

CHAPTER FORTY-ONE

MAY, 1943

"HE *WHAT?*" SAID KAY.

The man standing in front of her desk was balding and couldn't hide the cunning in his eyes, though he seemed to be trying. At her reaction, his expression turned wary. He kneaded the battered hat that he held.

"Well, I suppose I could be mistaken, Madame President," he said. "It was years ago. Maybe my boy didn't spend so much time over there after all."

Kay had half-risen as she exclaimed. Now she straightened all the way, feeling hot. "No. Don't tell me what you think I want to hear. I want the exact truth and I'll know if you're lying. Collis *grew up* with Amity Vancour?"

Collis's father hesitated, then nodded. "Back in Gloversdale."

"I know where he's from."

"We had a little place out there, next to those *Van-coors*. I never liked them, I'll tell you that. Snooty rich folk. Didn't surprise me one bit to find out what *he'd* been up to."

"He" was presumably Amity Vancour's father. "Collis and Amity," Kay prompted tightly.

"Oh, he was always crazy about her, even though she was a tomboy and kind of plain, if you ask me. Goldie, my wife, said once –" Hank Reed mimicked a high-pitched, whining voice – "Hank, I bet if we played our cards right, he could marry that girl!"

Through the window behind Collis's father, Kay could see the mountains of Denver: white peaks pushing against a blue sky. She'd come here to inspect the troops that were marshalling for a last-ditch push against World United.

She had lost her nuclear weapons factory; it had fallen to WU troops like a house of cards. The news had threatened to crush her. World United had gotten a message to her soon afterwards asking if she'd surrender. She'd refused point-blank.

Her plans for Black Moon were gone – she could never best Johnny now, never. But she could hang on to Can-Amer. With everything slipping through her fingers like sand, Kay was desperate to at least do that.

Summoning Hank Reed to her office while she was

here had been impulsive – something to distract her from all the harrowing news.

A bastard and he's still alive, Collis had said. Kay knew all about bastards. She'd been curious about this one. In the back of her mind was the thought that Collis had gotten rid of Cain for her, and so she could return the favour with this man he hated. Collis was in the far north again, scrambling to hold on to what was left there.

Or that's what his letters claimed.

Kay paced to the window. In the plains between the city and the mountains, she could see her troops' camp, and Keaton's headquarters. Denver had largely been evacuated. Factory workers like Reed were some of the few people left in the city.

"Go on," she said finally.

Hank Reed cleared his throat, looking cautious. "Well…I'm not sure what else there is to say, Madame President. Collis was always over there. I think he'd have moved in if he could. Once, after we left Gloversdale, I overheard him telling someone about his 'family' – meaning the Vancours. Well, maybe he was fourteen then and almost as tall as me, but I gave him a walloping, I'll tell you, the stuck-up little no-good."

Reed seemed to catch himself. He gave an ingratiating smile. "My, though, he's done well *now*, hasn't he? I sure am proud of my boy, and even prouder that you saw fit to marry him, Madame President. Hey, I guess I'm your father-in-law."

Hank Reed looked nothing like Collis, but disconcertingly his voice was the same: husky, with a faint western accent. If Kay closed her eyes, it could be Collis telling her these things.

She didn't move from the window. "All right. You can go."

When she didn't hear Reed leave, she turned around. For the first time she saw his resemblance to Collis, in the quick, friendly grin he gave. "Well now, Madame President, I'm sure if my son were here he'd put in a word for his old man. Times are tough, you know, and—"

"Get out or I'll have you killed," said Kay.

The blood drained from Reed's face. He started to speak, then stopped.

He left.

Slowly, Kay went to her desk and looked at the file she'd taken from Collis's office again. She studied his handwriting on a carbon copy: the single word *No* in response to whether he wanted any action taken on Mr Reed, senior.

He'd known Amity Vancour all his life. He'd thought of her family as his own.

The *No* resonated through Kay's brain like a drumbeat. When Collis had first woken up from his gunshot wound, his promptness at betraying Vancour with the correct address had reassured Kay – he was exactly who she'd thought. She could control him.

He'd told her that he first met Vancour on the Western Seaboard Peacefighting base. That her brother meant nothing to him.

Kay recalled glimpsing Collis and Mac whispering in a shadowy corridor of the Zodiac once, their expressions intense. Later, the memory seemed to corroborate Collis's story that he'd been playing Mac for Gunnison.

Had he been playing Mac?

Just before the assassination attack that had killed Cain, Kay had been talking with Keaton about Black Moon. If Collis had overheard…might he have decided that her death just then could be disastrous?

Kay snatched up the phone. "Get me a long-distance line. Yukon one-four-five-one."

An hour later, after a series of calls, Kay slowly hung up the receiver. There had been three unaccounted-for days in one of Collis's recent schedules. He'd covered himself well, but he'd apparently been alone during that time. No one could say where he'd been.

Kay had lost the nuclear weapons factory less than a week after this secret absence.

She quickly took a map from her drawer. A WU base lay near the area from which Collis had vanished. If he'd driven day and night, he could have made the return journey.

She made another call. Through the long-distance whine, she said, "I want to know the mileage on Mr Reed's jeep when it was first checked out in April, and also when it was returned."

When the numbers came, she checked them against Collis's itinerary – the only places he claimed to have been.

The total was off by over a thousand miles. The difference matched the return journey to the WU base.

Kay put her pencil down, staring at the number. How was it possible to feel this betrayed? She'd known all her life that no one could be trusted. Why had she made an exception for a man she *knew* was a liar and a cheat?

The memory came in a rush: a conversation about Black Moon back in January. Kay had been reading intelligence reports on the size of the WU army and air force. Keaton was right: Black Moon, when it came, would not give her the power she needed. She'd stared at the chart, trying to reconcile it with the facts in her hand.

Frowning, Collis had said, "Actually, wouldn't it be better to wait until summer, when we really *have* more bombs? They only know about two. You could set off three, then tell them there was another factory they hadn't known about, that you have dozens. You'd have them on their knees."

He hadn't mentioned it again, but Kay had found herself casting the chart for another lunar eclipse in July. Leo with Scorpio rising. This chart showed power too – but *ease*. A sense of everything clicking into place.

She'd made the change, rescheduling Black Moon. And then in April, she'd lost Atomic Harmony Devices to the WU's army.

Other memories attacked like wasps. They all shared Collis. His lips, fervent and demanding on hers – the look in his eyes when they'd said their vows. *We're one now.*

She made a final phone call.

"This is Kay Pierce," she said to the commanding officer of one of her remaining northern bases. "Is my husband still there?" She toyed with her wedding ring despite herself.

"Yes, Madame President," came the crackling response. "I believe he's in his quarters. Would you like to speak with him?"

Kay let her hand fall. She felt as if she might fly into pieces. Her voice remained level. "No. You're to arrest him and have him shot. He's with the Resistance."

After Kay hung up, she sat staring at Collis's handwriting on the file, trying to tell herself that she didn't feel a deep sense of loss amongst the anger. She'd ordered that the execution be kept quiet; her embarrassment at having trusted Collis was intense.

How could she have been such a fool?

She mentally shook herself and stood up. To hell with Collis Reed. She took off her wedding ring and threw it in a drawer.

An hour later, she was inspecting the troops with Keaton: line upon line of men and women around her own age who had been trained for over a decade, because Johnny, no matter his faults, had had foresight.

"Good," she muttered. "Good." She glanced at Keaton. "When will it begin?"

Keaton was a thin, rangy man who always smoked a cigar.

"Thursday," he said. "We'll start attacking the WU's northern holdings in sequence." He gave her a level look. "I warn you, Madame President, it'll be bloody."

Kay nodded, not caring, feeling only frantic lest the attack failed. And meanwhile, the problem to the east remained. The WU still held New Manhattan and now other cities too – Boston, Philadelphia. New Manhattan was the hub. With it, they could attack her holdings in the area with impunity.

She thought of Amity Vancour and of Collis's betrayal – of the assassination attack that had likely been meant for her too.

"I want New Manhattan knocked out," she said. "Throw all the air power we've got into it. I don't care if you destroy the whole island and everyone on it."

CHAPTER FORTY-TWO

JUNE, 1943

INGO AND I HAD RETURNED to New Manhattan to the news that Tess had died in battle the day before. Sadness had lanced through me as I recalled straight-arrow Tess loaning us the plane and wishing Hal well.

No time to grieve; the attacks were unrelenting. One of Pierce's hidden airbases had been in Syracuse, it turned out. She'd poured everything into it and try as we might, we couldn't knock it out.

Rank was assigned based on each pilot's old Peacefighting status. Tess had been the highest-ranking Tier One. I'd known I was fourth in line, but hadn't thought much of it.

Suddenly I was third and our new squadron leader was a man named Toshi. Barely a week after Toshi took charge, both he and the second-in-line pilot were killed when Pierce's bombers scored a direct hit on our airfield.

To my shock, I was the new east-coast squadron leader, with over four hundred pilots answering to me.

The next few weeks were a haze of tiredness and adrenalin. Near-daily air attacks still battered New Manhattan. I coordinated sorties, assigned pilots to flight details. I was also the one who wrote to families when someone was killed. I struggled over these letters for hours, trying to give comfort over deaths that had too-often been brutal and bloody.

"I was only a Tier One because Hendrix wanted me to take bribes," I said to Ingo once in the privacy of our room. I'd taken over Tess's old suite. "This is a *joke*."

It had been a gruelling day, with two deaths and non-stop sirens splitting the air. Sometime after midnight I'd fallen asleep over some urgent memos, my head slumped on my forearms. Drowsily, I'd felt Ingo's arms around me, picking me up and carrying me to our bedroom.

"You're capable," he said. "And they're following you. Nothing else really matters."

I pressed against his chest silently, thinking of the future we'd talked about with Ma.

Neither of us had mentioned it since. The idea felt very distant now.

I could never show my fear to anyone else. I steeled my spine and didn't. Despite the hit we'd taken to the airfield, we couldn't abandon New Manhattan; too much depended on its ports. I put people to work repairing the damage and commandeered one of the new shopping centres that had opened before the war started. It had acres of long, flat parking lots. Now it was an airfield.

The parade of deaths, of wounded, seemed never-ending. Things began to feel more like the old Peacefighting base, with those still left keeping to themselves. Harlan's face was closed and grim every time I saw him.

So many pilots I knew died. Percy took a hit through the arm and was in the hospital for four days. Ingo was shot down and had to bail and landed badly, cracking two ribs. Back in our Peacefighting days, he'd have been grounded for six weeks. He was off for two days and then insisted on flying again with his ribs taped up – and I had to let him, even though I knew what agony he'd be in with the Gs pulling at him. I couldn't afford to say no to experienced combat pilots, even ones I was in love with.

"We need to advance west in an arc from here to here," Jean Buzet said, drawing a curve on the map between Boston and Washington. "Can we do it?"

"Yes, if you add more ground troops," I said tiredly "I'm doing what I can from the air already."

"Amity—"

"Look, apart from New Manhattan, we only have three airfields and they're all getting attacked daily," I broke in. "What do you want me to do, Jean? More sorties? My pilots are stretched to the limit already, and we keep hearing that the worst yet is on its way."

We were at Baltimore Airfield, wrested from Kay Pierce by our troops two weeks before. The man Ingo had originally brought from the EA was now the World United rep for my region.

The airport office had once held tourist pamphlets and employee schedules; now it was a war office. The small space was summer-warm, even with the windows open. A fly buzzed listlessly.

"Pierce's troops can't hold out much longer," said Jean, taking off his glasses and rubbing the bridge of his nose.

"I've been hearing that for months."

Jean's eyes as he put his glasses back on were sympathetic, but I could see the pressure being put on *him* from the top too. World United was still based in Kay Pierce's old palace. Its high-ups were from over two dozen different nations – they'd all sworn to defeat Pierce for the sake of the whole coalition, keeping their own countries' interests separate. They were committed, determined.

The plight of one east-coast squadron leader wasn't going to stand in their way.

"It's not a request, I'm afraid," said Jean. "We *are* advancing, and our ground troops need air support."

Back in New Manhattan, I sat in the airport cafe making out the flight rota. It was a waste of time; we didn't use one – when those sirens went off, you scrambled. But Corporate liked paperwork and so I scrawled names down quickly, irritated.

"Some poor lackey will have to type that, you know," observed Percy, sitting opposite me in the cracked leatherette booth. He was picking at a piece of apple pie.

"I know. I don't care."

"I forgot to ask, d'you suppose I can have a few weeks off?"

My pencil stopped as I stared at him.

"Joke," he said.

"Don't do that to me."

Percy's left arm was still bandaged, but he was flying again. It wasn't his firing arm, he said, so he was fine. I knew he was lying – I'd seen him wince, climbing out of his cockpit.

He gave a sad smile. "Sorry. Have some pie." He slid the plate towards me.

I started to shake my head, then changed my mind. I snagged a fork from another table and took a bite. I hadn't eaten all day. It was delicious.

An assistant appeared. "Miss Vancour, someone's in the office to see you. Says he's on WU business."

I held back a groan and put the fork down. I'd been looking forward to finishing the rota and relaxing for a change. I got up and Percy pulled the pie back towards him.

In that brief moment he looked so bereft that I impulsively put my hand on his shoulder and kissed his cheek, wishing that Hal could learn to deal with what he was going through – that over six weeks on, Percy might hear something from my brother instead of radio silence.

Percy looked up, startled. Then the corner of his mouth lifted a fraction.

"None of that now," he said. "People will start to talk."

In the airfield's administrative offices in the Grand, a secretary handed me a card. "He's just in there, Miss Vancour."

The name on the card was Vince Griffin.

Mac. I struggled to keep my expression neutral. I'd received a letter from him back in December with no return address, saying only that he'd recovered from his bullet wound and that he and Sephy were all right. The relief had been immense.

Now the use of his code name meant that he was here covertly.

"Everything all right, Miss Vancour?" asked the secretary.

"Yes, thanks." My heart beat faster as I glanced up, tapping the card against my fingers. "Who did he say he was?"

"He's with the WU."

I nodded and went into the lounge. The functional space with its plain wooden chairs was as busy as usual. A ceiling fan hummed above as several visitors sat reading magazines, waiting to be collected for meetings.

A short man with rumpled brown hair stood at the

window, gazing out at New Manhattan with his hands in his trouser pockets.

I cleared my throat. "Mr Griffin?"

Mac turned. It was really him. I somehow kept a grin from splitting my face as he crossed to me with his hand out.

"Miss Vancour? Nice to meet you. Thanks for seeing me."

"Of course, no problem."

We shook. You would never have guessed from his expression that we knew each other.

"My office is just this way," I said.

Squadron Leader Amity Vancour proclaimed the lettering on the frosted glass in paint that still looked new. When we got inside I made sure the door was firmly shut and then threw myself into his arms. "Mac!"

"Hey, kiddo," he murmured, holding me tightly.

"What are you *doing* here?" I said as we drew apart. "How are you? Where's Sephy?"

"Long story, fine, and at home."

"Where's home?"

"Nova Scotia."

"Really?" I hesitated. "Ingo and I were just there last month."

Mac's eyebrows rose. "Yeah? Why?"

I found myself unequal to the task of talking about Hal just then. I fiddled with the stapler on my desk and shrugged. "Just managed to snag a few days off, so we went to see Ma. I wish we'd known you and Sephy were there."

I started to say something else, then saw the gold ring Mac was wearing. I took his hand, studying it with a smile. "Oh, Mac…"

He squeezed my fingers. "Yeah. The lady finally went through with it. And she's seven months pregnant," he added. "Says she feels like she's going to have an elephant instead of our kid."

I grinned, picturing it – imagining Mac a father. "I'm so happy for you both." I shook my head. "I wish you hadn't come though. We're getting it really bad again here – the rumour's that a major attack will happen soon. Be ready to dive into a bomb shelter."

Then I glanced at him, apprehension stirring. "Why *are* you here? I assume it's not just a social call."

"I wish," he said. "No, I've been doing a lot of work with the WU bigwigs – liaising with my old surveillance network for them. There's trouble, kiddo. Big trouble. I've got Collis down in the tunnels."

"*Collie?*"

Mac looked sombre. "Yeah. We need to talk to you. The WU doesn't know I'm here; we snuck in through the tunnels. I couldn't exactly bring Madame President's husband into this city in public."

Staring at Mac, I sank onto my desk, my thoughts whirling. "What happened the day of the assassination attempt?" I said finally. "Did he explain?"

"He did. I'll let him tell it." When I didn't respond, he said softly, "It's okay, Amity. I promise. He's still with us."

I pretended that Mac and I were going to grab a coffee away from base and we left the Grand together, heading towards Monument Park and the hidden tunnel entrance. Mac walked the same way he always had: hands in his trouser pockets, fedora angled down, casting a shadow over his face.

I knew I wouldn't get anything out of him until he was ready, and didn't try. "How did you get into the city, anyway?" I asked as we walked up Concord. I knew the entrance across the river that Ingo and I had found was guarded.

Mac shrugged. "I've got a few contacts in the WU who agree with what Collis and I are trying to do."

I took this in uneasily. "So the WU in general *wouldn't* agree with it?"

"I sincerely hope they would. But some of the high-ups sure don't." Though Mac seemed troubled, suddenly his gaze narrowed and he glanced at me.

"Wait...you said Ingo went with you to see your mother in Nova Scotia?"

I felt my cheeks tinge. "That's right."

"Should I be happy for you too?"

"Yes," I admitted, and he grinned broadly, tipping his hat back.

"Glad to hear it, kiddo. Holy hell, it was painful watching the two of you sometimes."

I spotted Harlan then, heading down Concord towards us through the steady flow of pedestrians. Since Vera's death, he'd kept mostly to himself, though Ingo and I kept trying to reach him.

As he drew near, I started to introduce Mac to him... and then remembered with a sinking feeling that they'd already met.

Harlan strode forward, scowling. Before I'd fully registered his intent, he drew back his fist and punched Mac hard across the face.

The *crack* of skin against skin rang out. Mac staggered and half-fell against a plate glass window. "Harlan, no!" I cried. I grabbed his arm as he drew back for another punch. "Stop it! Didn't Vera tell you?" I knew instantly that mentioning her hadn't helped.

"What?" spat Harlan. He jerked away. "That he's supposed to be on the right side? I don't give a shit! That bastard sentenced thirty-six of our friends to die!"

Mac slowly straightened, looking shaken but unsurprised. His jaw was already reddening.

"He risked his life to save as many as he did! I suppose you'd have done better?" I snatched up Mac's hat from the ground. My voice shook.

"Yeah, maybe I would have! Like *standing up* to Gunnison, instead of being his little lackey!"

Before I could respond, Mac put his hand on my arm,

silencing me. "Listen, fella, for what it's worth, I sure as hell don't blame you," he said to Harlan.

Mac stepped closer to him.

"Go on," he said, his voice quiet. "Take another pop at me, if it makes you feel better. I mean it. I wish you would."

Harlan's face was red. "Go to hell," he snapped. He brushed past me on the sidewalk and kept going.

Endless pedestrians kept streaming around Mac and me, carrying their shopping or briefcases. I didn't know what to say.

Finally Mac blew out a breath and slapped his hat against his palm. He pulled it on and gave me a small, twisted smile. "Just as well I didn't bring Collis. I have a feeling he'd be even less popular."

The tunnels felt the same as always, even with their terrain so changed from all the explosions the year before. Mac had hidden a lantern and knew the way. When he and I finally reached the cavernous chamber of our old rendezvous point, Collie stood in the glow of a flashlight, fidgeting and glancing down at his watch.

It was like stepping back in time – as if Mac were Dwight, and the assassination attempt had been only hours ago.

Except that this time when Collie looked up, relief crossed his face.

He hurried over; we met in the middle of the high, weeping space. "Amity," he said, putting his hand out.

We shook. "Collie, what's going on?" I said slowly.

We sat on the chilly pipes that had served as benches so many times. Collie and Mac glanced at each other. Collie rubbed his palms on his trousers and then leaned forward, elbows on knees.

"All right, well…I guess we should just jump right into it," he said. "I know you must have wondered what the hell was going on back in September, when you saw me after the assassination attempt."

"You could say that," I said dryly. Part of me was still amazed I hadn't shot him that day.

Collie seemed to guess my thought. His small smile was rueful. "A few minutes before the attempt, Kay was called out of the meeting," he said. "I went after her and overheard her talking on the phone with General Keaton. She was telling him about World United's attacks in the south west and far north, and asking about something called 'Black Moon' – whether it could still go ahead against Florence in February."

I tensed. Florence – forty miles from Ingo's home. "What's Black Moon?"

Collie's gaze didn't falter. "The code name for a planned nuclear strike."

Shock lashed through me. I saw the stolen photos again in a mental jumble – the bombs, the smiling scientists.

"She was actually going to *do* it?" I whispered.

Collie rubbed his fist. "Yeah."

None of us spoke for a moment. From somewhere water dripped, echoing.

"See...Kay's kind of superstitious about astrology," Collie said into the silence. "I'd been seeing charts with that heading for months. I guessed it meant a lunar eclipse; I just didn't know what she had planned for it."

He gave a short, unhappy laugh. "Anyway, that's what it meant. When the moon was totally dark here, a nuclear bomb would go off in the EA."

A mushroom cloud against a shadowed moon. The image chilled me in its power. I could see its appeal...if you were Kay Pierce.

"And this was a good reason *not* to kill her?" I said shakily.

"Yes," Collie said simply. "Everything about the plan was in place. She was going to launch the strike, then send ground troops in at strategic points to take over the European Alliance. And from there the world, I guess – she was still trying to make more nukes. I was afraid that getting rid of Kay wouldn't stop it. That with her and Cain gone, Keaton would just grab power from Weir and go ahead on his own."

Collie frowned and glanced down at his hands. The glint of his wedding ring looked surreal in a way that Mac's hadn't.

"I didn't know the scale of World United then," he went on in a low voice. "And I don't have any influence with

Keaton. The only way out I could see…was if Kay lived. Then I could stall her and help the right people get rid of the nukes."

Suddenly it all came together. I studied his strong-featured face in the lantern light, realizing with dread the position he'd been in. He'd known exactly what tipping Kay off would do to the Resistance.

"All right," I said, my throat thick. "I get it."

Mac looked grim. "There's more, Amity."

"The day I saw you down here, I mentioned I was leaving the city," said Collie. "I've been making trips out to the far north."

"Go on."

"We hadn't known World United even existed until they attacked." He lifted a shoulder. "Lucky for me, Kay needed someone she could trust. She's been sending me up there to help fortify the area and liaise with Atomic Harmony Devices."

We, I noticed he'd said. He seemed unconscious of it – yet here he was, helping us.

"So I played along for months," said Collie. "I managed to persuade her to put the strike off until another eclipse this summer. Meanwhile she kept sending me up north to check on things. I knew all the fortification details. But the whole region's thick with security, even for me. Finally back in April, I managed to get away on my own and gave myself up to the WU. They got in touch with Mac to verify me."

He gave Mac a slight smile. "I thought Mac wasn't going to do it at first."

"Well, hell, buddy; I got shot because of you," said Mac easily.

Collie glanced back at me. "Anyway...I told the WU all I knew."

"That's how they were able to seize the nuclear weapons factory and the mine at Harmony Five," added Mac. "Collis told them exactly where the weaknesses in the defences were."

A wondering smile grew across my face as I stared at Collie. Our greatest triumphs in the war had been because of him. I wished fervently that Hal was here, that he could know this immediately.

"Good for you," I whispered. "Collie, I mean it."

"Not as good as I thought, as it turned out." He sighed. "Amity...the thing is..." He hesitated, glancing at Mac.

"All right, kiddo, here's the deal," said Mac quietly. "The WU has the nuclear weapons now. There are still two bombs. They plan to use them."

CHAPTER FORTY-THREE

THE WORLD DROPPED OUT FROM under me. "*What?*"

Mac's eyes were sympathetic. "Go on, Collis, tell her."

Collie rapped a fist against his thigh. "Okay, well... you've heard that the WU destroyed the factory when they took it over. It turns out that's not true. As the scientists retreated, they blew up a lot of it themselves, so that the WU couldn't get their hands on it."

"But the WU wouldn't want to..." I started, and then trailed off. "What about the bombs?"

"The scientists didn't have time to move them when they retreated. Those things are *heavy*, and have to be specially handled. So the WU has them now."

Thinking back, I realized that the WU never claimed

that the bombs themselves had been destroyed…only the means to make them.

"I managed to meet with the WU one more time, after they got the nukes," Collie said. "They were asking lots of questions about Kay's ground troops – whether I couldn't make her back off. I couldn't have even if I'd tried. She's…" He stopped, glancing at his ring. An expression I couldn't read crossed his face.

"Very determined," he said quietly. "But their tone made me suspicious. I sneaked a look at some paperwork I wasn't supposed to see. They've had heavy losses – they want the war over with as soon as possible. And so…there was a proposal to launch nuclear strikes against Calgary and Puget to put an end to it."

The darkness pressed against us. I felt clammy as I stared at him. Calgary and Puget were the remaining strongholds for Pierce in the north. "This can't be true," I said faintly.

Mac sighed. "I've got some high-up WU buddies. When Collis came to me with this, I was able to check it out. It's true, all right…and now they've decided to go ahead."

My voice rose. "They can't. They *can't*. We're supposed to be on the right side!"

"They're calling it a 'strike for peace'." Mac gave a short, humourless laugh. "See, the idea is that it's going to end the war. So it's for peace."

"Calgary's got over two hundred thousand people!" I cried. "Puget's got *millions.*"

"I know, Amity. I know."

Collie rubbed his forehead. "And remember I said I convinced Kay to wait until another eclipse?" he said tonelessly. "The WU's going ahead then too; the timing works for them. They're even using the same Black Moon code, as a kind of...statement against Kay."

"When?" I said finally.

"Calgary the day after tomorrow," said Mac. "Then Puget after that, if Kay doesn't surrender."

"Which she won't," Collie put in softly. "I know her."

A few days. Ingo and I had spent over a month in Calgary, holed up in a Resistance safe house. It was where we'd first started to fall in love. We knew people in the Resistance there. And Puget was a major city. I recalled its teeming docks, its skyscrapers.

Mac's gaze was steady. "I've been doing some nosing. I'm afraid it's even worse than that, kiddo."

I stared at him. "How can it be *worse*?"

"Pierce was close to producing more bombs when the factory was destroyed. Now the WU's rebuilding it. They plan to pick up where she left off."

"But...that doesn't even make sense! The WU is the whole world, apart from Can-Amer. If they're ending the war, who would they use new bombs *against*?"

"They think it'll be a deterrent – that more bombs will ensure peace for ever." At my expression, Mac gave a weary shrug. "I know. It's nuts. Listen, this is all classified – most of the WU don't even know. And not everyone who does agrees; some are reacting just like us. But the high-ups who count have pushed it through."

Mac played with his lighter. In a low voice, he said, "To my mind, the scariest thing is that it may be 'World United' for *now* – but the world's sure as hell never gotten along, has it? Look at how busy you Peacefighters always were."

My thoughts had been ticking coldly along the same route. "The WU will probably disband within a year or so after all this ends," I murmured.

"Yep," said Mac. "Then there'll be some jockeying for position…one or two powers will get hold of the bombs… someone else might grab the mine and the technology…"

Stricken, I glanced around us at the debris in the tunnel – relics from a lost time.

This was exactly how the ancients had destroyed themselves.

Collie cleared his throat. "I'd have gotten to Mac sooner with this, but Kay found out I helped the WU and I was arrested. I was able to bribe the guard when it got out whose side I was on   she's lost a lot of support at ground level. But then it took me…oh, hell. Way too long to steal an auto and get back here. Three thousand miles."

I was hardly listening. "No," I murmured. My fist was tight. "This *cannot* happen. We have to do something!"

Collie's smile was tinged with worry. "Yeah, we were kind of counting on you feeling that way."

Mac propped his forearms on his thighs, his brown eyes

locking on mine in the lantern light. "Look...we've got a plan, Amity. It's dangerous as hell though. And it all comes down to you. But if we succeed, we destroy those nukes – no one gets bombed. And we do away with the world's capacity to ever make the damn things again."

My heart clenched. "Start talking."

Collie explained how, if I agreed, he'd fly with me to the Yukon. Any plane I took would need to stop for refuelling – as "Mr Kay Pierce", he could help me cross Can-Amer.

"Kay hasn't publicly announced my arrest and execution order." Collie's smile was slightly bitter. "So to most of Can-Amer, I'm still one of the most important people in the country."

Mac picked up the thread then, describing how once I was in the Yukon, I'd go on alone to Atomic Harmony Devices. There, with Mac's help from New Manhattan, I'd hopefully be able to convince the powers that be that the orders had changed and Wildcat was now scheduled to pilot the bomber.

"You're the only pilot in the world who could get away with it, kiddo," Mac said intently. "It makes sense that they'd want someone who's got the public behind her to do this. I'm surprised they didn't ask you for real."

I rubbed my arms, chilled. "Okay...let's say I manage it. What then? I've never even *flown* a bomber."

"The ones they plan to use for the nukes are single-crew planes," put in Collie. "A little larger than a long-distance Merlin – you'd be fine."

Mac had lit a cigarette. He gazed down at its red glow in his hands and said slowly, "So you'd fly the bomber with both nukes up into the mountains. You'd drop one of the bombs somewhere harmless in the wilderness, from a high enough altitude that you're safe…and then the other one on the mine at Harmony Five."

I stiffened.

"The camp and mine are empty of people now," Mac added. "But since they're rebuilding the factory, it's a sure bet they'll start mining there again."

The dark chamber around us faded into a jumble of memories: marching through the snow into the mine every day. Its indescribable noise and swirling dust. A Gun whipping both Ingo and me as we worked at the rock crusher.

Hard joy came at the thought of annihilating that place. From the look in Collie's eyes, he knew how I felt.

"Would that really do it?" I said roughly. "Get rid of those bombs for ever?"

Mac nodded. "Gunnison did survey after survey – the world's uranium is almost depleted. Without that mine, that's it; no one can make any more."

I tapped the pipe I was sitting on, thinking. "Okay, this doesn't sound all *that* dangerous. Unless you mean I'd probably be arrested afterwards."

"It's dangerous, all right." Collie rubbed the back of his neck. "Amity…these bombs…" He sighed. "See, when one explodes…say, over a city…first there's a blast of radiation.

Then a massive shock wave, like a huge wind rushing from the blast. The scientists said it'd topple skyscrapers like toys for miles."

I sat frozen, picturing the buildings of Calgary and Puget.

"Then seconds later, a giant fireball erupts in the epicentre," said Collie. "Over six thousand degrees Celsius. It vaporizes everything in its path."

"How 'giant'?" I got out.

"Half a mile across, maybe?" Collie looked down, playing with his cuffs. "The blast effectively creates a vacuum. So after a minute, the wind comes rushing back from the opposite direction, destroying whatever's still standing. It fans the fireball. The scientists reckoned you could get a firestorm two or three miles across in just a few minutes. And that's not even going into what happens to people who get radiation poisoning…"

I felt sick. "Stop," I whispered.

Mac's gaze was troubled but direct. "Kiddo, look. A city's a pretty big target. The mine isn't. And it's surrounded by mountains, protecting it – so to hit it, you'd have to go fairly low. There's a danger that you'd get caught up in the shockwave before you could fly far enough away to avoid it."

I tried to laugh; a strangled sound came out. "Right," I said. "So, yeah…pretty dangerous."

Looking greatly conflicted, Mac reached over and squeezed my hand. "Amity…you know I wouldn't ask you this if there was any other way."

I took a breath and nodded. Then I glanced at Collie, the other pilot among us. "Tell me straight – if I agree, do you think I have a chance of surviving this?"

He hesitated. "Yeah, I do," he said finally. "I won't pretend that…that we wouldn't have to ask you anyway. But you're an excellent pilot. With luck, you can do this."

Ingo wasn't in our room when I got back to base. I called a woman named Fern, who was the next highest Tier One after me, and asked her to come over.

Then I quickly called a few of our friends' rooms. Ingo wasn't in any of them. He wasn't in the hotel bar when I called down there either.

No, I thought, trying not to panic. I couldn't go without seeing him. Yet I'd have to, if it came to that. We had no time to spare.

I flung a few things into a bag. When a knock came, my heart leaped – but of course he wouldn't knock at his own door.

It was Fern. I sat her down and explained that I had to leave for a few days. She went ashen. "You're putting me in *charge*?"

"Yes. You're totally capable, Fern."

She was a fearless flyer, yet she stared at me in shock. "But…that big attack is coming up from Pierce! Everyone says so."

How well I knew it. It was the worst possible time for

me to leave. "I know," I said roughly. "You'll be fine. Look, here are all my plans – all the paperwork you'll need."

We went quickly over them. I could see Fern gaining in confidence a little as she took things in, making a few suggestions. World United Corporate would wonder where the hell I'd gotten to. I planned to send them a telegram saying only that I'd been called away on an urgent family matter.

I'd probably be court-martialled, if I lived.

"All right," Fern muttered finally, staring down at the documents. She shoved her dark hair back. "I think I've got it all." She gave me a wry look. "You're positive you can't stay?"

"Believe me, if I could, I would." I wished I could at least give a handover speech to my pilots. It was going to jar everyone terribly, having me just vanish. Yet there was no time. It was dark outside and they'd be scattered all over New Manhattan.

"Something's wrong, isn't it?" ventured Fern, studying me.

I sighed. "Yeah. I wish I could tell you more."

"Don't worry; I know you wouldn't do this lightly. Well…good luck with whatever it is, I guess."

She stood up and gathered the papers. At that moment Ingo walked in and my shoulders slumped. He stopped short as he took in Fern, the paperwork, my half-packed bag.

"Good luck to you too," I said in an undertone to Fern at the door. "Take care of my pilots."

She squeezed my arm. "I will. So long, Amity." She nodded at Ingo as she left.

The door closed. I rushed to Ingo and threw myself into his arms. He held me tightly. "Amity, what—"

"I have to leave soon," I said thickly.

"Is this to do with Mac?"

I pulled away a little.

"I saw Harlan in the bar downstairs, looking like thunder – he told me what happened. I've been trying to find you." Ingo sat me down on the sofa; our fingers interlocked. "Tell me."

I did so as quickly as I could. His lips paled as I told him about the WU's plans to bomb Calgary and Puget to keep making more bombs as a "deterrent".

"That can't be true," he said.

"It is. Mac's checked it out."

Ingo's face was slack. He murmured something in Germanic and then barked out a short, bitter laugh. "Just when I think that the world's turning sane again…all right. Go on."

When I explained what Collie and Mac had proposed, he stared at me. "Mac actually asked you to *do* this?"

"He didn't have a choice," I whispered. "Neither do I."

Ingo slowly let go of me. Elbows on his knees, he scraped his hands up his face and buried his fingers in his dark curls.

"No," he said finally. "I can see that."

He looked at me. From his expression, he'd never smiled in his life. "I'm going too."

"You can't."

"The hell I can't."

Pain shot through me. My voice sharpened. "You *can't*. New Manhattan's about to get battered. We're short of experienced pilots as it is!"

He gripped my arms. "Yes? And what exactly am I fighting for, if you die carrying out this insane plan? Tell me!"

"For your home. Your family. For…" I squeezed my hand hard over my eyes, struggling for control, thinking of all the hollow-sounding condolence letters I'd had to write – of the rumours we'd heard that the fiercest battle yet was coming.

"We're going to need every fighter we've got here," I said. "You're the highest-ranking Tier Two. If Fern dies, you're in charge."

"And if I refuse?" Ingo said in a low voice.

I was still squadron leader until I left. I let my hand fall. I touched his face, gently tracing its familiar lines.

"I hope you do refuse," I said. "Then I can have you arrested…and no matter what happens to me, I'll know you'll be safe."

Two a.m. The airfield was almost empty at this hour. I stood near the outside fence with Ingo, my bag over my shoulder.

Neither of us spoke. He'd agreed that he would stay and

fight – that with the upcoming battle there was little choice – but there was still tension between us and I hated it.

Finally a pair of shadows appeared: Mac and Collie. I glanced over my shoulder at the silence of the field and opened the gate to let them in. Collie had had to take a chance on slipping here through the night-time city streets. He had a bag over his shoulder too.

Mac and Ingo shook hands. "Good to see you, pal," said Mac. "I just wish it was under better circumstances."

"So do I," said Ingo with a ghost of a smile. He looked at Collie. After a beat, he put his hand out. "Reed," he said quietly.

Collie nodded, and they shook. "Manfred."

Ingo looked wry, one corner of his mouth still up. "Do I congratulate you on your marriage?"

Collie winced. "I wish you wouldn't," he said.

I glanced at the ring on Collie's hand again, wondering why he still wore it. It felt strange to think of the journey ahead of us – I'd hardly spoken to him alone in over a year.

The four of us headed across the field. The silence felt heavy.

Only a few of the spotlights were on. The plane waited near the runway, dark and ready. I'd asked two of the fitters to prepare the long-distance Merlin that Ingo and I had taken to Nova Scotia. They were friends of Hal's; I knew they wouldn't blab.

"I'll get the chocks for you," said Ingo.

"Give us a minute?" I said to Mac and Collie.

"Sure thing, kiddo," said Mac softly. I saw from Collie's expression that he knew I was with Ingo and wasn't surprised. I supposed Mac must have told him.

"I'll start her up," he said.

Ingo and I stepped away into the shadows. I could just make out the long planes and angles of his face.

Suddenly I was struck with a terror that I'd never see him again – so strong it took my breath away.

We embraced tightly as the plane erupted into life behind us. "Be careful," I whispered hoarsely against his neck. "*Stay alive*, damn you."

"You're saying that to *me*? Keep safe…please." Ingo drew back and cradled my face.

"I think you know but I still have to say it," he said, his voice almost angry. "That future together that we spoke to your mother about…I want it, Amity. I want it more than anything."

"Me too," I got out.

He let out a breath and kissed me. I was trembling. I pressed close as our lips moved together, wrapping my arms hard around his neck and trying not to think it was the last time.

The fear felt cold and certain.

"All right," Ingo whispered fiercely, stroking my hair back with both hands. "All right. We both have something to live for. That's got to help."

I put one of my hands over his and tried to smile.

"Maybe…maybe someday we won't have to say 'be careful' every time we say goodbye."

Five minutes later I was in the cockpit, trying to bury my feelings. Collie glanced at me uncertainly in the faint light of the control panel. "I'd offer to fly, but I haven't piloted in over a year," he said. "Night-flying probably isn't a great way to get back into practice."

"Don't worry about it," I said curtly.

Collie had already done the prep, but I checked that the radiator shutter was fully open, and gave the primer pump a few extra strokes, glad of something to do. Down below, Ingo was grabbing up the chocks.

"Clear!" he called.

I started to taxi. I allowed myself a single glance at Ingo and Mac. Mac raised his hand to us. Ingo didn't, but our eyes locked. *We both have something to live for. That's got to help.*

The Merlin's song trembled through my bones as we picked up speed. I eased back the throttle. We lifted from the earth and climbed into the darkness.

CHAPTER FORTY-FOUR

FOR THE FIRST FEW HOURS, Collie and I didn't speak much,
apart from checking our coordinates or him sometimes
offering me water from the canteen. He mostly stayed
slumped in his seat, gazing out at the blackness as the
Merlin droned around us.

I was relieved when the sky paled with dawn. Finally, I
could take my eyes off the artificial horizon and look out
the windscreen without that awful feeling of disorientation.

I felt disoriented enough already.

Collie straightened a little. "Want to put it on autopilot
and we can swap places?"

I shrugged. "I'm okay."

"You're probably tired," he said, then gave a small smile.

"Sorry. Didn't mean to sound like Rose." My mother was notorious for insisting you were tired no matter whether you were or not.

Far below, the landscape was low, rolling hills, violet in the dawn. Though we were far from any known base of Pierce's, I was keeping a wary eye out for enemy planes. Thinking that Collie might as well get some practice while things were quiet, I nodded and put the controls on autopilot. "All right, go ahead. Thanks."

We swapped places.

By now I'd flown with Ingo more than with Collie. As he started to fly – glancing automatically at the dials and adjusting the oil pressure slightly, his fingers light on the stick – I was struck by how skilled he was. He hadn't flown for over a year; you'd never have known it.

"We could have used you as a fighter pilot these last nine months," I said after a pause.

The corner of his mouth twisted. "It might have blown my cover. I have a feeling Kay wouldn't have liked it much."

"What's the deal with you and her, anyway?" I hadn't meant to ask – the words just came out.

Collie gazed out the windscreen. His golden hair was shorter than the last time I'd seen it, his eyes dark blue in the faint light.

"I don't really want to go into it," he said.

A chill touched me. "Does that mean your marriage isn't a sham?"

His glance was irritated. "I'm not asking *you* personal questions."

"All right. Sorry."

I fell silent, thinking that that sounded like a *yes*, and wondering how in the world that could be, given Kay Pierce's actions and Collie's presence here. It occurred to me to wonder whether he'd conned Mac and this was a trap. I didn't seriously believe it. Something about Collie's demeanour – a kind of distracted sadness – didn't lend itself to it.

After a few minutes he looked back at me. "Any water?"

I twisted the top off the canteen and passed it to him. He took a swig and handed it back.

"Thanks," he said, then gave a short laugh. "Too bad it's not something stronger, with what we might be heading into."

"Drinking and flying? Not a good mix."

"Yeah. Probably not. Bad habit."

"I thought you hadn't flown in over a year."

He cleared his throat. "No, I mean...just the drinking."

I felt my eyebrows rise. The Collie I'd known hadn't been big on admitting his faults.

"Really?" I said.

"Yeah." A cumulus cloud grew as we neared it; he eased the stick back. We briefly entered scraps of mist and then came through it. "Not so much any more though," he said finally. "So there's that, I guess."

He grimaced and rubbed one hand briskly on his trousers. "Hey, how are Rose and Hal?"

I'd been studying his familiar profile, frowning. I realized what he'd asked and hesitated. He looked quickly at me.

"What? Are they all right?"

I wished desperately that I'd told Mac about Hal after all – then he'd have told Collie and I wouldn't be the one who had to.

"They're fine," I said. "They're both in Nova Scotia."

Collie's forehead furrowed. He looked out the windscreen and then back at me. "Amity, what aren't you telling me?"

He'd always known when I was lying – even if, apparently, I'd never been able to do the same with him. I sighed and told him about Hal, wishing I knew how to couch these things gently.

Collie's face drained. "Oh no," he whispered. "Oh shit…now I really *do* want a drink." He glanced at me tensely. "How's…how's he coping?"

I fiddled with the canteen. "About as well as you'd expect, I guess." From his letters, Hal was clearly still having highs and lows – though in his last one to me, he'd added *Eye on the prize* as a PS.

"He'll be okay," said Collie roughly. "He will, Amity. He's a game kid."

"Not so much a kid any more."

"Yeah, I guess you're right…sixteen. But he'll be fine." Collie nodded, as if wanting to convince himself. "He'll be fine," he murmured.

I thought of Dwight's death – of the silver ring that Hal still wore. The daylight was stronger now, touching the clouds below with pink and gold. Finally I said what I was thinking: "It's really going to mean a lot to Hal to know for sure that you came through."

Collie's expression turned bittersweet. For several moments, the engine's steady drone was the only sound.

"I'm sorry that you doubted me," he said. "I mean, sorry I gave you so much cause. Not just this time, but… you know."

I sighed. I definitely knew.

"I didn't doubt you this time, really," I said at last.

He glanced at me. I could see the surprise in his eyes. "You didn't?"

I shrugged. "I wasn't sure. But I didn't see why you'd come to the tunnels for Hal, if you were really with Pierce." Then I stopped, uncertain, looking at the gleam of gold on his finger. In some way he wouldn't define, he *was* with Pierce.

Collie seemed to be thinking the same. He frowned slightly, banking the Merlin west as we followed the line of the mountains. The world tipped on its edge below us.

"Well, thanks, for what it's worth," he said.

The Merlin could fly for six hours, if you used the extra fuel tanks. Collie and I seemed to have used up all our available conversation long before that. As Can-Amer turned from mountains to plains below, I wondered anxiously if the promised air battle had started in New Manhattan yet.

Halfway through the second reserve tank, the sun was blazing strongly across the Merlin. "Maybe we should land and refuel," said Collie. "There's an airport close to here." I was flying again by then, and he was checking the maps.

"Can we make it all the way to the Yukon in one more hop if we do that?" I said, and Collie did the calculations, working them out on a piece of paper with a pencil.

"Yeah, we'll be okay."

"All right. Maybe you'd better land. I'll get in the back, where I won't be seen."

He took the controls. I crouched behind the passenger seats; they smelled of dust and canvas. I gazed tensely out a side window. As he angled in for the landing, a rustic airport rose up to greet us through swathes of trees. The Merlin bounced only once as we landed in Kay Pierce's territory.

Collie clambered down from the wing and greeted the attendants who came jogging up. I didn't hear what he said, but peeking out I was startled by how commanding he seemed – the Collis Reed I'd seen on so many newsreels, in the flesh.

The attendants got to work refuelling. Collie came back to the plane. "Come on, there's a restroom," he said softly, holding his hand out to me. "I've told them I have a high-profile prisoner and that this is all confidential."

I rose slowly, rubbing my hands on my trousers. "Will they keep quiet?"

"Just keep your head down. And yeah, they will. No one would dare cross me in this place." His tone was rueful, matter-of-fact.

I saw again Kay Pierce in Henderson Square Garden, with the fifty people she'd just ordered shot lying sprawled and motionless. *Do you know what your wife is capable of?* I wanted to say.

But of course he did.

I crossed the landing strip with Collie holding me by the arm, my wrists behind my back as if cuffed. The attendants kept their focus fixedly on their work. I couldn't tell if they'd recognized me.

In the cracked-tile restroom, I relieved myself and then splashed cold water on my face. I emerged out into a corridor where Collie waited. The faint sound of a telio drifted out from an office, and I went still, listening.

"*...and though the battle still rages, New Manhattan cannot hold out against Harmony for much longer. The near-total destruction of both major airports on the island has left the terrorists with nowhere to hide...*"

My heart fell into my stomach. Collie took my arm. "Come on," he muttered.

In the plane, he didn't speak again until we were safely back up in the air. "You know that most of the news is propaganda, right?" he said, raising his voice over the engine.

"Not always," I said tersely.

"No. But—"

"We've been expecting a major battle any day," I interrupted. "We really *can't* hold out much longer. Our main airport took a bad hit a few weeks ago. If it's not just propaganda, and they've gotten both airports this time…"

I stopped, scraping my fist against my lips. *Ingo.* Harlan and Percy. Fern, so newly in charge. How old had that news been, anyway? What the hell was happening?

"All right," said Collie finally. "Try not to think about it."

At least he wasn't telling me that everything would be fine. I exhaled. Finally I nodded. "Let me fly for a while, okay?" I said.

Yet as the Merlin ate the miles, I realized that not thinking about New Manhattan just made more room for images of toppling buildings – a giant fireball.

Lunar eclipses were only visible at night. The attacks against Calgary and Puget had been scheduled for tomorrow; the eclipse would follow a few hours afterwards.

I recalled again Calgary's peaceful streets and felt sick. On a personal level, I somehow felt that if we could save the city where Ingo and I had grown so close, the two of us would have our future together. The thought made no sense but I clung to it.

As if reading my mind, Collie said suddenly, "Are you happy with him?"

I glanced over, startled.

"Manfred," he said, as if I might not know who he meant.

"I thought personal questions were off the table," I said after a pause.

"All right. Sorry."

The Merlin hummed to itself for a few beats. "Yes, I am," I said.

Collie's voice was soft. "Good. You deserve to be happy." He studied his hands. "I don't know him very well. But he's always seemed like a good guy. Dependable."

"He is," I said. "Ma likes him," I added before thinking.

Collie shot me a look. "Yeah?"

I shrugged, suddenly remembering the night that Ma had brought out the sherry when Collie and I had gotten together. "Well...she didn't bring out the sherry," I said. "But yeah, she likes him."

I kept my gaze away from Collie's wedding ring. I hoped that the idea of asking him if he was happy with Kay Pierce was ludicrous, so I didn't.

A few more minutes passed. We were entering the mountains now, the landscape below rumpled like an unmade bed. Collie sat gazing out the windscreen.

"Remember darkest Africa?" he said finally.

"What?"

"When we were kids. You wanted to go explore 'darkest Africa'. You'd read about it in a book, or something."

It started coming back. I banked, keeping north-west, and the starboard wing rose. "We planned to take a boat there, didn't we? A plane and a boat both." It had made sense when I was ten.

"You planned."

I glanced at him. "I thought we both did. Up in the hayloft that time."

His soft snort was almost a laugh. "Amity...I had enough on my mind dealing with home. I was just playing along so that I could stay for dinner."

"It was only pretend," I said, confused. I felt my forehead furrow. "Why are we talking about this?"

The cockpit was bright with sunshine; it winked at his stubble. He sat fiddling with his wedding ring. "I was just thinking about it." Finally he looked up. "Hey, did Mac tell you that Sephy's pregnant?"

"Yeah, he said." I smiled, glad of something hopeful to think about. "Do you suppose that's why she finally married him?"

Collie's mouth quirked. "Maybe." He took a sip of water from the canteen. "Remember how we used to joke about having ten kids?"

We'd talked about it all the time. A faint nostalgia came. Those days had once seemed so golden. "I remember." I took the canteen from him. "Ten was probably a little excessive."

"Ten too many," Collie said. At my quizzical expression, he looked slightly sheepish. "I've never wanted kids. But I knew *you* probably did someday, so it seemed like a good thing to say."

I stared at him. "What would you have done if we'd actually gotten *married*?"

"I don't know. Had a secret vasectomy?"

"You would have, wouldn't you?" Despite everything, I was almost laughing.

"Yeah. Knowing me, I would have." Collie glanced back at his ring. He cleared his throat. "Listen…I know you're wondering about me and Kay."

Faint trepidation stirred. "It's your business, not mine."

"I know. I want to tell you." Collie sighed, looking tired. "She's different in private. When it's just the two of us… I guess I care about her more than I should."

"Are you in love with her?" I asked, chilled.

"No," he said finally. "But…I had to get very involved, right from the start. She expected it."

"You were sleeping with her even last February?"

"Yeah." Collie gave a rueful laugh. "Not any more though. I think she'd shoot me on sight."

My thoughts were tangled. I had no idea what to say, so I said nothing.

"When I married her, I was playing a role, but maybe in a way I wished…" Collie grimaced. The world hummed gently past.

"I've told her things I've never told anyone," he said. "She just seems to understand me. And I know who *she* is, and I despise what she's done. But part of me still cares about her anyway." He looked down, rubbing a fist against the opposite palm.

"I wish I didn't," he said softly.

From nowhere, I thought of the boy I'd once kissed in our barn. Sadness stirred.

"Well, you're here now," I said. "That counts for a lot."

"Yeah." Collie exhaled and seemed to straighten a little. "Actions, not thoughts."

When I spotted another plane in the distance, I frowned – but it was so far away that we could evade it easily, if need be.

"They're high up," I said, watching. "Must be at least thirty thousand feet."

Collie hadn't seen it. When I spoke, he followed my gaze. He sat up slowly, eyes widening. He grabbed for the map. "Change course – go east and take it higher – *now!*"

His urgency jolted me. I jammed down on the rudder and threw us into a barrel roll; mountains and sky spun. I pulled out, watching the altimeter. Twenty thousand feet – thirty.

"Collie, what *is* it?" I cried.

He craned against his straps to look back at the other plane, his body rigid. "Oh no," he murmured. "Oh no, no..."

Suddenly I realized where we were: Calgary was a few miles to the west, sprawling against the horizon in my mirrors. I hurriedly twisted to look back too.

The other plane was just over the city. A shape tumbled

from it, so small it was almost invisible. It glinted like a dust mote.

"*No!*" I whirled towards Collie. "You said it wasn't till tomorrow!"

"It wasn't!" He reached for the stick. "*Keep climbing, damnit!*"

No. *No.* This could not be happening. I kept climbing, and climbing, until the cockpit was cold and I'd taken it as high as the Merlin could handle. I thought I might throw up and it was nothing to do with the altitude.

I didn't really see that, I thought frantically. *Collie's wrong, he has to be wrong...*

Suddenly I grit my teeth and took us into another barrel roll, heading west again.

"What are you *doing*?"

"I have to know," I whispered, my fingers tight on the stick. The clouds had thinned. From this high up the earth was a curved, serene mass, softly green, with few features. At first I saw nothing and desperate hope filled me.

Then from the direction of Calgary a ripple came: something big, blooming outwards. It grew. A moment later, the mushroom cloud was clear against the horizon.

CHAPTER FORTY-FIVE

HALF AN HOUR LATER, I landed at the small, remote airport which was expecting us – the last one in Can-Amer's holdings. Collie had arranged everything; this time the fitters were sympathizers.

I was numb. From Collie's face, he was too. We sat out of the chill in the small office while the fitters refuelled the Merlin.

They were clearly shaken. The flash had been visible from here, they'd said, lighting the sky. Collie and I had seen the plane turn back towards the bomb factory – I prayed that meant the second nuke wasn't on it and the Puget bombing of millions hadn't happened yet.

"Why was it early, do you suppose?" I said. The words

tasted acrid. I kept thinking of the rushing wind that toppled buildings – the fireball half a mile across.

Collie scraped his hands over his face. "The only thing I can think of is the battle in New Manhattan," he said finally. "If it's really that bad, maybe they decided to ramp up the plan early to force a surrender."

The fear for so many people I cared about on top of what had just happened threatened to drown me. I leaned forward on the desk, rubbing my temples.

After Collie and I had seen the mushroom cloud, I'd somehow gotten the plane heading east again, though my mind was screaming, *two hundred thousand dead.*

Seconds later, though we were probably ten miles away, the Merlin had bucked as if hit by another plane and I'd cried out.

Collie had looked sick. "The…shock wave from the bomb," he'd said. Then he glanced at me. "Amity, if they've already bombed Puget, and you show up claiming to have new orders…"

"I still have to try – check it out at least," I said hoarsely. "If there's any trouble I'll say there's been a mistake. Mac will back me up on the phone when they call him."

It sounded flimsy even to me, but what choice did we have? Collie nodded without speaking.

Neither of us had commented on what I'd be attempting if the plan still went ahead…and what that shock wave would be like at a much closer range.

Now Collie sat massaging his eyes. "I wish I could go with you the rest of the way."

"You can't," I whispered.

His presence at the factory would raise too many questions. Beyond this point was WU territory. The factory was still almost a thousand miles away. An auto waited for Collie, for him to take wherever he was heading.

Collie let his hand fall. "I know I can't," he said shortly. "But I wish I could." He got up abruptly and went to the telio set that sat on a shelf. He turned it on and fiddled with the dial.

Unbelievably, all that came on was music. I stared blankly at the curlicue speakers as an old waltz played.

Neither of us spoke for a while. Then we both looked up as one of the workers came in. "Your plane's ready," he said. "We fuelled the spare tanks too."

Back outside, the Merlin sat waiting, its nose pointing towards the afternoon sky. A line of ragged spruce trees grew beside the runway.

Collie walked me out to the plane. I hadn't asked where he was going next, and he didn't volunteer it. Thinking of what might be coming, I wondered if this was a final goodbye. Collie had been so much a part of my life – I'd been so in love with him, once.

I slapped my gloves together. "Well…thanks for everything," I said awkwardly.

"I wish to hell it was more." Collie hesitated, studying me with worried blue-green eyes, the cool wind ruffling his hair. "Your family is the best part of me," he said at last. "I guess that'll never change."

The spruce trees whispered to themselves behind us. I put my hand out. "I wish you all the best," I said. "I mean it. You deserve to be happy, too."

Collie's expression grew still. He shook my hand. Our fingers gripped each other briefly, then interlocked. He squeezed hard. "Good luck, Amity," he said softly.

I touched down on the runway a few hours later. The factory that Ingo and I had discovered over a year ago rose to one side. Scaffolding covered some of the buildings. The landscape looked transformed, the brown hills now green – though to the north, I could still see snow in the mountains.

The bomber was in view, sitting in an open hangar.

I undid my straps and slid back the cockpit hood. It was late afternoon, still full daylight this far north. I clambered out and dropped onto the wing.

"Hi," I called as a couple of fitters came jogging up. "I'm Amity Vancour. I need to see Commander Sheridan as soon as possible. Blunt at Corporate sent me."

Commander Sheridan was the head of this facility now that the WU had seized it. Mac had briefed me on all the names. The fitters looked surprised, but helped me down from the high wing.

"Well…sure thing. Come on in, Miss Vancour," said one.

He was about my age, with a shock of vivid red hair. He grinned. "If you don't mind my saying, it's an honour to meet you."

I forced a smile, wondering if he knew about Calgary, and how he could look so cheerful if he did. *Please, don't let them have bombed Puget yet.*

We walked through the fresh, chilly air to the office. The fitter got me a cup of coffee as the receptionist called Commander Sheridan. I managed to give only a casual glance to the bulletin board where Ingo and I had found the photos the previous winter.

Now it held pictures from a company party: smiling people wearing festive hats.

The receptionist put her hand over the receiver. "He's not expecting you, Miss Vancour."

I let consternation cross my face. "Isn't he? Mr Blunt was supposed to get in touch with him." I glanced at my watch. "It's pretty urgent. I was escorted across enemy territory to Redwing. I've just flown for fourteen hours."

She relayed this, eyebrows up, then nodded to me. "He's on his way."

A telio sat on a cabinet in the corner. I longed to ask her to turn it on – I was desperate for news of New Manhattan, along with everything else – but stayed silent, sipping the coffee.

Arvin, I thought dully. He was the Resistance worker who'd sheltered Ingo and me for almost a month in Calgary. He'd been frightened but kind.

Did you feel anything when a nuclear weapon dropped on you? Did you have time to be afraid?

A man in a blue uniform appeared through the door, younger than I'd expected. His dark hair grew in a widow's peak. "Miss Vancour? I'm Commander Sheridan." He put out his hand and I rose and shook it.

"Nice to meet you, Commander."

"Please, call me Ed. Sorry, my office is back outside again." He gave me a quizzical look. "We weren't expecting you, or I'd have had a jeep waiting."

"That's all right. Sorry, Mr Blunt was supposed to be in touch."

We went outside again – "Ed" opened the door for me – and drove to a building a few minutes away, travelling through streets of large grey buildings. The one we stopped at had planters to either side of the front door, as if flowers grew there in springtime.

When we got into Commander Sheridan's office, he motioned me towards a chair. "Can I get you anything? Coffee?"

"I've just had some, thanks." I managed to keep my voice neutral as I said, "Ed, I'm sorry to get right to business, but there's some urgency. Corporate want me to be the one to drop the second bomb. In fact, I thought they wanted me to drop the first one too."

Ed froze as he started to sit down. He sat the rest of the way, and said, "Oh?"

My blood beat rapidly as I reached into my jacket.

"Here's the order," I said, pulling out a piece of paper. "They're worried about the public's reaction – they thought having me be the one to do it might help."

I stayed silent as he read the fake order. Mac had drawn it up before he entered New Manhattan, to have it ready if I said yes.

Ed rubbed his jaw. "Well, this is news," he said finally. "I'll need to verify it, Miss Vancour."

"Amity. Please, go ahead."

As he dialled the operator, relief flooded me: apparently the second bomb hadn't gone yet.

"Long distance," Ed said into the receiver. "I need to reach Blunt at his home number... I must say this explains a lot," he added to me. "I'd heard that you disappeared on a family matter right before the battle."

I nodded, trying not to think of New Manhattan. "I wasn't allowed to say anything."

As the minutes passed, operators connected each other in a chain stretching across the WU's holdings. The final one sat in a branch office in Philadelphia. Mac knew her. When the crackling long distance call came in, she was going to connect it to Mac in New Manhattan. He'd met Blunt several times and thought he could get away with it.

I didn't doubt him. Mac was a consummate actor.

"Hello, Nolan?" said Ed finally, leaning back in his seat. "Ed here. Yes, fine, you? Good... Listen, I've got Amity Vancour in my office. She says it's on your orders."

His eyes flicked to me. He smiled slightly. "Very spry, considering she's just had a long flight. How are you?" he asked me.

I smiled too, my muscles going limp that it had worked. "Fine, but please tell Mr Blunt I'm a little surprised the first bomb's already gone. I thought I was dropping both of them."

Relief. I'd been terrified that I might not be able to let Mac know the first bomb had already fallen.

Ed relayed this, adding apologetically, "There've been crossed wires, obviously, Nolan…I've got your order here, but I hadn't seen it. Rossetti said to move the first stage of Black Moon forward. Yes, of course you were aware…well, what about Puget? Do you still want to change pilots?"

A long pause. He tapped a pencil, nodding thoughtfully. "I agree – it'll be good to put a known face to it to help bring the public around… No, that's the only change Rossetti planned to make; still seven p.m. tomorrow… All right. You too."

Ed hung up. "Yes, you're flying the Puget mission. We couldn't wait on Calgary; we've had heavy losses in New Manhattan." He grimaced and tossed the pencil aside. "No one will be able to say we're not giving Pierce a chance to surrender."

If she did, they wouldn't load that bomb onto the plane and our plan would be ruined. "Fingers crossed." I hesitated, my pulse pounding. "What's…what's happening in New Manhattan?"

"Nothing good, I'm afraid. Pierce has bombed both airports. Pilots are dropping like flies."

I felt faint. Not propaganda then. Why hadn't Ingo refused to fly, so that I could have had him arrested? The cold certainty that our goodbye had been final came back and fear rocked me. With a fierce effort, I buried it deep.

"You'll be taking off tomorrow afternoon, so you have time to rest up," Sheridan was saying. He rose. "Shall I have someone show you to a guest room?"

I managed a smile, though we'd counted on my leaving at first light, before anyone from Corporate on the east coast had a chance to get in touch.

"Yes, thanks," I said, rising too.

"Nolan wished you luck, by the way," Sheridan added. "He said to tell you that we're all counting on you."

CHAPTER FORTY-SIX

JUNE, 1943

MAC SLOWLY HUNG UP THE PHONE. He scraped a hand over his jaw and looked out the window.

He was in one of the bedrooms of the Grand Hotel in New Manhattan. He blindly studied the devastated airfield a few blocks away – the scraps of metal that used to be Firedoves. At least a third of the Doves had been in for refuelling when the bombs had hit.

But now, gazing out at it, all Mac could see was a mental image of a mushroom cloud.

When Amity had relayed the news through Sheridan, Mac had struggled to keep his tone steady. Still shaken, he glanced at his watch. *All right, focus.* It might be too late to save hundreds of thousands, but millions more were still at risk. If Ed Sheridan up there in Harmony Five took it into his head to call back in the next hour, he had to be ready to field it. After that, their sympathetic switchboard operator would finish her shift and they were in the hands of fate.

Mac sat in a plush armchair in the almost empty hotel, smoking a cigarette. Distantly, the sound of aerial battle came from the central part of the island. He rubbed his forehead, remembering.

Over twelve hours ago, with eight hours spare before the earliest he could expect Sheridan's call, he'd gone down to the airfield, where fitters were readying the planes in the faint light of near-dawn.

"Anything I can do to help?" he'd asked the squadron leader. *Fern Bradshaw*, read her name tag.

"Who are you?" she asked distractedly, studying a clipboard.

She looked a little like Sephy. "Mac Jones, WU," he said, showing his ID.

"No unauthorized personnel."

Mac shrugged tensely. "Come on, I hear Pierce is going to hit hard. Willing pair of hands, right?"

Fern hesitated, studying him. Finally she said, "Help the fitters. Do whatever they tell you. And try not to get hit by a prop blade."

Barely an hour later, Pierce attacked. The work at the airfield became frenzied. Dressed in a blue jumpsuit, Mac had rushed food and coffee over to refuelling pilots; taken tools to the fitters; anything. He kept a sharp eye on the aerial battle, over the northern part of the city – if it drew too close, he'd have to take cover.

The bombs came out of nowhere. Suddenly the pavement had wrenched and buckled in fountains of concrete. The airfield became a turmoil of flames – screams – planes exploding one after the other. Mac dived for the ground and scrambled under a truck as a trio of Scorps flew low, strafing everything in sight.

When the drone of retreating airplanes faded, Mac crawled hastily out. Shouts of *"Medic!"* echoed. Pilots and fitters pelted from all directions towards the hit planes and the wounded. Mac's blood beat hotly. He ran for a jeep that had taken a hit; he could see someone in it.

Fern Bradshaw lay slumped across the seat, eyes open, her torso sodden with blood. Mac stopped short, stricken.

"Ah, hell," he murmured. This time her resemblance to Sephy chilled him. Mac took her pulse but knew it was pointless. He gently laid her hand back on her stomach.

Then he realized. "Oh, *shit*," he breathed.

The airfield was still chaos; sirens bleated through the air. Mac turned hastily and saw a tall, scarred pilot racing past, heading for a plane.

"Ingo!" he bellowed, taking off after him. Ingo glanced back and stopped; his eyes widened.

Mac reached him and said shakily, "Listen, we've got a problem, pal. What happens when the squadron leader dies?" He nodded back at the jeep.

Ingo froze, gaping. Then he swore and broke into a sprint with Mac at his heels. They reached the jeep. Ingo winced at the sight of Fern's limp form. He tried her pulse too, then straightened slowly, staring down at her.

He closed his eyes and ran a hand down his face. After a moment he seemed to steel himself.

He glanced towards the office. "Come on," he said, clapping Mac's arm, and they ran, Mac taking three steps to every two of Ingo's.

They burst inside. "Give me the mic," Ingo said to the man at the desk. The guy started to protest, then saw his expression.

"Get the hell under cover until you get that phone call," Ingo muttered to Mac as he sat down. "I'd rather not have Amity arrested because you've gotten yourself killed."

Mac stared at him, a sudden suspicion forming. "Yeah, you're right," he said slowly. "But, buddy…"

Ingo's thin lips looked grim. He flipped a switch, glancing out at the field.

"What happens is that I become the new squadron leader," he said. "Did you hear me? Take cover, Mac – *now*."

When the hour of waiting was over, the black, boxy telephone had remained silent. Mac exhaled and rose.

So far so good then. They had to pray now that Sheridan and Blunt didn't contact each other before the second scheduled strike tomorrow – Mac's switchboard contact wasn't at work the next day. Originally, they'd thought the danger slim, with Amity leaving the facility so early. But if she somehow gave herself away during her wait, Sheridan would call, all right.

Stay tough, kiddo – you can do it, he thought.

The sound of a nearby explosion hurtled him back to the here and now. He bolted from the room and rushed down to the lobby. "What's been going on?" he asked a WU guard.

Apparently Ingo had commandeered the broad parking lot of Henderson Square Garden as an impromptu airport. Mac made his way to it, jogging through the empty city streets to the sound of the shriek of engines, the rattle of gunfire.

He arrived close to sunset. No sign of Ingo, but Mac was given one of the trucks and told to keep an eye on the ongoing battle – to go out and find bailed WU pilots and bring them in.

On his third trip back, Ingo was just climbing out of his Dove, wincing. Mac went over. "You okay?"

Ingo nodded shortly; they moved away from the plane as fitters raced up. "Couple of broken ribs from a few weeks ago," he said. "Did you get the call from Sheridan?"

"Wouldn't be here otherwise. She's there, buddy," Mac added, gripping Ingo's arm. "She's okay."

Ingo visibly relaxed a fraction and squeezed his temples. "Thank you," he said softly.

Mac started to tell him about Calgary, then changed his

mind. Ingo didn't need to know right now that over two hundred thousand people had died – that the woman he loved was in even more danger than before.

As if validating Mac's choice, Ingo glanced behind him as someone shouted, "Squadron Leader Manfred!"

Already looking distracted, he paused briefly before starting off. "Are you staying?"

"With your permission, sir," Mac said, and Ingo gave a faint grin at that.

"Go to hell. And stay, please. We need the help."

Eight hours later, it was nearly dawn again. In the light of large spotlights set up in the Garden's parking lot, fitters clambered over the remaining Firedoves, readying them for battle. Mac tried not to notice how many fewer planes there were now.

He sat on the Garden's front steps, watching the action – wishing he could do more before the battle hit again.

Mac glanced at his watch and then up at the lightening sky. Not much longer, probably.

A young English pilot came and sat next to him. He was fidgeting, drinking a cup of coffee as he watched the fitters. "Thanks for the lift last night," he said to Mac.

"Anytime," said Mac. "Percy, right? How's your arm?" A fresh bandage was on the guy's left forearm; it had been bleeding the last time Mac saw it.

Percy snorted slightly. "The medics said my wound had

opened up…it feels ridiculously trivial, if you want the truth." He shook his head, gazing around them. Perhaps fifty pilots were milling in the broad space. "Not enough of us," he murmured.

The day before had seen dozens of deaths. Ingo had somehow kept morale going. Mac had no idea how. The guy had helped gravely injured pilots from their planes while keeping a level, joking tone; gone up time and again himself, despite his broken ribs.

Mac saw Harlan then, sitting on his own, his expression stony as he watched the planes being prepared. Percy followed his gaze. "Poor bugger," he said softly.

Mac glanced at him. "Why?"

"Lost his girlfriend of over two years a couple of months back. In a bombing raid. It was, um…quite a bad one." Percy grimaced then and looked down at his coffee, swirling it. The laugh-lines at the corners of his eyes looked incongruous on his tired, drawn face.

Mac's gaze returned to Harlan as he winced, thankful that Sephy was safe in Nova Scotia. Yes, and what the hell was *he* doing, still here risking his life in this place, when she was pregnant? He'd lost his own dad when he was eleven. He wanted to be a father to his kid.

Yet looking around him at the too-few pilots and the makeshift airfield, Mac knew he couldn't leave.

Later, as the pilots started gearing up, Mac hesitated and went over. Harlan froze when he saw him, one arm through his parachute strap.

Mac cleared his throat. He put his hand out. "Listen, Mr Taylor…I'll understand if you don't want to shake my hand. But I wanted to tell you I'm sincerely sorry for your loss."

Harlan's expression darkened. He finished putting his arm through the strap and didn't answer.

Get out of here, Jones, you're making it worse. Mac let his hand fall. "Well…good luck up there."

When he'd taken a few steps away, a gruff voice said, "Wait."

Mac turned. Harlan came over and regarded him for a moment, his blunt, handsome face grim. "Her name was Vera Kelly," he said. "She was one of the pilots you saved on the Western Seaboard base."

"Collis saved you, not me," said Mac. "He told me not to choose you."

Harlan grimaced at this. "Yeah," he said finally. "Anyway… she forgave you for what you did. When she knew the truth. I don't. But I thought you might like to know."

Mac's throat tightened. "Thank you," he said quietly.

Harlan nodded. He gave a faint smile. "She was always a lot nicer than me." He turned away and walked to his plane, holding his helmet in one hand.

Three hours later, Harlan Taylor was dead.

He was one of dozens more WU pilots who died that day, defending the island and its people. Mac wasn't the one who found him. He got to the downed WU plane after the medics and scrambled out of his jeep amidst the wails of sirens and the thud of artillery from overhead.

From the set of the medics' shoulders as they rested the pilot on a stretcher, he knew it was already too late.

Mac stopped short at the sight of Taylor's still features. He lay staring up at the battle. Then a medic drew a blanket over him.

Sorrow wrenched Mac's gut.

"Ah, hell, buddy…I'm sorry," he muttered.

Later that day, he brought in a European Alliance pilot with red-rimmed eyes.

"I saw him go down," she said, huddled in the corner of the jeep. "I…I knew from the hit he'd taken that he wouldn't make it. I was going for a bomber – he held off a pair of Scorps that had ganged up on me." She stared blindly out the window. "The big jerk saved my life."

Mac hardly even knew what he said – something he hoped was soothing. Empty fucking words. They pulled into the Garden with only the sound of battle overhead.

As the pilot got out she gazed over at the waiting planes and added, "You know…a group of us played poker together sometimes." She glanced back and gave Mac a wan smile. "Harlan kept promising that he'd make us some of his rotgut to drink."

Mac sat where he was after she'd left. The medics' truck was parked not far away, its back doors open. Several blanket-covered bodies lay inside.

Mac somehow knew one was Taylor – and remembered the burly pilot saying of Vera, *She was always a lot nicer than me.*

Abruptly, Mac slammed the jeep in reverse and glanced behind him, one arm across the top of the seat. "Yeah, you were wrong about yourself, pal," he murmured aloud to Taylor. "I think you were probably pretty okay too."

The summer day burned as bombs rained on the city. Mac found and brought in what pilots he could. Around three o'clock, a plane went down in flames in Centre Park. When Mac reached it, the pilot was Ingo. He'd been grazed by a bullet, leaving the right arm of his shirt soaked in blood, and seemed to have cracked another rib.

As Mac drove him back to the Garden, Ingo sat clutching his side, not speaking, his face deathly pale.

Mac glanced at him. "Listen, buddy – suggestion? Maybe you shouldn't just tape yourself up and go right back into battle."

"Shut up, Mac," said Ingo in a low voice.

Mac knew better than to push it. He glanced overhead, keeping a wary eye on the sky as he hurtled them through the potholed streets. Ingo sat with his head back against the seat, his eyes closed. Mac thought for a second he'd passed out.

"They've got to be okay," he murmured.

"Amity and Collis?"

Ingo rubbed his temples. "Yes, them, of course. But I meant everybody who's left." The news of Taylor's death earlier had hit him hard. He let his hand fall, looking twenty years older than he was, and gave Mac a faint smile.

"I can see now why I've never wanted to be in charge," he said. "I feel personally responsible for every one of them."

The medics had set up a station inside the Garden. Mac left Ingo getting his ribs and arm seen to, and left to go after another pilot – one of Pierce's this time, a scared-looking kid who put up no resistance when Mac turned him over to the WU police.

When Mac returned to the Garden, he saw Ingo talking urgently on the shortwave wireless that had been set up in one corner, his shirt open over his taped ribs, his curls chaotic. Something in his expression made Mac go over.

Ingo was just signing off when Mac reached him. Ingo stared at him as if he didn't know who he was. "Keaton's surrendered," he said.

Mac stared. "*Keaton?* What about Pierce?"

"They haven't heard from her. It came through Keaton. A nuclear bomb was dropped on Calgary yesterday."

"I know," Mac admitted. "Amity saw it. They were still planning to bomb Puget today when she got to the factory."

Ingo stared at him. All at once he got up in a flurry and headed for the door. Mac followed him outside. They stood looking up at the sky, Ingo clutching his taped ribs, his breathing too shallow. Scorps and Doves were still battling above the buildings. Even with no bombers in sight, the orders now seemed to be to destroy the New Manhattan air power.

Numb, Mac pushed a hand through his hair. "So...it's really almost over?" In terms of this city, he could only be glad – but if Atomic Harmony Devices didn't load that last nuke onto the bomber, any chance to end those things for good would vanish.

"I don't know," said Ingo, his expression taut. "Yes, I think so. The Can-Amer pilots don't seem to know yet – they could be out of range." He shot a frustrated glance at the battered Firedoves in the parking lot – the fitters were repairing several.

Suddenly Ingo glanced at his watch and then at Mac, fear in his dark eyes.

"Amity," he said in a rush. "She's still there, isn't she? If she's only supposed to be dropping one bomb, she wouldn't have left as early as we thought."

Mac winced. "I'm sorry, pal. I didn't tell you yesterday, because—"

"Skip it! They could know by now the whole thing was a ruse – what happens to her then?" Ingo grimaced and swiped at his mouth. "No, don't even answer that."

Mac kept quiet, his own thoughts grim. Using deceit to get hold of a nuclear weapon in wartime... Amity would be arrested and court-martialled for treason. The penalty for treason was death.

Ingo stood beating a fist against his palm, the expression on his half-scarred face hyped-up, borderline violent.

"Buddy…" Mac started helplessly.

They both looked up as a fitter called over that a plane was ready. Ingo at first stared at the woman as if he hadn't understood, then shuddered and visibly steeled himself.

A second later he was running towards her, buttoning his shirt over his taped-up ribs. Mac followed. Ingo winced, still paper-pale as he put on his parachute.

Mac didn't tell him that he shouldn't be flying in his condition. Ingo knew that. Mac watched, his fists tight in his pockets, as Ingo yanked on his helmet, staring up at the too-many remaining Scorps. A Dove took a hit as they watched.

"Once this is over, it's finished for good," Ingo muttered – and Mac guessed he was thinking of those pilots he felt personally responsible for.

Gunfire echoed above. Ingo climbed onto the wing, wincing, and slid into the cockpit. Watching him, thinking of the dozens who'd died these last twenty-four hours – Harlan, Fern, so many others – Mac's chest felt made of lead.

"Good luck, pal," he called to Ingo.

Ingo waved, distracted. In no time, his plane was roaring, picking up speed as it passed the tarmac's painted parking spaces. It took off and angled sharply, gaining height.

It entered the fray.

Oh, kiddo, you've got to succeed somehow, Mac thought dully to Amity.

Ridding the world of those weapons was the only thing that might make all of this worthwhile.

Chapter Forty-seven

June, 1943

I STOOD IN AN EMPTY HANGAR, drinking a cup of coffee and gazing out at the bomber as it was prepared for flight.

The hills beyond the airstrip were covered in small pink wild flowers, though in a few deep ruts I could see patches of unmelted snow. Summer in the Yukon was still chilly, as I recalled all too well from Harmony Five. Up there, where it was colder, there'd been places where the snow never melted.

I was all too aware that I was thinking about this to try to take my mind off everything else. Sheridan had asked me to come to his office an hour earlier. I'd been terrified that I'd been discovered.

Instead he'd steepled his fingers, looking troubled.

"I wanted to tell you this myself in case you heard any rumours," he said. "There's a lot of confusion and mixed messages flying around today. But General Keaton's surrendered."

Thinking of New Manhattan, my heart had leaped. "He has?"

"*Keaton*, not Pierce. Kay Pierce has indicated that she'll never back down."

He looked steadily at me. A clock ticked in the background as my thoughts spun. Two hundred thousand people had already died in Calgary. Pierce's main military man was throwing in the towel. Sheridan couldn't be suggesting what I thought, could he? Would World United actually still *sanction* this?

Though I knew the role I had to play, I heard myself say slowly, "But surely if Keaton's backing down, then—"

Sheridan shook his head tersely. "It has to come through the official channels. There's been no verified surrender. The Puget bombing goes ahead."

The Cusp was about half as big again as the two-seater Merlin, specially made for these bombs. A single pilot could fly it, like Collie had said. The Cusp was heavier than what I was used to, not nearly as nimble, but otherwise essentially the same.

On its side and tail, the Harmony symbol with the

scorpion at its centre had been painted out. A dove shielding the earth was in its place.

Beyond the plane, a ghostly moon hung in the daytime sky.

Black Moon. From nowhere, I recalled watching a lunar eclipse as a child with Collie and Hal, the three of us lying outside on the grass one warm summer night.

Now an eclipse had forced Collie to betray the Resistance – had been instrumental in Pierce selecting this date for the nuclear attack – might even be the date of my own death. For a weird moment, as I stared up at it, the moon itself seemed my enemy.

I shook the thoughts away. Another pilot wandered over – a fresh-faced guy who looked about seventeen. He stood beside me, studying the Cusp.

"You stole my flight," he said. "I was supposed to do it."

"Orders. Sorry."

I wondered if he was the one who'd destroyed Calgary. I decided I didn't really want to know. I took another sip of coffee, suddenly deeply aware of the hangar's other planes behind us. I'd spent half an hour earlier pretending to check them out – no one had questioned a visiting pilot's interest. With luck, they wouldn't realize what I'd done until it was too late.

I'd deliberately not asked for any news of New Manhattan today, though I was desperate for it. My fingers tightened around the coffee cup.

The other pilot and I were silent as we watched the

workers load the bomb. They used a hydraulic platform to raise it into the plane's open underbelly. The bomb was smaller than I remembered, oblong and bloated-looking, with fins.

A chill swept me.

"It's okay," the other pilot said finally. "Can't say I'm sorry not to do it again."

At three o'clock, when the Cusp was ready, I walked out into the cool summer afternoon. The relief was fierce. I'd somehow made it through this day without detection. Sheridan had already wished me luck. We'd shaken hands.

The engine had a low, throaty roar, a different key from the Merlin's. I held up a leather bomber jacket I'd found in the airport to one of the fitters. "Okay if I borrow this?"

"Sure, no problem."

I pulled it on and glanced towards the plant's manufacturing section. I'd noticed earlier the scaffolding covering some of the buildings. Now the sound of construction floated over. Collie was right, they were rebuilding it.

You bastards, I thought dully.

"Heard the news from New Manhattan?" asked the fitter.

I stiffened. Finally I swallowed and looked down, fastening the zip of the jacket. "No, what?"

"Fighting's been heavy as hell. They've lost two more squadron leaders."

I stopped mid-motion. I stared at him, my lips numb. "Are…are you sure?"

"Yeah, they died in combat. One just this morning. Man something. Manson?"

The world seemed to stop.

"Manfred," I whispered.

"That's it." The fitter kept talking – telling me that Manfred had commandeered Henderson Square Garden for an airport before he died; that his fatal crash had been in Centre Park; that the new squadron leader was named Barton but the fighting there seemed to be over now, so maybe Barton, at least, wouldn't kick it.

The words beat dully at my brain. I realized that he'd stopped talking. I was still staring at him.

Belatedly, I looked down again and fumbled to work the jacket's zip. Its noise was faint against the sudden roaring in my ears.

Ingo.

"Miss Vancour? Are you okay?"

"Yeah," I got out. "Fine."

Alone in the cockpit, I wanted to curl into a ball and sob. I took a ragged breath and straightened, flicking switches, checking dials. I had to do this. *Had* to…though whether I lived or died didn't feel very important any more.

The fitter grabbed the chocks and signalled the all-clear. I violently shoved away my thoughts and started to taxi. The Cusp's reaction was slower than I was used to, its movements heavier, but it started obediently across the runway.

A flurry of motion in my mirrors. Glancing back, I saw Sheridan and a pair of armed guards running across the airfield. Sheridan's mouth was moving and I couldn't hear the words but I could see them.

"Stop her! She's under arrest! Stop her!"

The fitter, his hair flattened by the Cusp's propellers, looked back at Sheridan, startled.

My pulse spiked. With a lurch of the engine, I opened it up, taxiing faster towards the runway. Glancing hurriedly back, I saw people racing for the hangars. *Damn, damn!* Sheridan had found out. My minor sabotage of the planes would be too easily fixed.

Focus, I ordered myself.

The long strip of the runway was clear. Wild roses grew to either side. It ran past me, faster and faster, a blur of grey. Finally I had speed and pulled back the throttle.

Airborne.

If I thought about Ingo, I'd shatter like glass.

Numb, I spent the first half-hour of the short flight looking over and over in the mirrors, expecting to see Doves speeding after me. If Sheridan knew my flight order had been phoney, he might well have guessed where I'd be heading.

No Doves appeared.

Maybe I'd actually gotten away with it. I was at forty thousand feet, glad to have the leather jacket I'd borrowed. The Cusp was more spacious than I was used to. It felt oddly empty around me.

It was just me and the bomb.

I glanced back, hating this thing that had taken me from New Manhattan when I should have been there. It sat waiting on a cradle, bloated and complacent, the only one in existence now.

The ghosts of the ancients must be laughing. We'd thought we were so enlightened.

Far below, I knew train tracks sliced across the landscape in a thin, straight line. I kept mentally seeing the cattle car that had brought me to Harmony Five – its pungent smells, the taste of fear.

Anguish stirred. I glanced down at my tattoo, recalling Ingo tracing its lines after we saw the camp's liberation – how he'd kissed the tears from my face. And our goodbye only hours ago, when I'd known in my heart that I'd never see him again.

I shuddered and closed my hand into a fist.

With about ten minutes left to go, I put the Cusp on autopilot and made my way to the back. The bomb lay nestled in its cradle. I crouched beside it.

Words had been painted on its blunt nose: *Big Betty.* I stared at them, my stomach turning a little. Had the bomb that destroyed Calgary been called something jaunty too?

Collie had told me that there was a lid built into the nose, and that priming the bomb was as simple as turning a dial. I found the round lid and eased it open, the metal cool against my fingers.

Sure enough, a dial lay inside. You could adjust the bomb to go off at a certain altitude, or on impact.

I swallowed and rubbed my hand on my trousers. Very carefully, I turned the dial from *Off* to *Impact*. It clicked as it locked into place. Such a small change, but now Big Betty was ready.

I made my way back to the cockpit. Harmony Five shouldn't be far now. I began easing the Cusp down.

Like Mac had said, the lower I got, the better my chances of hitting the mine...but I'd also have less chance of escaping the shock wave.

I knew I should care.

I emerged from the cloud cover into a slight headwind. Snowy mountains appeared below. I kept glancing at the altimeter. Twenty thousand feet. Fifteen. I'd planned to take it no lower than ten...but now I set my mouth and descended to five.

Harmony Five glided into view: a cleared space between two mountains. Its buildings looked tiny and huddled. Staring down at them, I started my turn.

An explosion rocked the plane.

I yelped, thinking at first that the bomb had gone off. Then a familiar shape flashed in my mirrors. A Dove – no, two, with the WU emblems. They weren't letting that mine go without a fight.

Wind whistled through the Cusp. I was breathing hard. "Oh, you couldn't hold off just five more minutes, could you?" I muttered. I half-turned in my seat and risked a glance.

A hole gaped in the rear; they'd gotten part of the fuselage. Another Dove howled past and bullet holes scattered across the opposite wall of the cockpit. The whine of metal on metal pierced the air.

I banked, trying to evade. Compared to the nimble Doves, my motions were lumbering.

The Cusp rocked again. Part of my tail went with a metallic shriek. Red lights flashed hysterically from the control panel. *Ignore it!* I screamed at myself. *Just hold it steady!* The mine was coming up any moment.

"Eye on the prize," I muttered. This was *my* prize, all that was left to me – to finally do away for ever with what my father had put into place. I gritted my teeth, hanging onto the stick though the bomber was wobbling badly now. "Eye on the prize, Dad."

The woods through which I'd been forced to march appeared below. *Forward motion,* I remembered. Big Betty was travelling at three hundred miles per hour; she'd keep doing so even after she dropped.

She, I thought wildly. Don't name these things after women, thank you very much.

As a Dove swooped in, I hit the button.

I didn't hear the bomb fall, but when I glanced behind me, it was gone. So was what looked like half my plane.

I could see the sky through the mangled walls. Both Doves whipped past and shot off into the distance.

Despite the cold, sweat dotted my brow. I faced forward again, struggling to keep the plane steady. *Please, at least let me have gotten the mine,* I thought. If I was going to die, let me at least have done that.

Mountains and deep snowdrifts sped past below. Unbelievably, I still had an engine. If I could just keep going – if I could somehow keep on—

Light erupted, brighter than the sun.

I cried out and tried to take it faster, flying blindly through the brilliance. The engine howled in protest and then I was slammed forward, my straps biting at my shoulders. The stick tore from my grasp.

The plane bucked, pummelled from all directions. A great rush of wind sent the Cusp tumbling. Sky and earth spun. My tail came off with a wrenching groan.

Thoughts came quickly, vividly.

Hal. *You're strong, little brother. You'll be fine.*

Ma, singing us to sleep when we were sick.

And as the plane tore to pieces around me, Ingo and I were back in the Grand, dancing to the low, hypnotic music.

The feel of his lips on my neck.

You were faster as a lock-picker.

I smiled softly. I remembered all of it.

All.

CHAPTER FORTY-EIGHT

JUNE, 1943

"HI, KAY," SAID COLLIS.

His wife was in their bedroom at the Zodiac, packing clothes in a small leather bag. The telio set was on. She whirled around, her eyes wide and startled. "What the hell are you doing here?" she said hoarsely.

Collis tossed the auto keys onto her dresser. He was exhausted from the long drive, tense with worry over whether Amity had managed to destroy the Harmony Five mine. On the auto's wireless set he'd heard non-stop about the devastation in Calgary and Pierce's refusal to corroborate Keaton's surrender...but the news had stayed silent on the second nuke.

Kay's question hung in the air.

Collis shrugged. "I guess you forgot to tell your staff that you want me dead. I'm your husband. They seemed to think you'd want to see me."

Kay's expression was stony. Her hair was up in the stiff curls that he disliked on her. "I have a pistol, you know."

"Use it."

She gave a humourless laugh. "Yes, and bring everyone running in here, just when…" She glanced at the telio set suddenly, her voice trailing off.

"…and here in Topeka, as crowds gather near the Zodiac, we await word from our *glorious* Madame President. Incredibly, she has still given no official reaction to the nuclear destruction of Calgary, with a bomb created by her own regime's predecessor…"

As crowds gather near the Zodiac.

As the newscast continued, Collis sank onto a velvet-covered chair and studied her. He cleared his throat. "How long have those broadcasts been going on?"

Kay had gone rigid, her fingers pressed to her mouth. She glared at him and let her hand fall.

"Since the bomb," she said shortly. She snapped the telio off and returned to her packing, flinging clothes in the bag. "So I guess your WU pals aren't so trustworthy, are they? All those thousands of people dead."

Collis didn't respond. Finally he glanced back out to the large sitting room. Through its windows, another dome of the Zodiac was visible.

"I saw the crowds, you know," he said.

Kay gave him a swift look.

"As I drove in." He nodded at the sitting room. "If you look out, you can probably see them."

"And the Guns aren't…" Kay didn't finish.

"No," he said. "They don't seem to care much."

Kay's expression hardened as she gazed at him. She left her packing and strode to the sitting room, brushing past as if he wasn't there. He followed. She stood at the window and craned to see to the west.

The crowd was gathering near the Zodiac's main entrance. Kay stared at the seething mass of people.

In her heels, she came up to Collis's shoulder. She wore a neat green skirt, a matching broad-shouldered jacket. Collis looked down at her instead of the crowds, taking in both her fear and the fierce jut of her chin.

She slid the window open a crack and the sound of rhythmic shouts came.

"*Pierce must go! Hanging's too good! Pierce must go! Hanging's too—*"

Kay banged the window shut, trembling visibly. "*Never,*" she muttered. "Oh, just let them try it."

She ran to the front door of the suite. He'd relocked it after he'd slipped inside. Her bodyguards had been nowhere in sight. Downstairs, half the staff were making a run for it.

Kay checked the door, then gripped one side of a heavy bureau. "Help me!" she snapped.

Collis walked slowly over and did. They dragged the bureau in front of the door.

Kay raced back to the bedroom. "Is that why you've come?" she flung over her shoulder. "To gloat?"

Collis swallowed. He leaned against the doorway, watching as she found her ephemeris and shoved it into the bag.

"No," he said.

She gave him a hard, hounded look. "I wouldn't have thought you'd show your face."

"What did Keaton say?" Collis asked after a pause.

Kay grimaced, rolling up a pair of nylons. "That we've lost too much to have a chance. That we can't control the populace with what's happened to Calgary."

"He's right. He's probably sending troops here for you right now."

"*I know!*" She flung a brassiere into the bag. "But I will *never* surrender, Collis, do you hear me? I will never say the words." In an undertone, she added, "I wouldn't give Johnny the satisfaction."

Collis didn't move. Finally he said softly, "Johnny's dead, Kay."

She cinched the bag with a vicious jerk. She took off her jacket, then crossed to the mirror and started pulling hairpins out. Her hair tumbled down her back. She swiped off her make-up. She looked younger, her freckles more visible.

Collis watched her face in the mirror. "Why didn't you announce my execution order?"

"Do you think I *wanted* the world to know what a fool

I was to trust you?" Kay yanked off her silk blouse and hurled it onto a chair. In a sweet sing-song, she added, "Besides, if I'm going down, you are too, husband darling. I hope World United throws you to the wolves."

Collis didn't respond. They would, if Amity had succeeded and his role came out. They might anyway. He was under no delusions that any of them were fond of him.

Kay stepped out of her skirt. Her small, slim form had excited him so many times. Now he just felt hollow. He took in the mole on her ribcage, remembered kissing it.

Kay wasn't wearing her wedding ring. As she crossed to her closet, she glanced at his hand and gave an ugly laugh. "You don't have to *wear* that thing, you know."

"We're married," he said quietly.

"I only married you to play you."

"Really?"

Her face tightened. Her motions abruptly more furious, she grabbed clothes from her closet and dressed quickly: a plain, inexpensive skirt. A worn blouse like a struggling secretary might wear.

Collis had listened to newscast after newscast on his long drive. They'd simmered with turmoil, confusion. Conflicting reports of the final battle had streamed out of New Manhattan. Collis had twice heard that Manfred had died – then a mention that Barton, the new squadron leader, had merely been "left in charge". No explanation was given. Other reports told of the Calgary bombing. The details of the city's destruction had sickened Collis but he hadn't snapped off the wireless.

"It beggared description," a woman had said, her voice heavy. "There was a ball of fire, a tremendous noise… words are inadequate tools, I'm afraid."

They really are, thought Collis now, gazing at Kay.

She pulled her hair back in a plain style and then donned a scarf, tying it under her chin. She glanced quickly at the bedroom window. Oak trees nestled close, their branches wide and inviting.

Collis cleared his throat. "Where will you go?"

"As if I'd tell you," Kay muttered. Then she glanced at him, her lips a thin crease. "Where will *you* go?"

"I'm not."

"What?"

"I'm staying."

She laughed, looking honestly amused. "They'll arrest you."

"I wouldn't be surprised."

Kay stepped very close. He could smell her perfume, just like when he'd woken up that first time, his bullet wound throbbing, and she'd come in and adjusted his pillows.

Her blue eyes glinted. "They'll make you the scapegoat," she said with relish. "If they don't have me, they'll blame everything on you. The whole world will hate you."

Collis nodded slowly. He gave an almost-smile. "It doesn't matter," he said. "As long as I don't hate me."

She frowned, studying him. Then they both jumped at

a cascade of knocks from the next room. The doorknob rattled. "We have a warrant for the arrest of Kay Pierce!" shouted a voice.

Kay sucked in a breath. She snatched up the bag, flung its strap over her shoulder. She ran to the window and heaved it open.

"Wait," said Collis.

She gave him a wide-eyed, frenzied look. He went to her and pulled out his wallet. As the door started banging behind them, he took out all the bills that he had.

"Here," he said quietly, offering them. "You never carry much cash."

Kay's face seemed to crumple as she stared up at him. Briefly, the look in her eyes was the same as when she'd married him, and something in him tightened.

Then her chin jerked up. She grabbed the money and stuffed it into her bag.

She slapped him hard across the face.

Collis didn't react. Kay sat on the window sill and strained for a branch. She glanced back at him, her eyes bright.

"I hope they hang you," she said.

Leaning far out, she snagged one of the tree's branches and then hooked her leg over another one. As Collis watched, she made her way down, the leather bag thumping against her side. Distantly, from the front of the Zodiac, he could still hear chanting.

When Kay reached the ground, she didn't look back up

at the window. She smoothed her clothes and hooked on a pair of sunglasses. Then, her hands in the pockets of her plain skirt, she walked briskly from the trees to the road.

Behind him the door banged and shuddered, the heavy bureau slowly scraping across the floor. In the late afternoon sky, he glimpsed a faint full moon, already rising, and remembered: the eclipse was that night.

Black Moon.

Collis watched Kay grow smaller. He lost her through the trees for a while and then her blue scarf appeared beyond the complex's gates. As she moved against the flow of pedestrians streaming towards the Zodiac, her stride looked brisk, resolute.

She vanished into the crowd.

Collis straightened. He felt oddly happy – and didn't know whether it was because he'd never see her again, or that she'd escaped.

He slid the window shut.

The door was almost open now. As Collis crossed to the front room, he paused. He took off his wedding ring and placed it on Kay's dresser.

He glanced at himself in the mirror and smiled slightly. Probably not what Mac would have done. It still felt okay.

Collis headed for the door, breaking into a brief jog. "Wait," he called out.

He heaved the bureau aside and opened the door. A group of armed men stood there, breathing hard and glaring at him.

"You took your fucking time, Reed," snapped one as they pushed past.

A few of them held rifles on him as the rest searched the apartment in a frenzy, banging doors open.

"She's not here!"

"Damn it!"

"Where is she, Reed? Where?"

He shook his head. "I don't know."

"When did she leave?"

"A few minutes ago."

A man got close, his face red. "*Did you help her escape?*"

"I guess you could call it that. I gave her some money. I didn't try to stop her."

Someone grabbed him and jerked his hands behind his back. Collis felt handcuffs go on. He didn't struggle.

"Well, we've got a warrant for you, too, Reed. You're hereby under arrest for the crimes of Kay Pierce's regime," spat the man.

The cold metal weighed heavily against his wrists. Below, the shouts continued, but here in this apartment it seemed quiet, almost peaceful.

"I've committed plenty of crimes that had nothing to do with Kay Pierce's regime," Collis said. "I'll tell you all of it. Whatever you want to know."

The men hesitated, staring at him. Collis knew that Kay's wish that he'd be hanged would probably come true. He still felt light. Free. Somehow he knew he'd never have the nightmare again.

Finally one of the men grabbed his arm and yanked Collis forward; he stumbled.

"Come on, you filthy scum," he muttered.

Chapter Forty-nine

June, 1943

THERE WAS NO PAIN. I lay in the cockpit, dimly aware that there was a fire nearby. Its steady crackling was the only sound.

As I gazed up through the shattered windscreen, I watched the moon get eaten by a red invader. First a small arc was slowly nibbled. Then I blinked and all of it was covered.

Black Moon, I thought dreamily.

Not black though. Coated in blood. When I looked again the moon had been washed clean. It stared down at me – a bright, shining eye that frightened me. I whimpered. I tried to turn my head to hide from the moon. I couldn't move.

I shuddered and closed my eyes. My eyelids felt sticky…

wrong…but I knew that the moon couldn't see me if I couldn't see it and this was comforting.

The fire crackled. I drifted away.

Dawn on the snow. Reds and pinks. I gazed fearfully at the colours and knew the moon must still be there, hiding.

The fire was almost out but it was a magic fire because I was still warm.

So warm.

"Amity!"

The voice came from far away.

"*Amity!*"

Closer now. The speaker sounded familiar and something ached within me. I tried to speak. My mouth wouldn't move and I moaned.

"Shh, it's all right. It's all right."

I felt myself being gathered up in someone's arms. Part of me seemed to be there and part of me didn't.

How could that be?

The thought was distant. The person carrying me staggered a little, their breathing ragged. But my head was against their shoulder and the smell of them was warm and spicy and so familiar I wanted to cry.

I knew then I was safe. The moon was gone. There was the sun.

When I woke up, I was in a hospital room. Everything hurt.

I saw Ingo and started to cry.

Wincing, he got into bed beside me and held me close, his touch gentle on my bruised body.

"I thought you were dead," I whispered.

"No…no." His curls brushed my skin as he kissed my temple, my cheek. "I thought you were."

Alive. As the world dimmed at the edges again, I pressed against him and let out a long breath. I didn't know where I was, or how he'd gotten here.

I didn't care.

The next time I opened my eyes, Ingo was gone.

A nurse stood at my bedside, checking my pulse. I licked my lips and looked around me. The movement brought pain. "Did I dream him?" I murmured.

"He's fine," the nurse said, and terror swamped me. I tried to sit up and she gently put her hands on my shoulders.

"*He's fine,*" she repeated. "He was exhausted and injured; it's a miracle he did what he did in his state. He collapsed this morning and one of his broken ribs punctured a lung. He needs to be on oxygen for a few days. But he'll be all right."

I melted against the pillow. "How…how is he still alive?" I whispered. "A fitter told me that he'd died in a crash."

The nurse shook her head as she poured me a glass of water. "He didn't say. But there was so much confusion during the battle…conflicting reports every hour."

"I have to see him," I said hoarsely.

Her gaze snapped to mine; she put the water down. "Miss Vancour, you're—"

"I have to. Please."

"This will hurt," she said finally. She got a wheelchair and helped me into it, half-lifting me. Pain burst through me and I clenched my teeth to keep from crying out. My left leg lay in a stiff cast. Bandages covered my left foot and my right hand.

The nurse wheeled me to another room. The wheelchair had *Property of Yellowknife Hospital* stamped on it. Outside a window we passed, I could see snow-capped mountains and pots of flowers.

Ingo lay in a bed with his eyes closed, his dark curls stark against the pillow, an oxygen mask over his mouth and nose. His breathing was shallow and obviously hurt him. His arm was wrapped in a bloodstained bandage.

The nurse manoeuvred my chair close to his bedside. He opened his eyes; they widened as he saw me. "Five minutes," the nurse said softly. "Please don't try to talk yet, Mr Manfred."

Ingo reached for my hand. I gripped the miracle of his fingers and the nurse faded from existence. He looked haggard. He gave a faint smile and rubbed his thumb across my palm.

I wanted to kiss his fingers – stroke his hair back. It hurt too much to move.

"I love you, Ingo Manfred, do you know that?" I whispered.

As the weeks passed, we healed together.

Though still sore, Ingo was up and around in a week. At first he didn't discuss the battle. Then one rainy afternoon, he told me everything, his tone steady but his eyes haunted. So many dead. *Harlan.*

We held each other.

Like so much of the news that day, the story that the fitter heard had been only half-accurate. Ingo had commandeered Henderson Square Garden, been shot down over Centre Park – but he'd flown in the final battle.

"The second it was over, I called Atomic Harmony Devices," Ingo said. "At first they said you hadn't been there. Then they claimed it was classified."

He'd departed New Manhattan at once, leaving Barton, the next highest ranking former Tier Two, in charge. Everything had been chaos then, Ingo said. The early news reports had gotten garbled.

When he'd finally reached the factory in one of the long-distance planes, I'd taken the bomber eighteen hours before and no one was looking for me. The Doves sent after me hadn't returned either. The WU personnel had seen the flash of light. Venturing up to Harmony Five was pointless, said Commander Sheridan. Clearly we were all dead.

Ingo forced him into action, pointing out that if people knew Amity Vancour was missing after saving humankind from itself, and that World United hadn't even tried to find her, there'd be uproar.

"I don't know when I've ever been so angry," he said softly, looking down and playing with my fingers. "I think I might have killed him if he hadn't agreed."

Sheridan had. He outfitted two planes with runners for the snow, and Ingo and another pilot flew north. They'd found us miles from the blast. The pilots of the Doves had been killed, but I was somehow still alive.

The Cusp had been ripped in half. The nose of the plane, with me inside, had buried itself in a deep snowdrift. I hadn't hallucinated the fire. A large part of the tail had apparently been in flames nearby for some time.

There was hardly a part of me that wasn't bruised. My left leg was badly broken; the doctor said the bones might need to be reset later. I'd lost my right little finger and half the ring finger to frostbite. I'd also lost two toes on my left foot – which was unfortunate, said the doctor, because my left leg was already weakened from both the break and the old bullet wound. Walking would probably always bring pain now.

I was lucky...in more ways than one.

Later, experts said that the mountains that had forced

me to fly so low to hit my target would also have absorbed the initial radiation blast. With only a low wind, the fallout had been contained by the deep valley where Harmony Five lay.

Though the mountains had worsened the shock wave's impact – making it buffet me from all directions as it ricocheted around them – in the end, the terrain that had once housed Harmony Five had saved my life.

"It's not exactly made for crutches, is it?" I sat propped up on pillows, contemplating my right hand's strange new shape. It throbbed, stumps aching.

Three weeks on I was still bed-bound with my shattered leg. I'd just tried crutches for the first time and had almost fallen.

Ingo half-lay beside me, dressed in street clothes. "Not the ones they have here, anyway." He rubbed my arm. "We'll get special ones made if we have to."

I nodded. The cast would be on for several months, but I needed to be mobile sooner than that. When I'd been in the hospital for a week, Mac had called. My eyes had welled to hear his voice.

"You did it, kiddo," he'd said, huskily. "I knew you could – I'm proud as hell of you. And listen…I've got a proposition for you and Ingo both."

We'd talked for almost an hour on the crackling long-distance line. A few times I'd put Ingo on the phone.

We had agreed to what Mac proposed.

When I hung up, Ingo and I looked at each other. "Your home," I murmured – now Ingo still wouldn't see it or his family for some time.

"It'll wait." He took my uninjured hand and kissed my fingers. He jostled my hand gently. "Besides – didn't you know? My real home's right here."

For the present, my world was still this hospital room. A deck of cards lay on my bedside table; Ingo and I played sometimes. As my gaze caught on them, I thought again of Harlan – all those nights spent playing poker together.

Hey, Vancour! How the hell d'you join the Resistance in this town?

Damn you, Taylor, I thought bleakly. *Why couldn't you have held out for just a few more hours?*

Ingo seemed to realize. The sorrow for Harlan, for all of them – Vera, Dwight, Tess, Fern, everyone – came over both of us at times.

He put his arm around me, and I leaned into his side. "You'll be fine," he said.

Surprise stirred. I glanced at him. He smoothed a strand of my hair back.

"It's not a platitude, my love," he said in a low voice. "You will be."

He still looked haunted sometimes. The images that he'd shared of the battle haunted me too. Now it hit me anew, with an aching wonder. I touched Ingo's face, tracing its angles.

So many deaths…yet somehow this one man had survived.

And so had I.

I pressed against him and he wrapped his arms around me. Caressing the long line of his back, I shut my eyes, savouring his steady heartbeat.

Finally I straightened and cleared my throat. "We'll both be fine," I said. "No platitudes here, either."

Ingo smiled ruefully. "We've never been very good at them, have we?"

"No. So we're not starting now."

"Agreed." He bent his head to my lips. The shiver that ran through me felt like a promise. I ran my hand through his hair.

"I want to be out of this hospital," I murmured against his mouth. "I want to be in a bed alone with you again."

"The thought's crossed my mind too," Ingo said. "Once or twice." He kissed my cheek, my neck. "We'll make up for lost time later," he whispered.

"I'm so glad you never say anything you don't mean," I said, and felt him grin.

"So am I, in this case."

When we drew apart, Ingo held me, my back to his chest. "Look," he said, nodding at the window. He laid his scarred cheek against mine. "Perfect flying weather."

We gazed out at the sky: pure blue, with high, sweeping cirrus clouds. I nodded, reaching up to stroke his curls. "It looks like that painting in the book of prints you gave me."

"It does. The one by Magnini."

I smiled, still studying the clouds. "Yes. Exactly."

We talked about our future.

CHAPTER FIFTY

AUGUST, 1943

MAC AND SEPHY STOOD IN the strong summer sunshine, watching with thousands of others as a young girl carrying a folded flag walked past down New Manhattan's Concord Avenue. A band marched behind her. The plaintive notes of the Appalachian national anthem were almost the only sound.

Behind the band came the surviving pilots who'd protected New Manhattan. They wore dress blues. Some were in wheelchairs being pushed by others; some had arms in slings or missing limbs.

There were seventeen of them.

Mac watched the passing pilots in silence. Six weeks ago, with the end of the war, there'd been tickertape parades.

People had hung from open windows high above the streets, blowing party horns and flinging confetti that fell like brightly-coloured snow.

Now, as the Appalachian flag was about to be reinstated in the presence of the pilots who'd helped save it, the crowd was still. Sephy stood beside Mac holding Louise, their newborn daughter. As the baby slept, Sephy dabbed at her eyes and gave Mac a small, sad smile.

"So few of them," she murmured.

Mac nodded, his own throat tight. In his heart, he added the members of the Resistance who'd fallen.

He put his arm around Sephy. Along with others, they quietly fell into line behind the pilots.

The World United offensive had worked, everyone said now. Yes, it was a terrible thing – unleashing such ferocious power – but perhaps nothing else would have stopped Kay Pierce. And after all, World United had destroyed the nuclear weapons factory, and gotten Wildcat to bomb the uranium mine only hours after Calgary fell.

That was the official story. Amity had agreed not to challenge it if World United disbanded, and if the factory was destroyed and those responsible for the Calgary bombing were never allowed to hold public office again. They'd complied.

No more nuclear weapons. No more threat to the world.

Kay Pierce had escaped. Mac was darkly unsurprised. Kay was definitely not a woman to hang around and wait to be executed.

He thought of Collis and sighed.

The silent, expectant crowd streamed into Centre Park. The new mayor got up on a platform with the pilots and spoke about the brave heroes, both living and dead, who'd helped win the war.

He mentioned many by name, including Amity, calling her, "Not only a hero, but now the head of the new Global Peace Committee, a true 'wildcat' who won our hearts and trust." Mac could imagine Amity's expression if she'd been there – she'd always disliked being singled out.

She'd have to get used to it, he thought with a small inward smile.

Finally the mayor took out several typewritten sheets of paper. As a warm breeze rustled through the trees, he said, "These are the pilots who fell defending our city."

The list of names went on for several minutes. The park went still, hats placed over hearts. Sorrow touched Mac as he heard "Vera Kelly" and "Harlan Taylor".

Dwight Perkins, he added mentally, his fedora clasped over his chest. *Anton Bergen. Mabel and Ernest Chevalier...*

The names ended.

The young girl with the flag stepped forward. A pair of police officers attached it to the flagpole beside the bandstand. The chain rattled, hoisting it into place: green mountains against a blue background.

As the national anthem began again, the sombre mood faded, replaced by joyous singing. Mac and Sephy glanced at each other.

She squeezed his hand. "'Bout time."

"Yeah. 'Bout time," said Mac, staring at the flag.

Holy hell… He'd fought ever since he was sixteen. Now, finally, the regime that had caused so much death and pain was gone. Old borders had been restored, all across what used to be Can-Amer.

Yet now the world had to decide what next. How could so many nations coexist peaceably? The remnants of World United – those who hadn't supported the bombing – needed an unbiased committee to chart the way forward.

When Mac had called Amity in the hospital, he'd explained that they wanted her to be in charge of it, with some of the old Resistance team working alongside her – people who'd proven themselves ready to die for peace. Ingo. Mac himself. Sephy. Grady, and others from around the world who could be trusted.

"A committee? I'm not a politician, Mac," Amity had said.

"I think that's the whole point, kiddo," he'd replied.

Plans were already under way. Once Amity got out of the hospital and she and Ingo returned to New Manhattan, the real work of the Global Peace Committee would begin. They'd need to hold hearings, filter through years' worth of corruption – learn how to prevent it from ever happening again.

Later, a more permanent board would be formed to decide how the world should resolve conflicts. There was talk of locating it in Rome. Mac and Sephy would take on liaison roles at that point, staying in New Manhattan.

The last notes of the national anthem faded.

Food was brought out. The band started up a dance tune. Mac caught sight of Hal Vancour then, on crutches, with one trouser leg pinned mid-thigh. He and his mother were talking with a few of the pilots. As Mac watched, Hal scanned the crowd, his strong-featured face drawn.

By now, Mac and Sephy had visited Hal and Rose several times in Nova Scotia. They headed over.

Rose looked red-eyed – Mac recalled that she'd known Harlan Taylor – but was showing a letter to one of the pilots, saying, "Amity's at a specialist hospital in Puget – she had to have her leg reset. But Ingo's with her, and says she's doing well…"

Mac glimpsed the letter: *Dear Rose,* it began.

Rose and Hal saw them then and Rose exclaimed over the baby. As she and Sephy started talking, Mac held out his hand to Hal and then impulsively hugged him.

"Hey, buddy," he murmured.

Leaning on a crutch, Hal clung to him for a second, suddenly seeming again like the fourteen-year-old kid with serious eyes Mac had first met.

"When the mayor was talking about the heroes of New Manhattan, he should have mentioned Collie," Hal said roughly.

"I agree, pal," said Mac.

The rest of the world didn't. Collis was in prison,

charged with crimes against humanity and a host of other offences. If found guilty of even a few of them, he'd face the death penalty. Already, his trial was gearing up to be a circus, with invective spewed about him daily in the press.

"Why the hell'd you let Pierce *go*, buddy?" Mac had said when he'd visited Collis, worry making him snap the words. That was the real sticking point, the thing he knew would cause the most difficulty at Collis's trial.

Collis had shrugged, looking a little sad.

"It just seemed right," he'd said. "Her conscience is up to her."

Overhearing what Mac and Hal were saying about Collis, Rose sighed, her expression pained. Then Louise woke up, and she smiled a little. "Oh, let me hold her," she said to Sephy, stretching her arms out. "She looks just like you."

"Really? I think she looks like Mac," said Sephy, handing Louise over. "She's got his nose."

"Poor kid," said Mac with a rueful smile, studying his daughter. He couldn't describe how he felt every time he saw her.

Rose and Sephy fell into conversation again. Hal started to say something to Mac – then glanced up and went motionless. Through the shifting crowd, a pilot with russet hair was approaching.

Mac recognized him suddenly: the English pilot he'd spoken to the day of the surrender. The pilot's eyes were on Hal, but when he reached them he glanced at Mac and his forehead creased. "Hello," he said, and put his hand out. "Percy Allen. Have we met?"

"Mac Jones. Only briefly," said Mac as they shook. He didn't explain, and Percy didn't ask. He seemed to brace himself as he turned to Hal again, who'd barely moved.

"Hello, Hal." He kept his gaze on Hal's eyes, not looking at his leg.

"Hi, Percy," said Hal, his tone stilted. "Long time, no see."

Percy nodded and shifted his weight. "I spotted you from the stage. I…wasn't sure whether you'd come."

"Yeah, of course." Hal's hands on his crutches were tight. He gazed down at his one shoe and cleared his throat. "I was, um…really glad to hear that you made it."

"Looked pretty dicey a few times. It makes you wonder – why you, out of so many other…" Percy grimaced and pushed a hand through his hair. "Never mind. Pointless maunderings. Do you fancy getting a coffee?" He said the last words in a rush.

Hal glanced at his mother, still talking with Sephy. For a long moment he didn't respond.

"Please?" Percy added.

Mac had eased away a few steps. Trying not to watch, he saw that Percy's hands were tight fists in his trouser pockets.

Finally Hal gave a ghost of a smile. "'Some' coffee or 'a cup of' coffee. Not 'a' coffee, you limey."

Percy's answering smile was sad. "I've missed having you tell me these things," he said.

Rose looked over then. Hal said, "Ma, this is Percy Allen. The one, um…"

"Oh!" Rose put her hand out. "Yes, I've heard a lot about you."

"You have?" Percy glanced at Hal as they shook. "All good, I hope."

The tips of Hal's ears reddened. Before Rose could respond, he said, "We're going to go grab some coffee, all right, Ma?"

Rose's attractive face creased. "Oh, Hal…is that wise? You've been on crutches for hours."

Hal shook his head, looking slightly impatient. "I'm fine. I'll see you back home." He and Rose had moved to New Manhattan recently, where there were better doctors for Hal's leg. Hal said goodbye to Sephy, hugging her briefly, then glanced at Mac. "I'll call you soon, all right?"

Mac nodded and gripped his shoulder. "See you, pal," he murmured. *Be happy,* he thought.

As Hal and Percy set off, Mac took the warm bundle of his daughter from Rose.

Louise peered solemnly up at him with her young-old eyes. The corner of Mac's mouth lifted and he kissed her head. His gaze met Sephy's. Her faintly sad smile matched what he was feeling.

Glancing after Hal and Percy again, Mac saw that Hal's spine looked tense even given the crutches. Percy said something Mac couldn't catch, nodding down at them.

Hal looked quickly at Percy, his expression hesitant.

After a beat, he seemed to relax a little as he responded.

Rose sighed, her eyes on her son too. "It's so hard to let go." She glanced at Mac and Sephy and gave a small smile. "You'll find out."

EPILOGUE

THE LIGHTS SHONE BRIGHTLY ON MY FACE, *making the audience a dark mass. I was used to it by now. My hands on the podium stayed steady as I said, "I'd like to tell you a story. It's a story my father used to tell me. On this opening day of the Global Peace Committee's eighth annual session, I think it's important."*

I didn't have to check my notes. Without trying, the scene came vividly back: myself in bed at age nine with my father perched beside me, his voice intent.

"My family originally came from Oceania," I said into the darkness. "One of my ancestors there was named Louise, and as she walked home from school one day, soldiers attacked..."

The green, rolling land glided past below. The Dove was a MK14, and finally I could agree with Harlan that I liked a version better than the MK9. Its stick felt light under my fingers. Flying it was like strapping on wings and stepping into the sky.

As I banked, I felt my tensions ease. The meeting in Rome that had followed my opening day speech had been long and acrimonious at times – funny, when we were talking about peace. Yet being up here with the late-afternoon sunlight so golden and slanting made all that fade into its proper place.

It was my job. It was important. But the people I was heading home to were my life.

"Troops swarmed through the streets. Shots echoed. People were screaming, running for cover. Louise sprinted home, but when she opened the door, everyone had been killed.

"She saw her mother lying on the kitchen floor with her stomach sliced open. She saw her older brother's body slumped against the wall; it ended at the bloody stump of his neck. His head lay on his lap, staring at her. Her father was simply gone. Bloody scuff marks led out the door, as if he'd been struggling when he was dragged away.

"As you can imagine, hearing this had a great impact on me. 'Those soldiers were evil!' I told my father. 'They did

terrible things.' And he said, 'But, Amity, that's what happens in war. Louise's side might not have acted any better, if they'd had the chance.'

"We know now to our sorrow that it's true."

Eight years on, the world had decided on an improved system of Peacefighting. The Global Peace Committee, now made up of one representative per country, was overseeing the formation of the new Peacefighting force. I was starting to realize that getting it up and running would take years more.

I'd be glad when I could leave it behind and just fly transport, like I'd always wanted.

The MK14 hummed around me. Flying still made me feel close to Dad; he'd have loved the MK14. So often now, I felt only pity for him.

But that was in the past and I didn't live there. Mostly as I flew, I just thought of the evening ahead: talking with my husband over dinner; scooping up our son and burying my face in his curly hair; sitting out on the balcony with a glass of wine and watching the sun set over the fields.

"The war Louise lived through led to what we once thought was the Final War. It was not. But along with many others, Louise told her story and warned: the ancients destroyed themselves. We must never do the same.

"The International Peace Treaty was signed by every nation. It was broken, but we have now re-signed it – all too aware of how close we came to forgetting Louise's warning.

"Your presence here today is a bond."

I brought the Dove in lower, its shadow swelling and shrinking over the hills. A rambling farmhouse below always reminded me of my childhood home, and I smiled. I'd heard from Hal the day before. He'd decided against becoming a pilot and had recently entered med school.

He and Ma kept in touch with Collie – I knew he'd always be a son, a brother, to them. In the end, helped by testimony from those of us who knew Collie had been with the Resistance; he'd been convicted of only one charge: being an accomplice in the murder of Lester Henley in Harmony Three. On the stand – which he'd insisted on taking – he'd admitted to everything he'd done, both good and bad.

He'd served seven years. When he'd gotten out, Mac had offered him a job with the Committee's liaison branch. Collie turned him down, saying he needed to make his own way. Though to the world he'd probably always be Mr Kay Pierce, Mac said he didn't seem bitter.

Kay Pierce had never been found. I didn't let myself lose sleep over it.

* * *

"When I was first asked eight years ago to lead the Global Peace Committee, I felt wary. Surely we've had enough of alliances that claim to be for peace? Yet if the ones we've had so far have failed, it's not for the lack of good people trying their best.

"If we're ever to truly have peace, we must keep on trying.

"My middle name is Louise, and I'm proud of it. Thank you for listening. Let's begin."

I flew over the final hill, and there was home, with the runway stretching out in the fields behind it. The house's worn, gentle stones glowed golden in the late afternoon light.

I came in over the lush vineyards and saw them: a tall man with a scarred face and a little boy. The man was crouched beside the boy, one arm around his shoulders, pointing at me up in the sky. The little boy was jumping up and down.

My heart was the sun. As I passed overhead, I grinned and waggled my wings.

I brought the Dove in for a landing.

ACKNOWLEDGEMENTS

The *Broken* series has been exhilarating, challenging and ultimately my most fulfilling writing journey yet. After more than three years, it'll feel very strange not to have this world and these characters in my head.

Black Moon is already pretty flipping long, so I'll keep this brief (for me!). Thank you so, so much to everyone who helped me along the way with this book and this series. Particularly the team at Usborne – Stephanie King, editor extraordinaire; Anne Finnis, Rebecca Hill, Sarah Stewart and Becky Walker – you're all stars and your feedback has been invaluable. Thank you for believing in this impossible-to-encapsulate-in-an-elevator-pitch series, and in me. I've got the best publishers in the world.

Thanks to Stevie Hopwood and Amy Dobson in Publicity – you're both awesome, and joys to work with.

Thanks to Katharine Millichope for the stunning front covers. Each one has been more amazing than the last. Thanks to Sarah Cronin, for doing such a stellar job setting out the text, not just in this book, but all my Usborne books.

Thanks to my lovely agent Jenny Savill – looking forward to Whatever Next with you!

Thanks to my wonderful friends, who've read drafts, offered feedback, and helped keep me sane (I always say this, because it's always true). I won't name names because I'm sure to inadvertently leave someone out. Instead I'll just say thank you SO MUCH to all of you – you know who you are – and especially the Charlotte Street Gang. You all rock and I love you.

A huge thank you to my readers. All of them. Yes, you, reading this right now. It seems magical to me that these words are bridging time and space to reach you. I'm waving, can you see? I'm thrilled that you came along for the ride that was the *Broken* series. I hope you enjoyed it.

Love and thanks to my family for being generally awesome, and in particular my husband Pete. Spouses of writers deserve a special place in heaven. Or at least lots of chocolate.

Pete, I hereby give you ALL THE CHOCOLATE. You deserve it and so much more. I love you.

THE BROKEN TRILOGY:
COLLECT EVERY EXHILARATING EPIC

Welcome to a "perfect" world.
Where war is illegal; where harmony rules.
And where your date of birth marks your destiny.
But nothing is perfect.
And in a world this broken, who can Amity trust?

*Set in a daring and distorted echo of 1940s America,
L. A. Weatherly's BROKEN trilogy is a compelling
journey of deception, drama and rebellion.*

"Action, romance, heartbreak, betrayal, agonizing guilt and
heart-stopping tension... And TWISTS; dear Lord, the twists."
AWFULLY BIG REVIEWS

To Inbali Iserles, my "trilogy twin".
With thanks and love.

First published in the UK in 2017 by Usborne Publishing Ltd., Usborne House,
83-85 Saffron Hill, London EC1N 8RT, England. www.usborne.com

A CIP catalogue record for this book is available from the British Library.

ISBN 9781409572046 03208/1

FMAMJJASOND/17   Printed in the UK.